Punta Rassa

Ann O'Connell Rust

The Floridians Series Volume I

Amaro Books

Published by
Amaro Books
5673 Pine Avenue
Orange Park, Florida 32073

First Printing 1988

ISBN No. 0-9620556-0-3

Library of Congress Catalog Card No. 88-070994

Printed in U.S.A. by Edwards Litho

Cover Artist: Linda Taheri

AUTHOR'S NOTE

The setting of this story is Florida — 1877 and 1878. The background is authentic, but all the characters are fictional. The following towns have since had name changes — some many times.

ROSE HEAD — is now PERRY
DARBYVILLE — MACCLENNY
ROWLAND'S BLUFF — BRANFORD
TATER HILL BLUFF — ARCADIA

The town of CROSSTOWN is fictional but the author placed it in the same vicinity as the present day CROSS CITY.

Dedicated to my parents:

Francis Hummel O'Connell
Onida Aurora Knight

ACKNOWLEDGEMENTS

The author wishes to acknowledge her indebtedness to Mary Barbara O'Connell Sganga, whose faith in her ability as a storyteller was never doubted and always encouraged; to David Hummel Rust, whose knowledge of today's writing trends was invaluable; and to Allen Fennell Rust, whose assistance was gratefully appreciated ... he saved the computer from an early demise on numerous occasions. A special thanks to Jim Brown and staff of Empulse, Gt. Barrington, Mass.

CONTENTS

PROLOGUE

Lt. Layke Williams was in intense pain as he weaved in and out of consciousness. The waves of reality surfaced, then blackness stole the hesitant, quiet light. A young volunteer nurse sat on the edge of the cot and winced at his every moan but continued to bathe his feverish brow in a rhythmic motion, the same endless motion she had used on the hundreds of faceless men in the airless tent. The lumpy, filthy mattress was soaked with sweat. She tried to cover his still body with the soiled sheet and used a corner to wipe her damp forehead as she nervously restrained his hand that searched, then reached toward the pain. The air was motionless - heavy. Awareness again visited Layke, and he recognized the angry voice of Capt. Tucker.

"No, not this one, Doc. You'll not take this one's leg. This is the Bull's boy, for Christ's sake." Layke heard the hopelessness in Capt. Tucker's voice as he shouted, and saw his battle weary eyes as he glared at the diminutive, stooped doctor, who was bending over and examining Layke. Again Layke had lost the battle to face consciousness.

"This one will die with dignity - dignity! Do ya hear?" Capt. Tucker hurriedly left the tent and leaned against the South Carolina pine, ceasing to fight the bitter liquid that clawed at his throat, and retched noisily. Too tired to wipe his teared eyes and runny nose, he leaned his throbbing head against the tree's rough bark, then turned and embraced the tree, relinquishing his grief as he sobbed uncontrollably.

Capt. Rollins Tucker had proudly served under Layke's father, Col. Andrew Williams, affectionately called Bull, for the first two years of the War Between the States before being transferred to Uncle Joe Johnston's regiment. He was excited about Layke's performance in the field and felt he had the same intensity of command as the Bull. He hadn't seen that assurance in any of his other officers, not in all his years in the army.

"What in hell would the army do with another cripple?", he rationalized. The Williams family was army through and through, and it sickened him that Bull's two oldest sons had been killed at the Battle of Chattanooga. But Layke... he'd rather see Layke dead than crippled.

"Not your last boy, Bull," he shouted, piercing the unreceptive black night. "The least I can do for you is to let Layke die with dignity. You don't deserve a one-legged soldier-son. Not the best damned officer I ever knew. The best," he weakly added, his head bowed in submission.

The filtered light fought its way through the canvas of the makeshift hospital when Layke finally awakened. The air was pungent with the acrid odor of urine, and the seared flesh of the cauterized limbs permeated the stillness with its inescapable odor. The soldiers were lined up along both sides of the long enclosure, and more men crowded at the entrance waiting to replace the dead. His first conscious thought was about his leg. Unaware of the watching figure standing silently at the foot of the cot, he cautiously allowed his weakened arm to lower itself. Biting his lip in apprehension, his hand inched closer to the pained area.

"I thought we'd lost you, Lieutenant," Capt. Tucker interrupted formally. Then he smiled, put his comforting hand on Layke's shoulder and warmly said, "The leg's still there, son. Battered - but there. You've been out of it for over a week."

He cleared his throat and with a husky voice reeking with despair, said tiredly, "It's all over - the War's over. You can return home. But I expect great things from you, Layke. Great things!" Abruptly he turned, thought again and before opening the tent flap, swung around and crisply saluted Layke. "Lieutenant, when you get back to Tennessee, give the Bull my best."

That was the last time Layke saw his captain. He spent the next year regaining his strength under the protective care of his doting mother. He was bitter! He had loved the army - it was his life - it was his heritage. Walt and Ben were gone, and it was up to him to carry on the family tradition for the Bull and for himself. But the horror of the War continued to fester in Layke, and he sadly realized he'd have to regroup - begin again. A new plan would have to be addressed.

His first decision was the most difficult. Even with his love of Tennessee he knew he'd have to leave those unforgettable smokey hills for which he'd fought so courageously. The thanks he'd received from her and the South was the nearly severed leg and the intermittent teeth-gnashing pain ... and he resented the intrusion.

ii

Reluctantly, he left his disappointed, grieving family and wandered aimlessly down the Appalachian foothills. He stopped at several small settlements along the Georgia trail but found none to his liking. They were as beaten and tired as the town he'd left behind. He ended his journey in the small settlement of Marianna in the rolling hill section of northwest Florida. Marianna was an exciting town - full of life. It was an important cow town, surrounded by large tobacco and cotton plantations - and beef was king.

Using his little money, he purchased a small piece of land and tried his hand at farming. It wasn't long until he realized that farming was not for him. He needed the abandon of the open range to heal his deep wounds. He needed the energy that he felt when visiting with the unconventional cowmen, most of whom had also served in the conflict, but who seemed untouched by it. So Layke decided to become a cowman - a Florida cowman. He welcomed the freedom from sameness as he rode the range, experiencing a new and exciting adventure every day.

Blocking out the previous six years of army life, he relaxed and immersed his long, well muscled body into that freedom so recently embraced, so soon made comfortable, and dismissed the regimentation and discipline that had been his heritage as he worked the range and wandered from ranch to ranch for over eleven years, searching.

BOOK ONE:

BERTA McRAE

CHAPTER I LAYKE WILLIAMS

Was the fall of '77 when Layke Williams and his cow dog Tag left the Wilpole ranch. They headed south alongside the Suwannee, and Layke made up his mind that this would be the last time he'd take to the trail. He was going to settle down. His long years of searching had not borne fruit. His loneliness was still intact, and he longed to give his life meaning.

He pulled up rein in Old Town, a small settlement on the banks of the Suwannee River. Not much of a town and not many folks about, but when Layke Williams sat a horse he turned heads, and the few heads that were around took notice.

He was hot and dusty and needed a good soaking bath to take the pain out of his throbbing leg. He tied Bucko to the hitching post in front of the town's only boarding house and told Tag to stay. Tag crawled underneath the front porch and made himself at home in the cool shade.

A middle-aged lady, who identified herself as "Miss Trudy Stucky, proprietor of the Stucky Hotel," greeted Layke. She excused herself and hurriedly got his room ready, announcing loudly from the upstairs, "There's some taters and pone and slab on the stove if'n you're hungry."

"I'll settle for some good, strong coffee - range style - if you don't mind, Miss Stucky. I'm not real hungry - just need to soak off some of this Florida dust."

Layke filled the tin tub near to the top, and when he anxiously lowered his taut, long body into the steaming water the throbbing pain soon eased. He relaxed, leaned his head against the tub's smooth rim, trying to fit into the too small area. He felt released. He allowed a new beginning to emerge, and he welcomed it, smiling gratefully to himself in resignation, as he closed his dark hazel eyes.

After rubbing himself down briskly, he got his razor out of his saddle bag. His beard had been itching something fierce for the last three days. It was about time he saw his face again - hadn't seen it since before the Wilpole job. As he gazed at his emerging features, he noticed how bloodshot his eyes were.

"Sure has been a dry fall. Don't remember ever seeing so much dust,"he said to himself as he stropped the razor to restore its fine edge.

Miss Trudy was busy pouring his coffee and wiping off the long pine table in the dining room when Layke quickly descended the narrow stairs. She hummed an old tune as she lovingly prepared for her new guest. Hardly recognizing him without his dark brown beard she thought, "Oh my, what a handsome man he is! Haven't seen a man that handsome in a coon's age. Seems to have a little limp - must've been injured in the War or maybe on the range."

"I sure could stand some pone and slab with my coffee after all Miss Stucky, if you still have some. That nice hot bath has awakened my appetite."

She chuckled, bustled her matronly body around the table, and in no time returned with a platter overflowing with fried sweet potatoes along with corn pone and the pork slab, crisp and brown and dripping with cane syrup.

Miss Trudy lowered her ample body onto the chair facing Layke and chattered away, singing the praises of Old Town, exclaiming that there were over twenty families settled around there now and more moving in every year.

When Layke inquired about work in the area, she told him about Berta McRae needing help over at South Spring; "what with the cow hunt and spring drive to Punta Rassa coming up, and since young Reuben, her oldest son, moved up to the Oliver ranch near Rose Head to be close to that pretty Leonora."

Berta, being a proud and strong woman, had assumed all the jobs any man could handle since she was widowed. Some of the locals faulted her for it, but the truth is she had no choice, and Miss Trudy sang her praises loud and clear.

"The widow has done the best she could. After all, four mouths to feed when Reuben died. Not to be wished on anyone, and her having to do nearly any kind of work to keep the wolf from the door. Now, her second son, Jonah, has taken up the slack, and if the hearsay is right, he's doing a right smart good job of it for one so young. She's just got the two old colored families living on the place to help her out - not that they're much use, being so old and all."

She filled Layke's tin cup to the top with the bubbling, rich coffee, all the while talking away. He sighed and leaned back in the ladder-back pine chair.

"Best meal I've had in almost a month, Miss Stucky," he exclaimed with obvious satisfaction.

4

"Call me Trudy, Layke. Most folks around here call me Miss Trudy." Her faded blue eyes twinkled, and she got more spring in her step as she went about cleaning up the kitchen.

"He sure knows how to please a lady," she thought and smiled to herself as she asked him about the crops up towards Rowland's Bluff, and if it was as dry there as it had been around Old Town and other passing-the-time-of-day chatter.

Layke followed her into the kitchen and asked, "Miss Trudy, I'd be much obliged if I could have a few scraps for Tag. An old piece of corn bread or just about anything will do."

Tag was wagging his tail almost off when Layke came out onto the boarding house porch carrying the tin plate generously overflowing with scraps from the Stucky kitchen. Miss Trudy followed him, and enjoying Tag's hearty appetite commented, "His appetite must have woke up, too, Layke," and her plump body jiggled all over as they watched, amused by Tag's enjoyment.

Night was fast falling, and he realized he had to get Bucko over to the stable. "Bud Brewster will take good care of your horse, and you're welcome to come back when you're through there and visit on the porch."

The townspeople would usually gather after supper on Miss Trudy's porch and discuss the crops and the events of the day. The men would smoke their pipes, and one of them would always have a jug of home brew. Frankie Brewster, Bud and Luta's boy, would bring out his harmonica and play some of the old tunes. Luta would wander over after she put Bethy in her crib, and she and Miss Trudy would shell peas or snap beans or just relax and chat about one thing or another.

Layke leisurely looked around and knew that his decision to settle in Old Town was a good one. "Down boy, down!" he said to Tag as he pushed him aside. Tag resumed playing with the Brewster dog, dust swirling all around them. He lapped the warm, stagnant water out of the trough as Layke walked toward the stable carrying Trudy's lantern to light his way. "Guess all soldiers and cowmen are creatures of habit," he thought. The idea of going to bed without checking his horse was unthinkable. As usual Tag was practically in Layke's boots when he came out.

With fists clenched, reinforcing his decision, he straightened his broad shoulders and said to himself, "There'll be no more thinking on it - this is the end of my wandering. It's a good town

5

and these are good people. I'm staying!"

He returned to the porch, smoked his pipe and visited with Bud Brewster, who was also the town's blacksmith, and the brothers, Davis and Palmer McCoy, who operated the dry goods and feed store. As promised, there was a jug and Frankie's music to fill the star-studded fall night.

It had been a long day, and he wanted to get an early start to the McRae spread. As he tiredly turned toward Trudy and inquired about the directions to the ranch, Bud Brewster spoke up and proceeded to tell him. Layke rose to leave, and before he could bid the gathering goodnight, Davis quickly offered him another swig from the jug, "so's to warm you on your way."

"Thank you, Davis." He raised the jug high and said in his deep voice, "To the fairest of fair - Old Town."Taking a long swig, he licked his satisfied lips. "I hope this will be one of many toasts I'll have the honor of offering to the fair Old Town."Bowing to the ladies with a perfect soldier's posture he left the amused townsfolk as they excitedly discussed the interesting cowman.

As Layke climbed the worn stairs Miss Trudy turned to Luta and winked at her. "If that pretty Berta McRae doesn't hire him on I'm a mind to my self." She chuckled as she said it, and Luta joined in, amused at their private joke.

"Hmmm, what a good looking couple he and Berta would make. She so blue-eyed and blond and him with that thatch of dark brown hair and those all-color eyes. Don't know when I've seen a handsomer man, so straight and tall like the good soldier he once was."

When she said that, Palmer left his spot and crouched beside Trudy's and Luta's chairs and in a secretive voice, barely above a whisper, told the congregated townspeople what Bo Lutes from over at Fort Fannin Springs had told him that very evening about the crippled stranger.

"You know Bo has been on every spring drive since the War, and he said that the cowmen all over Florida have umpteen tales to tell about our new visitor, Mr. Layke Williams. You noticed that he didn't tote no gun, didn't you? Well, that's a good one all right!"

Palmer proceeded to tell his fascinated audience all about how Layke took to the cow whip instead of the gun when the War was over and he'd given up soldiering. He unfolded the story of

Layke that had been told around cowmen's camp fires for the past ten years or so.

"It seems he decided he'd try to do a little farming when he first got to Florida. Got himself a small spread and played the hermit. Didn't take to folks as they were always bringing up the War, and Layke just wanted to forget it. You knew that he'd been in some of the most fiercest battles, serving under Uncle Joe Johnston, didn't you? And, it's been told, lost two of his brothers and his best army buddy - and, of course, 'bout lost his leg. Anyways, he needed time to regroup.

"Well, he took to farming just about like a bobcat does to a cow dog. That land fought him 'til he durn near starved to death. Don't ever offer him anything with a berry in it," Palmer interjected humorously - "that and fish was about all he had to eat that spring. Since he swore he'd never take up a gun again and wasn't too good at trapping, he did have himself one hard time of it. Kept a few chickens around for eggs and meat and had an old lean-to for them to nest in.

"One spring night there came up a fierce storm all a sudden like, and bein' down to 'bout his last chicken he headed for the coop to make sure his next meal was dry. On the way he heard all this squawkin' and in the lantern light saw that chicken a'flyin' all over the place, and hangin' onto its tail feathers was the biggest wolf a body could imagine. It was a'starin' him right in the eye. No gun, mind you. Not even a log. Well, he knew his time had come. He started to back up real slow like when 'bout that time another animal jumped out of the pitch-black and went for that wolf. Now he couldn't see real good what with the wind and rain a'howlin' all over the place, but he could hear. It was a dog!

"Now Layke didn't own a dog. The closest neighbor he had was 'bout five mile east, so it wouldn't have been theirs. He started huntin' himself a big log 'cause it sounded like the wolf was a'bestin' the dog. Then he remembered the buckskin whip, so ran back to his cabin to fetch it. Now Layke was new to the whip, but he was smart enough to know that a man had to take care of himself with somethin' besides his bare hands. So he'd bought one at the dry goods store in Marianna. He'd seen the fired-up cowmen use 'em on a Saturday night after a few rounds of stump whiskey, so he had the idea of what to do. And he'd done some practicin' at snappin' off some low limbs, but to use it for real, he hadn't.

7

"So he snuck up on the fightin' animals and there before him was the dog on the ground. The wolf was hurt but was a staring at him with its fierce eyes. He knew he'd have to act - and act real fast.

"Now Layke was on react, and react he did! He aimed for the head and split that wolf right between the eyes making a deep gash. Then he took that log and beat him 'til he was dead. He could see in the half light that the dog was still alive, so he picked him up, careful like, and took him back to the cabin.

"The storm blew over just as quick as it sprang up, and he wrapped the poor dog up in his old army blanket and fell into a dead sleep. When he finally woke up, he remembered the dog. He'd made it through the night. He decided to name him Sergeant.

"Never did find out where Sergeant came from. Said he ought to have named him Providence, cause Sarge gave him the nudge to become a cowman. But somehow that name didn't seem fittin' for just about the best catch dog this state ever saw. Why, that dog could grab a hold of a bull's nose and hang on 'til he turned the whole herd around.

"He nursed Sarge for almost two weeks. Took up the cow whip and went hunting for game and made a rich broth to mix with meal and fattened that dog right up. Got so's he could strip the skin off'n a squirrel or rabbit at ten paces. And from that day to this Layke Williams is known to be the best hand with a buckskin whip of any cowman in the whole of Florida. Old Sarge died while he was up at the Wilpole spread. Bo said that's why Layke moved on.

"Got him a good cow dog in Tag. Everywhere he goes, that dog tags along, as no doubt you've noticed. Yep, there are umpteen tales to be told about our new visitor, and Bo knows 'em all if'n you want to hear more."

Palmer returned to his chair, and he and Bud continued the telling of the tales, as they did most every night after supper, while Frankie listened and played sweetly on his harmonica.

Trudy and Luta rocked and snapped the beans for the next day's dinner. They continued to discuss in hushed voices who, if anyone, would be capable of ending the longing they could see in the cowman's hungry heart.

"He does have a lost look in those all-color eyes, don't he,

Luta? A real hungry-for-love, lost look. Hmmm, I'll wager that there's not an available lady in all of Old Town who wouldn't just love to help him fill up the empty space in his heart."

CHAPTER II BERTA

It had been day to day for a long time for Berta McRae. The sameness just about got her down. "Oh, how I'd welcome a good norther to come blowing in to cool things off. Seems to me I notice the heat more and more. I'm always damp. Even my hair smells sour," she thought as she brushed the golden, damp strands away from her forehead.

She busied herself to hurry up the preparation of dinner and decided that after dinner she and the children would go down to the stand of wild persimmons beside the south spring. The dark blue water was cool there, and they'd get a real good soaking. They needed a change from the monotonous, every-day chores.

When Reuben was alive they would quite often go to the south spring. After their Sunday dinner she'd straighten up the kitchen while he played with the children. Then they'd stroll leisurely down to the spring. The children would gather joe-pye weeds and black-eyed susans as they skipped along the ox trail. She'd spread an old quilt underneath the giant oak at the bottom of Sand Ridge, where the grass grew thick and soft, and they'd enjoy a lazy day - napping and splashing in the cool water.

When they returned near nightfall she'd put on the sweet smelling camisole her Auntie had sent, all sweet with rose petals from the bushes back home in Macon. She could still see them blooming in all their glorious colors in the side yard between her ma's and Auntie's houses, where the whitewashed fence separated the two properties.

Berta still missed home. She had tried to make Old Town seem like home for these past seventeen years. But when Berta said home, she still meant Melrose Street in Macon, Georgia. She'd been back only once in that long time. It was immediately after the War and they had finally been allowed to travel. Reuben, with his keen insight, had known how homesick she was and had insisted that she make the trip. Young Reuben was only five and Jonah not more than a babe.

How she had longed for the comfort of the big four-poster feather bed in her beautifully decorated room - so delicate and feminine with the Brussels lace edging the sheer panels that framed the deep windows overlooking the side flower garden. She remembered lying awake on the lacy pillows by the hour, dreaming of her

10

make believe husband or the Grand Golden Ball...or just counting the millions of tiny pink and white flower sprays that cascaded across the dusty rose wallpaper.

Her ma always saw to it that there was a cup of steaming chocolate awaiting her when she arose, and she would sink her tiny feet into the deeply piled wool rug and dance around and around, her sheer nightie swirling out behind her with not a care in her secure world. Everything surrounding Berta had been pretty and soft and delicate. Nothing like the home she had shared with Reuben at South Spring... nothing!

As she looked toward the darkened parlor, her heart ached. My, how proud they had been of that room ten years ago. Reuben had hired Miles Lindstrom all the way from Tallahassee to do the plastering and papering of the walls. He understood how much his young bride missed her beautiful surroundings, and he was determined to do everything within his means to make South Spring comfortable and pleasant for her.

Berta selected Victorian blue paper with sprays of pussy willows and green ivy. The ornately carved mahogany love seat and matching chair were beautifully covered in cranberry satin brocade. Along with the pedestal tables with their brass claw feet, they had been brought all the way from Macon - first by wagon to Rowland's Bluff, then put on the steamboat to Old Town. Her ma had given her the exquisite Galway crystal oil lamp for the long parlor table placed by the front door, and she had hung Irish lace panels at the only window in the small square room.

Berta quickly looked away. The tears filled her half closed eyes as she tried to control her emotions. The once beautiful paper was now faded and stained underneath the window. An unexpected norther had taken care of that. Had Reuben been home instead of on a cow hunt he'd have been able to repair it. Old Dan wasn't good at that sort of thing, and she was so busy helping Young Reuben coax their remaining milk cow into her stall that stormy night that she was unaware that the blowing rain had found its way into her safe home to defile the beauty of her parlor.

Jonah and SuSu were real young then and spent most of their time in the warmth of the kitchen, where she kept their play things during the winter months. It wasn't that they weren't allowed in the parlor - she just kept it for mostly looking at instead of playing and sitting in. When a visiting neighbor came on occasion, she would lower the window shade and light the lamp for the duration of the visit. The children loved watching the shadows that the glowing light created on the walls and would take turns guessing what the various shapes resembled.

Berta sighed and shook her head. "Enough of remembering," she said. But as she continued with the preparation of their main meal, her mind wandered back to the needed comfort of her youth and the cherished days of the good times in her beloved Macon.

She was not quite seventeen when she and Reuben wed, and he ten years her senior. He and his family had been friends with the Norwood family for many years. The McRaes owned Lochmon, a large cotton and tobacco plantation southwest of Macon. As a youngster, Berta, her sister, Lamorah, and the male child of the family, Thaddeous - called Tad - would spend a week or two each summer visiting Lochmon.

Berta's father was a cotton and tobacco broker and traveled from Macon to Savannah two or three times a month. Mrs. Norwood was kept busy with the childrem and the running of the home so seldom accompanied her husband on his trips, but when he returned, he'd always bring back beautiful gifts.

Savannah was a busy port in the 1850s. The shops were laden with figurines from France and Italy, china from England, Brussels and Irish lace and other fine fabrics from all over the world. Consequently, the Norwood home was one of the most beautifully appointed homes in all of Macon.

When Berta made her debut at sixteen, relatives and friends from Atlanta, Savannah, and as far away as Jacksonville, Florida arrived for the important occasion. Her ma and Aunt Bertrice had been busily preparing for the upcoming event for months and were as nervously excited as the servants and children.

Berta's gown was from Paris, France - royal blue, silk taffeta with pale pink satin rosettes on the wide moire taffeta ribbon surrounding the discretely low neckline. "Very fashionable. Just right for the occasion," Miss Julia, of Warsaw's Fine Fashions, assured them. "Just perfect!"

Her youthful skin glowed; her golden curls cascaded below her waist. Ornate Spanish combs held them securely above her tiny ears to show off her grandmother Augusta's pearl and diamond earrings, a gift for her coming-out day.

The lovely, but unpretentious Norwood home was alive with

activity. Her ma, Sadie, and Little Woman had cooked for weeks preparing the fancy tarts and rum cakes. Bushels of walnuts and pecans had been shelled and finely chopped for the tea cakes. Hams had been brought from Lochmon by Reuben, who accompanied his sister Maribea, Berta's best friend, and who had made her debut the year before.

Berta had always liked Reuben, but had not spent much time around him because he had been at school in Atlanta. When he was home, he was busily assisting his father in running the plantation. She had not seen him since Maribea's debut, and then for only a short time, as she was helping Mrs. McRae with the many chores, and barely realized Reuben was there.

He was very easy to talk to and she had always been comfortable around him. But because he was Maribea's older brother she really hadn't thought of him as a suitor. Everyone in the family assumed she'd one day marry Matthew Livingston, who was only three years older and accompanied her to all of Maribea's debutante parties. It was obvious that Matthew was smitten by her high spirit as well as her beauty, and certainly her social position was found to be very acceptable by the Livingstons.

They were an old Macon family, and had at one time been one of the wealthiest families in that area, but had made unfortunate investments in recent years. Berta and Matthew had not discussed any plans, but because they were constant companions attending the many social functions, their friends and relatives assumed there would be an alliance.

Berta often remembered the first time she had thought of Reuben as someone other than Maribea's older brother. It was at her debut, and her ma had asked him if he would be so kind as to run the numerous errands she had been unable to accomplish, and he had graciously agreed to assist her. Frankly, Berta was bored with the never-ending planning and preparation. She prevailed upon her ma to allow her and Maribea to accompany Reuben - just to get out of the house for a little while.

Mrs. Norwood, who knew her vivacious daughter through and through, sensed that her nerves were becoming frayed, and agreed. At the last moment, Muldeen insisted that Maribea stay to help her with the pink rosettes; they were to catch the lace scallops on the cloth covering the punch table. Aunt Bertrice couldn't accompany them as she was completing the floral arrangements for

13

the tables and pedestals. So, reluctantly, Berta was allowed to join Reuben unchaperoned. She was more excited about riding unchaperoned with Reuben, except for Benge, the driver, than about the debut the next day.

"Oh, Reuben. Isn't this delightful? So much more fun than staying around the old house. Isn't it?" Berta exclaimed excitedly as she looked up at his broad Scottish face as he held her arm securely, assisting her into the buggy.

"Benge," she said with affected authority, "first drive to the haberdashery to fetch Pa's new shirt and hat. Then, Benge, we'll drive to Miss Julia's to pick up Ma's dress."

Berta was having such a good time that she was unaware of Reuben's smiling at her as if it were the first time he'd seen her. They talked animatedly and persuaded a very reluctant Benge into driving them to the sweet shop for pralines. Being very extravagant, she filled two bags full, explaining to Reuben that she did not plan to eat them all, that some were for Little Woman, who loved them.

Little Woman was Berta's favorite of all the Darkies on the place. There were only a few years' difference in their ages, but Little Woman assumed the matronly role with absolute dominance over Berta. Berta could not imagine home without all of them; Little Woman, who was actually the housemaid, and Sadie, who ran the kitchen with the same pride as the missus. They were all free, because her pa didn't hold with slavery.

The gardens were tended with Benge's magical touch, and in the spring and fall people from all over Macon would drive by the Norwood home on their afternoon drives to view them. The front yard wasn't extremely large, but Benge had done a magnificent job of utilizing every inch of space. In the spring the lilacs, peonies, iris and tulips were as glorious as the roses. And in the back of the house beside the summer kitchen he had arranged unbelievable shades of azaleas, some as tall as trees and others only foot- high miniatures. A towering mimosa tree surrounded by dogwood, cherry and plum trees grew south of the stable, and he always had a fence of brightly colored sweet peas along the back of their property. The Norwood gardens were breathtaking, and May was a perfect time for the debut festivities.

After Berta and Reuben left the sweet shop they told Benge to drive them to the Broad Street Park, where there was always lots of activity. The organ grinder with his colorfully dressed monkey on a leash entertained the strolling couples. They walked beside the band shell, but because it was a week day, there was no performance. Selecting a bench beneath a dancing willow, they slowly ate their pralines as the cool spring air wafted the aroma from the pastries, roasted peanuts and hot buttered pecans that the street vendors were peddling. They talked and talked, unconscious of the passing time.

Reuben told her about his college in Atlanta, where he had become much more interested in the cattle industry than in the tobacco and cotton business that his father had sent him to study.

"And one day it is my desire to own my own cattle ranch. My Uncle Elon, father's oldest brother, has a large spread in Florida right on the Suwannee. Now it's true that Florida is still very primitive, but I recently read in an Atlanta paper that an enterprising person with derring-do could make his fortune in the last frontier. Ma says that Uncle Elon didn't get along with Grandma and Grandpa, so he left home when he was very young. Do you know, Pa 's seen him only once in the past twenty years? All of a sudden he showed up - about a month ago - right out of the blue."

"It was all very strange. They didn't even recognize each other 'til Uncle Elon spoke. I got to ask him all about Florida during supper, and there is no doubt, Berta, that Florida is indeed the land of opportunity." Berta sat mesmerized, munching her praline and hanging onto his every word.

When Reuben had discussed his dreams and aspirations with his father, Hamilton McRae showed no enthusiasm for the venture. After all, the reason he had sent him to college was to acquire knowledge that would be beneficial for Lochmon and its prosperity - not to go high-tailing off to the bastard state of Florida to become a cowman. He just couldn't believe the young men of today. Why, when he was their age...well...

But Reuben ignored his father's disinterest and continued to question Elon, extracting as much information as he could during the short visit. It seems that he had married a girl from one of the turpentine camps, and they lived on a ranch called South Spring just outside the settlement of Old Town.

Reuben had become particularly interested when he told him of the abundance of game in that area. "Why, Reuben, it's a true wilderness. Do you know, I can go for days on end and not see a livin' soul? Not a livin' soul!"

15

Of the two boys in the McRae family, Reuben was the out-doorsman and Ham the quiet one. Their pa often said "Reuben was born to the shotgun and fishing pole - while Ham, well, do you ever see Ham when he's not toting a book and sippin' his bourbon and branch water?"

As Reuben enthuiastically spoke of his plans with Berta, she became as excited and interested as he. His sun-tanned Scottish face lit up with every adjective, and she found herself asking questions and interjecting ideas as they animatedly discussed Florida with all its possibilities for Reuben's future.

It seemed like only minutes, but when Benge left the buggy to fetch them he was real upset. Berating them all the way back to Broad Street, he said, "Miss Lillian is goin' to have mah hide if'n I don't get ya'll back to Melrose Street in jig time. Miss Berta. Ah can't believe you'd cause ole Benge this much misery...Ah sho can't."

Berta patted him on his boney back...soothing him, but they were amused by his frustration and continued to talk non-stop all the way home. She had not even thought of the debut from the time she sat beside Reuben in the buggy that morning 'til they finally arrived home and were met by a very distraught Miss Lillian.

"Where on earth have you been? Don't you realize that Little Woman has to do your hair and Benge has to go to the station to meet Uncle Jock and Aunt Lawanda and all those younguns coming all the way from Florida for your highness's debut?"

Berta, resenting the intrusion of the party plan chatter, virtually ignored her 'til she mentioned Florida. Her ears pricked up, and she started to glance at Reuben, who was busily apologizing to her ma. They simultaneously turned toward each other, and there was a new and different feeling in their expressions. Reuben's dark brown eyes sparkled as he peered deeply into Berta's young, innocent, blue ones. Berta, embarrassed, was the first to look away, but she had a knowing smile on her lips.

Miss Lillian was unaware of everything but her plans for dinner and getting her guests situated in the various family members' homes, and was in utter dismay when Berta abruptly turned and dashed up the stairs - two at a time. She shook her head in disbelief as she turned toward Reuben for sympathy.

"I don't know what has come over that girl! She's behaving like a child and here she is making her debut tomorrow. I'll declare

16

she acts just like a jittery colt!"

Reuben turned Miss Lillian around to face him, and put his big square hands on both her shoulders as he explained to her, "Berta is just nervous and keyed up about tomorrow's events, Mrs. Norwood. Maribea acted in the very same manner just before her debut last year."

Actually, he wasn't aware how Maribea had acted, but he knew the comforting words were called for. Reuben McRae was never at a loss for words, and the correct ones always came easily to him. Miss Lillian sighed, relaxed, and thanked him for being so understanding. She continued to bustle around the parlor giving that room its final inspection.

Reuben joined Wesley Norwood and Bertrice's husband, Olaf Pope, on the side porch. As he entered the room, Mr. Norwood turned toward him, drink in hand, and it was obvious to Reuben that it was not his first of the day.

Wesley and Olaf were deep into a heated discussion about the obvious secession of the southern states and were arguing about when it would occur. With a furrowed brow and slurred speech, he asked, "Reuben, when are ya gonna get into a uniform?"

Realizing the necessity of a calm response, he answered, "Well, gentlemen, I shall of course defend the South when and if it becomes necessary. But really, anything can prevent an all-out war. In the meantime, I shall build a life for myself and hoped for wife and children in the finest southern tradition to assure us the priviledge of choosing our own way of life, and not be dictated to by our good brothers in the capital."

When Reuben said "wife", his mind turned to Berta. He had not seriously considered taking a wife, at least not in the forseeable future. His parents were anxious for a suitable alliance and were very accomodating when they were asked to attend the many social functions in and around Atlanta, but Reuben had found none of their daughters to his liking.

He was not an extremely handsome man - more rugged in appearance than handsome. Most people thought of Reuben McRae as a pleasant, unassuming man of medium height, medium brown hair and eyes, but delightful company. He was much sought after, always a gentleman, and as much at ease around the ladies as the ladies' fathers and brothers. He was considered a catch by the affluent families in that region of Georgia, and was extremely

17

popular.

Unlike Reuben was his younger brother Ham, tall and wiry with sandy, straight hair and pale blue eyes, and thought by many as the handsomer of the two. He loved music, literature, a good cigar and whiskey. He was also suspected of frequenting the slaves' quarters from time to time. Although he and Reuben differed about most of the important issues, they shared a mutual respect for each other's beliefs and a close brotherly bond.

If Ham had a deep interest besides his books and bottle, it had to be his love of Lochmon, and though he was more withdrawn than Reuben, he had very definite ideas concerning the operation of the plantation and would debate them at length with Reuben, his father and anyone else within earshot.

When Reuben dreamed of seeking out the exciting Florida wilderness in which to build his own place, he knew in his heart that Lochmon would be well taken care of by Ham. And with Reuben gone Ham would surely assume the leadership he was capable of. Nothing would make Reuben happier than to see his brother become the man who had been locked up inside for far too long.

When Miss Lillian and Berta entered the side porch to join the men, Berta and Reuben exchanged intimate glances, and for once in his life Reuben was speechless. Maribea arrived a few minutes later and sensed that something had occured between them, but after studying her best friend decided she would wait until Berta wanted to confide in her, as she was sure she would before they were asleep that night. She was positive that they had discovered each other.

She smiled to herself and had difficulty containing her joy. As she watched them she wondered just what had taken place on that lovely May afternoon. She loved Berta as a sister, and nothing would give her more pleasure than to have her as a sister-in-law. When she came bursting into the room an hour earlier with her face all flushed, Maribea had thought it was because her mother had admonished her for being so late. She could now see that that was not the case.

The other family members soon joined the assembled group as Sadie placed the heavily laden platters of sandwiches and relishes on the mahogany sideboard in the dining room. With the ladies present the men ceased speaking of the troubled times and instead referred to the local politics, the price of cotton and tobacco and

18

other general topics.

Bertrice was trying to hurry Olaf so they could get to the depot to meet the express from Savannah. But Olaf Pope was not to be hurried, and the more Bertrice tapped her foot and pursed her lips angrily, the more he expanded on every suitable subject to delay their departure. Berta and Reuben found the situation very amusing and began to giggle like two school children as they shyly looked at each other. Maribea was the only one who noticed their nervous exchange.

Olaf finally, reluctantly, left the festivities with Bertrice giving him a piece of her mind the minute she thought they were out of hearing. They soon returned with Uncle Jock and Aunt Lawanda and their eight children, who, tired from the long journey, joined the other family members and guests for the cold supper. Later they retired to the spacious Pope residence next door.

Jock had brought oysters and shrimp from Savannah and Mamie and Sadie worked way into the night to get them pickled and into the deep crock before they spoiled. The fresh lemons and limes had to be squeezed for the punch and burnt sugar cakes that were Sadie's specialty before they retired for the night. It was a warm and happy kitchen as the two lovingly chattered about the next day's events. The Norwoods were their family and they were as proud of Berta's debut as though she were their own.

Berta and Maribea had retired early but were so filled with excitement that it was impossible for them to allow sleep to interfere with their high spirits. They giggled and talked, and finally Maribea could hold her curiosity no longer. "All right, Berta, why were you and Reuben so late this afternoon? Why I thought Miss Lillian was going to have a conniption fit 'fore ya'll returned."

"Isn't it excitin', Maribea? Why didn't you tell me about Reuben wantin' to go to Florida to start his very own ranch? How wonderfully adventurous he is and not the least bit afraid. Why, I would be scared silly to go to such a mysterious place."

"Why, Bertrice Lillian Norwood. I had no idea Reuben had ever entertained such a ridiculous idea. Why, what on earth will Papa do?"

She angrily turned away fron an astonished Berta and through her sniffles said, "When I saw you and Reuben this evening I thought that just maybe you had found each other, and that perhaps, in the future of course, you just might be asked to be a

19

McRae. Now I'm not sure I'd like that one little bit. 'Cause if it does happen, I'll not gain a sister...I'll just lose my very best friend and favorite brother to the Florida wilderness, and I just know I'll never see either of you again. I just know it!"

Maribea began to sob in earnest. Berta tried to calm her with soothing sounds, but Maribea was not to be consoled.

"Berta, oh Berta! You wouldn't even dream of going off with Reuben if you'd seen Uncle Elon. Berta, he's such a wild, uncouth old man , and I'm certain that uncivilized place has made him that way! Please, dear friend, for all our sakes make Reuben change his mind!"

Berta was concerned for Maribea, but could not understand why she was so upset. She held her shoulders gently and reassuringly said, "Dear Maribea, I don't for the life of me understand why you're so upset! Why, Reuben and I hardly know each other. Gracious me, I'm not at all sure of Reuben's intentions...or for that matter, my own. But, dear, if indeed one day I should become a McRae I would certainly hope to have some say-so as to where I lived. Frankly, I'm not at all sure that Florida sounds all that appealing; no culture or shops or just about anything but cows - thousands of cows, as far as I can discern."

Maribea finally calmed down and fell into an exhausted sleep. But Berta was much too restless, and as Maribea slept peacefully, Berta lay awake and wondered about the mysterious Florida wilderness and what it would be like to accompany Reuben there as his wife. After all, her very own grandparents and great-grandparents had been pioneers right in Macon, Georgia and hadn't become weird like their Uncle Elon. Why, they were as proud and as fine as folks anywhere. She was sure Maribea was over-reacting. She finally drifted off, and when Little Woman resorted to shaking her she was in the middle of a glorious dream about Reuben and their big, beautiful ranch in Florida.

The day went by so fast that when she was being dressed by Little Woman she was still in a daze from the previous day's activities. Her large room was filled with her cousins and friends helping each other dress for the party. Crinolines and stiffly starched petticoats hung in great profusion from the high four poster bed. The room was alive with chatter and nervous giggles, but the merriment was lost on the somber Berta. The girls were delightfully amused by her solemn appearance and teased her unmercifully. Berta accepted their good natured actions with grace but wished the party would soon end and things would quickly return to normal.

The time had finally arrived, and the guests were assembled at the foot of the wide staircase in the parlor. Little Woman pinched her cheeks, trying to add color to them and nervously checked every detail of her voluminous skirt. Its deeply ruffled train was edged with pink satin rosettes that perched in the center of the deep scallops and circled her tiny waist.

There was a knock on her door, and she heard her pa softly call her name.

"Berta, are you ready?" Again he called. "Berta, my dear girl, are you ready to make your appearance?"

She responded in an almost inaudible voice as he opened the door. Little Woman was having difficulty holding up the long trailing skirt and was babbling a mile a minute. Her pa put his large hand underneath her delicate, quivering chin, tilting it up as he kissed her lightly on her cheek and whispered in her ear. "You're almost as beautiful as your dear mother was at her debut, my precious girl." But Berta was so tired and nervous she barely heard him. She quietly thanked him and took his steady arm, grateful for its sturdy support.

At that moment the more than one hundred assembled guests took their silver spoons and began tapping their wine glasses. The tinkling music brought a hesitant smile to her trembling lips - then a grin - and finally youthful laughter arose.

When Reuben saw her in all her finery laughing and holding onto Wesley Norwood's arm, he knew he had never seen such an enchanting creature and that he wanted to spend the rest of his life enjoying her and making her happy.

Six months later he and Bertrice Lillian Norwood were wed. She descended the same stairs, wearing an ice blue satin gown, and over her beautiful golden curls a heavy Spanish mantilla enveloped her soft, flawless shoulders. That evening, immediately following the reception, she and Reuben boarded the train for Savannah and finally Jacksonville where they were met by Uncle Jock, who insisted on accompanying them to Lake City. As fate would have it, Elon and his wife, Effie, died of diphtheria shortly after his visit to Lochmon. They had no living children. Effie was never able to carry full term and all five children had been stillborn, or so folks

21

were told.

When Hamilton McRae received the letter about Elon, he contacted the Crosstown Bank as instructed and was informed that he was the sole heir. He knew immediately his course. Reuben's continued infatuation with ranching and the threat of war aided his decision. He called Reuben into his study and seriously discussed his role as master of South Spring. An elated Reuben left the following day by train. But before he departed he called on Wesley Norwood to ask for Berta's hand in marriage - they had been given permission to court the evening of the debut.

Both families were ecstatic over the news of the betrothal - there was so little good news those days with the secession imminent and the talk of war on everyone's lips, and their families were relieved that they would be far away. They hoped they would avoid the hard times they were sure would befall Georgia.

****

Reuben and Berta bought supplies at Lake city for the long, arduous trip by ox-cart to Rowland's Bluff on the Suwannee River. There they boarded the steamship *Madison*, a small sternwheeler that made a weekly trip from Cedar Key to as far as the high water would allow, stopping at the various landings all along the Suwannee. She was referred to as a floating country store by the crackers who lived in the area.

The *Madison* had a loud and lusty whistle and could be heard for miles around, and her arrival was an exciting event for the people who lived near the river. The farmers and ranchers would gather their produce and goods for trading or shipping at the sound of her whistle and make tracks to the nearest landing. Capt. Jim would stay as long as people wanted to trade and pass the time visiting, discussing politics, exchanging news of the outside world and local gossip.

Berta was exuberant! On Reuben's previous trip to South Spring he had gleaned as much information about the area as possible to share with his bride. He kept her entertained with the humorous tales of the area, some true and some obviously doctored. Around every twist and turn of the black river he'd delight her with his new knowledge. "Berta, see!" he would exclaim excitedly. "That's a pileated woodpecker... or, honey, look! Over there beside the fallen log. See the two round eyes and then follow from there ..see the ridge.." "Oh, Reuben, is that an alligator? Oh my! Look,

22

there's a baby beside it."

He identified the birds and their musical trills and the red shouldered hawks that screamed from the dense woods. A flock of little blue herons hovered above and seemed to guide the *Madison* , assisting Capt. Jim in the pilot house on the top deck. This was the land that the tall, proud, hamdsome Timucuans occupied before the eighteenth century, and Berta was already feeling its frightening power over her. She was hesitant to accept its deafening quiet - its sometimes glassy smooth waters - when around the next bend a shallow would appear and then a sand bar, deceiving an inexperienced boat pilot.

She had left the cosmopolitan Macon for the unexpected ...the unknown. It was a slow paced, hard life and was totally different from life in and around Macon. Reuben prayed that his bride with her youthful innocence would accept this new land that he already loved with a deep fervor that Lochmon had never afforded him.

****

Wes grabbed Berta around her legs and was laughing so hard she couldn't help but join in.

"Wesley Hamilton McRae, what on earth has got into you?" "Ma, I was just playin'. You were a big old black bear, and I caught you so's you wouldn't eat SuSu." He scrambled out to the porch as quickly as he had run into the kitchen. Berta shook her head and smiled to herself. "That child has been my salvation, Lord, and I thank you for him," she sighed. The six-year-old towhead had brought her back to the present, and she was grateful. She knew she dwelled too much in the past.

In the distance below the forming clouds, Berta saw the dust rise, and from its midst emerged a rider.

CHAPTER III THE MEETING

It was a clear morning with a hint of rain in the air when Layke left the Stucky Hotel and headed west alongside the lazy Suwannee. He could smell it as he and Tag took their time exploring some of the side roads on the trail. The full branches of the sweet bay and live oaks that grew thick beside the meandering river gave them little protection from the relentlessly pounding sun.

They had been an hour on the ox trail when they came to a clearing. Layke saw the spread in the distance. It was the usual small heart-pine cabin with a porch, barn and a few other out buildings that Bud Brewster had described. But as he drew closer he saw a well tended flower garden bordering the house-long porch. "As pretty as the flowers Mama used to grow at home," he thought. The house was similar to his home in Tennessee but not nearly as large. As he noticed the clouds gathering to the south of him, he remembered the wonderful, rhythmic sound that rain drops made on a steep tin roof.

Berta continued putting the dinner dishes back into the cupboard. She turned to SuSu, who had helped dry them, and said, "Why don't you go play with Wes, honey? Or maybe you'd better take a little nap. I'll just see who on earth that is. Can't imagine who'd be riding out at this time of day."

She finished clearing the kitchen and drying her hands on her faded, flowered apron, and went out on the back stoop. Berta didn't recognize the stranger, but as she looked toward south gate she, too, noticed the blackness of the gathering clouds and gave a sigh of relief. The river was low as there had been no measurable amount of rain for over a month, and she and her neighbors were concerned.

Layke approached the gate and saw a woman emerge from the kitchen. Tag was barking and dancing around him and Bucko, stirring up the powdery dust. When the dust cleared he saw her. She was wearing a softly flowered house dress and pushing her taffy colored hair back from her questioning brow. He didn't notice her rough, calloused hands as she opened the gate. He looked only at her eyes.

"I never in all my life saw such eyes," he said under his breath with amazement. "Cornflower blue. As blue as any cornflower in the hills of Tennessee."

24

Her chin was held high and thrust forward. He smiled -- just couldn't help himself. And he wasn't one to smile often -- almost never did. But that determined set to her spine amused him. As he studied every inch of the beautiful woman standing before him, an unexpected surge of emotion seized him by surprise. A once-felt feeling from, oh, so long ago returned. Layke Williams knew he had at last found home.

He was the first to speak. "Berta McRae? Your servant, Ma'am." He tipped his sweat rimmed hat, never taking his eyes off hers. "Miss Trudy sent me. She thought you might have need of a cowman."

The dust finally cleared, and Berta got a good look at the stranger. She got a catch in her throat and cleared it several times before regaining her composure. In a forced voice she said, "Good morning, Mister...?" But silently she exclaimed, "those all-color eyes have found their way into my very soul. Dear Lord in the morning!"

"Layke Williams from up Tennessee way," he replied, as mesmerized as she.

She managed, "Mr. Williams, welcome to South Spring."

"Please call me Layke - spelled with a 'y'. Was my grandpa's name on my mother's side." He reiterated, "Miss Trudy suggested I ride out to see if I could be of assistance. I'm an experienced cowman and could use the work."

"That depends, Mr. Williams - I mean Layke. I took in Ned Perkins last year and thought he'd do fine, too, only to find he'd rather run off on payday and not show up 'til mid-week, and then he had the nerve to leave me high and dry when the drive to Punta Rassa came due."

As Berta heard the strange words spill forth, she was amazed that she was the one saying them. "He's a Godsend," she thought as she allowed herself to actually study the tall, handsome man before her. "He's the answer to South Spring and all my prayers. I'm not sure Big Dan and Jonah and I can get through another year without help. Now, why did I say that about Ned Perkins? I know full well I'm going to hire him. I've just gotten so bossy since Reuben died, I can't believe I'm hearing this," and she averted her eyes from his practiced stare.

"Ma'am, if you'd like references I'll be happy to write the Wilpoles up in Rowland's Bluff. I'm sure they'll give me a good reference, as I worked for them for three years. I just felt I'd like to be nearer the coast and the good fishing here-abouts." Layke wasn't sure Berta believed him, she wore such a perplexed expression.

But she put his mind at ease. "Of course, I'll give you a try. Miss Trudy is a very good judge of character, and I'm sure she would not have sent you had she thought that you weren't right for me and the children." Berta retreated to her matter-of-fact, no nonsense voice and added, "She's a dear friend. Now let me show you around, and I'll get Jonah, my oldest -- at least my oldest here -- and he'll help you get settled in."

When Layke got off Bucko, she noticed his limp. She tried to avert her stare, but Layke saw her and understood.

"I took a ball in my upper thigh in Bentonville, but it's fine now and doesn't interfere with my work, Mrs. McRae."

Berta felt her face become flushed as she smiled up at Layke to let him know that it didn't matter.

"It'll be such a relief to finally have a man around the place. An intelligent man who can carry on a conversation and - oh my - someone I can rely on to handle the long drive to Punta Rassa. Old Dan is just too old to be of much help on the range, and Jonah is much too young and inexperienced to accept that kind of respon- sibility," she rationalized.

But Berta knew the real reason she needed Layke Williams around, and it frightened her. The sudden realization that perhaps she could love again rushed warm and throbbing, deep inside her. A feeling so intense and questioning. She clasped her damp, clammy hands together to stop their shaking, but Berta recognized her woman's desire and knew instinctively that Layke was sharing the intensity of the moment as he walked slowly beside her.

Jonah rounded the corner of the barn and saw them walking toward him. He bristled as he looked from one to the other. The stranger turned and petted a black and white cow dog who followed him and was almost in his boots. "Ma must have known him from somewhere else...maybe Macon," he thought. The stranger seemed to have a limp, "more than likely wounded in the War." As they got closer his ma turned to Jonah to introduce them.

"Jonah, this is Layke Williams, our new foreman." Jonah's throat seemed to close, he was so stunned. He had trouble swallowing, but managed to shake hands with Layke after wiping them off on his britches. The dog came over to Jonah to be petted, but he shoved it away as he angrily looked straight into the eyes of the stranger. He yanked off his dirty, worn hat and pushed an astonished Berta aside, and almost in a run, headed for the kitchen door.

Berta was so shocked by Jonah's behavior she turned to Layke and explained, as she apologetically petted Tag, "Jonah has had a very difficult time since my husband died and young Reuben moved away."

Embarrassed, she looked first at Tag and then up at Layke, pleading for understanding as she rattled on about how hard it had been since she'd been widowed - and then she stopped.

She pursed her lips and angrily said, "Enough is enough. That boy needs a good talking to!"

Remembering her manners, she asked Layke, "Would you like something to eat before I show you to your room, Mr. Williams..."

"Well, yes Mrs McRae, I would, but I can get settled in myself..." "Oh, please call me Berta, Layke," and, having said his name aloud, she abruptly turned and walked toward the kitchen knowing his penetrating eyes were watching her self-conscious steps.

Berta was hot and tired and really put out with Jonah. "What on earth has got into that boy? He has a mean streak in him just like Uncle Elon!" Reuben had said that just before he died - "That boy has the same devil streak as Elon!" Berta had never known Elon, but she noticed that every time one of the townspeople made mention of him they spoke in hushed tones and that the colored folks around the place tried to avoid saying his name altogether. She never got around to asking Reuben about him - now she wished she had.

Layke knew it was best not to be around Jonah until the boy had a chance to accept him as foreman. He had never seen such open hatred - not even in the War. He took his time as he and Tag went into the barn, and he wondered if he had made the right decision about accepting the job. He thought on it as he went about emptying his saddle bags.

"She needs me and I haven't been needed by a woman in many a year. She's a spunky one and so far has been able to handle the responsibilities she's been left with - somehow it just wouldn't be right for me not to share her burden...not right at all." And he smiled as he warmed to the challenge.

27

The room set aside for the cowmen was spotless, as he knew it would be. It was sparsely furnished: a cot with its corn-husk mattress, a small pine table with an oil lamp and a cane seat chair. There was a trunk for his few clothes and a pine rack to hold his coats. All handmade by Reuben and colored Ezekiel.

It was all he and Tag needed. "At least this room has a floor," he observed. The room he shared with the other cowmen on the Wilpole ranch had an earthen floor. In late February, when the cow hunt season began, he'd have to add a few cots for the expected help for a few nights before they started rounding up the beeves on the open range. But for now, it would do just fine.

Tag made himself right at home. He immediately jumped up on Layke's bunk only to be quickly removed by his big, swift hand. Layke laughed as he swatted him.

"OK, old boy. I know you're at home anywhere I place my boots and hat, but the bed is mine alone."

Tag jumped up to be reassured by his master, and a pat on his head and a rub around his furry neck were all he needed. He curled up in the dark corner of the room and proceeded to go to sleep, tired after the long, hot trot from town.

Layke got the wash bowl out from under the table and went outside for some cool rain water from the barrel at the corner of the barn. He glanced up at the house hoping to see Berta but instead saw a towheaded boy of about six years playing with a bird dog. He'd throw the stick, the dog would retrieve it, and the lad would repeat the act over and over again. Layke was sure he was aware of his presence, but he did not acknowledge him.

"Jonah has probably spread his dislike of me, and he feels the same," he thought. But Layke was wrong. As he started back to his room, the lad came running over to him with a big grin spread across his freckled face and bright cornflower blue eyes dancing just like his mother's.

"Howdy, I'm Wes, and I'm six years old. How old are you?" There was warmth and openness in those laughing eyes, and Layke immediately warmed to him. He extended his big, friendly hand and responded, "Old enough to know a good bird dog when I see one, Wes. What name does he answer to?"

"Oh, this is just Old Red. He's not mine. He belongs to my big brother, Jonah. Ma says I'm too little to hunt, but I got a pet snake. Ya wanta see it?" And he quickly reached into his pocket and produced a little black snake about eight inches long and a half inch in diameter.

He proudly held it up in both his grubby hands as high as his slight arms could reach toward Layke's amused face and said that the snake's name was "Darky" and that Layke could pet him, if he was of a mind to. Layke commanded curious Tag to sit, and when he reluctantly obeyed, he took Darky from Wes's possessive hands, and with a humorous glint in his eyes he declared Darky to be a fine specimen.

"I'm sure he's as good a pet as Old Red, or Tag, for that matter." After the initial greeting and examination of each other's pets Layke and Wes and Darky and Tag returned to Layke's room. Wes babbled along as Layke washed up for dinner. As Layke listened to the lad he realized why he had to remain at South Spring. It wasn't just for Berta's sake, but for Wes' as well.

He realized that if he ever had a son that he'd want him to be just like Wes. He'd want to give him the opportunity to be a carefree lad in the Florida wilds, learning how to survive in an untamed land. After all, Wes was not responsible for his mother's plight nor his brother's uncontrollably bad temper, and he'd want to teach him how to handle a not-asked-for situation.

He looked at the innocence before him, and he was ashamed. Ashamed for all the grown men he knew who at one time had been as innocent as this blue-eyed lad before him. Layke had seen them kill just for the sport of killing, raping this land of its magnificent riches. He'd want to teach him how to use the cow whip instead of the gun, how to hunt only for needed food and to leave the wildlife to serve its purpose -- not to waste.

Wes called him by name the second time, and Layke, who had been so deep in thought, finally responded. Wes continued to chatter along happily, hungry to share his adventures with a man.

"I got a turtle, too, down by the south spring. Me and Zekiel built it a pen, and Ma lets me go with SuSu to feed it. But I only get to go once a day, usually right after supper. Ya wanta go?"

"Don't mind if I do, son."

Layke said "son" easily, as though he'd been saying it all his grown-up life. They left the barn together chattering all the way up the brushed-clean sand path leading to the kitchen porch - Layke and Tag and Wes and Darky.

Jonah was peering out the kitchen window at them as they

29

leisurely approached the house. He kept clenching his fists and his back was ramrod straight. Berta glanced over at him from the big black stove where she was stirring the hen and vegetables in a large kettle. She sipped a small amount off the wooden spoon to test the seasoning and decided that now was as good as any to confront Jonah.

"Jonah," she said in her most authoritative voice, "you've done as good a job with South Spring as any human being could, young or old. Now, my hiring Mr. Williams doesn't mean that I think any less of your work. It doesn't. It just means that we're able to afford an experienced foreman to help make life a little better for all of us and that you'll be able to go back to school, as I'm sure your pa would've wanted you to.

"After all, Wes and SuSu are much too young to be of much help around here when it comes to cow hunt time, and we'll certainly need help on the drive to Punta Rassa. Mr. Williams comes highly recommended as a cowman, and I'm sure we can all learn from him."

Berta left the stove and went over to Jonah. "I want you to promise me you'll assist him anyway you can. After all, he's new to this area of the state and doesn't know our land as you do. I'd be much obliged if you would show him the spread before winter sets in and the cow hunt begins, son."

But before Berta placed her reassuring hand on his stiffened shoulder, he whirled around toward her with his eyes filled with that devil streak Reuben had told her about and stormed past her out to the side porch with his teeth clenched and fists held firm. Not a single word did he say. Berta's heart beat heavily in her heaving breast as she ran after him shouting, "Jonah! Jonah!"

It was then she saw Layke and Wes approaching the kitchen door. They had not heard her pleading call as they were so engrossed in their own conversation, and she was relieved.

Berta paused at the porch door to catch her breath and restrain the tears she was afraid would come. She busied herself in her kitchen - her solace. Reuben used to say, "When Berta has a problem, she takes to her kitchen, and by morn her heart is light."

Then the McRae family would witness a feast that her imaginative and creative hands produced. There would be hard-boiled eggs with the yellows scooped out and blended with finely chopped ham with little green onions mixed with mayonnaise and powdered mustard seed. Paper thin slices of smoked ham rolled into funnel shapes, that the children had called "funnel ham", would surround them.

She'd blend an aromatic mixture of berries, blueberries, huckleberries and raspberries in orange juice with thin slices of orange rind heaped with heavy cream and sprinkled with sugar and mace. She'd bake the corn bread instead of frying the corn cakes as she usually did and add bits of smokey ham and sausage with plump kernels of sweet corn. The table would be set with her finest china and silver.

But Berta's heart would not lighten this day. When Layke and Wes entered the kitchen, he knew immediately something was wrong. It was obvious that she was very upset as she kept wiping her hands on her fresh white apron and nervously pushing back the strands of hair away from her furrowed brow. Wes chattered on happily not noticing the tension.

Berta took down a tin cup from the cupboard and went through the motions of serving Layke, while Wes watched his every move with both elbows on the table and his hands cupped under his chin. He continued to tell Layke about all the things he had seen and done for the past few days. Layke did not respond. He just watched Berta.

He mopped up the cane syrup with his hoecake, and Berta silently refilled his cup with the steaming coffee. A beautiful young girl of about ten shyly entered the room. She was so unlike her mother in coloring - enormous chocolate-brown eyes and long, thick, red-brown hair. She was very fragile in appearance and had a haunted quality about her.

Berta spoke at last. "SuSu, this is Mr. Williams. He's come to help out with the cow hunt and drive."

SuSu immediately ran from the kitchen back to the sanctuary of the open porch, where she had fashioned a playhouse. She had strung up a line in one corner and draped an old quilt over it. There she would spend hours playing with her treasures: her china-head doll her auntie had sent her from Georgia, pieces of lace, bright shiny buttons, scraps of fabric of every color and feathers she'd found on her walks with Wes as she watched over him.

"SuSu is very shy Mr. Williams. After all, she was very young when her father was taken from us, but I'm sure she'll outgrow it. My Aunt Bertrice was a shy child, and Susu favors her in looks."

31

Berta was withdrawn and said words without expression, and Layke was concerned for her. She had returned to the formal Mr. Williams placing a barrier between them, and he was hurt, but replied with understanding, "It takes some people longer to get acquainted than it does others, Berta. SuSu might be of that nature."

He thanked her properly for the delicious meal and rose to leave. Her back was toward him, and tiny, golden curls had escaped her smooth bun and were damp against the nape of her neck. He ached to touch her - to comfort her - to hold her, but he dared not. She whirled around and desperate for understanding as she looked up into his eyes said, "Thank you Layke. I wish it had been more ... much more."

She had called him "Layke". His decision was made at that moment. "It was all I needed or wanted, Berta," and his heart sang. He knew he'd never leave South Spring as long as she needed him. He'd be as patient as an impatient man could be and as understanding as a selfish man could be for as long as he was able.

All the way back to the barn, he repeated over and over to himself, "Berta McRae, you'll be mine before the spring drive to Punta Rassa - I feel it - I know it! I saw in those cornflower blue eyes the unmistakable promise of tomorrow. Jonah will be won over, and if he isn't, then to hell with him! He'll just have to accept us. You'll be mine, Berta." And a resurgence of Layke's dormant determination reentered his life on that day. Not since the War had he felt such confidence.

****

Layke rested on his bunk and rubbed his aching leg. The heat was oppressive. Half asleep, he daydreamed about the golden haired Berta, her warm, rounded, woman's body and her beautiful work-worn hands. He was restless - God, he was restless. It was hot and sticky for a November day. He could feel the approaching rain in the air, but the rain-filled clouds eluded South Spring. He was so antsy that even Tag sensed his master's restlessness.

Layke Williams was not chaste. Neither was he a rowdy cowman who frequented the upstairs rooms to visit the ladies on a Saturday night. He rode with them and was respected by them, but he was his own man. When Layke rode into town on pay day, it was to break the monotony of the cowman's life.

32

He would first head for the boarding house and order a steaming hot bath. The ranches he worked were quite primitive, and the best he could do during the week was a wash up or a dip in a creek or river. After his long, soaking bath, he'd dress in his finest and go downstairs and have a big meal in the dining room. Then he'd wander over to the local saloon for a few drinks, engage in a game of cards or join the other cowmen in singing some of the old War ballads.

The girls who frequented the cow towns were fun-loving, easy-living girls and would favor any cowman who would buy them drinks or treat them right. But Layke never had to seek their companionship...they sought his. They would quite often draw lots to determine who would be in his feather bed when he returned to the boarding house at the end of the evening. Even though the other cowmen knew what was going on, they ignored the silly girls' pranks. But Layke played their game and delighted them with his theatrics. He'd display total surprise when he discovered them and chastise them for their forward behavior, and they loved his reaction. They'd steal out of his room before daybreak. Their private game heightening the otherwise dull, monotonous life they led.

Word was in every cow camp throughout Florida that Layke Williams was a gentleman, and there wasn't a camp girl in the entire state who wouldn't fight for the right to share his bed on a Saturday night.

It had been over a month since Layke had celebrated his Saturday nights in town. Too long! He and Tag had taken their time getting to Old Town. They had explored the area alongside the Suwannee, venturing into the old ox trails and logging camp roads, enjoying the wildlife that inhabited the black river and the surrounding area - the anhingas atop the stately cypresses spreading their wings to dry, floating logs topped with families of turtles sunning themselves, blue birds darting among the river birches to the tune of the tiny pine warblers whose boisterous song belied their minute size.

As Layke fondly remembered the Saturday nights in Rowland's Bluff his leg ceased to throb. Suddenly he jumped off his bunk, startling the sleeping Tag.

"I can't get her out of my mind," he said, desperately trying to control himself. In all his adult life no one had affected him the way Berta did. No one! He didn't trust himself around her.

33

"I'll have to leave now -- this minute!" He felt driven - out of control. He rushed into the barn to saddle Bucko. He allowed himself to glance at the house, and there she was, rocking in her favorite chair, shelling the crowder peas for the next day's dinner, unaware of his plight. SuSu and Wes were playing on the porch beside her.

Startled, Berta looked up when she heard Layke. He was astride Bucko with Tag at his heels, galloping hard even before he got to the south gate. Instead of sitting straight in his saddle, he was leaning forward, and Bucko's mane was flying straight back as he raced down the ox trail with Tag doing his darndest to keep up with them. He rode as a man possessed.

She stood, dropping the bowl of freshly shelled peas on the porch floor. She was perplexed, but was mostly astonished by his behavior. She knew that she had behaved in a very distant manner when she served his dinner and had planned to apologize for her behavior later. "I guess I waited too long. He's a sensitive and wounded man and he needed to be nurtured...not treated coldly."

An unexpected tear escaped and gently rolled down her flushed cheek as she watched him race out of her life. Her heart ached when she could no longer see him through the dust as he charged across the terrain.

She felt numb, whereas just a short time before she had felt so alive - renewed. For the first time in her entire life Berta had felt a burning fire well up inside her and she was having difficulty controlling her woman's desires. She had no way of knowing that Layke was having the same desires - and his were out of control.

She slowly walked back into her kitchen, leaned against the cupboard, and hitting her forehead against it, sobbed uncontrollably, allowing the pent-up anguish of the past four years to flow out of her limp body.

"Layke, what have I done to us? I've chased you away with my cold, selfish ways even before we had a chance to know each other. Now, what will I do? What will happen to South Spring if you don't return? What on earth will become of me, Layke? Dear Lord! What will I do?"

CHAPTER IV   POOR TAG

Layke had ridden Bucko hard for quite a distance. He slowed down to a trot and turned in his saddle to look for Tag. He was nowhere in sight.

"I've got to take hold. There's too much at stake for me to behave like this. Now where on earth is that dog?" he said angrily.

He got down and rubbed Bucko's lathered neck, all the while apologizing to him, trying to erase the obvious pain he had inflicted. Still no Tag! He led Bucko down the steep embankment to the river, and as the tired horse drank the dark river water, Layke climbed back up the grade to search for Tag. Still, he was nowhere in sight.

Layke was feeling very childish and foolish. It wasn't in his nature to run from a problem. He berated himself, "Why on earth did I behave like that? I really can't blame Jonah for his feelings. After all, he was head of the spread until I arrived, and he's so young I shouldn't put blame on him." But he knew deep down that it was not Jonah's reaction that had triggered his irrational behavior, but his uncontrollable desire for Berta, and he was upset by his immature actions.

"I'll have to hurry back and apologize," he thought as he rested his hard, sweat-soaked back against the giant oak while contemplating his problem. Then he heard Tag - he was whining. Layke quickly got up from his cool spot, and he saw him in the distance. Something was wrong. Layke started running.

"Why's he walking so peculiarly? He's not an old dog." Tag fell a few seconds before Layke reached him. He could not believe his eyes. The dog's back leg was bleeding profusely, and the bone was exposed. He'd been shot. Layke scooped him up and ripped off the bottom of his shirt, wrapping it tightly around the leg as he ran toward the river and Bucko. Tag's eyes were barely open.

It seemed to take forever 'til they reached the river. He tried to get Tag to drink, but he was too weak. He unwrapped the leg to examine it more closely and saw no shot. Hurriedly, he rewrapped it and managed to straddle Bucko, who seemed to sense that something was wrong. Layke decided that Old Town was closer than South Spring, so he headed east, holding Tag gently as they sped toward town.

****

Trudy Stucky was a light sleeper - she never seemed to need more than five or six hours at most. She'd rise early and go downstairs to her comfortable kitchen, light the wood cook stove and proceed to roll out the breakfast biscuits, get the coffee cooking and the pork slab sliced real thin and fried 'til it was golden brown and crisp. But this morning she didn't feel like doing her usual morning chores, not after what had happened to poor Tag.

In a daze, she automatically went through the motions of preparing the breakfast for her boarders. She was so unnerved to think that someone in Old Town was capable of committing such a despicable act that her mind flitted from one suspect to another. But the answer to "who?" would not come to her.

Never in all her born days had she seen a person as distraught as Layke when he came galloping up to her porch at almost dusk yesterday, shouting.."Trudy, Miss Trudy - Tag's been shot!" Frankie had been helping her sweep up and came running into the kitchen all out of breath with excitement and repeated the news. She hurriedly poked the wood in the stove, shoved the pots to the back, burning her hand in the process, and grabbed the butter to rub on it as she ran as fast as her heavy body would allow after Frankie to the front porch. Sure enough, Layke was cradling Tag in his arms. His face was distorted. He was stunned.

Trudy, who was a take-charge person, having had to be all of her life, took poor Tag from Layke, wrapped her apron around him and headed for Bud Brewster's stable.

She told Frankie, "Fetch your pa and have him ready when we get there." There were no doctors in Old Town, the closest one being in Crosstown, which was half a day's ride away. When anyone needed a doctor in Old Town, they asked for Bud Brewster, except when birthing time came. There wasn't a more capable person in all of Florida for a birthing than Miss Trudy Stucky, and she bore that distinction proudly.

Bud ran from the stable to meet them. Layke was right beside him telling him where Tag had been shot. Bud figured it was near Two-mile Bend. After examining him, he shook his head, turned toward Layke and said, "He's lost a lot of blood, Layke, and it

36

doesn't look good."

He started giving orders to all three of them, all the while humming an old tune. Trudy turned to Layke and explained, "Buddy does that purposely, Layke, as the humming seems to comfort the animals."

He worked on Tag's leg for almost an hour and by then there was quite a congregation of townsfolk on the Stucky porch all giving their opinions as to what could have happened.

A very concerned Layke finally joined them. He told them, "Bud said if he gets through the night it will be a miracle, and if he lives it might be that his cow hunt days are over. He's lost so much of the muscle in that upper leg--it's been blown away."

The stories began then. Every man there was trying to out-do the other about tales of cow dogs' experiences. Layke was lost in his own worried world and heard only bits and pieces of their oft-told stories. He was consumed by concern and bitter with anger. He tried to not blame Jonah, but in his heart he was sure that he was the one who shot Tag.

There was just no way Tag could have been mistaken for any other kind of animal. He was black and white and running down the open road - clearly visible. Every grown man hereabouts had to be an expert shot to survive in this wilderness, and ammunition was costly. You never took a shot unless you had good reason. No, whoever shot Tag meant to, and that was what was disturbing to every man, woman and child assembled on the Stucky porch. A good cow dog was a necessary and precious thing for a cowman to have, for it took patience and long, tedious training to teach them how to work the beeves.

One of the men piped up and said, "Maybe it was a stray shot." They looked soberly at each other, shook their heads, and one replied, "Not anywheres near Two-Mile Bend. That's McRae land, and there ain't no good huntin' in that area except for a few dove."

There was the Swede's farm north of McRae's and the Beatty farm to the south on the other side of the river. Nicer folks you'd never find, and there was certainly no reason for any of them to hunt near Two- Mile Bend. They all had good hunting right in their own back yard - so to speak. No one had reported seeing any strangers about, on the river or on the land. If there was a stranger in these parts, more than likely he'd use the main trail and not the ox trail out to Reuben's, and for sure someone would have

37

known he was there. The conjecture continued into the night.

Trudy walked over to Layke, put her plump, comforting hand on his shoulder and told him, "I have some venison stew on the back of the stove and some hot biscuits to help it down, Layke. It's time you ate something." She knew he'd probably not eaten much all day.

"Trudy, I'm just not hungry." She prevailed and led him into her warm kitchen, set a plate before him and filled the cup with hot, strong coffee. Layke managed to eat a little and asked for another cup of coffee. He was so fidgety that he couldn't stand being in the kitchen with her nor on the porch with the townsfolk. He just had to be at the stable with Tag.

"Trudy, I'll take my bed roll to the stable and stay the night there," he said as he rose.

She looked into his weary eyes and understood. "That's where you ought to be, Layke. Miracles do happen, you know."

He rubbed his left thigh and smiled slightly as he did and replied, "That's a fact, Trudy. That is indeed a fact."

As he left she thought, "Tag is just like his master. Maybe he, too, will pull through. They're both made of stern stuff."

****

Trudy was in her rocker in the kitchen having her first cup of the day. The sun was just peeping up, and soon it would be over the tops of the tall sand pines, live oak and hickory trees out back of the boarding house. Although Trudy liked calling it a hotel - seemed more dignified somehow - all the townsfolk called it "Stucky's Boarding House." It was the largest building in town.

Old Town was a family town, not a cow town. There was no saloon, just the hotel, dry-goods and feed store, stable-blacksmith shop and the church, that served also as the school. The Swede's wife, Minna, was the school teacher, and Charlie Beatty was the Sunday preacher but was mostly a farmer who ran a few cows. So the four buildings served dual purposes as did the people who worked in them. Miss Trudy was the town's midwife and, of course, Bud Brewster took care of the folks' aches and pains and even set their broken bones.

About once a month a roving preacher would come to town, which was a big event for Old Town. The Reverend Townsend and his wife, Sarah, and their three talented children were a circuit preaching family. They served five community churches, similar to the one in Old Town, that they visited for five or six days at a time.

Everyone of those Townsends sang and played a musical instrument beautifully. They had no permanent home and usually stayed with whichever family wanted them wherever they preached. Every night there was a revival and the excitement was high.

The reverend was not a big man, but he had a booming voice, and when he got going about midway through his sermon and the spirit was upon him, the percentage of souls saved was right up there with the best of 'em. All the big events, weddings and baptisms, were saved up for his visit.

If the weather was nice, a picnic was held on the last day of the revival. The women would take a covered dish of food and spread their specialties on make-shift tables underneath the tall hickory trees surrounding the small wooden church to shade the picnickers. It was a looked-for event in the quiet and peaceful community, where not much happened.

As Trudy rocked, she wondered how Tag had got through the night, but she also wondered why the Townsends were a week late in arriving. She decided that if she hadn't heard anything by this next Sunday she'd send the Beatty boy over to Fannin Springs to telegraph Crosstown to see what had happened. Maybe someone had become ill, or they had wagon trouble. But it was real strange that there was no word from them.

Her mind was troubled this morning, and as she was rising from her rocker she rubbed her arthritic knees, reached into the big sack of corn beside the back door, and started outside to feed the penned-up chickens in their coop. She heard a noise at the front door and decided to feed them later.

Trudy was hoping it was Layke. She saw him with his head lowered, and her heart ached for him. Guess poor Tag didn't make it through the night. "Come on in, Layke," she said as she opened the door for him.

He spoke before she could ask him. "He made it through the night, Trudy, but Bud said it's infected, and he'll have to take the leg off to save him."

She poured his tin cup to the rim, and put a pan of biscuits in the oven. The grits were bubbling on the back burner, and the brown eggs were in the earthen bowl ready to be fried in the black, iron skillet filled with pork drippings.

"This morning you're going to eat a hearty breakfast, and then I'm going to send Frankie out to Berta's to tell 'em what's happened. If I know her, she's worried sick about your whereabouts."

Layke looked astonished. He had been so consumed with concern about Tag and guilty about his feelings for Jonah, that he had not given Berta a thought - not once had he allowed her to enter his mind - the guilt had blanked her completely out. He put his strong hands to his muddled head as he bowed it.

****

Berta had had such a restless night that the bed covers were all in a ball at the foot of her bed come morning. "It's chilly this morning," she said as she pulled her light blue robe over her night dress. "Or is it my nerves?"

She automatically went through the motions of preparing breakfast for her family. When she looked out the window toward the barn, she saw Jonah and Red coming toward the kitchen door. She didn't have to ask if Layke had returned. Jonah was smiling to himself and had more bounce in his stride than she'd seen since before Layke's arrival yesterday.

It seemed as if she'd known Layke forever. She couldn't believe she'd known him for such a short time. Berta was a practical person, having left her romantic ideas back in Macon. There was no room for romance in a rancher's wife, so why was she behaving like a silly school girl?

Jonah light-heartedly talked about the next cow hunt and mentioned that the Townsends were late arriving this month. Berta hadn't given them a thought. She had heard that Ruthie Townsend was sweet on Jonah, but hadn't noticed that he was aware of it. Perhaps in her worry over running South Spring she hadn't noticed a lot of things, she concluded, as she looked at her middle son.

He favored his pa, but was not the talker Reuben had been. He was more like his Uncle Ham. He kept everything to himself, much like what she'd heard Elon was like. But this Friday morning Jonah McRae was chattering like a magpie. His world was back in order, now that Layke Williams was gone.

Berta was helping SuSu finish up the breakfast dishes when she heard a horse approaching the south gate. In anticipation she

40

quickly dropped her dish cloth on the table and ran out the kitchen door. Her face relaxed in disappointment when she saw that it was not Layke.

As the rider pulled up, she recognized Frankie Brewster. "What on earth is he doing out this way?" she thought. Then she let her worried mind imagine the most awful things. "Something has happened to Layke!" she just knew it. A bitter-as-gall liquid arose in her throat, and she was afraid she'd be sick right there on the kitchen stoop.

Jonah went out to greet Frankie. They were about the same age and had known each other all their lives. They weren't real good friends, but did fish and hunt together from time to time. They came up the path together talking animatedly. Berta couldn't make out what was being said, but did hear "Layke" and "Tag" - and her heart sank with fright.

"What's happened, Frankie?" she finally got out. Then he told her about Tag, and that Miss Trudy and Layke had sent him out to inform her of his where-abouts. He said that Layke wanted him to assure her that he'd return when or if Tag pulled through, but that he needed to be in town just now, and he knew she'd understand.

Berta sighed so loudly that the boys looked at her anxiously. She hadn't realized she'd been holding her breath the entire time slow-talking Frankie was unfolding the story. Jonah grabbed her as she started to go down. The obvious concern in his eyes brought her to, and he walked her into the kitchen and poured her a dipper of cool water from the bucket by the cupboard.

Jonah spoke up then. "Who would be low-down mean enough to shoot a good cow dog?"

It was then that Frankie asked them if they'd seen any strangers about. Jonah said, "No, no one. I was dove hunting yesterday west of Ellie's pond and didn't see or hear anything peculiar. Late in the afternoon me and Big Dan was checking our fish traps in the river when we saw Layke and Tag high-tailin' it up the trail. We dropped everything and got back in a hurry. Thought something bad had happened, the way he was stretching his horse."

Berta nodded in accord as she remembered how relieved he had looked when he and Red returned - not fifteen minutes after Layke had left. She had thought that he was just happy that Layke had gone. Berta became aware right then that she didn't know her

41

middle son very well, and it would improve their relationship if they talked more often. She had been holding back her caring ever since Reuben died, and it was time past due for her to show more affection to her children.

Frankie accepted her invitation to stay for dinner, and he and Jonah went about the morning chores while Berta prepared their meal. Aunt Willa, Big Dan's wife, helped SuSu and Wes gather the greens from the garden. While they stripped out the heavy ribs and washed them, Frankie came back to the porch to visit and suggested, "Why don't we go ask the Answer Man who shot poor Tag? I bet he'll know."

Aunt Willa spoke up, "That ole coot don't know nuttin' - Answer Man - humph! Best call him the Lazy Man."

Back of the big garden underneath a large stand of scrub oak and one towering, ancient river oak was the Answer Man's house. Now, he hadn't been called the Answer Man for a whole lot of years - maybe ten or so. The old timers called him Zeke, but Berta referred to him by his given name, Ezekiel. He liked that. Next to his "leftover" house was Aunt Willa's and Big Dan's - down a sandy knoll and back a little from the main house. That always rankled Aunt Willa 'cause she somehow got into her head that the closer you were to the "main" house the higher in favor you were with the Mister and Missus; in this case Berta and Reuben McRae and before them Elon and Effie.

All four of the McRae children had grown up on the porches of the "leftover" houses, so called 'cause that was what they were. When anyone in the vicinity of Old Town built anything - a chicken coop or a new barn - the local Darkies were given anything left over so they could have a place of their own.

SuSu and Wes, and before them young Reuben, kept Berta informed as to the goings-on at Aunt Willa's and the Answer Man's. It was a source of amusement and entertainment that helped lighten her heavy burden, especially since Reuben's passing.

Looking out the single window in her kitchen she could see the blurred image of Ezekiel's bright blue, shiny shirt. There he sat, just like the "high and mighty grand potentate" as his disgruntled sister-in-law, Willa, described him. He appeared to be practicing one of his answer-seeking trances, and she could faintly hear his sing-song cadence wafting in from the cabin. Berta laughed to herself and wished she could share her amusement with another

42

adult - Trudy, or now, Layke - who would truly appreciate the humor in the series of events that turned poor, old, lazy Zeke into the revered Answer Man.

When the new bride and groom, Berta and Reuben, first arrived at South Spring, Aunt Willa Roker, Big Dan's wife, and her sister Myrtice Benson, wife to Ezekiel, took the very young Missus under their protective wings and proceeded to instruct her in the running of the house. She was very accomplished in the fine needle work, floral arranging, menu planning, and Sadie had given her a quick course in making fancy sauces and desserts just before her marriage and departure from Georgia. But the arts of candle and soap making, preparing the basic fare of chicken fixed every which-a-way, biscuits, corn bread and sundry other things were all done by loving, black hands for as long as she could remember. Berta proved to be a grateful and apt pupil and they all grew to love and respect her.

No one seemed to know when the Black families moved to South Spring. When Berta questioned Myrtice one day she just said, "Oh, we's always been here, Missus," so the subject was dropped and never thought to be asked again. Their children were grown and gone before Berta's arrival - most had long ago moved to Jacksonville, where they could be paid a wage for their work and not have to rely on barter, as was the custom in that area.

Between the two families there were nine grown children, and it had been almost four long years since any of them had paid a visit. A few had come for Myrtice's funeral, the few who lived closer to Old Town.

Berta chuckled as she remembered Ezekiel's youngest son Jasper's visit. Jasper had been gone from South Spring since before the "Cession" as some folks referred to the secession of the southern states, and hadn't been back since. One day the Answer Man was on his throne - as Aunt Willa called it. It was just an old cane backed chair that he'd painted a bright orange. He pretended to be in one of his trances, but Willa and Berta knew he was just dozing as usual.

Up rode a fancy dude with a mighty dressed up lady friend in a rig that shouted at you, it was so loud. When Ezekiel opened his eyes and got a gander at all that money staring him right in the face, he put on a real show for them.

When Jasper had left home, his father had been a tall, muscled, handsome man - at least in his memory. The man before him was old and grey, and Jasper didn't recognize him anymore than Ezekiel recognized the fancy dude before him. Since Myrtice's passing he didn't eat right and was probably loaded with worms. He wouldn't listen to or take any advice from Willa, whose remedy was to swallow a wad of chewing tobacco. He said, "Answer Men don't get no worms, woman." He had gotten thin and ashen and just seemed to have shrunk up, but that did not dampen his fervor for his new position.

There was new blood before him and the Answer Man began his show. He slowly got up from his orange chair - arms raised and extended - giving Jasper the beginning of his trance posture. He started in with his moaning, and before Jasper could identify himself and introduce his very suspicious lady friend the Answer Man spoke in a sing-song rhythm.

"The Answer Man knows all
But the answer you seek
Might take a day or a week.
Promise you won't yell
When he goes into his spell.
The Answer Man knows all."

And with that he sat on his throne, closed his eyes, tuned in for the question so he could give the appropriate hmmm and ymmm at the right intervals. But Jasper, with his mouth hanging open getting ready to ask who in the world the kook was and what was he doing in his pa's house, was interrupted by the Answer Man's follow-up rhyme. Ezekiel knew he had a big one on the hook, and he wasn't about to let him go - so he'd best help the shy, young, rich boy with his question.

"The Answer Man knows all.
If it's help you're a-needin'
His answer will be a-speedin'.
Just hurry up and ask
So's he can get to his task.
The Answer Man knows all."

While Ezekiel was impatiently waiting for the rich boy's question, Willa came running over with her arms extended and calling, "Jasper - oh, Jasper, Myrtice's baby boy, Jasper...Oh, my..Oh, my," and she proceeded to cry and hop up and down at the same time.

Ezekiel quickly came out of his spell. Later, when Jasper asked his Aunt Willa what in the world had come over his pa, she just shook her head and laughed. "The old coot has gone and got hisself the name of The Answer Man. Miss Berta's younguns started it. They used to get under her feet when she was busy, asking her a million questions, and she'd see yore lazy pa sittin' on the porch doin' nuttin' while yore poor dead ma was workin' her fingers to the bone. So, she'd say to 'em, 'Why don't you go ask Ezekiel? He'll have the answer.' So they did. So, if'n one of 'em ever had a question they'd go ask Zeke."

"Was Young Reuben who gave him the name. Pretty soon their friends started spendin' time on his porch and the next thing yore ma and me knew, yore pa was takin' all this foolishness to heart and he began to think that he had all the answers - the old coot. Now he's up and made hisself a grand potentate just a-sittin' on his throne waitin' for some dumb folks to pay him a visit - just a-rarin' to go into one of those fool trances - the old fool."

****

"I just don't know what we'll do, Jonah. She's the best milk cow we've ever had," Berta said as she followed Jonah out of the barn. They joined the others on the porch after checking Rosie's tender hind leg. "Do you think we'd better send for Bud? I'm worried, son."

Frankie could see how worried she was and remembered how upset Miss Trudy was about the Townsends. "Miss Trudy is real worried, too, Miss Berta.... about the Townsends' being over a week late. She said that if they haven't showed up by after Sunday that she was going to send Raymond Beatty over to Fannin Springs to telegraph Crosstown to check up on them."

"Jonah mentioned that very thing this morning at breakfast, Frankie. It's not like them. They're such a dependable family."

Frankie left the McRae ranch right after dinner. He decided to head south to the Beattys'. He somehow didn't want to return by way of Two-Mile Bend where Tag had been shot. His excuse to himself was that he should go tell the Beattys about Tag and Layke and ask if they'd seen any strangers about. But if the truth had been known, Frankie was afraid to go back that way.

On his way out to the McRaes' he had got the spookiest feeling when he approached Two-Mile Bend. He felt like a hundred eyes

45

were on him, and Pal got real funny acting, too. Now, it might have been his imagination, but he didn't think so. He was of a mind to tell his pa when he got home, but was afraid his pa would think him a sissy. But Pal seemed to want to start galloping right at that point, and Frankie couldn't control him. He slowed down of his own accord when they got closer to the McRaes'. Usually Pal did his bidding, but that horse was spooked, and Frankie Brewster knew a spooked horse when he rode one, by gum.

****

He tied Pal to the hitching post in front of Stucky's porch even before he went to the stable. He wanted to tell Miss Trudy what had happened. He was sure she'd give him a little something for his trouble. She came out the front door even before he got up the steps.

"Well? she asked.

"Well, Miss Trudy, I did just what you said and then some. Decided to go to Beattys' farm on my way back to ask them if they had seen any strangers about and to tell them about the Townsends' being late."

She was getting plumb exasperated waiting for slow-talking Frankie to get to the point. "It's a good thing you can blow that harmonica faster than you can talk, Frankie Brewster. Well, get on with it. What did you find out, and did you see anything peculiar?"

He proceeded to tell her, "Pal got plumb spooked when I got to Two-Mile Bend." He knew Miss Trudy wouldn't think him a sissy so he continued. "Jonah didn't see anything when he was hunting that morning or when he checked his fish traps that afternoon, right after Layke and Tag left the ranch, Miss Trudy."

By then Trudy was beside herself. She knew full well by the way he was dragging everything out that he had something of importance to tell her. His eyes were as big as saucers, and he was rubbing his sweating hands together nervously.

"I'll declare, right here and now, Frankie Brewster, if you don't get on with the important parts, I'm going to give you a piece of my mind instead of a doubloon."

That did it - a doubloon...my! He proceeded to blurt out what the Beattys had seen and heard that very afternoon just before his arrival. Seems that Raymond Beatty was coming back from checking on some smoke he'd seen over near the salt marsh south of the Suwannee. Raymond said that he was concerned because of the dry conditions, and he knew that lightning hadn't started a fire, so he approached the cypress stand cautiously. As he got closer to the marsh, he heard voices. So he got off his horse and quietly listened. Was a group of men. They were laughing and cussing and carrying on. He couldn't hear everything they were saying, but he sure didn't like the sound of 'em, so he didn't ride in to see who they were or what they were up to. He had just come back to the farm when Frankie rode up from the west side. If Frankie had taken the east fork, he'd have come up on 'em for sure, and goodness knows what would have happened to him.

Charlie Beatty, Frankie and Raymond and the second oldest Beatty boy, Renford, decided they'd better find out just what was going on. So they saddled up and rode toward the cypress stand about a mile from the house. They told Mrs. Beatty and Agnes to stay put and not to let anyone in the house. Bertrun stayed with the ladies just in case the gang showed up. He was only sixteen, but was big for his age, strong as an ox and a crack shot.

As they approached the cypress, they listened carefully, but heard nothing. So, very slowly, they entered the hammock. No one was there, but there sure were signs of them - broken limbs, mashed down grass and the remains of the fire. Renford was as good a tracker as there was anywhere. He made out that there were five of 'em. Least ways, there were five horses, and they were headed southeast of the Beatty farm toward Otter Creek settlement.

After the war there were a lot of rag-tagged gangs that terrorized the Southland. But by 1877 most of them had been captured and hanged. Never had any of them come close to Old Town. The settlements were sparse on the west coast of the state, so there wasn't much of anything for them to steal. In the past they mostly plundered the northeast coast and central part of the state in the more populated areas.

Miss Trudy left that porch in a hurry and told Frankie, "After you left this morning the Hartman boy rode in from Fannin Springs to tell us that the Townsends' mare had been found, killed, and that they're missing. You'd best get your hide over to the stable fast. Folks down Otter Creek way have to be warned." He hoped she

47

hadn't forgotten his doubloon, but he did exactly what she told him to do and was smart enough not to ask for it.

Davis and Palmer were out on the dry goods store porch asking her a million questions as she unfolded Frankie's story. They were all in accord that one of them had to ride to Otter Creek to warn them. There was not much more of a town there than Old Town, except for the big lumber mill, but after what happened to Tag they'd not put anything past that gang.

Palmer McCoy volunteered to ride to Fannin Springs, two miles south of Old Town and across the river, to fetch Bo Lutes. They figured the gang was already a good five miles south of there. It would take Palmer longer to get to Otter Creek than Bo Lutes as Bo was an expert trapper and knew the territory like the back of his hand and wouldn't take time to make camp. He should be able to make good time by taking the back roads and get there before the gang.

Trudy was nervously pacing, and it seemed to her that they were all taking their own sweet time getting the horse saddled. "Palmer could get to Fannin Springs soon after nightfall if he'd just stir his stumps," she thought. They were finally ready. Bud and Layke were needed to keep an eye on Tag, so Trudy went to the back of the store to tell Martha McCoy that Palmer was riding to Fannin Springs to sound the alarm and to alert Bo Lutes.

Now Palmer McCoy was a mild, soft spoken man, but Martha almost never opened her mouth. Behind her back Trudy referred to her as PeeWee. "A good puff of wind would just about blow Martha away," she often said. But that woman had the biggest and healthiest younguns Miss Trudy ever delivered, and every one of 'em was as mean as a snake - always tormenting some poor thing. Trudy was surprised Martha had let them live long enough to get grown. As they got older they seemed to grow out of their meanness somewhat. Two of them moved up to Rose Head, and one was a banker all the way to Jacksonville. Imagine that! Palmer bragged about Homer all the time, but Martha just sat there rocking and doing her hand work, and always with that secretive know-it-all grin dancing across her face.

Folks wondered if Martha had all her smarts, but probably no one would ever know. They'd never find out by anything she said, that's for sure. As Trudy left McCoys' she said to herself, "At least I've told her about Palmer riding to sound the alarm. Now if she

48

wants to get excited she can do it on her own time." She often wondered if Martha ever got excited. She didn't do more than let out a few grunts when she delivered those huge babies, but the little PeeWee would grin from ear to ear. Trudy shook her head from side to side as she wondered what Martha McCoy could possibly be thinking about, and all the while Martha was rocking and secretly smiling.

She went back to the stable to tell Layke, "You're most welcome to share supper with me, Layke. You look so drawn and worried about poor Tag, I'm sure you can stand a break."

After their supper of leftover chicken perlo and fall greens she and Layke retired to the porch. He smoked his pipe and slowly began to confide in her about Jonah's obvious jealousy. He was hesitant to speak of it at first, but Trudy was a good listener, and he soon began pouring out his anxieties. Trudy was not only a good listener, but a good advisor as well, and knew Berta better than anyone in the territory.

Trudy was a maiden lady by happenstance, not choice. She was only fifteen years Layke's senior, but she seemed much older, somehow. She had inherited the hotel from her folks, whom she had cared for when she was of marrying age, and after they died there just wasn't anyone around Old Town suitable to wed.

When she was in her mid-thirties a man from South Carolina came through on his way to Ft. Myers. He had a brother there who worked for The *Ft. Myers Gazette*. Josh Peacock never did get to Ft. Myers. He and Trudy just seemed to hit it off. About then the war broke out, and he was one of the first ones from Old Town to join up. He was killed at the Battle of Olustee in north Florida. He wasn't exactly a hero at Olustee, but to hear the townsfolk talk, he was.

Miss Trudy didn't much like to talk about Josh, but that night she unburdened all her pent-up feelings about the man she almost wed thirteen years before. Afterwards, she and Layke sat in the quiet...no one else joined them, and they immersed themselves in their memories and dreams and listened to the night noises and watched the lightening bugs flit through the night trying to compete with the sky filled with stars.

When Layke got back to the stable to check on Tag, it was almost midnight. Tag's nose was still warm, but not as hot as before. He fell into an exhausted sleep, the soundest he'd had since his arrival in Old Town. As he drifted off he thought, "I can't believe all the events that have occurred in such a short time - I have a feeling that the Gods are against me..."

CHAPTER V THE VISIT

Palmer McCoy arrived back in Old Town the next morning and bore startling news for the townspeople. He had arrived in Fannin Springs and had found Bo Lutes immediately.

"Bo was so excited that he was headed for Otter Creek before I even heard back from Crosstown. A drummer put up at the hotel and told me the whole story. You know -- the whole story. The poor, poor Townsends. Oh, my. Oh, my."

"Well, hurry up Palmer. I'll declare you're as slow-talking as Frankie," someone shouted. "Get on with it."

"Well, it's just like we thought. The Townsends left Rowland's Bluff and headed for Crosstown on Friday, but first they went to Curtis to see Sarah's sick sister. When they didn't show up on Sunday for the revival, Brother Luther figured that her sister was sicker than Sarah had thought, so they stayed over to help out.

"But come Tuesday and they still hadn't showed up, Brother Luther figured that something was amiss. He sent Roy over to Curtis to get the lowdown on their whereabouts, and Sarah's sister said that they had left at daybreak on Saturday, just like they'd planned.

"When Roy got back to Crosstown with that news, Brother Luther telegraphed Rowland's Bluff to tell Sheriff Tatum about them being missing, but him and his deputies were clean to the other side of the county. Seems like some drunken lumber man shot up the camp and wounded a couple fellows and then high tailed it into the thick woods."

"For heavens sakes, Palmer, where are the Townsends? Are they all right, or ain't they?"

"I'm gettin' to it, for Pete's sake! Just hold on! Roy didn't see hide nor hair of 'em, when he rode the same road that they always took. Not a living soul has seen them since they left Rowland's Bluff on Friday, over a week gone past. Sheriff Tatum and his deputies have beat every bush in the whole county, and still no sign of 'em."

Everyone close in to Old Town was on Trudy's porch that Saturday morning, when on the heels of Palmer, not more than an hour past, James Lutes, Bo's brother, came galloping into town in a cloud of flying sand yelling the astonishing news.

"It just came over the telegraph that the Townsends have

been found, and they're alive. Did you hear? They're alive! The R.J. Skinner gang kidnapped 'em, and when they found out that they didn't have no money, they tied them to their wagon and left 'em for the buzzards." James said in a loud voice, so they could hear him over the ruckus they were making, that he didn't have any more details, but that he was going to ride over to Crosstown come morning to find out more.

The spirits were high and the jugs of home brew were passed around frequently among the townsmen that night. James Lutes, a natural born story teller, kept them entertained as he rambled on about the kidnapping - everyone having a different theory about the happening. When Layke came over from the stable to join them, everyone inquired about Tag, and Layke informed them that he was holding his own since Bud took the leg, but not wanting to elaborate, quickly changed the subject back to the kidnapping.

The next morning James rode out for Crosstown before daybreak with a hearty breakfast under his belt, that Trudy had lovingly prepared. He told her, "I'll be back before nightfall with the real skinny on the kidnapping, Miss Trudy. On that you can bet."

Everyone in Old Town proper would be on the Stucky porch that night, for there hadn't been this much excitement since the medicine show came to town two years before, and the Swede's daughter, Carla, ran off with one of the hawkers. They'd thought she'd been kidnapped, too, only to find out that she had gone of her own free will.

Layke arrived at the boarding house earlier than usual, right after James left. Tag seemed to be much better and had drunk a little water. His fever was almost gone, and Bud was optimistic about his recovery, so Layke had time to think about his next step.

He joined Trudy for a cup of coffee and broached the plan. "Miss Trudy," he said using his considerable charm, which was not lost on the very receptive Trudy, "I think it'd be a good idea if I rode out to South Spring and brought Berta and the children into town for church. Maybe I could talk her into staying over for the evening's goings on." He paused and studied Trudy's expression and rushed to finish before he changed his mind. "She needs to get out of that house, Trudy. Jonah can return to tend the stock, and perhaps Berta, SuSu and Wes can stay over for a little visit with you," he said with apprehension and a slight questioning look of his raised brow.

She thought on it for a while, watching him squirm as he awaited her answer, and said that because of Jonah's obvious dislike of Layke, that perhaps she should be the one to extend the invitation instead. "You know, I haven't had Berta for an overnight since before Reuben died four long years ago. You're a very caring and thoughtful man, Layke Williams," she said while clearing her throat and brushing a tear away. To herself she thought, almost as much as my Josh...almost.

Layke could see the wisdom in her suggestion and quickly agreed. Once Berta had been allowed into the safe recesses of his mind, she seemed to invade his every thought, and he was obsessed by his longings and grateful to Trudy for her compassionate understanding. He knew he needed an ally.

Trudy rushed around and got on her Sunday dress. She collected the parasol out of the carved, wooden umbrella stand beside the front door while Layke got her horse from Brewsters' and hitched it up, nervously waiting for her. They wanted to arrive before Berta and family left for church, as they did almost every Sunday morning. She would have time to pack some extra clothing for herself and the children, if they left immediately, and she could get accustomed to the idea of spending a little time away from South Spring, Trudy concluded.

****

Berta admonished herself. "Now why on earth should I feel guilty every time I get excited about going into town on Sunday morning?" It was the only time she got to be with her neighbors anymore.

When Reuben was alive she went to town at least twice a week. She sometimes helped Minna Haglund at the school, or she'd do her fancy shopping, as Reuben called it, at McCoys'. She'd pore over the few magazines that were there - it didn't matter how old they were. She'd check the new dress fabric that had arrived on the steamboat, examining each bolt over and over before making up her mind. Those were cherished memories. There was never that kind of time now. No time for herself and not much more for the children.

But things would get better - she just had to believe that they would, she said over and over. Every time she thought those comforting thoughts Layke's handsome face with that hurt expression still in his eyes would appear in her daydreams, and she longed to stroke that face and ease his past sufferings. There, she said it - she felt possessed.

"Wes, if you don't hold still, we'll never get to town in time for church. I never in all my days saw such a wiggle-worm." Berta popped him teasingly on his bottom and finished straightening the big navy blue bows on SuSu's rich auburn braids. As she checked her blue serge dress from last year she realized how little she had grown. It was just a tad shorter - while Wes - "Well, that child has already outgrown last spring's pants," she thought with a chuckle.

She heard the buckboard and quickly draped her robe around her shoulders as she peered out the window. She couldn't make out who it was, so she hurriedly dressed, selecting the royal blue dress she had made before Reuben died. It didn't fit as well as it had. She had lost weight since she'd made it, but, as she observed, it would just have to do. The Victorian jet buttons on the bodice and cuffs had been very fashionable at the time, and she remembered how proud she'd been of how it fit. She could still see Reuben's laughing face as he turned her around and around to inspect it, exclaiming with pride, that she had become quite a good seamstress.

Berta walked out onto the front porch and recognized Trudy and Layke. Her heart raced for fear that her expression would convey her thoughts, so she directed her eyes toward Trudy. Jonah had hitched the team to their buckboard and was coming out of the barn when he saw them. Berta made it a point to look at him to see if there was the open hostility he had shown before, but Jonah liked Trudy Stucky, so maybe that was why he wore a pleasant expression as he opened the south gate for them.

The expression didn't last long. It disappeared when Trudy told Berta why she'd had Layke drive her to South Spring. "It's time you got away from the house for a spell, Berta. Why, I sure could use some good company. I can't remember the last visit we had...must've been more than four long years ago, I'll declare, it must've."

But no one was fooling Jonah. A cold chill ran down Trudy's spine as she looked at those wild, Elon McRae eyes as he glared at Layke, unrelentingly, with total hatred.

No matter how many times she said that she'd asked Layke

54

to drive her out 'cause all the other men were busy with their families, and as how James Lutes would be coming back from Crosstown with the news of the Townsends' kidnapping, Jonah still thought that Layke had tricked Miss Trudy into coming out with him.

She continued chatting with Berta, trying to avoid Jonah's glare. "Berta, there should be a big gathering at the hotel..the biggest that this town has ever seen, and I sure could use your help. Why, you'll see friends you haven't seen in years."

Jonah wasn't believing any of it. He had his mind made up that Layke Williams wanted to take his mother away from him, and there was no changing that stubborn mind. "Just like Elon!" she thought. "Just like Elon! He's got that same devil's streak he had. May the Lord have mercy on poor Berta and Layke. That same devil's streak Elon had," and she shuddered as she thought of it.

There weren't many who knew the real story about Elon. Just a few old-timers were alive to tell it. It seems that Elon landed in Old Town back in '40, just a lad of about 17 or 18, built like a brick and tough as nails. He started working old man Sam Barker's turpentine camp outside of Crosstown as soon as he got to Florida. Now anyone who worked a turpentine camp had to be mean to start with, and as some would have you believe old man Sam Barker and Elon were a match made in Hell.

It seems that after Elon had been there a few weeks his stripes began to show. He'd get liquored up in that devil's den, Crosstown, and would start mistreating some of Carlie's girls. Some would have bruises as big as Florida oranges when he was through with them. Carlie Evans was not one for anyone to go up against - and that included Mr. Elon McRae.

Finally, one Sunday after Elon's Saturday night romp, Carlie, all six feet and two hundred pounds of her, and Bruiser, the half breed who worked for her, yanked Elon up, and him still in a drunken stupor, and gave him some Florida orange bruises, too. They tied him up just like a hog going to slaughter, tossed him into the back of the buckboard, and they proceeded to drive him through town, yelling and cursing, right past the folks who were going to church, and him using every curse word he could think of.

Sam Barker took one look at him and proceeded to laugh so hard that his old crossed eyes were a-dancing all over the place trying to find the right spot to land. Seems that Sam's girl, Effie, short for Ephram, seeing as how she was supposed to be a boy, had taken a liking to the Scot, and Sam had been trying to discourage her. Seeing him hog-tied and beat to a pulp should take the honey out of her stares - or so he thought.

That Elon had a temper everyone in the camp knew. But just how bad a one they would soon be a witness to. He crawled into his bunk, tail between his legs, and as he got his strength back toward morning - it's been told, anyways - that he snuck into Sam's room, and him snoring his head off, and right beside his missus, too. Elon proceeded to choke him. Well, the missus woke up and started yelling, the men from the bunk house came a-runnin' in, and it's been said it took four of 'em to pull Elon off of Sam. He wasn't dead, but he hurt him so bad that to the day he died you couldn't understand his talk. He got real good at sign language, and if he wasn't a sight with those old crossed eyes a-dancin' and his head askew, and him manipulating those long, bony fingers frantically in the air. If you didn't know better you'd have thought him crazy.

After they pulled Elon off of Sam he grabbed Effie, and her still in her night shirt, threw her over his horse and galloped right out of that camp. Sam never forgave him. If he had any kind of soft spot in his hard heart, it was for Effie, his first born who lived.

That's when they staked out South Spring. No one knows to this day where Elon got that much money, but some would have you believe that he had Effie return to the turpentine camp and steal it right out from under Sam's mattress.

****

Layke and Trudy returned to town in silence. Trudy could not stop the memories of the past from entering her troubled mind. A time she had tried to bury in her subconscious. A time of deep fear, hurt and anger.

Effie McRae had been large with her first child when she accompanied Elon into town that Saturday. When Trudy saw them ride past the hotel, she thought to herself, "I'll be visiting South Spring before this week's up, I'll vow."

It was Wednesday past when Elon came riding into town to fetch her with his eyes wild and saliva running down both sides of his freezing, dust-covered mouth. It was as cold a January night as Trudy could ever remember seeing in Old Town. She hurried over to Palmer's to ask him to keep an eye on things, as it might be

56

a few days before she returned, it being Effie's first born, and to keep a fire going in the stove for the boarders.

Elon had difficulty restraining his trot beside Trudy's slow moving buckboard. Not a word did he utter the entire trip. Trudy ignored his silence and made small talk. But his unreceptive ears were purposely sealed, so she flicked Toby's black rump with her buggy whip to speed him on.

When they arrived, Effie was barely visible under the mountain of quilts in the ice cold cabin. Trudy told Elon to get a fire going in the kitchen stove and to be quick about it. She examined the still, silent Effie and soon found that she was well into her labor. Elon would not, or could not leave the room. He stood brick-like, filling the doorway with no expression in his dark eyes, that were knitted together with his usual fixed scowl.

"You'd think that for this occasion you'd at least be able to smile, Elon McRae," she thought. She'd never understand this man if she lived to be a hundred.

She had been with Effie over four anxious hours when the robust, healthy male child was received into her waiting hands. She was about to inform Elon that he had a beautiful boy when she saw its turned foot - her heart almost stopped. "Oh, no, I do not like this man but I'd not wish a clubfoot on any man's child. Dear Lord, how to tell him - how to tell Effie, who's wringing wet with exhaustion?"

When Trudy reluctantly presented Elon with his son and in so doing told him of the child's deformity, he did not even blink. Soberly he took the child from Trudy and went into the warmth of the kitchen. She returned sad-faced to Effie, and as she stroked her warm brow, she decided to let Elon break the news to his young wife in his own time and in his own way.

Trudy soon followed Elon into the kitchen. She'd not forget that moment for as long as she lived. Elon was nowhere to be found. She called softly...no answer. From out of the black night he appeared, and walked into the kitchen as straight and upright as she'd ever seen him. Both of his coat sleeves were soaking wet up to his shoulders.

Trudy's mouth was open to ask about the babe, but she knew, even before she got the words out, what had happened. All he said then or ever said since to Trudy Stucky that winter night was, "He's gone."

57

Her heart sank, and she hurriedly got her belongings as she dashed out the door, tears streaming as she called into the icy night, "You're the devil himself, Elon McRae! You're the devil!" and she flicked Toby's rump as her aching mind envisioned Elon holding that helpless babe under the icy water in the rain barrel beside the porch.

To this day she could not erase that horrible picture. She knew Effie had had four full-term pregnancies since, but there was never a living child to prove it. When Trudy would ask Aunt Willa or Myrtice about it, they would just shake their heads and mumble, "Poor Miss Effie..Poor little thing."

Trudy had confided in but one person about Elon's murdering his own son, old Joe Garvin, who in turn told his son Pierce of the inhuman act. She never figured why she confided in Joe. Maybe because he was an outsider and a trusted friend, and the unburdening helped cleanse her memory somewhat. Joe had long since died and she had no one to assist her in the dilemma she was confronting now. Should she tell Layke Williams, or should she wait?

****

Jonah drove the family all the way to Old Town in total silence. Berta made excited small talk, and Wes and SuSu could hardly contain themselves about the overnight stay in town. She turned to Jonah and suggested, "Why don't you ride Blackie back to tend the stock? Then you could ride back to town to attend the shindig and spend the night."

He only grunted. Well, she'd say no more. That boy would be the death of her yet. She wanted to shout with joy she was so excited. She felt like she'd been released from prison. She knew she shouldn't feel that way, but, oh - how she did! She was not going to let Jonah spoil her good time. If anyone deserved a good time, she, Berta McRae, did. The past was the past, and as of this day, November 21st, 1877, Bertrice Lillian Norwood McRae was going to have a beautiful, carefree day, and Jonah be damned! She quickly put her hand to her mouth as she gasped at what she had thought, and immediately asked the Lord's forgiveness for being so sinful. Berta was astonished that she could mean such a terrible thing - but she knew she did.

Charlie Beatty preached too long as usual, especially since

everyone was anxiously awaiting James's return from Crosstown with the news of the Townsends. Davis and Palmer announced to the congregation that Martha and Davis's wife, Erma, had cooked a ham, and if the ladies wanted to help out with the cooking that they'd be much obliged.

Every woman in the church spoke up and told what she'd bring, and Trudy announced, "The hotel is free to anyone who'd like to stay the night. Berta McRae will be helping me with the cooking." Berta felt relieved when she made the announcement. She had been so excited about getting away from South Spring that she'd completely forgotten to take any food to help out, as was the custom in the small town.

"My, my, what has come over me? Normally I would have at least furnished preserves and pickles, since I didn't have time to prepare anything special. After all, I do live five long miles out, and it's too far to drive out and back for just a few dishes of food," she rationalized, but Berta was the only one who was concerned about her omission.

Layke was standing at the back of the small church. He'd been inside a church only a few times since he was a young man in Tennessee. He wondered if Jonah had listened to the preacher's sermon, or if he had closed his ears to everything he said that didn't agree with him. But as Berta had thought before him, Jonah be damned! And Layke didn't gasp or ask for the Lord's forgiveness as he studied Jonah's somber expression.

"Berta is going to be mine before the spring drive, Jonah. And the sooner the better!" he added to his silent declaration. As Layke was thinking that, Berta turned and their eyes met and held fast. Berta shyly turned back around, and facing the preacher she patted Wes on his blond head, just to give her fidgety hands something to do. She had a smile of expectation on her beautiful face, and she just prayed Charlie Beatty couldn't read her mind.

The ladies who lived close to town returned to their farms and gathered the food they had promised. They added pickles, preserves and the desserts that they had prepared for their own meals that day. By two in the afternoon the McCoys' and Stucky's porches were crowded, and inside Miss Trudy's spacious dining room there were two long pine tables bountifully overflowing with the many dishes of hearty food.

Martha and Erma Davis had their menfolk move the barrels

of nails, cases of thread and bolts of fabric to the back room to accommodate the makeshift tables of boards and kegs for their food display. They expected over a hundred people in town that cool November afternoon to await James Lute's return with the fascinating news of the kidnapping.

As Trudy and Berta happily went about overseeing the festivities, the men took their overflowing plates of food to the open porch, and the ladies retired to the four upstairs rooms that were usually reserved for drummers and weary travelers.

The children soon gobbled their dinner so they could go to the fields around town to play tag and "Mother, May I," while the older ones went to the river to see who could get the most skips from a flat rock. Frankie Brewster had a rope strung from the tall oak beside his dad's stable, and there were those brave enough to try climbing it, with their over-stuffed stomachs, only to fall down, laughing as they did.

Jonah stood by watching with a scowl on his face, not wanting or willing to join in their merriment. He was busily scanning the crowd for his ma, but mostly for the whereabouts of Layke. He soon saw him as he emerged from the stable alongside Bud Brewster. Then, Jonah remembered Tag. If Jonah had a redeeming trait, it had to be his love of all animals.

He unthinkingly ran over toward them and blurted out his concern for Tag. When Layke told him that Bud had to amputate the leg, his eyes filled with tears, and when he tried to hide his distress by quickly turning his head, Layke saw and understood. He started to put his hand on Jonah's shoulder, but before he could, Jonah started running toward the stable door. Layke wisely decided to leave him to himself.

Later, Bud took Layke aside and told him about Jonah and Tag. "When Jonah ran into the stable he got down on his knees and put his arm around Tag; the tears were streaming down his face. And Layke, he said, 'Anyone who'd shoot a good cow dog should be hanged 'til they're blue in the face, even if the dog belongs to the worst skunk in the whole wide world. It's not your fault he's a wife and mother stealer, Tag. It's not your fault.'"

"I was in the shadows by the hayloft so he couldn't see me, but I could see him. I never thought I'd see such hatred in a son of Reuben's. Never!"

Layke wasn't one to confide in another, but it seemed to him that he was fast changing. First Trudy, and now Bud. He told Bud how he felt about Berta and that he felt she cared for him, too, but the obvious dislike Jonah held for him was standing in their way. He liked Bud and respected him. When he watched him work on Tag, he realized that if he had more education he would be a wonderful doctor. "But he lives in Old Town, just a wilderness town, loved and respected by all who know him. That should be enough for any man. It's enough for me; it's what I want. Finally, at long last, I know exactly what I want. I want Berta and all of the responsibilities that go with being her husband and the master of South Spring - even if that includes being a father to Jonah. This just might be my most difficult test."

When Layke made his solemn declaration, he got the same taut sensation in his throat he had experienced before each battle during the conflict.

CHAPTER VI   THE KIDNAPPING

James Lutes rode into Crosstown to silence. The tomb-like atmosphere made his skin crawl. No one was around, not a living soul. He rode slowly over to the stable. He had ridden Dolly pretty hard, so she needed a rest and a good rub down, but no one was there. He proceeded to the bank, but the door was closed and bolted. Then he remembered that it was Sunday, and he could understand the bank's being closed. So he back-tracked Dolly to the general store, but it, too, was closed and padlocked. He was beginning to get concerned. Crosstown was a ghost town - not even a barking dog about.   The turpentiners who were usually overflowing the saloons and streets, even on Sunday, were nowhere to be seen.

James was not a church-going man, but today being Sunday he was sure that's where he'd find the townspeople.   As he cautiously approached the small white church nestled among the tall oak trees he got the eeriest feeling, like he was being watched. To ease his anxiety he started whistling low, almost under his breath, and began stroking Dolly's sleek, sweaty neck. James was an expert trapper and hunter, so his senses were necessarily keen. He was for sure positive someone or something was watching his every move.

He silently lowered his tense body from the saddle. His worn boots reached for the ground. When the brittle twig snapped, his entire body reacted, and he let out a yelp. Swiftly he swung around - his hand instinctively went for his gun. A lazy, striped house cat sauntered by unconcerned by his presence as he let his breath out slowly. When he turned back around toward the church, the front door burst open and at least a dozen angry men simultaneously rushed out from behind the heavy oak doors.

One of them said in a threatening voice, "That's far enough, stranger. State your business and be quick about it."

It was then that James understood. Crosstown was a town afraid. He very calmly explained to the tense men who he was and why he was there. "The Townsends' worried friends from Old Town sent me to find out how they're faring and just exactly what happened," he lied. James was by nature a very curious man and had not been sent by them, but he knew they were glad that he had volunteered to come.

The small building seemed to erupt with the frantic people rushing outside hungry for the fresh air. They had spent the long night in the stuffy church with the windows and doors closed, locked and barricaded. When he told them that the last report had the R.J. Skinner gang headed south toward Otter Creek settlement, their obvious relief was pathetic to him. He lived for the chase and the unexpected, and he was uncomfortable in the presence of mild mannered men.

He was told that the Townsend family was staying at an isolated farm about five miles away. The Logans had gladly taken them in, and Sheriff Tatum left one of his deputies to guard them while they pursued the gang. They were all doing so poorly that Doc Turner had decided to stay with them. The Sheriff had posted two of his deputies at each end of town to turn the turpentiners away that morning, and everyone else stayed in the church.

****

Sarah waved weakly. Only Ruthie had turned around to return the good-bye. The cool morning mist swirled around the heavily loaded wagon as the family eased its way down the rocky path to the main road to Crosstown. It was not much more than an ox trail and was used mostly by the stage coach and the drummers who sold their wares in the small settlements.

They had not been gone more than a few hours when their mare came up lame. The Reverend Townsend and his son, Harry, had pulled the wagon off to the side of the trail into some thick myrtles so the women could have some shade. They had been sure that they had passed close-by farms on previous trips, so they went in search of them in the hope of securing another mule or ox.

Mrs. Townsend, Ruthie and Anna had stayed with the wagon and mare and passed the time by discussing Sarah's illness and the last revival in Rowland's Bluff and how they always looked forward to the revival in Crosstown, as it was a lively, sinful town, and they felt their presence was necessary in order to save the town from damnation.

The men hadn't been gone more than an hour when five men rode up. At first the women weren't afraid, but they soon found out that they were certainly not gentlemen.

The apparent leader of the group informed the ladies that they had been on the road for quite some time and had had a run

63

of bad luck - they could sure use some provisions, and they would be most grateful if the ladies could supply them with some food.

Mrs. Townsend, who had become very uneasy at the way the one called Opie was ogling Ruthie with his lustful smirk, informed him in her soft manner, "You are most welcome to whatever food we have, as the Lord in his bounty will always provide for my family." When she said that a distinct change came over the men.

Opie repeated over and over again as he sneered at them, "So your Lord is going to provide for you, is He?" And with his animal-strong arms he yanked something out of the wagon and crushed it with the butt of his rifle. He began pulling items off and kicking them into the brush, exciting the others to follow his lead as he cackled evilly.

The leader, R.J., stood by, and did not try to stop their high spirited vandalism. Anna and Ruthie became frightened and began to cry softly. Their tears seemed to incite the gang to even more violence, and when the Reverend and Harry returned they found the area littered with their belongings.

"What on earth? What's going on here?" the Reverend asked in disbelief as he addressed the ruffians.

R.J. walked over to them and in a very pompous manner extended his hand as he said, "Sir, let me introduce you to the R.J. Skinner gang and to myself...I am R.J."

The gang became hilarious with laughter at his pretentious manner and started dancing around the astonished men, extending their hands to be shaken. When Harry and the Reverend didn't return their handshakes, the one called Sheldon became angry and without even a blink of his eyes pulled out his pistol and shot the poor mare. Then he grabbed Harry, and with the help of R.J.'s brother, Joe Bob, they put the mare's rough, leather collar around his neck and began whipping him with the bullwhip, forcing him to pull the wagon into the heavily wooded area. The only stern-faced one among them was R.J. The others were laughing uncontrollably, like hyenas, making sport of the disbelieving family.

The gang mounted their horses and corraled the frightened Townsends like cattle, leading them into a clearing in the woods. They retrieved their belongings and proceeded to make camp, ordering the women to prepare their meal.

Sheldon, in his surly manner, informed them that he'd return promptly with fresh meat and in no time came back with several squirrels. Tossing their still warm bodies at Anna and Ruthie, he ordered them to dress them and to be quick about it, that he was hungry. They were used to skinning and cleaning game, as Harry was good with a trap, and they often prepared game for the family, and were relieved to have something familiar to do. But when he yanked the slimy entrails out of the squirrel, and forced them to open their mouths as he shoved them inside, and shouted, "Your Lord says for you to eat this squirrel's guts," they became hysterical and began to retch, trying to close their ears to his insane laughter as they shook with fear.

The Reverend tried to stop him, but Sheldon struck him a hard blow with the butt of his gun and cut a deep, jagged gash over his eye. Blood spurted everywhere. Harry, like a shot, went for his throat; but Bunt, the small child-like one, shot Harry in the calf of his leg. It was only grazed, but it bled enough to make him extremely weak.

R.J., tired of his men's antics, took charge. He sat beside the bleeding preacher and grilled him about the layout of Crosstown, its banks, and if he knew the owners and their families. Over and over again he unrelentingly questioned the sniveling man. "I am just a circuit preacher and get to know only the people who graciously take my family into their homes," he said repeatedly. But R.J. didn't believe him one whit. The others tried to interrogate him but were unsuccessful as well.

Opie spoke up and in his cocky voice said he knew a for sure way to get the holy man to talk. He deliberately walked over toward Ruthie. Grinning, his eyes filled with lust, he started tearing her clothes off slowly, piece by piece, laughing his hellish cackle as poor Ruthie shook with fear, cowering beside the wagon wheel. The Reverend broke down. He was shaking with uncontrollable rage. He began shouting toward heaven in an unintelligible gibberish. His arms were raised as he ferociously shook his fists at his unseeing God, and fell face down in the dust, a broken man.

The gang howled at the trembling family sprawled before them, but Opie didn't let their tears and prayers stop his tormenting the half-clothed, sobbing Ruthie. He dragged her behind the wagon by her disheveled, long, brown hair. She kicked and screamed while trying to pull the torn blouse over her exposed breasts. He threw her thrashing body down on top of the thick layers of pine straw.

Sheldon grabbed one of her legs and yelled at Opie, "Let me

at her first, Opie. I'll get her opened up for you. Bet this little holy gal ain't had a real man before. Hey... maybe she ain't had one at all. We'll baptize her, Opie. We'll just fix her right up for her Lord,"

"She's mine, Sheldon. I seen her first. I'll get her primed for anyone else who wants her." The salivating Sheldon watched as Opie raped her, and thrilled at his every brutal thrust, egging him on as he vicariously enjoyed her defilement.

The burning, searing pain ripped deep in her as she screamed and begged for mercy, but none came. Harry, weak from the loss of blood, tried to go to her, but Bunt had tied a rope tightly around his ankle and secured it to a stake. He was hobbled just like an animal with his hands bound behind his back.

R.J. stood at the edge of the clearing deep in thought, ignoring it all until he'd made up his mind about their next move. He yelled at Opie and Sheldon, "Let her go, boys. You've had your sport. We've got some important planning to do, and that sure as hell doesn't include poking some little ripe, holy tart."

The Reverend began heaving and gasping for breath, and Mrs. Townsend pleaded with Joe Bob to allow her to go to her husband, explaining that he had a very weak heart. He retorted sarcastically, "Why don't you tell your Lord to make him all well?" His heavy brows were knitted together with his disgust for the helpless family.

It was then that she and Anna resigned themselves to their fate. From that moment they didn't speak one word. They just sat and stared into space and moved only when they were forced to.

R.J. decided to hit the Crosstown bank without casing the town. What he didn't know was that Crosstown was surrounded by turpentine camps, and Ruthie wasn't about to enlighten him. A rougher, tougher, corn swigging group of men a body would ever see anywhere frequented Crosstown and its saloons on a Saturday afternoon. Now, Crosstown wasn't as wild a cow town as some, but it sure was one helluva lively turpentine camp town on Saturday 'til Monday. Ruthie knew this. She had heard her pa preach about the Devil's visiting their camps often enough, goodness knows.

Ruthie had an instinct for survival and decided to play into the cocky robbers' hands. After straightening her torn, dirty blouse and skirt, she asked Opie if he would go with her to the creek for

66

a wash-up. She cozied up to him, and he was just stupid enough to think she had enjoyed the pain and degradation he had inflicted upon her. Then she skillfully worked R.J. to the outside of the group and sweetly eased up to him. Opie was so all-fired jealous that he turned pea green. She informed R.J. about all the gold she'd heard was in the bank on a Saturday when the turpentine camps deposited their giant payrolls for the following week.

R.J. was so eager and easy she couldn't believe how he played right into her inexperienced hands - and she had thought that he was the smart one. Ruthie was feeling her new found power. Her full breasts felt tight against her torn blouse, and she purposely breathed deeply to accentuate their ripeness every time she got close to him. That animal, Opie, was like her shadow. Finally she clenched her teeth and commanded him, "Leave me be when I'm talking business with your leader," and she glared her hatred for him.

R.J. liked her spunk, so he told Opie, "Mind what the little lady says, Opie. And, Opie, you keep away from her, do ya hear?" Opie resented his interference and angrily turned away from them to join the others. But before he left he said low between gritting teeth, "I'll have another go at you, you little tart, and when I'm through not even Sheldon's big prick will fill you up, you'll be so God-damned stretched."

She continued her tantalizing game. Licking her full, moist lips she seductively stroked her barely covered thighs as she teased R.J. If he knew what she was doing, and she was sure he did, he was nevertheless enjoying her performance. Ruthie could feel her pa's and Harry's astonished eyes following her, and she averted her eyes for fear she'd not be able to follow through with her plan. She was convinced that they'd all be killed before their ordeal was over if she didn't ingratiate herself with R.J.

R.J. took Ruthie's advice and decided to hit the bank in the early afternoon. At two o'clock on Saturday afternoon the gang conspicuously rode into Crosstown leaving Bunt behind to guard the Townsends. They were surprised by the throngs of people on the planked sidewalks, on the sandy streets and in the many buildings lining the main road. There was barely room for their mounts among the unruly crowd of drunken turpentiners. They had inched their way to the first saloon when R.J. disgustedly turned to Joe Bob and gave the signal to leave. The streets were just too crowded for them to make a get-away once they had robbed the bank. The attempt was aborted.

When they returned to camp unexpectedly, Ruthie ran out to greet them and excitedly asked, "Why are you back so early? How much did you get?" and babbled away with child-like exuberance, knowing full well why they had to return.

R.J. pushed her away roughly. "Too many people," is all he said and walked to the edge of the camp site to study his dilemma. Ruthie followed but kept her distance. She wasn't about to be far from him what with that Opie glaring his threatening scowl at her every chance he got. His men were hesitant to approach him and started breaking camp quietly. She retrieved her blanket out of the wagon and placed it a few feet from his. Opie followed her with his evil eyes but made no effort to speak to her or to touch her. She knew he was afraid of R.J. or he wouldn't have obeyed him in the first place. She slept fitfully. Once she cried out in the night and R.J. rolled over and asked her if she was all right. She felt protected and warm and soon drifted off.

Sunday, after a meager breakfast of cold corn dodgers and bitter, boiled coffee, they left the Crosstown area and headed southeast toward Old Town. They made camp outside town at Two-Mile Bend. It was there that R.J. came down with the fever. It was awful. His piercing, black eyes rolled to the top of his head as he shook uncontrollably.

Ruthie ministered to him. He was the only friend her family had, and she dared not let him die. She got rags and wiped his forehead with the cool creek water and made herb tea from the supplies from her ma's box, insisting that he drink it every hour. He fought her weakly, but she persevered. His fever finally broke on Tuesday, but he was so weakened from the ordeal he could barely be understood.

Ruthie had made R.J. a pallet in the back of their wagon. He was resting under the quilts when he raised his head and called Joe Bob over to the wagon. Joe Bob had to lean close to make out the few words he managed to utter. "Return to Crosstown to check out the bank in midweek," he managed. "Take these holy people with us."

The men, anxious for excitement, started packing up immediately. Ruthie studied R.J.'s expression and in their silent exchange understood his reasoning and was grateful. He wanted to get the Townsends closer to Crosstown to assure himself that they'd be found, as no one would be looking for them as far away as Old Town.

They arrived outside Crosstown Wednesday afternoon. The men tried to talk R.J. into staying at camp, but he insisted on accompanying them. By the time they rode into town he could hardly sit his horse, he was so weak, so another robbery attempt was aborted. A disgruntled group of men sat around the camp fire that night and frightened the Townsends with tales of their past exploits. Sheldon bragged about how he had just shot an old dog that wasn't good for anything anyway, and Opie, looking right at Ruthie, talked about the best whores he'd ever poked and said that she sure as hell wasn't one of 'em.

R.J. interrupted their bragging reports to inform them of his decision. "I am bored with these holy folks. It's about time that we checked out the big money down south." At that declaration all hell broke loose, they were so excited. The inactivity of the past few days was for docile men, not for high- strung bucks on the prowl.

Sheldon tied the family to the wagon, exclaiming "Now let's see your Almighty Lord get you loose from this one!" as he pulled the rope extra hard on Harry's wrist. "The hungry panthers will get to you first," he shouted at him, his face just inches from Harry's head, which was bowed in resignation. Then he turned to Ruthie, who had her head raised and was staring at him...daring him. He methodically opened her blouse, smiling and licking his drooling lips. He reached inside and grabbed her full, young breast, squeezing it as he stroked and said, "You ain't ever had what I got bulging between my legs, little lady. That Opie ain't even got the makings of a boy, much less a man. I'll be back for you. You just keep looking over your shoulder, and one of these days old Sheldon will give you a poke you'll be bragging about for the rest of yore life."

Try as they might, the Townsends didn't get loose from their wagon 'til early that foggy Saturday morning. A turpentine worker wandered off the main road in a drunken stupor after a Friday night at Etta Mae's saloon and stumbled upon them. They had been tied so securely that even clever Ruthie couldn't get herself out of that predicament. It took a drunken turpentiner to assist the Lord in his work.

****

A very excited James Lutes arrived back in Old Town mid-afternoon. The McCoys' and Stucky's porches were crowded with the laughing, relaxed townsmen, full of their abundant dinner. The children were running up and down the trail in front of the few buildings excitedly yelling the news that he had returned. He was quickly surrounded by the curious neighbors, everyone asking questions at once. James was a practiced storyteller and kept his audience captive as they sat around Miss Trudy's open porch. He added his own interpretation and embellishments to the horrible tale of the Townsends.

The women gasped and wrung their hands and cried quietly as their hearts filled with compassion for their dear friends. The Townsends had been visiting Old Town for almost seven years and were highly thought of. The men became angered and kept saying, "Someone oughta go after those stinking bastards," and, "I hope I'm the lucky one to put the rope around their chicken-scrawny necks," and on and on into the night their anger was expressed at the unbelievable acts performed on their friends by the feared gang.

The women were gathered inside the hotel and in hushed tones they quietly discussed the tragedy. Berta had put Wes and SuSu down for the night on the pallet in one of the front bedrooms. Jonah had ridden Blackie back to South Spring at dusk, as she had suggested, and told her he'd be back for them the next day. He looked so dejected and forlorn as he played unsucessfully on her heart strings. Actually she wished she could stay even longer, but she knew it wasn't practical. Her mountainous responsibilities were always with her, and she could not wish them away.

Emma Haglund asked Berta if she could assist her in the school while she was in town, and she promised that she would. While Reuben was alive the children went to school in town, but now she didn't have time to take them and couldn't spare Jonah. She helped SuSu with her reading and numbers, and when she went to town on Sundays, Emma - bless her heart - would give her the next week's lesson so the children wouldn't get behind. Wes was quick to learn, and, though SuSu didn't show a lot of interest, she seemed to retain the lessons well, so it made teaching easy for Berta. She often thought that if she could have chosen to be anything other than a wife and mother, it would have been a teacher. The one subject that she was not proficient in was music, and Wes and SuSu both loved to sing, just like their father.

Reuben would sing the old songs at the top of his lungs as he went about the daily chores. They all loved to hear him. There was nothing but silence at South Spring now. Young Reuben would happily sing right alongside his father, but Jonah didn't sing at all, not even in church. He always said that it hurt his throat.

Trudy glanced at Berta as she came down the stairs to join the other ladies in the parlor. She thought that she looked weary so went to her saying, "Berta McRae, it's been a long time since we had a good gabfest. Let's go into the kitchen and have a nice, hot cup of coffee and catch up on things."

Berta nodded and smiled. Trudy Stucky wasn't fooling her for one minute. She was curious to know just how she did feel about Layke. It was plain to see that Trudy was smitten by his charm and good looks as was every lady gathered there. He was the talk of the town, and all the mothers with eligible daughters had made it a point to invite him out for Sunday dinner and had even offered to help care for Tag to spell him and to do whatever else they could for the poor man.

Layke took it all in his stride. She guessed he was accustomed to all that female attention since he was thirty plus, unmarried and extremely handsome. He appeared to be a hard worker and had a good education and certainly had a way with young and old alike. Yes, Layke Williams was quite a catch for one of the young ladies of Old Town, or so they thought.

They had no way of knowing that it was Berta McRae who had already caught his eye and captured his heart, and Trudy wasn't about to tell them and spoil their scheming. "Let them have something to look forward to," she thought, as she watched them maneuver their daughters into going to the stable to look after Tag and seeing if Layke wanted anymore persimmon pie or coffee or whatever else their manipulative minds could conjure up. He was undoubtedly the best looked-after man in all of Old Town.

Berta joined Trudy in the kitchen. As she followed her, she tried to see if Layke was on the porch but could not for the gathered crowd around James Lutes. Nor did she hear his deep voice. "Maybe he's at the stable tending to poor Tag," she thought, and secretly resented their time apart.

Some of the families had started gathering up their children and cooking utensils and leftover food for their next day's meal. Miss Trudy commented, "I'm believing every farmer in Old Town must have had a good crop of crowder peas, as most every woman here brought a pot," and she and Berta chuckled as she went to the back door and waved her apron in the air to clear out some of the obvious odor.

"That Trudy sure has a way of injecting humor into any given situation," Berta thought. She knew she was getting her into a good, relaxed mood so that she would unburden her tale of Layke and Jonah, and as she sat there relaxed and feeling protected and loved in the Stucky kitchen, she did Miss Trudy's bidding. Her pent up feelings tumbled out and she hardly took time to catch her breath.

Trudy just sat and rocked, letting it all soak in. She gave a "hmmm" or an "is that so?" or a "now, now," but no advice or opinion did she give Berta that dark November night.

She got up from her rocker and walked over to her, putting her motherly hands on her shoulders, all the while looking at the imposing figure standing tall and straight in the doorway. It was Layke. How much he had heard she did not know, but some of it he surely heard, as he had an expression on his face that sent Trudy Stucky from that kitchen as fast as her two plump legs could carry her.

She managed to get the last of the children into the Haglund wagon so they could return to North Prong, but mostly so that Layke and Berta could have some privacy from curious eyes and ears. Then she joined the others on the front porch to entertain the cowmen and a slightly inebriated Davis and the remaining survivors. She smiled as she said to herself, "Berta McRae, if you don't take advantage of this'n, I'm not believing there's red blood in those veins of yours. I've done my part."

Berta didn't need to turn around to know that Layke was there - she could feel his presence. As soon as Trudy left the room, Layke calmly walked around her chair to face her. He gently pulled up Trudy's chair, never taking his eyes off Berta's. He reached for her hands and held them firmly as he began to speak. It was obvious to Berta that he had rehearsed every word and had no doubt carefully planned the meeting with Trudy's assistance.

He began, "Berta, I don't want any interruptions so please hear me out. I know we've not known each other but a few days. But I also know that there are times when two people meet that there's no need for a long acquaintance for them to realize there is something very special between them."

He didn't fidget or look embarrassed while he was speaking about his feelings. He was very matter-of-fact and expected no nonsense from her, but it was also obvious that he was having a problem keeping his emotions in check.

Berta was having difficulty dealing with his seriousness. She wanted to laugh and shout and say, "Layke Williams, why don't you just take me in your arms and kiss me?" but she didn't dare. It was clear that he had deliberated over the precise words, and that she shouldn't upset the flow of things. But it was hard for her to keep a straight face. The devilishness she had been allowed to indulge in as a child was on her lips ready to explode. But contain herself, she must. "Yes, Layke," she managed.

"Are you patronizing me, Berta McRae?" he asked as he hungrily reached for her.

The rain that had been threatening for the past week arrived without warning. Wind-driven white sheets chased the remaining cowmen into Trudy's dining room, and Berta reluctantly joined her as they dashed upstairs to hurriedly close the open windows. The curtains billowed around them as they made the rounds of the four upstairs rooms. Wes and SuSu stirred and asked Berta if it was time to get up, but she covered them again and said, "Shhhhh, it's just a November storm," as the lightening and thunder made their announcements.

The Florida sky was alive with activity. It was the first storm Berta had allowed herself to enjoy in the past four years. Berta had confessed to Reuben the first year they were at South Spring that the most exciting thing that ever happened around there was those wonderful Florida storms. How she loved the excitement and unexpectedness of them rumbling across the electrified sky!

She shivered as she drew her shawl around her shoulders and joined the others in the dining room. When she looked at Layke she knew the magical time they shared in Trudy's kitchen was past. But as their eyes held, they both knew that there would be other times, and she felt warm and protected and ignored the warning of the torrential rains that were swelling the Suwannee and threatening South Spring.

Miss Trudy told the few men who were there that they were welcome to stay the night, and Berta joined her upstairs to get their

73

rooms ready. Neither of them spoke a word about Berta's and Layke's conversation in the kitchen, but Trudy knew Layke had made his intentions known, because Berta was the most relaxed she had been in a long time right in the middle of a frightening storm that could wreak havoc at her ranch.

Not once did Berta think of South Spring. She thought only of Layke Williams, who was staying the night in the room next to hers. She allowed a seductive smile to play across her otherwise ladylike face in the pitch black, stormy night as Trudy gently snored beside her, and she knew beyond a doubt that Layke was also awake and restless with his yearnings.

CHAPTER VII   THE FLOOD

Jonah gently felt around Rosie's swollen back leg. She twitched and lowed softly. He said to himself, "What more can happen to us?" and in disgust struck his open palm with his fist.

Rosie twisted her head around to let him know he was hurting her. "Now, Rosie, now, Rosie," he said in a sing-song cadence, stroking and calming her with his soft caring manner.

He had made up his mind that when he rode into town for Berta and the children, he'd fetch Bud Brewster. The leg was badly swollen and it was obvious, even to Jonah's untrained eyes, that it was not a bee sting as they had previously thought. He remembered a salve his pa had used on their horses and cows, and after searching the shelves on the south side of the barn, he found it.

His pa used to say, "This salve'll make Peg Leg Pete grow a new leg," and my how he'd laugh. Jonah often remembered the many stories he told them about the mythical pirate who roamed the Mexico Gulf right off their property, or so he made them believe. And as a child Peg Leg Pete was very real to Jonah and young Reuben.

After he applied the salve sparingly, as Rosie was in such pain, he turned in for the night. When the rains finally arrived that black, Sunday night with the unexpectedness of a spring storm, Jonah became understandably frightened. Their land bordering the Suwannee was prone to flooding and the herds feeding alongside the river were in immediate danger. He had taken hold of assisting Berta on the ranch, but she had been there to shoulder the major responsibilities, and before then young Reuben had been her rock to lean on.

Jonah knew he had to act. He had to move the beeves up to the high ground. But he also knew he couldn't do it alone. Big Dan and Ezekiel weren't able to do range work anymore, but he could ride either to the Swede's or Beatty's for help. He decided to wait for a while. He had been in bed for only a short time, but it seemed like hours. Finally after tossing and turning, he got up, pulled on his pants, grabbed his slicker off the coat rack and went to the kitchen door and opened it. The commanding wind and rain lashed out at him. He had difficulty closing the weathered door, and as he struggled to secure the iron latch, the lightning

75

streaked capriciously, teasing the surrounding night sky.

With his head held down Jonah trudged through the ankle deep bog to Rosie's stall. The damp cold found its way inside his thin shirt and slicker. It was obvious that she was in deep distress, in much more pain than when he was last in the barn, and he knew the longer he delayed his departure, the more difficult would be his chance of getting help.

The run-off along the Suwannee was torrential. It had been such a dry fall that the deep sand could not absorb the immediate downpour. The river was already overflowing its banks in the low-lying areas along the western sections, South Spring being one of them. The often used ox trail along the river was under water at Effie's Pond area, and Two Mile Bend, where the largest herds were feeding, was already impassable.

There was no end in sight of the now steady rain. But Jonah continued to stay with Rosie with Old Red hovering protectively by his side in the hay- filled stall. He couldn't decide what to do. Should he try for the Swede's? Maybe he should try to make it to Old town. The howling winds pounded the weathered barn as he strained to see through the wall of rain pouring off of the barn's steep roof, but there was no one there - neither Big Dan nor Ezekiel. He knew he could no longer postpone making a decision ...the right decision. He sat curled up in Rosie's stall, perplexed, his head bowed trying to block out the immediacy of his dilemma. He fell asleep.

****

Reuben McRae was one of the few ranchers in the northern part of the state who had seeded part of his acreage. He had experimented with planting different types of grasses and supplemented the corn and hay with velvet beans for the winter feeding. The smaller ranchers drove their cattle to the central part of the state to the feed lots on Payne's Prairie and the Kissimmee basin, where the pasture was fertile and lush, to fatten them up before the long drive to Punta Rassa, but Reuben preferred to utilize his own land to its fullest.

There was open range in the entire state, but most of his herd was on South Spring land with only a few hundred head wandering among the piney woods not more than twenty or thirty

76

miles beyond his boundaries. The Suwannee cut through the middle of his holdings on its way to the Gulf and was subject to flooding all along the way, particularly during the spring rains. But a fall storm was rare, and the cowmen who would normally be on the alert for such an event were all in Old Town sleeping off their over indulgence at the evening's gathering.

****

Wes playfully jumped onto Berta's bed, awakening her, as he and SuSu had an early morning romp. She wore a confident smile as she remembered Layke's serious declarations of the previous night and pulled her knees up, hugging her arms around them as she snuggled into the extra bed covers, for it had got chilly during the damp night.

The rains were still visiting their diagonal sheets against the bedroom windows. She cautioned the children to be quieter because there were guests trying to sleep. Then suddenly she became shocked at her total self-indulgence when she remembered the seventeen-year struggle she and Reuben had devoted to build South Spring. With this torrential rainfall the entire herd was in jeopardy and could be wiped out.

She quickly grabbed her blue floral wrapper, and while gathering her clothes told the children to dress themselves - immediately! Frantically she dashed down the narrow stairs toward the domestic noises wafting upwards from Trudy's kitchen, hoping that she was alone and berating herself with clucking noises for her consummate selfishness.

Trudy took one look at Berta's disheveled appearance and before she could question her about it, Berta blurted out her frightened concern for Jonah and South Spring. "Trudy, the beeves must be moved to higher ground. After all, a fifteen-year-old boy can't handle that job alone! I just hope he had sense enough to get help from Swede's or Charlie's."

Trudy rearranged her pots, moving them to the back of the stove to stay warm and took the distraught Berta by the arm. "Get yourself upstairs, young lady, and get dressed as fast as you can! I'll get Layke." But Layke was at the stable with Tag, so she rapped on Barney's door. No answer. He must have had too much of the jug, she figured.

"Barney Coombs, are you in there? If you are you'd better stir yore stumps this minute, do ya hear?" She heard a grumbling noise and shuffling sounds as he approached the door.

"Who's there? Who's there?" he mumbled. It seemed like forever 'til he finally opened the door. Trudy latched onto his ear and began pulling him downstairs after her. Barney kept saying over and over again in his slightly deliberate, unsteady voice that he was hurrying, but that he'd not step off that porch in all that weather without a cup of coffee and at least one of her biscuits.

"I'll declare right here and now, Barney Coombs, if you and Layke don't get a move on you'll cost Berta McRae and all her children their livelihood." She shoved a hot buttered biscuit into his open hand and told him he could drink his coffee when he got back with Layke, as it was just too dadburned hot, and that he'd better high-tail it over to the stable as fast as his short bowed legs could carry him.

No one ever stopped to argue with Miss Trudy when she said to move it - you just automatically did her bidding. Barney moved those bantam legs as fast as they had ever moved and sloshed his way to Brewsters' stable to alert Layke about South Spring. They were good cowmen, and between them and Jonah they should be able to handle it - if they could get there. The roads along the river were probably already impassable, so they'd have to go the much longer route by the Swedes' place.

Tag was on the mend and up on his three legs eating a normal breakfast when Barney stormed in. Bud, Layke and Frankie were all gathered around as if at a birthing, and in a sense it was. They all had satisfied grins on their faces, that were quickly erased when Barney shouted word for word what Trudy had said to him. Layke didn't wait to hear Bud's response as he dashed out into the early morning downpour. Bud and Frankie answered in unison, "Sure, Layke, we'll take care of Tag," but Layke was gone with his head down and his hands shielding his face from the stinging rain. The two distraught women greeted him as he stomped the mud-covered boots off on the porch floor and yanked off his soaked jacket and shirt revealing his shivering, sculptured torso.

Even in her unsettled state, Berta was conscious of this man's animal needs and she longed to satisfy them. Quickly she turned and almost ran into the kitchen. She knew she had to exercise complete control until she had time to sort out her feelings and

78

to help Jonah through this trying time in his growing up. She needed to talk to him - reason with him. But she wasn't sure how long she would be able to deny her longing for Layke.

The rains continued pounding relentlessly against the weathered hotel as Layke and Barney packed their saddlebags. Berta and Trudy were in the kitchen gathering food for them to pack along with their other provisions. Their obvious nervousness triggered the children's pent-up energy. Finally Berta had had enough, and the tongue lashing she gave them told Layke how distraught and really frightened she was.

Layke studied Berta's worried expression as he held her white-knuckled fists, trying to give her hope. She had difficulty looking directly at him and he understood her enormous guilt. The only time in the past seventeen years she had allowed herself to be the carefree Bertrice Lillian Norwood of Macon, Georgia, and it had to end with impending disaster for her and her family.

His heart went out to her. Oh, how he ached to hold her, to reassure her that all would be well. She, of all people, should not suffer. "It's not fair! Why shouldn't fate allow her this one frivolous moment?" He clenched his fists angrily - his past bitterness returned, and he wondered if there indeed was a God.

Only a short time had passed from Berta's realization of her troubled South Spring and the time Layke and Barney departed Old Town for the Swede's spread, North Prong. While Layke and Barney were preparing for the round-up, they discussed the best route to take to South Spring. Layke was at an obvious disadvantage in his knowledge of the area, but Barney had ridden for South Spring on all the cow hunts and drives since Elon had owned it. He knew the terrain in all kinds of weather, for from late February thru April, when the cow hunts occurred, were precarious times in Florida. One day there would be brilliant blue skies with feathery white clouds and the unmerciful heat, and the next, the tumbling temperature would plummet to below freezing, when an unexpected norther blew in to envelop the entire peninsula.

The northern trail from Old Town was already flooded. It took its toll on Bucko and Barney's horse, Poker. It seemed like hours 'til they got to the Swede's spread, only a short distance from Old Town. Emma met them at the kitchen door with the hot soup already poured, and as they joined her and the girls, their muddy

79

boots ignored, she informed them of Swede's fear for their stock.

"He and the boys have been out since before daybreak rounding up the small herd down by the mill pond to bring them up to the high ground." When Layke asked her if she knew anything about South Spring she just shook her head and said, "Swede was so unsettled this morning before he left. But he did mention that he sure hoped Jonah had got help from Charlie as 'bout a quarter of Reuben's pasture is low. That's all he said, Layke. He and the boys were in a hurry to get to Battle Creek and the herd there."

Layke and Barney exchanged concerned looks and asked to be excused. Emma quietly tucked some shortcakes into their jacket pockets. She had wrapped them securely but before they left the Haglund barn and headed south both had reached into their pockets and nervously eaten them - anything to take their minds off of their problem. There was no let up in sight. The hard, white rain continued. The trails were indistinguishable - just solid water as far as they could see.

****

Rosie was lowing softly, and every time Jonah allowed himself to acknowledge it he went to her and said, "It'll be all right, old girl, it'll be all right," not believing his own voice. Midday was approaching and as Jonah and Old Red peered out the barn door, he turned to him and said, "Red, did you hear anything?" And when he said that, Red announced the horsemen with his practiced bark, then a low growl as Jonah held his hand above his eyes sheltering them. He couldn't make out who the riders were.

He called anxiously and with great relief, "Over here! We're over here in the barn!"

Layke and Barney sloshed their weary horses toward the voice. When Jonah saw Layke his first reaction was anger - then tremendous relief; anyone was better than no one, he conceded. He welcomed them with as much emotion as he could allow.

"I've a sick cow here; that's why I didn't get help to move the beeves," he said defensively as Layke and Barney glanced at each other understanding the young man's fear and guilt.

"No need to worry, Jonah. We'll take a look at her and rest the horses fer a spell. Miss Trudy and yore ma thought you might

80

could use some help seein' as how this storm come up so sudden like." Then Barney looked at Rosie's back leg. After they examined her further and discussed the extent of her problem, they both decided she had probably sprained it and that her great weight prohibited the healing.

Barney got some rags from the bunk room and bandaged it tightly as all three of them forced her to lie down. Jonah was so relieved that their remaining milk cow wasn't going to dry up that he was almost happy as he saddled Blackie and they rode for Effie's Pond, the lowest close-in land on their spread. If they could move them out of that area, they would probably be all right, since the rains were lessening.

They could see the beeves in the distance. Some had made their way north of the pond, but Barney spotted one mired deep in the mud, and while he and Layke uncoiled their ropes, Jonah used his cow whip to herd those on the perimeter. Old Red did his job, and they soon were moving the main part of the herd to the high ground. Layke and Barney were having a difficult time pulling out the bellowing cow, even with their experienced cow ponies. Once freed she weakly joined the others amid the noise of the frightened herd.

"If we'd been a hour later or if the rains hadn't slowed down, we'd a lost at least a dozen or more, Layke. I never seen the Suwannee so riled up - not in all my years working this land. Yep, she'd a drowned a bunch of 'em!"

Layke, with his rain-dripping hat almost covering his serious face, nodded in agreement. "We're not out of the woods yet, Barn. Berta said that there is another herd near Two Mile Bend. Let's catch up with Jonah and ask him."

Jonah and Red were already up to the rolling hill area north of the river when Layke and Barney put their mounts to a difficult gallop, yelling against the driving wind and rain. But Jonah couldn't hear their labored calls for his own yelling and the beeves' roar drowning them out. They finally managed to pull up alongside him, and the three finished the roundup and headed for the Two Mile Bend area.

The rain was now just trickling down as they moved slowly east. The trees were barer along the river than when Layke had ridden out to South Spring just a short time before. The high wind and torrential rain had aided in the annual fall defoliation. They

81

rode through a solid glade of water that stretched beyond the river valley to the high ridge on the south side. As they approached the valley, they spotted the herd.

When Layke and Barney looked at each other, their knowing glances reflected the true picture before them. A few beeves had made it to the rim, but the others were caught, partially submerged, in the clay-like soil, and there was just no way three cowmen could pull them out before the rushing water drowned them. Layke felt sick to his stomach as he viewed the impending devastation before him, but, being a seasoned cowman, he automatically went about the business at hand.

Barney called Jonah over and told him that he was in charge of the yearlings and that they would handle the larger and heavier beeves. The water was so deep that Red had to swim, and Jonah was having an impossible time making him stay on the high ridge. He chased him up to the huge live oaks on the knoll, and still Red would not leave his master. Throwing his hands up in resignation he glanced to the north and saw a group of horsemen approaching.

Layke and Barney were wrestling with a huge bellowing bull, and the noise that he and the frightened beeves were making drowned out his report of the approaching riders. When Layke brushed his hand over his half closed eyes to remove some of the grime, he saw Jonah motioning to him.

"Looks like the Swede and his big, brawny sons, Barn. I think they just saved Berta's ranch. Boy, am I glad to see them! We'd never in all this world have been able to handle all that," Layke said as he gestured toward the river.

They worked 'til almost dusk and the last of the beeves had been driven to the high land. The Swede addressed Layke, "The Suwannee was like a wild woman this morning. How many of 'em was drowned we'll not be knowing 'til the water drops and the buzzards lead us to their carcasses. But you can bet on finding some of 'em down to the west end of the spread. She let us off light this time, she did. But she always comes back to test us, Layke... she always comes back."

An exhausted Layke and Barney bid the Haglunds goodnight and turned west to South Spring with Jonah and Red close behind. Exhausted, they decided to spend the night at South Spring and ride back to Old Town in the morning with the good news for Berta.

Jonah was very subdued as he unsaddled Blackie. He knew

that he had behaved in a very irresponsible manner by not riding for help earlier, and he didn't feel like being by himself - not just yet. He was leaving the stable when he turned to Barney and asked if they would like some supper. They were about to decline, but when they pulled the fried chicken and biscuits out of their saddlebags, they realized that the food was soaked through. Barney swore that Old Red thanked him personally as he wolfed down the much deserved feast. Realizing that Jonah needed time alone, Layke headed for the house to start the coffee while Barney went with Jonah to check on Rosie. She was still down, and they helped her up. The leg didn't seem as tender as earlier, and Jonah proceeded to milk her.

Barney rubbed Bucko and Poker down, got a bucket of mash and fed them, and playfully swatted them on their rumps telling them that they had sure 'nuff earned a treat today. He watched Jonah. "That is a very confused and lonely boy for sure," he thought. "He must miss Reuben something awful."

"Barney, do you think Rosie ought to be on that leg tonight? Maybe we should put her down again."

"I checked it, Jonah. It's still sore, and the bandage ain't too tight...but, here, let me give you a hand with her. She'd probably rest better off'n it."

The rains were gone, but a damp mist hung over the land. The full moon came up over the ridge flaunting its rays as they trudged tiredly toward the aroma of coffee coming from Berta's kitchen. Jonah carried the bucket filled with Rosie's rich, creamy milk, and Barney discovered some more ruined food in the saddlebags for Red.

He smiled to himself. "Those ladies sure didn't want us to go hungry. Ladies sure do beat all, they sure do," and he chuckled to himself as he watched Red make short work of the chicken.

They stayed at the McRae spread 'til the following afternoon. The water continued to subside almost as quickly as it had arrived. It was still boggy around the low-lying areas, but the run-off of the Suwannee into the Gulf was rapid, and by the time they left, the north road was passable all the way to town.

As Layke and Bucko passed familiar areas, he found it impossible to believe that he had been there for such a short time. It seemed to him he had been there forever and that the Wilpole job and all the others, including the War, were but fuzzy memories.

He was relieved he felt as he did. He was completely comfortable for the first time in his adult life. His only concern was Jonah...Jonah McRae.

CHAPTER VIII   PROMISES

Bud and Frankie were retrieving the sheets of tin that had blown off of the stable when Layke and Barney rode up to the hotel in the foot-deep mud. They'd volunteered to help Trudy replace the shingles that were goodness knows where. Bud told Layke later that after he and Barney left, a hurricane-force wind kicked up, and he hadn't been sure that there would be an Old Town for him to return to.

Layke and Berta exchanged small talk all the way back to South Spring. Their declaration of the night before seemed so long ago with Berta withdrawn and distant, but he had seen this side of her before. She would need time and an extra dose of loving to remove her guilt. "And I'm just the man who can take care of your special needs my darling one," he thought as he caressed her cool hand, giving her his strength.

December and January came and went without any particular turn of events. There had been no word of the R.J. Skinner Gang - they were apparently lying low as was their pattern in the past, surfacing about twice a year. Tag was ensconced in the saddle seat that Bud and Frankie had made so he could ride with Layke on some of the trails, but he was more comfortable riding with Milton in the chuck wagon. He got along amazingly well and did a pretty good job of weeding out the herd considering his handicap, but he seemed more content helping Milton set up camp than being an active cow dog.

Layke needed another dog, but he couldn't bring himself to replace Tag even on the range - at least not yet. Two of the other cowmen, Wayne and Mush, had extra dogs they'd trained, so Layke used Bullet, who suited him just fine.

It was a bleak, cold, February morning, and the cowmen were up at North Prong helping the Swede with his hunt. They had separated the beeves and penned up the ones that would be driven south to Punta Rassa. The calves and their mothers were put in separate pens, and the foremen of each ranch would supervise the branding of the newborns. A mammy-up man was usually brought in from the central part of the state to match them up, as a calf will nurse from the closest available source, but it was discovered that Harlan, the Swede's youngest son, had the "gift" of mammying-up and was in great demand by the area cowmen. The Swede was very proud of Harlan's talent, who prior to the discovery had been referred to as "Bonehead" by everyone who knew him, especially his father.

Each year the prominent Old Town ranchers joined the Garvins of the Bullseye Ranch from over Crescent City way for the annual drive to Punta Rassa and the awaiting schooners that would transport the beeves to the meat packing plants in Cuba. Together they'd continue the drive to Silas Redmond's Split Creek Ranch east of Ft. Meade and proceed to Tater Hill Bluff, where J. Parker Meade and daughter, Callie, would join them. Parker's Tall 10 Ranch was the largest of all the ranches that participated in the spring drive, and Callie was as good a hand as any. They usually crossed the Caloosahatchee River at Ft. Thompson or Alva on their way to Punta Rassa. Sometimes Jordan Northrup from the Ft. Basinger area north of Lake Okeechobee would add his Big Lake beeves, and they'd ford the river together.

If the spring rains held off, the drive would begin by mid-April. There was plenty of good grazing then all along the trail, and they usually arrived at Punta Rassa about the first of May. The beeves would then be penned up to await the schooners that would take them to either Key West or Cuba to the meat packing plants. The settlers all along the trail looked forward to the exciting event each spring. When they heard the crack of the bullwhips resounding across the palmetto prairie they lined the dusty streets to await the giant herds and to watch the cowmen prance proudly down main street. It was a sight to behold.

****

Emma Haglund had sent her two oldest daughters out to the pens with the noonday meal. Their wagon was loaded with iron pots containing chicken stew with flat dumplings, fall collards and the huge batch of cornmeal cakes. Milton had a fire going with the usual lard can of strong coffee bubbling away and a demijohn of cane syrup close by for its sweetening. When the cowmen finished their branding and washing up in the creek, they headed for camp and a tin cup of the bitter coffee, some consuming as much as a gallon a day.

The girls were so excited about the news that they could hardly wait. Before they even served up the rations, they were

86

bending the men's poor ears reading over and over again what *The Tampa Tribune* had to say about the terrible thing that happened at Tater Hill Bluff. The First Bank had been robbed, and Luther Jones, the bank president, had been killed in cold blood by the R.J. Skinner Gang.

They all gathered around the Haglund wagon as Karine excitedly read from the weeks-old paper; her voice quivering at the proper intervals. *The Tampa Tribune* said Miss Sally Treadwell, who worked at the First Bank gave this account:

"*I was at my window, and James Marlow from up Myacca Spring way had just left and gone out the door. When I looked out the window, I saw these strangers tie up their horses. I was busy at my post when they burst into the bank with their guns pointed right at me. Mr. Jones came running out of his office to see what all the commotion was. Well, that R.J., the leader, did indeed have the blackest and meanest eyes I've ever seen in my entire life. He pointed his gun right at Mr. Jones and told him to open the safe and to hurry it up. One of them locked the front door and pulled down all the shades and even put the 'Closed' sign out so no one would come in. Well, there were five of them in all. One was outside holding the horses.*

"*It all happened so fast. Mr. Jones opened the safe, and R.J. and the one they called Sheldon, with the big, black hat, put all the money in the bags. The other two - one was real young looking, about fifteen or sixteen, I'd say - guarded me and the door. Alice, the other girl, was over at Mae's Boarding House having her dinner, so there were just Mr. Jones and me in the bank at the time.*

"*The four of them gathered at the front door with the one wearing the black hat, Sheldon - he was looking underneath the curtains to see if there was anyone on the sidewalk. He told us we'd better pay attention to what R.J. Skinner said 'cause he had a real itchy trigger finger, and he laughed to beat the band - a real mean laugh. Well, they scooted out that door, and Mr. Jones and me just looked at each other, and the next thing I knew Mr. Jones jumped up and rushed outside. And when he opened the door that Sheldon turned around in his saddle and shot him dead - right in front of me. Mr. Jones died right there on the front walk of the bank with me seeing the whole thing. They rode out of town shooting and yelling and acting just terrible. And that's all I saw.'*

*This is a word for word account of the horrible robbery
and murder that took place Friday the 16th of February in Tater
Hill Bluff, Florida, in which Mr. Luther M. Jones, President and
founder of First Bank, was killed.*

*Funeral services will be held Sunday the 18th at the Hickory
Hill Church. The Reverend Edward Small of Shiloh Creek Baptist
Church will direct the services.*

*A $200 reward has been posted for the capture of the R.J.
Skinner Gang, dead or alive. Contact Sheriff Franklin of Tater
Hill Bluff if you have any information."*

****

Berta went about her day-to-day chores and tried not to
think beyond each day. Since the November flood Jonah's open
hostility toward Layke was a constant worry, and the tension at
South Spring was thick. She had tried to talk to him, but he always
seemed to have a reason for his inexcusable behavior. He was her
shadow, never letting her out of his sight. And when Layke was
present, he'd needle and bait him, trying to incite his anger.

Layke had not told Berta of Jonah's fright and inability to
act during the flood. He knew that this new display of hatred was
due to the guilt he felt. He had been called on to perform as a
man, the head of South Spring, and he had failed himself and his
mother by his irresponsible behavior, and Layke was a witness to
his failure. Jonah despised him for it.

He had resumed his role as head of the spread while Layke
was away on the cow hunts. But when Layke returned, his anger
erupted, and he remained close to Berta, daring Layke to challenge
him. Layke decided to bide his time. He avoided any open display
of affection toward Berta, and Jonah eventually became bored and
relaxed his vigilance, as Layke knew he would. He was becoming
very comfortable with Layke's inattentiveness, and his cockiness
played right into Layke's patient hands.

Layke watched and waited, and to himself he thought, "Jonah,
she'll be mine before the spring drive. On that, young man, you
can lay a wager. My beautiful Berta will be mine."

After church one Sunday she was visiting with Minna
Haglund, who hadn't seen her smile so much in years. She was
delighted when Berta promised to help her with the school, and
as they waited for Jonah to bring their rig around, Berta animatedly

chitchatted with her about Layke.

"My, but does that man have patience. I know if Wesley has asked him once he's asked him a hundred times to tell him about serving under Uncle Joe Johnston and the battle against Sherman at Bentonville - you know, the one where he almost lost his leg. Layke sits there sucking on a piece of sweet grass and tells the whole story just like it was the first time, and Wesley sits there sucking on his piece of grass mocking everything Layke does. He's even started walking like him.

"Layke told Wesley, 'If you don't straighten up your walk, the other kids will start calling you Gimp.' "And Minna, Wes said, 'That's fine with me. If it's good enough for you, then it's good enough for me.' "Can you imagine?"

Minna smiled as she held Berta's hand and quickly kissed her on the cheek. Poor Berta. She deserved happiness, and it was obvious that she was taken with Layke Williams. And what woman wouldn't be? His presence had certainly put a lot of life into sleepy Old Town. There was something about him... Together they walked to the buggy, and when she looked at Jonah's stern face, she prayed that the rumor she'd heard about his open display of hatred for Layke was just that...a rumor. He had just never accepted the fact that Reuben was dead.

****

Berta was counting the days. The time was fast approaching when the unwanted days and long nights would arrive and take Layke away from South Spring. And when she'd glance at Layke and receive his adoring expression, her entire body would warm as she blushed at her desires, knowing he shared her feelings. She wondered how long it would be before they could share their love openly without fear or reprimand. He had become distant lately, but she knew it was to avoid any confrontation with Jonah, to spare her any grief. "But, my dear Layke, my grief is in not being able to fulfill our destiny."

She had become used to having him assume the responsibilities of running the ranch and loved doing the wifely chores of the past. Relaxed, she embraced the light, carefree attitude that Reuben had found so endearing and Layke had witnessed, all too briefly, before the flood.

89

The spreading dogwood tree south of the stable was in full bloom. Its ancient branches rested on the highest point of the pitched roof as a reminder that caring people had tended this land long before Elon McRae homesteaded it. Huge magnolia and pecan trees were abundant on the rise south of the house, and from Berta's clothesline the view was spectacular with the crimson and fuscia of the man-tall azaleas she and Reuben had planted their first year at South Spring.

Layke and Wes were playing in the side yard. Tag had joined in, and as she watched from the clothesline she was amazed at how well Tag got along with his handicap. She looked at Layke through the flying sand and sadly realized he'd be leaving the next day at dawn.

She deftly folded the clean, sweet-smelling wash and put it in the willow basket. "Even without Jonah's approval Layke and I are right for each other. I know in my heart it was not happenstance that brought him to South Spring; a power mightier than we destined it. He fits perfectly into the pattern of my life - of that I'm positive."

Layke turned as he lowered Wes from his shoulder and saw Berta's warm expression. Berta shyly, embarrassed, looked away. She tried to duck behind the tea towels, but there was no mistaking Layke's obvious message....she hadn't seen that look in four long years.

Hurriedly, she hung up the rest of the laundry and picked up the willow basket of folded, dry clothes. She started for the house, almost in a run, and dashed into the kitchen, quickly closing the heavy door behind her, leaning breathlessly against it. She could feel its roughness against her sun dampened blouse. Her pulse quickened - her mind raced. Reuben, shadowed, without form, flitted in and out of her consciousness. Then Layke appeared with that determined set to his jaw and the fixed glint in his hungry eyes. His patience had run out. She shivered.

He watched her as she hurried toward the cabin. Her warmth, her grace, her caring. He thought of her gentle beginnings in Georgia and her difficult frontier life at South Spring, how she lovingly made the soap, scenting it with bayberry and pine, candles from the wax myrtles with their fragrance permeating the small rooms with their soft blue light glowing. She reddened and calloused those once beautiful hands, creating her magic, embroidering,

90

tatting, crocheting, anything to add beauty to her pioneer life, her hands always moving. He marveled at the beauty and gentleness of Berta McRae, but also at the strength and determination and pride - and he wanted her. Now!

Layke had seen Jonah and Red as they quietly passed the barn earlier and headed for the area the kids had named, Jim Bottom - no doubt quail hunting, as had become his habit when he thought Layke was not around. Tousling Wes's straw-colored hair, he swatted him on the bottom. "Go play with SuSu, son. You've worn me out." Wes hurriedly joined SuSu in the cornstalks, where she was playing house, as Layke confidently approached the door. His worn boots were loud on the freshly brushed sand walk. There was no limping this time. He scraped his boots on the brush mat and gently rapped.

Berta, still clutching the laundry, closed her eyes and heard herself respond in a strange voice. He entered the warmth of her kitchen and Berta raised her eyes to his. There was no turning back. The laundry tumbled to the floor as she hungrily reached for Layke, and their embrace took them to remembered, comforting times - holidays and lilting music - whippoorwills' calls and the sweet fragrance of honeysuckle...of timeless past images as they clung desperately to each other......Effortlessly he lifted her light, trembling body, her head nestled into the crook of his neck. She heard the door close hard, vibrating, behind her.

The clean smell of the pine scented sheets enveloped them. Her pale, smooth, tingling breasts meshed against the dark brown cushion on his muscled chest. "My darling - my darling!" A newness, a strange sensation...pulsating...probing deeply... fathomless..."My darling...Now!" Rising...Undulating. The piercing eruption - the bolt of blinding light as their tumultuous climax suspended them to a world beyond forever... Then, falling...falling... Shallow, sweet, hesitant breathing filled the silence.

****

Jonah stood the gun up inside the barn door and went inside to check Old Red. He had cut his foreleg real bad, probably on sawgrass. "Nose hot and dry. Sure hope we don't lose him," he muttered to himself. As he came out of the barn he saw SuSu and Wes in the corn field playing.

91

"I wonder where that gimp is. He should be tending the beeves." He returned to the barn to get the bag of quail he had shot for dinner, and when he came out he saw Layke come out onto the porch, closing the kitchen door behind him.

He knew! He knew as he whirled around angrily and ran back into the barn. Berating himself for his negligence, he curled up on the pile of brittle straw. His fifteen-year-old imagination flitted from one circumstance to another, and always the outcome was the same. When that gimp was dead, everything would be right again - just like before.

He felt sick all over when he allowed his thoughts to dwell on his ma with that cripple. He grabbed his knees and rolled over on his side.

"Why'd he have to come and spoil everything anyway? I was doing fine. Even Young Reuben said so. Everyone said how like Pa I was, and how I had taken hold, and Ma was so lucky to have a fine son who could do a man's job." But Jonah knew he had failed, and the more he thought of it the more he was determined to eliminate the problem - Layke Williams.

There wasn't a day gone by that he didn't wish him dead - dead - dead! Just like the quail he had stuffed in his rucksack - still warm...not breathing...dead...His shaking hands began deliberately squeezing, pinching off their warm, soft heads. The bitter liquid frothed at his throat as his head hung low over the pile of fresh hay, and he released it, shuddering convulsively with unrelenting fury.

BOOK TWO:

CALLIE MEADE

CHAPTER I
YANKEE'S BOARDING HOUSE

Layke gently pushed the nearly empty coffee tin away, and Ruby came over from Silas's table to ask if he'd like a fill-up.

"Miss Ruby, Hannah makes the best coffee I've ever had, but don't you let on to Sam, or he'll ration me all the way back to Old Town."

"Boy, that Ruby Thomas is a funny looking one, but guess the cowmen don't have a heck of a choice around here, what with Callie Meade thinking she's a boy. I bet she'd turn a head or two if she ever put on a dress. Not likely though. She's a through and through cowman," he reflected.

Layke leaned back in the worn, cane-bottomed chair and relaxed over the last sip of bittersweet coffee. Pierce Garvin joined him and patted his too full stomach. "I know I must put on ten pounds every spring drive. Lose it on the trail and put it back on at Yankee's and Hannah's. I'll swear Hannah makes the best pie a body ever sank a tooth into. That deep-dish guava pie with heavy cream swimming all over it beats anything I ever ate, even if Ruby does miss some of the seeds."

Pierce pulled his chair over by the rail of the boarding house porch overlooking the expansive blue-green Mexico Gulf, propped his big number twelve boots on it and pulled a piece of gar weed out of his shirt pocket. "Yep, that Ruby missed a bunch in this piece," he exclaimed as he sat picking his teeth with the gar weed. "I sure wish we could grow guavas up in Crescent City. But then I wouldn't have as much to look forward to at the drive's end, would I Layke?"

"No, I guess not, Pierce." He sure liked this man. He must remember to tell Berta how all of the ranchers had accepted him as head of South Spring. He knew that Reuben could not have been treated any better or with more respect.

God, how he missed her! Looking over the Gulf, watching the sea birds casually dip in and out of the frothy waves for fish, while the soft, warm, gentle breeze fanned the palms along the south shoal, he thought of his Berta.

Pierce had ceased to make small talk. He missed his family and always felt a little guilty when he and Thom, his oldest, took to the trail. He could, like some, sell the beeves to Pratt Summers

95

when he came around from ranch to ranch buying up and moving 'em to Georgia, but felt they came out way ahead by moving the beeves themselves. Especially now that Thom was old enough to help and since Berta had got a new foreman, it wasn't so lonesome.

But this last drive just about did him in. He couldn't remember when they'd had so much bad luck. First, they were delayed by monsoon-like wind and rain and the Kissimmee was so swollen that it took them almost a whole day to get them across. And then that stupid Coot got careless and got himself snake bit. Doc Anderson had to come out from Tater Hill Bluff to tend him and ended up taking two of his toes. Lordy, the hollering and carrying on he did almost stampeded the beeves.

Pierce couldn't help but chuckle. Sam, the cook, had treated Coot just like a baby but took the ribbing he got from the cowmen in his stride. He had Coot in the chuck wagon, putting poultices on him, seemed like every hour, and by the time they got to Punta Rassa Coot's fever had just about gone.

Pierce turned to Layke and complained, "Do you ever remember having to wait six long days for those damned motor schooners, Layke? Someone said that he heard that the *Magnolia* ran aground up at St. Andrews Bay. Must have heard it at Alva when we crossed the river. Funny that Slick and Jam didn't mention it when they brought the Spaniard and Summers out for the settling up, though."

The Spaniard, Sr. Gato, represented the Cuban Meat Packing Co. and was stationed in Ft. Myers, north and east of Punta Rassa, and a growing settlement. As was the custom, when the cattle crossed the Caloosahatchee River, he and the representative from the shipping company, Pratt Summers, would ride out to the rancher's camp and settle the transaction. Sr. Gato spoke very little English, but Jordan Northrup, owner of the Big Lake Ranch north of Lake Okeechobee, enjoyed doing the interpreting and ciphering for the ranchers. Pratt Summers and Jam took the gold doubloons on to Punta Rassa to store them in Yankee's trunk at the boarding house. When the schooners arrived, the beeves would again be counted - some were always lost in the crowded pens. Then they were run up the wood sided planks into the schooner's holds and on to the meat packing plants in Cuba.

During the War Florida beef was in great demand by the Confederacy, and since the reconstruction period the years of hard work had finally paid off for the ranchers. The holding pens in Punta Rassa were too few and barely adequate, and the disgruntled ranchers were looking for other ports of departure. Tampa and Ft. Myers, also on the Gulf coast, were already saturated, and some of the cowmen had discussed selling their beeves to the turpentine camps and in Georgia. Slaughter houses were opening throughout the state, and there were ready customers all the way to Savannah.

"You know, Layke, I was just telling Mary that when the railroads arrive, our way of life will sure be different. No more spring drive. But I'll sure miss it, won't you?"

"Not like I would have before, Pierce. Before I met Berta, that is. Now, I'm just counting the days 'til I get back to her and South Spring."

Layke had confided in Pierce about his and Berta's feelings for each other. Pierce could hardly wait to get home to tell Mary. They'd both been shocked by Reuben's sudden death and knew that poor Berta was having a real hard time of it. But Pierce would miss the long evenings waiting for the schooners' arrival. It gave the cowmen a chance to catch up on politics, births, deaths, and the lazy hours spent spinning yarns and exchanging new ranching ideas provided a warm fellowship on Yankee's porch.

Silas Redmon, the only Black on the drive, and owner of the Split Creek Ranch, kept them entertained with his yarn spinning. There was no one who could tell a tale like Silas, and he had a group of men hooting and hollering over some fool tale while Pierce and Layke listened to them and lazily smiled at each other.

The excitement of the Tater Hill Bluff robbery and killing had died down. The R.J. Skinner Gang had not been heard of, and, knowing what was good for them, were apparently in hiding. The cowmen were busy playing cards and relaxing after the long drive and preferred to talk of their own adventures over a few belts of good Cuban rum, and didn't give the gang a thought. Shoot, they could buy a whole gallon of rum for fifty cents.

****

Ruby busied herself with the dishes and started setting the tables on the porch. Didn't take much more than that for the men to start gathering at their tables. They were always ready for one of Hannah's meals.

Callie Meade climbed up the steep stairs to the eating porch and started to sit but decided to take her meal back to her spot underneath the porch instead. She grumbled under her breath about having fish and corn dodgers again for dinner and was about to say it out loud when she saw that Thom Garvin wolfing them down just as fast as he could shove 'em in. Shaking her chestnut curls in disgust at how easily he was satisfied, she stiffened herself up tall and began climbing back down the stairs, wondering if he was watching her. "I sure am gettin' tired of these doggone fish and greasy corn dodgers!" she shouted, listening for a response while looking dead ahead and away from Thom. But not a single comment did she hear from the noisy men - not even Thom.

Her pa was with the other cowmen on the porch jawing as usual about everything, but mostly about nothing - not that she'd fault them for that. They loved the telling of the tales. But it was such a long-seeming time to wait for those schooners. Even when it was just a few days after the drive's end, seemed more like weeks to her, especially this go 'round.

"This porch isn't no place for a girl," her pa said, "what with the men playing cards, cussing and drinking."

So Callie spent most of her daylight time dreaming and walking the sparkling white beaches around Punta Rassa. Sure were a lot of things to see around there. The red mangroves grew to the water's edge in most places, extending their territory as they greedily amassed the sand and vegetation with their tendril-like roots. And at night she could hear the coons cracking the oysters that grew right on their tangled roots. She actually heard one man tell a Yankee that in Florida oysters grew on trees, but that they called them coon oysters. The Yankee thought he was fooling him, but that's what they called them all right, and they sure 'nuff did grow on trees.

Callie could always spot a bird's nest or scare a flock of egrets or herons and watch them soar into the blue, blue sky. She loved to take off her boots, roll up her pants legs and wade in the little rivulets catching the darting minnows with her bare hands.

Before first light she'd dig for sand fleas along the water's edge so she'd have bait for her early morning fishing. Fishing was real good around the shoal south of the boarding house. Bluer water you'd never find. It wasn't just blue, but blue-green, except when a sudden spring storm came up, then the beach bottom churned up, and it would get blue-black.

The only girl around near her age was Hannah's niece, Ruby, who lived with the Thomases and helped out with the cooking. But sure wasn't anything one could talk about to Ruby - she was so dad-burned boy crazy. And did she ever have her eye on that Thom Garvin! She gave him two huge helpings of cassava pie last night, and just like a pig he downed them. You'd have thought that after a plate full of fish and grits with tomato gravy and umpteen corn dodgers that he'd 've been bustin'. But no - he just had to smile sickly up at Ruby and say, "Sure could stand another piece of that good cassava pie, Miss Ruby."

And you sure couldn't call Ruby Thomas pretty either. What with that not red hair that didn't look like it could make up its mind whether to be red or yellow, and always looked like there wasn't enough of it to cover her head. And those lashes---white! Plumb white! Those eyes looked just like a sheepshead's 'fore you chopped off its head, all pale and glassy, and that old freckled skin never ever saw the Florida sun. No - you sure couldn't call Ruby pretty. She just cow-eyed every cowman around there. "I bet her Aunt Hannah would skin her alive if she caught her," Callie thought.

Her pa wanted her to stay with Ruby, but that was just too much to ask of her. Callie was real comfortable in her blanket roll underneath the high porch. The white sand had been swept free of shells and was soft as her feather bed back home. Everyone on the drive knew that that spot was Callie's, and that's the way she wanted it.

She was up every morning 'fore daybreak checking the stock with the rest of 'em, but while they were wolfing down pone, slab and coffee, she'd be baiting her hooks with sand fleas she'd dug earlier so's to catch those early feeders, sheepshead and flats. Most every morning she'd have a long string of 'em by the time the rest finished their morning coffee and smokes and settled themselves on the eating porch overlooking the Gulf, watching for the smoke of the schooners.

Callie liked being by herself - leastways she used to. Lately she'd been real restless. Her ma said a good spring tonic would fix her right up. Usually the spring drive was one thing she looked forward to more than anything. That was usually the only tonic she ever needed. But not this year. Being sixteen wasn't nearly as much fun as being fifteen or even fourteen, for that matter.

"Wonder why that is?" she said perplexed.

She was outside the kitchen door giving Cook the string of fish when that Thom Garvin with his too-white teeth gleaming in the sunshine, every one of 'em, moseyed up with an even bigger string of fish. He had that sick-smiling, prouder-than-a-peacock grin on his face. Some folks thought he was handsome - well she'd have to concede that he wasn't ugly. His eyes were the color of the Gulf, blue-green, and his hair as brown and curly as Callie's. But she hadn't paid much attention to him until this drive.

Callie asked him where he'd caught 'em, and he said by that fallen-down wharf up by the "Big Mouth" 'bout a half mile up the coast. He had ridden his gelding up there before sun-up, and my how he bragged that he couldn't bait his hooks fast enough. He'd used some old bacon rind Ruby had given him.

Callie got all red in the face and pursed her lips, wanting to say, "That Ruby Thomas would give you anything, Mr. Thomas Garvin." But instead she straightened up her five and a half feet and stalked off like she was plumb mad at him. Now why on earth would she do a thing like that? She didn't give.... that for Thom Garvin. Just 'cause he thought he could out rope all the hands around and do all those silly show-off tricks on his gelding didn't make him a big man. He really thought he was the last man in the whole wide world, he did!

She stormed past him and Cook, almost knocking a pan of freshly baked biscuits off the red oilcloth covered table on the side porch, and pranced into Hannah's kitchen just to get her mind off that uppity Thom. She mumbled to Ruby about maybe helping out, but they were bustling around, flour dusting all over, so, just in the way, she made her way out to the eating porch and past the men. Some were already playing cards, so not wanting to butt in she climbed down the steep stairs and went underneath the high porch. Yanking her sweat rimmed felt hat off, she rested her head against the tall, barnacle-encrusted piling only to start her daydreaming all over again.

"Sure wish that schooner would get here." She was sick and tired of all this waiting around. "Nothing to do in this dumb old place but tend the smelly old horses and beeves and fish," she thought restlessly.

Ruby turned to Hannah and asked her, "What on earth has come over Callie? I couldn't believe my hearing when she asked

100

if she could help with dinner. Imagine stuck-up Callie Meade
wanting to help in the kitchen. That does beat all!"

****

From where Callie was sitting she could see the schooner
Magnolia way off in the distance coming from San Carlos Bay and
'round Pine Island headed for Punta Rassa. "About time!" she
grunted disgustedly. "Six days' wait is dumb - the longest time I can
ever remember having to wait." It had up a heavy head of steam,
and the smoke made funny pictures in the cloudless sky. Normally
she would have gotten real excited but she was so put out with that
Thom Garvin that she just sat in the sand watching it make its way.
If she figured right, it would take nigh on an hour for her to
maneuver her way round Pine Island and pull into shore parallel
to Pratt Summer's long wharf. She just relaxed and watched the
big ship getting closer and closer. Not far out from the wharf it
blew its whistle.

The cowmen had been so busy eating and playing cards to
while away their time, they were caught by surprise. All of them
scrambled around scraping their chairs on the floor above Callie
and sounding like a runaway herd as they ran for the pens. They
had to get to their counting gates to count the beeves again.

Layke and Pierce jumped up quickly when they saw the
schooner approaching. Didn't take much to get them going.
"Summers should build bigger pens," Pierce grumbled to Layke as
they headed for the gates with the others.

Coot's foot had healed up real good, and he was feeling
better, so he and Thom headed for the pens. Thom was astride the
rail next to the Garvin gate, and Coot took up the counting spot
opposite him. All of a sudden all hell broke loose. Hannah came
running out the back door of the boarding house, hair flying and
arms waving in the air and yelling something about Cook being hit
in the head, and that Yankee's trunk was missing. Now, how on
earth could a heavy trunk full of gold doubloons be gone? Lordy,
everyone was screaming and carrying on - all talking at once. A
year's work was gone---gone!

Callie was busy getting her plate and cup to take to the
kitchen before joining the others for the counting, when she heard
Hannah let out the blood-curdling scream asking for the Lord's
help. She high-tailed it around the corner through the deep beach

101

sand to the back door and saw Hannah running to the pens. Cook was on the floor bleeding all over the place, and Callie took one look at him and ran for the corral to get BeeBee.

"I had best ride for Doc," she called to whoever was listening. On her way past the counting gate she called to her pa and told him she was going for Doc - that cook was bad hurt. Thom jumped off the fence and yelled to her to wait for him to saddle up, and he'd go with her. Not that she needed him, for heaven's sake. Just like always - he had to play the big man.

The water was deep beside the tangled mangroves, but soon they were on the trail to the settlement. There was not much there but a few buildings and fish shacks along the waterfront. Doc was at Mamie's having dinner. He threw down his napkin, and as big as he was he was light on his feet and in his buckboard in no time. Word had already spread around town about Yankee's trunk of doubloons being stolen, and Cook being almost killed - head bashed in and a year's work gone. "Who could have done such a thing?" they all muttered.

Callie and Thom rode up to the pen - Yankee was up on the porch yelling out orders. Pierce was trying to get everyone calmed down, and Callie's pa had Storm saddled and ready to ride for Sheriff Franklin in case Cephus had not been able to reach him by the telegraph. But he was in Ft. Myers, which was closer than Tater Hill, and Cephus had made contact - they were in luck.

About then Ruby came running out the back yelling with that old red-yellow hair stuck straight up in the air and her flowered apron flying out behind her, and said, "Cook came to and said it was the R.J. Skinner gang that attacked him and stole the trunk. You know, the same gang that killed the poor banker up at Tater Hill."

The schooner, *Magnolia*, blew its whistle again. Captain Spooner and Mate came running down the plank to tell them that they'd best get their stock ready, as he'd have to leave on the next tide.

Layke yelled above the noise and confusion, "Captain, I guess you haven't heard. The Skinner Gang stole the gold and high-tailed it out of here. And you aren't going anywhere with those beeves - they stay right here. I've got that money spent six ways from Sunday, and so do all the others. We're forming a posse right this minute, and Sheriff Franklin has already been sent for." With that,

Layke joined the others in the pens.

Pierce, Silas and Jordan Northrup had started forming the posse and telling them which ones should stay with the stock and which ones could go with the posse. There was no telling when they'd get back with the gold and those no good thieves, so some would just have to stay put until they returned. Everyone was arguing and yelling. No one wanted to stay, but Layke gave each cowman a job to do while they were gone, and that seemed to appease them.

Callie got BeeBee 'round back, and she hurriedly ran beneath the boarding house porch to fetch her blanket roll just in case. "Oh, Lordie! I'll need supplies. You have to have supplies when you're chasing desperados like the R.J. Skinner gang." She ran up the back steps, her long muscled legs bounding over every other step, and peeked inside the screened door. There was no one in Hannah's kitchen. Hannah and some of the men had moved Cook out to the porch and she, Doc and Ruby were fussing over him and telling him as how he'd be all right and as good as new in no time. And just as cool as a cucumber Callie stole meal and grits and some pone from Hannah Thomas' kitchen. The entire time she wasn't believing she could do such a sinful thing.

****

Capt. Spooner and Mate paced frantically back and forth on the porch not knowing what to do first. They were supposed to be delivering the beeves to Cuba, and they were already late, due to a spring storm that came up all of a sudden like and Mate getting himself liquored up in St. Andrews and runnin' aground. With his teeth grinding the Captain shook his head and thought, "That stupid no account Mate. If good mates weren't so hard to come by I'd singe his tail feathers, by gum. There's nothing to do now but go to the terminal and have Cephus telegraph Cuba and tell Don Luis that we'll have to return to Tampa to fill our holds, and that we'll have to tell the other schooners what's happened to all that gold."

He shook his head in dismay. "By the time they get that posse ready that gang will be burying those doubloons in the Big Cypress Swamp, and we'll all be out a bundle." He turned to Mate and grabbed him roughly by the arm, "I don't know if'n Pratt Summers

103

has his wits about him. Maybe you'd best send word to Sr. Gato in Ft. Myers. Lordy - nuthin' like this has ever happened before. In all my years doin' the Mexico - nuthin' like this."

The Captain yelled after Mate, "I can't believe that Skinner Gang was right in my boots a-stealin', Mate. It's just about more than I can take, what with Jesse Mae ailin' and all. I'm just too all-fired old and tired for all this ruckus." But Mate didn't hear his tirade as he ran against the wind to find Summers.

"This just might be my last run," he mumbled to himself. "It sure would please Jesse. She's a worrier. Brave she is, but a worrier too when it comes to me." He smiled. They had quite many a year together with her a bride of fifteen and him a strapping lad of twenty years. "But enough of that. I best hurry up Mate to find out if Pratt Summers got word to Sr. Gato about the robbery."

About then a breathless youngster came tearing around the corner and almost bumped into his protruding belly. Captain Spooner reacted quickly, grabbed him by the shirt sleeve and exclaimed, "Wait up, young fellow! What's yore hurry?" Cephus had sent the runner over to the boarding house to tell him Don Luis had telegraphed that he was to proceed to Tampa, and that he was to make haste on to Havana with a full load because they had orders to fill, and that if the doubloons weren't recovered he'd make some arrangement with the ranchers to purchase their beeves as soon as possible.

He felt sorry for the ranchers. The frustration of getting the beeves to their destination and then having to keep them there for perhaps another week or more would be awful. They'd lose more weight for sure, even if they drove them to some near-by pasture to feed.

He walked up the plank and gazed south. He sure didn't like the looks of those clouds, black as pitch and rolling in fast. "Well, they've got their problems and from the looks of it - I've got some too. This has been one peculiar season." He could usually read 'em, but not this year. "Guess Jesse was right, this coastal run is gettin' too much for me. I'd best stick to my groves and grandchildren."

He sure didn't envy that posse their hunt into the mysterious and treacherous Big Cypress Swamp. Like they say, "If'n the skeeters don't get ya, the gators will.

104

CHAPTER II   CALLIE AND THOM

That Thom Garvin really made Callie mad..."The men are going after the Skinner Gang," he said in his excited voice. Well, for his information she'd been doing a man's job ever since she could remember, and hadn't had any complaints either, by Ned!

With all the whooping and hollaring and carrying on the hands were doing, no one even noticed she was among them. She pulled her hat down farther over her chestnut curls, just in case, and kept her head down and her homespun shirt collar pulled up so no one could see her face and proceeded to carry on with the rest of 'em.

She was going to get away with her disguise and was amused to discover she was as excited as that Thom Garvin. Sheriff Franklin was getting everyone organized and setting up the advance group. He reminded all of 'em that they were dealing with robbers and murderers. Callie overheard him say that that Skinner gang was the meanest bunch of scallawags he'd ever come across in all his army days and sheriffing days to boot.

The men squatted in the deep beach sand drawing out the trails with a stick so the posse would know which trail they thought the gang would travel. The sheriff figured they'd head for Big Cypress Swamp. But just in case he was wrong, he sent two men up the Caloosahatchee River to alert the small settlements along its banks, Olga, Rialto, Owanita and all the way to Alva. Not much sense for the gang to go along the river, seeing as how there were settlements every few miles, but then no one knew for sure which way they would go, and it was the sheriff's job to protect the innocent.

Callie had a difficult time getting BeeBee saddled. He was itching to get on the trail, as were the rest of the horses. She guessed they'd picked up the excitement from her and the other cowmen. Her smooth, tanned skin tingled with anticipation, and her rising, firm breasts belied the fact she was just another cowman. But in all the commotion no one noticed.

Finally they were off and on the scent of the gang. Callie tried to stay toward the back and away from her pa. "This sure beats waiting around for the schooners, and it isn't steaming hot yet, thank the Lord," she thought. There had been a lot of good rain, and the growth they rode through was thick and lush, so green

105

it looked like it had just been washed. The river was swollen up just bursting to slide over its banks, but they'd soon head south through the mangroves, and then the sandy pines and palmettos.

"Oh, Lordy! We won't be two hours out before we have to make camp, and sure's shootin' Pa'll see me." She dropped back, and Jam caught sight of her and let out a whistle. She put her finger to her mouth so's he'd not whistle again, and he shook his head from side to side and came a sidin' up to her.

"Miss Callie, yore pa's gonna skin ya alive when he finds out you're here."

"He won't know 'til it's too late if you'll just keep a string on your trap, Jam. And besides, some of those doubloons are mine. I earned 'em same as you."

Callie knew she had to talk fast to get herself out of this one. About that time Thom eased back so's he could stick his nose in her business, but before she could tell him to go chase his shadow, he was defending her to Jam. Said as how she did the work of a man, could ride 'n' shoot, or so's he'd been told, just like a man; and why should she miss out on all the fun? And then he looked her square in the eye, and with that knowing-all grin he boldly winked at Callie. Callie turned beet red and didn't know whether to spit in his eye or to thank him. Seeing as how she was on the wrong end of the horse, so to speak, she decided to kinda smile - just a little one - and thank him. He sure looked at her from her head to her toes, and Callie's knees went to water. Even BeeBee knew something was different about his mistress.

Jam stared at her with his old crinkly eyes, and then he stared at Thom. He mumbled something about how her pa had better pay as much attention to the rear of that posse as to the front. Before Callie could think of a retort, Thom took off for the front of the posse to set the pace with the sheriff, her pa and the other cowmen who owned guns.

The sun was setting over the Mexico gulf, and every color on the Lord's palette was brushed across the endless sky. Callie never tired of appreciating the lush land that surrounded her. They rode beside the marching cypresses with their gray beards of Spanish moss flowing in the evening's warm breeze and finally arrived at Big Tree Hammock, where they decided to make camp. Another half hour of riding and it would be pitch black and too marshy to bed down. They all agreed that they'd best go after the gang in the light of day.

While they made camp and tended to their horses, Jam and Slick went around to the men to ask for volunteers to cut the palmetto fronds for their make-shift beds and to gather all the dry wood they could find for the big fire needed to frighten away the many predators.

Callie stayed as far from her pa as possible, pulled her hat down lower on her forehead, got her blanket roll off of BeeBee and her saddlebag filled with the provisions she'd stolen from Hannah. Jam and Slick doled out the palmetto fronds to all the cowmen for placing underneath their bedrolls so they wouldn't get damp. Callie piled hers up about six deep when Jam handed them to her. He didn't say a word to her - just grunted, and Callie grunted low and thanked him, making sure to keep her head down.

After getting BeeBee bedded down, she spread the old army blanket over her stack of palmettos and got some corn pone out of her saddlebag. She had settled down on her bed when she spied Thom Garvin. Looked like he was headed straight for her. Her knees began to water down just like before, and she got to feeling warm all over. "What on earth was wrong with her," she wondered. She knew he'd not squeal on her.

He brought his gelding over by BeeBee and was stroking him. She could see his back muscles rippling underneath his tan shirt, all sweaty and clinging to him. He untied his roll, and just as big as you please got his stack of palmettos, piled 'em up about six deep and placed them right beside Callie.

While her mouth was gaping open, he told her he had some smoked mullet if she'd like to share some with him. Callie, trying to be real ladylike, remembered her manners and thanked him. She asked him to sit, offered him some of her pone, and the two of them sat in silence eating the cold supper and marveled at the wonders of the Glades as they watched the setting of the sun over the Gulf.

The frogs made sure everyone knew they were present with their croaking, and then the mosquitoes tuned in. Thom cut six palmetto spears from the edge of the bedded-down group. He jammed them into the ground about half a foot, and strung the mosquito net over both his and Callie's makeshift beds. She was so close to him she could feel his body heat, but not a word was said for almost forever, it seemed to her.

107

Then Thom rolled over and said in a real low whisper, "G'night, Callie Meade."

She felt like a whole herd was stampeding inside her chest, and she was having a difficult time breathing ladylike. She held her breath for what seemed like an eternity, but remembered her manners and forced herself to speak. "G'night, Thom Garvin of Crescent City," she said in such a strange voice that it didn't sound like it could have possibly come from tomboy Callie Meade's lips. She wondered why she'd said that - he'd think she was daft. But while she was trying to think of something else to say, Callie heard Thom chuckle softly to himself and then swat a mosquito that had found its way under the net. He turned over, and the last thing Callie heard that pitch black night was Thom Garvin of Crescent City breathing ever so sweetly.

****

Everyone was stirring before sunup. Looked like it would be a long, hot day ahead. Sheriff Franklin was going over the plan with Silas, seeing as how he'd been a swamp man longer than anyone else who was with 'em. It was hard to track in the tall sawgrass, but Silas could do it if anyone could. He and his family in Ft. Meade were the only Negro family Callie really knew, other than Mattie and hers. Weren't many Negroes around Tater Hill and less than that on the southwest coast, as most had gone up north after the War. He had as good an education as most of 'em except maybe Jordan Northrup and Layke Williams, and he sure did know his cows and swamps.

It was said that he was the mammy-up champion of the whole wide world. Why, there wasn't a spread around that wouldn't pay him handsomely to mammy-up during their cow hunt. He vowed he'd give a cup full of doubloons to any owner if he made a mistake and got the wrong calf branded, and he hadn't paid out any to date.

Callie didn't want to get close enough to hear the plan, 'cause her pa was right there in the middle of it. Jam had kept his eye on her, as she knew he would, but he hadn't squealed. That Thom was right there in the thick of things shaking his head and waving his hands around just like he knew what they were talking about, and him not a swamp man either. "How men do go on!"

She had BeeBee all watered and packed. "Don't know why

we can't get a move on," she thought anxiously. "That gang will be half way to Key West by the time we get going." There was no coffee that morning, and some of the posse were complaining loudly. She heard Slick tell 'em that if they had to have their morning coffee that they should have stayed with the ladies at the boarding house. No more complaining after that. They just chewed the dry pone Hannah and Ruby had packed for 'em and washed it down with the spring water.

The sun hadn't been up more'n a half hour, and they were on their way with Silas and the sheriff leadin' 'em. Thom dropped back so's he could fill her in on the plan. His face was beet red, and excitement poured out of every pore. "If he doesn't watch it, he'll be havin' heart failure 'fore we catch 'em," Callie thought.

Thom said that Silas reckoned they'd have to make a stop to open Yankee's trunk. It appeared they were carrying the trunk in some kind of contraption slung between two of the horses, since the tracks were much deeper than the others, and they should be coming upon the trunk soon, as it was slowing them down. He figured that they were only about an hour ahead.

"If they're smart they'll be burying the gold in the swamp and high-tailing it to the coast around Harold Pass. Probably have a boat moored there and'll head south for one of the Ten Thousand Islands. When the heat's off and the posse's off their trail, they could go get the gold, split up and later meet up north somewhere. At least that's what Silas and the rest think they're planning."

Callie was ready to protest their thinking but before she could formulate a retort, he finalized his report. "No one in his right mind would purposely go into that swamp."

She thought on it and decided not to respond. Somehow she couldn't take her eyes off his hands as he clenched and unclenched them, causing the muscles to ripple underneath the tight shirt.

CHAPTER III   THE POSSE

Sheriff Franklin wanted the men with guns at the front of the posse, but he allowed Layke to be with them. It was known far and wide that Layke didn't use a gun but that his bull whip was almost as deadly. Word spreads fast on the range with cowmen going from one ranch to the other - either enticed by better pay or just liking to be on the move.

The tales they told around the camp fires at night would quite often be about Layke and his amazing accuracy with the whip. He was careful not to be coerced into the whip contests that his fellow cowmen set up between camps, as the bets would sometimes be a whole month's pay. Not that he was against gambling. He just felt his ability was for working the cows and self defense, not a talent to be trifled with.

The sawgrass at the edge of the swamp was so thick that they were having difficulty making any progress. Sheriff Franklin raised his hand to halt them, and Jam and Slick came back to the rest of the posse and said that they'd take a short break. The small hammock of cabbage palms and cypress trees afforded little shade, and the insects were thick. There was no time to cook a meal, so they rested the horses and ate the remainder of Hannah's pone. Callie stayed at the back with her hat pulled down swatting the insects that soon found their way up under her shirt.

Smartie Pants Thom Garvin was laughing at her and teasingly said, "That sure must be a new step you're dancing, Miss Callie Meade of Tater Hill Bluff." She got so mad she could have gladly strangled him, but instead bit her tongue so as not to draw attention to herself.

She saw Layke and Jordan Northrup up by the sheriff with Silas and her pa, all in a deep discussion. She was so curious she could hardly stand it, so she slowly walked BeeBee along the outside of the group, with him between her and the gathered leaders, and strained her ears. About that time a hand went over her mouth from behind as someone grabbed her. She jumped about a mile. She knew it wasn't her pa as she was looking right at him. It was that Thom Garvin. He was whispering in her ear that he was taking his hand away and she'd better not yell. Oh, how she wanted to chomp down on one of his dirty old fingers. She whirled around toward him knowing full well that he'd have that sick grin spread all over his face. But he didn't. He looked real grim just like he was at a funeral or something.

"Callie, don't say a word, but I think I've found something that belongs to the Gang!" and out of his britches pocket he pulled a piece of red cloth. He said he had gone into the hammock just curious as to what it was like, since they didn't have 'em quite like that up in Crescent City. Someone had told him that you could find wild orchids up in those trees in the Cypress, and as he was looking up, there was a red piece of cloth kinda tucked back of some funny looking, pointed plant. There wasn't real deep water there, as it was sort of on a knoll, and as his eye drifted down the tree he could see there had been some fresh digging.

"Thom, was it the doubloons?"

And real shaky like there was a ghost around, he whispered, "I kicked at it with my boot, and I only found one. I just know it's a marker put there by the gang, and I bet they're around here just looking at us and wanting to shoot us dead - all of us!"

At that Callie's brown eyes got saucer big, and her skin started to crawl, beginning at her feet and working its way up to her throat. "Oh my, oh my," is all she could think to say, and then to herself, "Is he teasing me again?" Aloud, she blurted, "Thom Garvin, if you're teasing me, I'm gonna yell!" But she could see he was dead serious and just as scared as she.

"What should we do? Shouldn't you go tell the sheriff?" she asked.

"No. I think if they are watching us, seeing as how they're out-numbered, they'll just sit tight, thinking we didn't find their marker, and just let us go off on a wild goose chase. I know Silas is good at tracking but it's nigh on impossible to track anyone in this sawgrass, and my gut feeling is that they're around here...just waiting."

With that statement, he said, "I'm going to mosey on up to where the sheriff is just to hear what they're talking about. Now you act just like nothin's going on, and you'd better get yourself back behind those trees. Your pa is going to spot BeeBee for sure. I'll come back as soon as I find out what's going on." And with that he was gone.

Callie didn't want to go anywhere near those trees for fear Thom was right and the gang was hid out just waiting for the chance to ambush them. But he was right that if her pa looked up and really stared toward her, he'd sure recognize BeeBee. She had no choice. She very slowly walked BeeBee back to the cypress trees, but just had to peek out from under her hat to see if she saw a boot or a gun or a hat or something that looked like it belonged to a killer. But she didn't, and her sigh could have been heard all the way back to Punta Rassa.

When Thom approached them, Layke turned toward him and shook his head. "Silas seems to think they've gone into the Big Cypress, and if that's the case we'll never catch 'em. But we've decided to go west toward the Gulf just in case he's wrong. We'll make camp tonight if we don't find 'em and then head on back to Punta Rassa tomorrow."

Thom shook his head and said, "I think that's the sensible thing to do. Maybe some swamp man can be hired to track 'em. It would be worth someone's time, 'cause there's a big bounty due 'em if they kill just one of the lowdown skunks." Layke agreed.

He slowly walked back to where Callie was crouched behind the cypress tree and very excitedly told her the plan. Then he proceeded to tell her of his own plan. When Callie heard what Thom Garvin wanted her to do, she got so upset she couldn't stop the saliva from seeping out of the corners of her mouth. She just kept wiping her mouth and listening to his hair-brained plan - and him including her in on it. She wasn't believing her ears! But the more he talked and the more she thought on it, the more she realized he was on track.

His proposal was this: Thom would tell his pa that he'd go back to Yankee's to tell them what was going on, since Silas was almost 100% positive that the gang tried for the Cypress. He was sure his pa would approve of his decision. Since Jam was the only one who knew Callie was with them no one would miss her. Instead of riding back to Punta Rassa he and Callie would hide in the hammock and wait for whoever buried the gold to reclaim it - and capture him or them.

Chances were that only one of 'em did, as according to Silas there wasn't any one horse riding a lot heavier than the others, and according to the description of the gang they were all pretty close to the same size. That would indicate that they'd divided up the doubloons. Now just maybe they'd not come back for the money in the next two days. If they didn't, then he and Callie would dig it up and take it back to Punta Rassa and be there by the time the posse returned. But Thom said, "I want to capture the skunk who stole the money more than get the money itself, Callie," and with that, Callie was in agreement.

Thom got approval from his pa, and as the posse moved to the west and the Gulf, Callie and BeeBee hid in the hammock. She had never in all her born days been involved in anything as exciting as this.

Thom cut palmetto fronds and made a shelter to hide BeeBee and Goldie. The hammock was not as dense as some they'd seen previously, and although the high grass was a good cover, it was not high enough to hide the horses. They were busy preparing for the capture all that long afternoon. Thom would be on lookout while Callie thatched the shelter, and then she'd spell him. They figured that whoever buried the gold wouldn't want to be in the swamp during the night - that is, if he had any brains at all - and that he'd approach the hammock from the west, as that's where Silas lost track of 'em. The less he waded through the snake, gator and mosquito infested Cypress, the better off he'd be.

Thom said, "He'll probably plan to come in just before dusk, spend the night on the dry knoll in the center of the hammock, dig up his gold and head northeast, maybe following the Caloosahatchee." But as Callie pointed out, "Maybe whoever hid the gold has gone west with the others to the Gulf, where they probably have a boat hid and won't come back to the Cypress 'til they think the coast is clear."

Thom reminded her, "They'll need their horses for whatever devilment they're plannin', so I don't think they'll leave 'em for any old boat."

"If I was a low-down, thievin' killer and robber I'd just steal me another horse," and Thom looked at Callie with newfound respect. She felt her face growing red, and quickly turned away. She was getting just about as scared being all alone with Thom Garvin as she was waiting for the robber.

As the sun began to sink and the expansive, clear sky became rosy and lavender, Thom positioned himself up in one of the tall cypress trees so he had visibility to the north, south and west. Only the east was obscured. Callie had watered the horses and had got as comfortable as she could while crouched inside the palmetto blind. She knew she'd be covered with redbug bites by the time she got back to Punta Rassa, as she already had bites around her

113

ankles, and they itched to beat the band - especially inside those sweaty boots. She found a long stick and was poking it down inside her boots to scratch 'em when she heard a noise out behind her.

Thom was up the tree acting just like he was up the mast of a ship, his hand shielding his eyes and looking all around.

"Oh, Lordy," she said. She tried to give their signal like a hoot owl, but for the life of her she couldn't get a sound to come out of her constricted throat. Her mouth was so dry, and her heart was making loud pounding noises. She was sure that if it was the robber he'd hear it pounding away.

She slowly turned around in the direction of the noise, and sure enough she saw a shadowy figure leading a horse. "Now why can't that stupid, deaf Thom Garvin hear him? He's making enough noise to start a stampede." But when she looked up to the top of the cypress, sure 'nuff he was looking in every direction but the right one. "I don't have a gun. I don't even have a big ole stick. He's gonna kill me for sure, and that gun-totin' partner of mine is perched up in that blooming tree playing lookout. I'm doomed!. I just know my time has come! I hope whoever gets BeeBee will take good care of him. I should have made a will", and Callie's mind hop-scotched all over creation, while the shadowy figure came closer and closer.

"Now if he looks up for his red marker, he for sure will see Thom. I bet Thom doesn't even have his gun cocked. Oh, Lordy!" She tried to give the hoot owl signal again and again but couldn't get a single hoot out of her dry, taut throat.

He couldn't have been more'n fifty feet away, and his horse was thrashing loudly through the underbrush. "Why in the world can't that Thom Garvin hear him?"

As she looked up to where Thom was perched, she couldn't believe she was seeing him climb down that tree and the robber coming right toward him. The robber's view was blocked by a stand of tall cypress, or Thom would have been in plain view. Callie tried to hoot again and this time got out a wee little one, but Thom was far enough down the tree to hear her, or she guessed he did, 'cause he stopped dead still. He must have heard the commotion, as Callie saw him ease around to the west side of the tree and take out his gun.

The robber was about 25 feet from the tree, and even in half light Callie could see his mean, evil face just as plain as the hand

114

in front of her. He stopped, and she thought, "Oh my, he's heard my heart pounding or Thom or something." But instead he started looking up, and all around for that red marker. When he didn't see it, he resumed his searching of the ground around him. It seemed like hours, but it couldn't have been more than a few minutes. He was almost right under Thom, and by then it was close to dusk. "In a few minutes it'll be pitch black," Callie thought. "You've got to make your move now, Thom." When the sun went down in the Glades, night was almost instantaneous, with no lingering twilight as up north. Callie could have touched him if her arm had been just a little longer.

Right about then, he looked up in Thom's cypress and Callie heard Thom let out a rebel war whoop as he jumped smack-dab on top of the robber. They were thrashing all over the ground and Callie jumped out from her hiding place and grabbed his horse and started running. He turned around in her direction, pulled his gun, and Callie heard the bullet whine past her left ear as she high tailed it through the hammock as fast as her long, muscled legs would go. She couldn't see, but she could hear the gunshot, and her heart went up in her throat. She called out to Thom, and he answered with his hoot owl sound. He seemed out of breath, and the sounds got farther and farther away.

Callie couldn't stand the not knowing any longer, so she led the robber's horse cautiously to the palmetto blind. By now it was pitch black, and she started to shake. She couldn't stop - she was cold all over - even her teeth were rattling. She managed to get out a small, shaky hoot. Nothing. Thom was nowhere around. Now she really was scared. He was probably shot and dying right near her. She decided to take a chance and call him by name. She heard noises coming from west of the hammock, but she couldn't see who it was. In desperation, she called him loudly, and he answered, "Callie, I'm all right. Keep calling, and I'll follow your voice." So she did, and when he got to her she flew into his arms, she was so relieved.

Realizing how cold and frightened she was, he took his coat off and wrapped it around her. With Thom's arms around her and her head buried in his welcome shoulder, Callie began to sob. He was so gentle. He kept saying, "It's all right, Callie. It's all right. He's gone - headed for the Cypress. I think I wounded him, but we won't know 'til in the morning whether I wounded or killed him."

115

They curled up together on top of the palmetto stack for a bed. Callie's pa's old army blanket was draped over it, and they both fell into an exhausted sleep in each other's protective arms.

Callie didn't awaken 'til after daylight. Thom had been up since first light and had checked the area west of the hammock. He had hit the robber. There was quite a bit of blood on the grass, and it looked like he had dragged himself into the Cypress. Thom went into the swamp as far as he thought wise, but the only sign of the robber was his big, black hat at the edge of the swamp. Thom knew that with any kind of wound he'd never make it out of there alive, and he smiled to himself as he envisioned a hungry panther making short work of the low down robber. He was anxious to get back to tell Callie that he was positive that at least one of the no good skunks had met his deserved fate, and he just hoped that it was the one who killed the banker - he had sure asked to die that miserable death.

He told Callie what he thought had happened, and as he was going over their situation, she got the coffee and can out of her knapsack and proceeded to gather wood for a fire. Thom kept looking at her kinda funny. Finally she had had enough, "Thom Garvin, what are you staring at, anyway? Haven't you ever seen a woman cook breakfast before?"

And with that he turned his face away and walked over to the tree where the doubloons had been buried. Finally, he said, "I just hadn't thought of you as a woman before, Callie. I'm sorry."

She felt so foolish that she didn't know what to respond. Finally in a very soft and feminine voice she called him, "Thom, your breakfast is ready," and they sat in silence eating their corn cakes and drinking the bittersweet coffee, not daring to look at each other.

Thom threw the saddlebag of freshly dug doubloons over the robber's horse, and he, Callie, and the three horses started the journey back to Punta Rassa. He couldn't figure out why they weren't delirious with excitement over finding the gold and probably killing the robber. But he and Callie were mouse quiet all the way back.

The return to Punta Rassa was much swifter than their original venture, since they were not tracking the Gang and had got off to an early start. They arrived back at the boarding house shortly after nightfall, and the cowmen who had remained to care

116

for the stock, and Yankee, Hannah and Ruby were hooting and hollering about their adventure. As was expected, the others had not returned - they had gone west to the Gulf and would probably use the coastal route back.

Yankee figured out that about one-fifth of the money was in the saddlebag. "But even so, Sr. Gato and Don Luis will sure appreciate it," Yankee assured the exhausted twosome.

All Callie wanted to do was fall into her blanket roll and curl up in her corner underneath the high porch and sleep forever. But that nosy Ruby Thomas must have asked her one hundred thousand questions about her adventure. Callie just wanted to put her mind to rest and not to think about anything, especially not about the last three days. She finally told Ruby to go ask Thom Garvin all about it, that he was the one who found the doubloons and shot the robber - that she just held his horse and cooked his coffee. So off she ran, with that old red-yellow hair flying all over, to drive Thom crazy with her millions of questions.

Callie was still asleep when she felt someone shaking her shoulders and calling her. It was her pa. "Oh, Lordy! I'm in for trouble - I'm sure," she thought to herself. But he seemed more relieved than angry, and he was talking to her real soft like. He said he didn't like the fact that she had ridden with the posse without his permission, but he was proud of her courage.

But as he pointed out, "Your ma would never forgive me if anything had happened to you, Callie, and it could have turned out just as easy that you and Thom were the ones left in the swamp for dead, and not the robber. Yankee asked me to wake you. There's a reporter with the *Ft. Myers Star* who wants you and Thom to tell him all about your adventure. Now get your face washed and your hair brushed and meet me up on the eating porch like a big girl," and with that he put his long, slender arms around her, and she thought she felt a tear fall on her cheek as he embraced her. He hadn't done that since she was just a little girl. And Callie got a catch in her throat when she saw his bent shoulders as he climbed the long, steep stairway to the porch and the waiting reporter.

CHAPTER IV   CALLIE'S DRESS

"Who was that lady I saw you with? That ain't no lady - that's Callie Meade!" And the kids would laugh. Oh, but that made Jay angry. He was touchy about his sister Callie - not that he'd ever let her know it. And could she sit a horse! Bareback, side-saddle, anyway. There wasn't a horse umpteen counties around that Callie couldn't break. Their pa would rather have her on the drive than George or Slick, and they were as good as any hired cowmen he'd ever had. No dosidoing or sashaying for Callie. And her ma got pure disgusted about her.

Lordy - how he hated the smell of a horse - it sickened him. His ma said that he had a sneezing fit ever since she could remember when he got as close as six broom sticks from a horse, and Doc said it was asthma. All he knew was he hated them, everything about them. Everyone said he should have been the girl. It didn't bother him anymore - it used to something awful, but no more, not since he got the letter from the capital - Washington, D.C.

Jay sketched pictures in pen and ink of every bird and animal he'd stuffed. People would come from all over to see Jay's stuffed animals and birds and the pictures he'd sketched. "They sure looked alive," they said. But it wasn't until Miss Agnes Taylor, his teacher, suggested that he sketch them real good and she'd send the pictures to the capital that Jay paid any real attention to the fuss. She even helped him put together the package.

His ma knew he needed something of his own just as important as Callie needed her horses, and his pa never said it was sissy, but he sure didn't encourage him. Jay actually overheard him defend him one day to George and Slick.

"Not everyone is in love with horses and bulls, and Jay sneezes so hard every time he gets near 'em that he'd for sure cause a stampede, and then where would you be?" But they still looked at him kinda funny just the same.

But he, James Parker Meade, got a letter from Washington, D.C., signed by John James Brown, Director of the Institute of Natural History. Callie ran all over town telling everyone who'd listen about Jay's letter. Sure made him hold his head higher. Mr. John James Brown, Director of the Institute of Natural History of Washington, D.C., said he would like to see more of his work. And ever since that letter, Callie had been spending more time in his

118

workroom.

He had already stuffed the panther Slick got up near Palmetto Hammock, but the great horned owl was still his favorite. Miss Taylor wrote for books all the way from New York City for him to study.

He loved being in his workroom alone with the birds and animals, and had learned their calls and all about where they lived and what they ate. Funny, but he never had a sneezing spell around them.

All at once everything changed. Seemed to happen real sudden like. "Callie sure acted funny," Jay thought. His Ma said, "Girls get like that - jumpy - sort of drifty-eyed." She'd been like that ever since the spring drive. She had been gone for only three plus weeks, but she came back - well - different. It wasn't long 'til he found out why. His name was Thom Garvin and he was from up Crescent City way.

****

The talk had died down about Callie and Thom finding the stolen doubloons and perhaps killing one of the robbers - thought to be Sheldon Hartford from Alabama, the one who gunned down the banker, Luther Jones. If the truth were known, Callie would just as soon forget all about it.

Don Luis sent the ranchers' doubloons by Capt. Spooner when he returned to Punta Rassa from Cuba, and the hands had tended the counting and loading of the beeves the day after the posse's return. Don Luis had also approved a $200 reward for the return of the stolen gold, and an additional reward would be given for the capture - dead or alive - of the remaining thieves.

Those two and a half days back from Punta Rassa seemed like a whole lifetime. That had to be the longest time Callie could remember. She did feel different all right. Maybe she was a hero, or whatever you wanted to call it. Her pa called her a heroine. But just because she and Thom had found some of the stolen doubloons, that shouldn't make a body a her... a whatchamacallit, she reasoned. And then that know-it-all Jam kept making remarks about something old and something new, and as how her pa best start planting rice alongside the wire grass, 'cause it looked like he might have a wedding on his hands. What a pot-boiler of a cowman

119

he was.

"If he wasn't my pa's top hand, I'd let out his steam," Callie said. Thom dropped back and rode alongside her making small talk. She just couldn't look at him with all those hands around staring at her with their sick, teasing grins.

"I think Ma's right. I must need a spring tonic," she conceded. Thom was trying his darndest to make her laugh, tweeking BeeBee's ears. Finally she had had enough, and with starch in her spine said, "Thom Garvin, why don't you just go back to Crescent City so I won't have to look at that...that ..." she couldn't think of anything mean enough to say - "baboon face!" she finally blurted out.

He threw his head back and howled with an amused glint in his laughing eyes. "Why, Miss Callie, I had planned on stopping off in Tater Hill Bluff to visit my Aunt Beulah Young and Cousins Maida and Marta 'fore returning to Crescent City. And I believe, if I know my Aunt Beulah, she'll be having a social for me, and I'd like to extend an invitation to you to be my guest right here and now."

Callie's dark brown eyes almost bugged out when he said that. " Oh, my! Oh, my! What on earth would I do at a social?" she questioned worriedly. Her ma had been doing her darndest to coax her into attending one for ever and ever, but she'd always thought up some excuse to avoid them. She'd always managed to come down with an incurable disease, or something almost as terminal.

One time she told her ma she was sure she had the bubonic plague. Her ma just smiled that sweet, retiring smile and softly said she'd be sure to stop by Doc's to inform him of her malady on her way to the social. Relieved, Callie spent the entire evening in the bunkhouse watching Slick and the others play Black Jack.

"I see by your silence you will have to get permission from your ma and pa," Thom said, loud enough for all the eager and amused cowmen to hear as he sidled up beside her.

Callie was completely speechless so she tentatively raised and lowered her embarrassed head in submission. Thom whacked Goldie triumphantly and trotted off to the chuck wagon. He picked up the gourd and on the hoof took a deep gulp of cool water from the barrel, all the time boring a hole plumb through her.

She beaded her eyes back at him and wished she'd put a big old frog in that barrel to surprize Mr. Smartie Pants Thomas Garvin, but he got all soft lookin' as he grinned his satisfied grin for all to see, and Callie swallowed hard and averted her eyes.

"Oh, Lordie! What on earth can I get sick with to get myself out of this mess?" Callie questioned. Not that going to a silly old social should be so all fired troublesome as roping, riding, branding, fording a stream, "or even having to look at Ruby Thomas cow-eye every cowhand in the whole state of Florida, for that matter," she reasoned.

Callie was anxious to get home this go-round. She never had been before. She had always wanted to stretch out the drive for an eternity, it seemed. But not this time. She wondered what word Jay had received from the capital. "Bet he got another letter," she thought. Callie sure was proud of him. And Ma - she bet she and Mattie had put up a hundred jars of relish or something or other. She might even have finished the sunflower quilt. As she brushed a fly off BeeBee's damp neck, she wondered why on earth she thought of that. She didn't even like sunflowers. Like her pa had said earlier that morning, she sure was skittish.

They pulled up to the first tall pine beside the west gate, and she saw her ma on the porch, wiping her hands on her apron, and as she looked at her, it seemed it was the very first time she had really seen her. Did she ever see her ma when she wasn't wiping her hands on her apron? And Callie thought, "I guess that's what a lady does - gets her hands into something all the time so's she has to wipe 'em on her apron. You never see Pa or the cowmen wiping their hands. Now that's something to ponder. And why do ladies wear skirts? Just doesn't make any sense at all. They have to hike them up to walk. Guess that's one reason they wipe their hands on their aprons - so's not to get the skirt dirty. But if they wore pants they wouldn't have to go to all that bother."

Not that Callie had anything against dresses. Some of them sure were pretty - all shiny - and she especially liked the pretty buttons her ma bought at the dry goods store. Some looked almost as pretty as cat's eyes. She got lace all the way from Europe, and some of her patterns were copies of dresses they wore in the big cities like Savannah and New Orleans and Washington, D.C.

"I'll bet Mrs. J.J. Brown wears those fancy dresses to the socials in Washington," she rationalized, "So they can't be all that bad. She must be real proud of her husband, him being the famous director of the Institute of Natural History. I wouldn't mind having one dress, but it would have to be the color of the Mexico Gulf at

121

daybreak, that blue-green that you can see plumb through. Yep! I could stand a dress that was that color." So from the time Thom mentioned the social, Callie was talking herself into getting her first dress.

****

Kate Meade insisted that Callie accompany her into town to select her dress pattern and fabric. Callie couldn't figure out why there was so much fuss about a dumb old dress, but just so her ma'd quit nagging her, she decided to accompany her to get it over with. And, besides, it'd give her a chance to visit with Clay Willett, who worked part time at Jeeters'. He was the only boy in town who treated her with respect, and she and Clay could talk by the hour on every subject you could think of. It seemed to her that he knew something about everything, and she never tired of hearing him expound. And besides, he'd already had several articles published in the *Tampa Tribune*...a real feather in his cap, she thought.

Mr. and Mrs. Jeeters were so excited about Callie's visit you'd have thought she was some kind of celebrity or something. They never acted like that before, and it just got on Callie's nerves. She'd bought many a thing at their dry goods store, and they hadn't given her the time of day or, at least, any special notice.

Her ma first deliberated over the pattern, then the fabric and finally the trim and buttons. You would have thought she was the Queen of Sheba the way they were all taking on about Callie's dress. It was true that Maida and Marta, Thom's cousins, did have lovely parties, her ma said, and she was very excited, but mostly relieved, from the looks of it, that Callie had finally agreed to attend one of them.

Beulah quite often had socials for her two eligible daughters, and anytime one of her relatives or friends had a wedding or tea, she would be asked to help with the planning. If she had a talent, it was her ability to organize any kind of social function. She was especially enjoying the planning of this social because her longest and dearest friend was Kate Meade, and her Callie was finally going to relinquish her boyish ways and for once in her life try to act like a lady. When Kate had told her that her prayers had been answered, Beulah realized that she had never let on, even to her,

122

her best friend, of her concern for Callie and her future.

After Callie and Kate made their purchases at Jeeters', they went to visit Beulah and the girls at the hotel. The Youngs occupied the back portion of the hotel, upstairs and downstairs, and it was a favorite meeting place of the ladies when they did their shopping in Tater Hill Bluff. Beulah Young was a warm and entertaining woman and kept the ladies amused by her stories. It was said by her acquaintances that "Beulah Young could find the Devil's funny bone." And they said it as a compliment.

Thom's mother, Mary, and Beulah were sisters, but alike only in appearance. When they were very young the townspeople had difficulty telling them apart, but as they got older their personalities took shape, and Mary became the more serious of the two. She met and married Pierce Garvin, and Beulah met and married George Young the same year up in Crescent City. But George had itchy feet and liked a faster pace of life, so he and Beulah took to the road and ended up in Tater Hill Bluff. They found a spot to their liking and homesteaded it, as did other adventurous young couples in the Florida wilds.

They first tried farming a spread on the out-skirts of town, but George and Beulah both loved people, and when old man Harrod Tedder, proprietor of the Tater Hill Bluff Hotel died, with no kin that anyone knew about, George and Beulah went to the bank and settled their claim on it. Since that day it had never been lacking for activity. Practically every wedding party held in or around Tater Hill Bluff had been right there in Beulah's big, beautiful parlor.

George had fashioned four folding doors to separate the hotel dining room and the private family parlor. For the large occasions the doors would be opened and folded back, giving room for dancing as well as feasting.

Thom had been staying at his Aunt Beulah's ever since the drive. His Uncle George was not well, and Thom was helping around the hotel with some of the repairs and painting the upstairs trim. He had always liked working with his hands, and his Aunt Beulah took advantage of his talent. He enjoyed the activity around the hotel. Drummers coming in and out always had a good story or were looking for action, and Tater Hill Bluff was a rough and tumble cow town with plenty going on with the Young Hotel right in the middle of it.

123

Kate joined Beulah in the big country kitchen, and they got the tea steeping. Beulah always had sugar cookies in the blue-ringed crock beside the black wood stove. As Callie was going up the stairs to join Marta and Maida, she called to her, "Callie, be a sweet girl and take some of these sugar cookies up to the girls. Your mother and I don't need but a couple to sweeten up our tea."

Callie had always liked Beulah Young. Come to think of it, she and Clay were the only ones in town who treated her as before - before the recovery of the gold, that is.

The girls were real excited about Callie's visit. They could hardly wait for her version of finding the gold and shooting the robber. Goodness knows they had heard Cousin Thom's telling it often enough. Poor Cousin Thom - he had to tell the story every time a drummer would rent a room at the hotel, and he was wearying of it, too.

Callie kept looking around hoping to catch a glimpse of Thom, but he was nowhere to be seen. She couldn't seem to take her mind off him. Every waking minute, it seemed like to her, his big grin would find its way into her brain. It also seemed that the whole family was talking about her behind her back. Just this very morning when she came into the kitchen for breakfast, all of them stopped talking and had funny, shifty-eyed looks on their faces - even Jay. Callie felt like a conspiracy was taking place, and she didn't know how to handle it.

The girls were giggling and carrying on when she knocked on their door and entered, carrying the plate full of cookies. Maida, the prettier of the two, immediately took the plate and set it on the tiny night table and said, "Callie Meade, you sit right there and don't move until we've heard every little detail about that tall and handsome robber."

Callie looked at her like she'd lost her mind and said, "Now who in thunderation told you, Maida Young, that the robber was tall and handsome? Why he was the ugliest, dirtiest, meanest looking skunk I've ever seen, and he smelled just like one, too!"

And with that, the girls extracted from Callie the tiniest of details about her adventure, giving them stories to embellish for months to come to delight their friends about the recovery of the doubloons. That was the last time Callie was ever asked to tell her story, 'cause the Young girls had a lock on it. As the saying goes, "Stories get told and get bigger in the telling."

The sugar cookies were eaten, and her ma was calling for her to hurry up her visit, as she had to get back to Tall Ten to help Mattie fix her pa's and Jay's supper before dark. Callie, exhausted from the reliving of her escapade, came out the door. There was that grin, standing by the stairway, just waiting to tease her. But he didn't, and when he said, "Callie", somehow it sounded different.

"Callie, you looking forward to Aunt Beulah's social? 'Cause I am, even if you aren't."

Since he didn't seem to be teasing, Callie calmed down, too, and said as polite as you please, "Why, Thom Garvin, I'm getting real excited about dancing with every man in Tater Hill Bluff," and she sashayed down the stairs just like a girl ought to. Thom let out a whistle, but she didn't even turn around when he said, "I'm going to be the first in line, Callie Meade."

She knew that scared look would be all over her face, since she never in her whole life had done even one little old dance step, and as she let her breath out she realized she was just as cold all over as she had been in the Big Cypress when that robber was walking toward her.

On the way back to the Tall Ten, Callie was so quiet her ma realized something was wrong. She nervously asked Callie if she was feeling well. She was so in hopes that Callie hadn't changed her mind about attending the social.

After biting the inside of her cheek 'til it almost bled, Callie finally blurted out, "Ma - I don't know even one little old dance step!" and Kate Meade, with obvious relief, had to hold back her amusement for fear Callie would rebel and decide not to go. She knew if Callie made up her mind to stay, a team of wild horses couldn't drag her away.

So she said with her understanding voice, "Callie, that's just what I had planned to ask you. I've set aside time in between getting your dress done to help you with your steps. Why Callie, it's just as easy as riding a horse," and Callie let out a long sigh of relief as she tweeked BeeBee with the crop to hurry them home so they could start her lessons.

Kate worked on Callie's dress without any let-up except for the dance steps she and Callie practiced day and night. Kate declared to Parker after they were in bed, following the first day of a nearly exhausting routine, "Well, I never in all my life saw anyone work harder to learn something than Callie and those steps."

125

Parker, who thought the sun rose and set with his daughter, found the entire episode thoroughly delightful.

He and Jay peeked in through the parlor window at the two of them doing their steps that night, and he never felt closer to his son, who was encouraging Callie vicariously with each labored maneuver. Jay, who had just turned fourteen, would attend the dance, but he would mostly hang around the punch bowl and observe, which was all right for a young boy, but a sixteen-year-old girl was supposed to be accomplished at dancing.

****

The day of the big event finally arrived. Kate had put the final stitch in Callie's dress, and it was indeed, in her estimation, beautiful. Callie had been right in selecting the blue-green color. It was so right for her rich brown hair and eyes.

"Callie, if you don't hold still, you'll get stuck by this needle and get blood all over your pretty dress." If Kate said that once, she must have said it a dozen times, but Callie was a bundle of nerves. She hadn't been able to eat even one of Mattie's biscuits for breakfast.

Kate had promised Beulah that she and Callie would ride into town to help her and the girls with the last minute details. When they got to the hotel, Thom was in the kitchen with his Aunt, and she was telling him about how the angel cake she had just taken out of the oven got the name of Phoebe Cake.

It all started with Silas Redmon's wife, Phoebe. Beulah said no one could tell the tale like Silas, and she chuckled as she remembered him telling it, sitting on the front porch of the hotel, not too many years after she and George bought it. But she, too, had a captive audience, because Callie, Thom and Kate surrounded her in the roomy kitchen as she related the oft-told tale.

"It was spring of '67. Silas said he'd never seen such a wet and cold spring in all his borned days. Steady rain for going on two weeks. Pierce Garvin's man, Coot, came sloshing in at daybreak. He'd been riding for two days. The word was that Reuben McRae and Pierce would be late getting to Split Creek. Pierce was having trouble fording the swollen Kissimmee, and Reuben and his hands from South Spring were waiting up for them at Mayacca Junction.

"Phoebe was in the kitchen singing to herself, as she was apt to do, fussing over the big black stew pot. Silas said she was always happy, not given to anger. Her ma, Viola, who had just been widowed up in Aucilla, was coming to Split Creek Ranch to make her home with them. Well, Silas didn't mind 'cause Phoebe could stand another woman around - especially one of her own kind, they being 'bout the only black family in those parts. The folks were friendly enough, but just wasn't the same. Silas said he'd always liked Viola. She was a lot darker than his Phoebe and about twice her size, but even tempered just like her, and he figured she'd be company for Phoebe during the long months he'd be on the cow hunt and trail to Punta Rassa.

"Everyone was excited about Viola's arrival. Their chores were done without too much reminding, and a special dinner was planned. Phoebe had been saving up eggs all week. The hens weren't laying well that year, and she needed only a few more eggs for the angel cake they all loved.

"Silas was supposed to get the eggs before going into town with the buckboard to meet Viola, but he just seemed to be dragging his heels and jawing with Coot 'bout nothing important, and Phoebe kept looking out the kitchen window at 'im squatting in the yard and drawing in the sand, just taking his own sweet time.

"'Well, enough's enough!' she decided. She'd just have to get the eggs herself. She put Arla in the crib, shaking her head as she did, at how early she'd begun crawling. Then she wiped her buttery hands on her apron and walked right past 'em, not lookin' right nor left. Silas looked up and almost said something, but noticed the angry ruff up her back. And Coot muttered a greeting, but decided he'd best not say anything after he saw Silas's knowing look.

"Well, they heard Phoebe scream, and both jumped like they were shot and dashed for the coop. There she was! Silas never saw her so all-fired mad. She picked up that long yellow chicken snake by the tail, crying her head off, mind ya - and before the men could stop her, she popped that snake's head plumb off.

"'Now Silas Henry Redmon,' she said, 'I hope you're satisfied. That varmint just ate the eggs I needed for Mama's angel cake. Gimme yore knife.'

"Silas was struck dumb. He and Coot, with their mouths hanging open, watched a riled-up Phoebe cut that snake right down the middle of its bulging belly and remove every last one of those

127

eggs - and not a one of 'em was broken.

"She real careful-like put them in her apron, and real proud of herself she pranced right back into her kitchen and proceeded to bake that cake. And so to this day angel cake is the favorite cake at Silas', and all across the entire state of Florida it's called Phoebe Cake."

Thom asked his Aunt Beulah if she had had to cut her eggs out of a big, old chicken snake, and she jokingly chased him out of her kitchen, laughing all the while.

The girls came downstairs to help Callie take her dress and other garments up to their room, where she would change for the dance. But first, they all helped move the dark parlor furniture alongside the walls, so there would be more dancing room.

Kate and Rube, Beulah's hired man, carried in the lemon tarts and coconut balls that she and Mattie had been making in their spare time to help Beulah out. In the dining room, two long pine tables were set up to hold the specialties of the Tater Hill Bluff cooks.

There would be buckets of boiled and roasted peanuts to accompany the sweets, and fresh fruit punch would be consumed by the gallon, as the party usually lasted into the wee hours of the morning. Entire families would attend - babes in arms, and grandmas and grandpas.

There never was a name given to the social after the spring drive. There had always been a get-together to thank the Lord for the success of the drive and to welcome summer. It was referred to as "the social", and it fell about two weeks after the return of the cowmen from Punta Rassa, before the weather became too hot. The same kind of get-to-gether occurred in the fall, but the fall function was referred to as the "gathering", and was after church on a Sunday, usually in November. At the "gathering", the ladies brought entire dinners, and it was held underneath the big oak and hickory trees in the church yard.

After dusk, those who were still around would gather at the Young Hotel for some dancing and singing around the piano. Now Beulah could sing - at least she thought she could sing. She was always on pitch, and you could hear her all the way to Alva on the Caloosahatchee - as some would have you believe. But she enjoyed it so much and had so much expression that it was hard not to appreciate her efforts. Sometimes, when she got really

128

warmed up, George would join in with his more than adequate baritone just to temper her shrill soprano so the folks would stay longer at his darling's party.

****

Callie had never been fussy about her hair. She just brushed it and twisted it up the back of her head and quickly pulled on her felt hat to anchor it in place. It was naturally curly, and she always seemed to have curly wisps poking out every which-a-way, and it bothered her. Maida and Marta decided to "do" her hair for the social. "Both girls have enough hair to stuff a mattress," their ma said affectionately, and they had learned some of the newest styles out of the books from Mr. Jeeters' store right next door.

Callie was having a hard time with all that attention afforded her, and as Thom passed by the girls' closed door he heard, "Now, Callie Meade, if you don't stop your fidgetting you're going to look like a pickaninny!" or "Callie, for heaven's sake! Hold your breath a little longer." And he, with his hand over his mouth so as not to give away his presence, was sputtering with amusement.

He thought to himself, "I bet she's going to look as done-up as Goldie the day I entered her in the Crescent City Fair with her coat brushed 'til she shone like the sun and the bright plumes I braided down her mane," and Thom laughed all the way downstairs. He decided to join some of the other cowmen at the punch bowl, where his Uncle George had detailed Rube to handle the spirits, so that the young men wouldn't get too rowdy and spoil his beloved's party.

Thom looked up toward the girls' room for Callie, the girls and Mrs. Meade. "Good grief!" he thought, "Half the state's already arrived, and old Jones Clampett's already snockered, and his cousin Cecil is just about as far gone." The fiddlers had been warmed up, it seemed, forever. "Where on earth is that girl? How can it take any human being that long to put a curl in her hair and throw on an old dress, anyway?" He resumed making small talk with the neighbors, but his eyes never left the stairway for long.

Finally he had had enough. He saw his Aunt Beulah over by the kitchen door, carrying out another tray of rum cakes, and was about to ask her what in tarnation had happened to the girls and Callie, when a blue-green dress appeared on the landing and every head in the room turned toward it in unison.

129

She was glowing - sparkling - just like the Gulf at daybreak, and Thom Garvin's mouth was wide open with amazement. The rush was on! While he was standing there gaping, every lad sixteen and up was after Callie for a dance - and did she know how to partner! Thom had thought she'd probably never even been to a social. Boy howdy, was he wrong! She was the Queen Bee, and did she ever know it! Why, every time he tried to squirm his way in amongst the other men to ask for a dance, she'd be off with either that Roy McNash or Billy Hand, probably the rowdiest cowmen around - and her the daughter of J. Parker Meade, just the biggest rancher in these parts. Boy, howdy!

Some women just didn't have any shame, he decided. He was feeling miserable, and Rube had added too much shine to his punch. "Oh, what's an old girl doin' spoilin' my good time," he said to himself as he made his way through the dancing crowd.

It was a beautiful star-filled night, just cool enough for a stroll down main street. Thom's legs were feeling kind of rubbery, and he was singing to himself as he passed Thomas' stables. But he could not get the picture of Callie out of his head. He'd never seen anyone like her. Of all the pretty girls Thom had known back in Crescent City, not one of them could hold a candle to Callie Meade this night. Her chestnut hair was all curls - all the way down her back. Thom hadn't even known she'd had hair except for what poked out from her hat. And that dress, with its low-cut top so's you could see she had ladies' shoulders, all white and soft looking, and long slender arms with lace hanging over them - just like in the ladies' picture books. Thom just could not believe what he'd seen.

He was feeling warm all over and decided he'd walk on over to Jeeters' porch next door to the hotel and sit and visit with some of the old timers, who were always hanging around there. Sure 'nuff, Jesse Barns and Arthur were there, and, as always, talking about the War. Thom joined them for a while, but kept looking toward the hotel, where the music floated softly into the night air and made him smile as he pictured Callie whirling around and around to its beat.

As he was sitting there with the oldsters, looking at the soft light filtering out onto the hotel porch, he got a glimpse of a blue-green dress in the shadows. His heart went to his throat, and he strained to see if there were any shiny boots beside it. When he

130

saw none, he bid Jesse and Arthur goodnight and moseyed ever so slowly over to the hotel. He pretended that he was going in the front door but paused to cough, glancing up so he could get a better look. It was indeed Callie - and she was alone.

As he approached her, he said in a whisper, "Callie, is that you?"

"It's me, Thom," she replied.

He drew closer to where she stood in the dark shadows. "What's wrong? Don't you feel well?"

She laughed just a little lady-like laugh and said, "My feet hurt, and when I took my slippers off, I couldn't get them back on." Then they both began to laugh and relax in the cool night air.

Thom said, "Are you having a good time? Boy, I've never seen anyone who can partner as good as you can! You must've been dancing since you were born."

And Callie very tiredly replied, "But you didn't ask me to dance, Thom."

He blurted out that he couldn't get close enough to her, what with all those rowdy cowmen hanging all over her.

Callie Meade had learned the ways of a woman that night, but she didn't feel like toying with Thom Garvin's affections. "Well, Thom, I'm here now, and there aren't any smelly old cowmen hanging on me."

He reached for her slender waist, and he and Callie followed the caller and danced 'til they became exhausted with laughter on the porch of the Young Hotel.

Trying to catch their breath, they leaned against the front of the hotel beside the window. Thom was still holding her hand, and they neither one knew it was going to happen. It just happened naturally. Callie was in his arms, and he was smelling her scented hair, and his head was swimming. In the excitement of the night they found each others lips. But Callie's thoughts were not on Thom's kiss or his strong muscled arms holding her tight - but on the too-tight stays in her dress and her swollen, blistered feet.

As she broke away with a giggle, Thom stated disgustedly, "What on earth, Callie Meade! A fellow kisses you and you break out laughing." But she couldn't seem to stop. She'd never had such a day - or night, for that matter. Then Thom started laughing, and the two of them slid their back sides down the outside wall of the hotel and ended up sitting on the porch floor - Callie as barefoot

131

as a yard dog with Thom stroking her dancing feet. That was the picture Kate saw when she found them after coming out onto the porch in search of Callie.

"Ma, Thom is trying to help me with my slippers, but my feet are so swollen from dancing that we can't get them back on," and she and Thom continued to laugh uncontrollably.

Kate was so happy that Callie was having such a wonderful, carefree time that she soon joined in their laughter. Then Parker and Jay came in search of the women folk and added their bass peals to the amusing situation as they took turns trying to assist Callie with her slippers.

Unsuccessful, a barefoot Callie and Thom got up and led the procession back into Beulah's parlor and joined the other dancers to the tune of the fiddlers. By then, Thom had taken off his boots, as had several of the other men, and even the very proper Marta and Maida had slipped out of their slippers. And the young and hearty danced 'til the wee hours that beautiful spring morning.

Before Parker Meade left the social that evening, several of the most eligible young men of Tater Hill Bluff approached him to ask if they might call on Callie. Thom Garvin was among them - but so was Clay Willett. When he mentioned this to Kate on their way home, she rested her weary head on his sturdy shoulder as she snuggled up beside him and sighed tiredly. She whispered so Callie and Jay, who were in an exhausted sleep in the back, couldn't hear, "It was that Mexico blue-green dress that did it. Callie sure knows her colors," and with that declaration she fell fast asleep while Parker drove the buckboard, trying to miss as many pot holes as he could, and smiled all the way back to the Tall Ten.

"Yep," he said softly, "That Callie sure does know her colors."

BOOK THREE:

JUANITA
AND
THE SKINNER GANG

CHAPTER I   THE BIG CYPRESS

Joe Bob looked at R.J. like he thought he'd lost his mind, and with complete exasperation called back to him, his words fighting the hot, humid winds that swept across the grassy glade.

"What in hell do ya mean we've gotta split up and divide the gold and go into that Cypress? There ain't no way in this God-forsaken, mosquito-eaten state I'm goin' into that swamp, R.J. There ain't no way!"

All the others joined in. "Joe Bob's right, R.J." Opie spoke up. "I, for one, ain't about to be eaten alive by any stinking gator. Not me! I'm gonna get me a little boat and sail amongst those pretty little islands in the Gulf and fish 'til my heart's content. Yessiree ..I can feel that nice cool breeze right now just a-whistling all around me, while some pretty little trick helps me spend all that gold."

"We've gotta split up, and go our own ways," R.J. emphasized. "It'll be a helluva lot easier for that posse to find us if we're some great, big target. It's a damned sight easier to hide if you're alone than if you're all together. For Christ's sake! Don't any of ya remember your army training?" he yelled, throwing his hands up as he hurriedly packed his share of the doubloons in his saddlebag.

He and Satan headed for the swamp. He turned in his saddle to issue his last warning. "That posse ain't gonna take a chance on going into the swamp. They'll just head for the Gulf and they'll pick you off one by one, just like the Yankees did. Me, well I'd rather take my chances with the snakes and gators." He saluted crisply and turned one last time. "I'm headed for that pretty little Juanita in La Belle. If any of you make it...well, I'll stay around there for a spell."

He and Satan hadn't gone more than a few yards, when he heard Bunt following not far behind, and he was crying uncontrollably, just like a big baby. But R.J. didn't stop him. After all, they were all indebted to him, as he had been their only means of getting food at the various settlements. He'd dress up as a girl, bonnet and all, and so help, you couldn't tell he wasn't one, he was so baby-faced looking. All along the peninsula he'd made their purchases at the various stores, and not once was he suspected. R.J. decided not to acknowledge him, and continued his southeasterly direction.

He entered the dense swamp and penetrated it about a

quarter of a mile, then headed due east thinking of the soft and willing Juanita to keep his fear in check. It was a slow, tedious route. The gray Spanish moss hung low, slapping him and Satan in the face, and the cypress knees, partially submerged in the murky, stagnant, swamp water, were especially treacherous for Satan - so he dismounted and led him. He couldn't take a chance on losing him. He knew there were quicksand bogs in the swamp, and to avoid their sleepy, deadly innocence, he'd throw broken limbs out in front of them every few feet. His head was throbbing from the constant tension required for survival. The slithering gators and snakes seemed to appear from every direction.

R.J. had lost sight of Bunt, but did not concern himself with it. He was too involved with his own survival to think of anyone or anything else. His plan was to head northeast to get out of the dark swamp before nightfall, but in the half light it was impossible to tell the time of day. He felt he'd been there about four or five hours, but there was no way he could be sure. He knew he had to take a chance and stay in the Cypress for as long as he could, but the thought of being in the swamp at night was more than he could stand. He figured it'd take at least three more miserable hours to get to the edge.

He slowly made his way for about an hour when he heard a shot. It sounded like it was from the west. He was positive that Bunt was the only one who had followed him, and he was almost sure that the posse would not take a chance on losing any of their men or horses to the Cypress. He'd heard that egret and gator hunters worked the Cypress for the valuable feathers and hides, but thought the western rim and areas closer to the big lake were the popular hunting areas. He sure hoped he was wrong...he needed help and he wasn't ashamed to admit it.

"God, how my feet itch!" he lamented. His boots and pants were soaked clean through by the dark, red swamp water. The insects were swarming so thickly that he'd had to pull one of his shirts up over his head - buttoned up so that just his eyes were exposed, but even then, some would manage to find their way inside his clothing, biting hungrily as he swatted and cursed. His shirts were bloody from the constant bites. He was itching so fiercely, he was sure he would lose his mind if he didn't get out of the savage swamp soon. Another shot. This time much closer, but again from the northwest. He cautiously changed his direction toward the sound in hopes that it was a hunter. In his confused state, he struggled to fashion a story to tell, just in case it wasn't Bunt who was doing the shooting. Every unexpected shadow took on the shape of a man...his heart was pounding harder and harder and he was having trouble getting his breath. He gasped for air.

In his irrational, superstitious state he became more frightened than ever. But he couldn't afford to become careless, and his constant scanning of his immediate surroundings was exhausting, but necessary to avoid the moccasins that would actually turn on a man. He heard no more shots, but decided to continue in the northwest direction anyway. "Let it be a hunter! For Christ's sake!" If it were, he would know the ways of the swamp, and R.J. was beginning to think that, if he survived, he'd need help.

"Why the hell did that cook have to all a-sudden come in the back room?" he lamented angrily. "Just our stinking, lousy luck! That's what it was. Just our lousy, rotten luck!"

****

The day before the robbery, the gang had taken cover in the thick mangroves surrounding the boarding house and observed the goings and comings of the cowmen. Joe Bob and Opie had worked their way in with the cowmen out in the pens, and casually questioned them about the schooner's expected arrival. After reporting back to R.J. that it was due any time, it was decided that they should strike immediately, and the best time was when the cowmen were on the big eating porch during the noon time meal. That way the back entrance was free and clear for anyone to enter unobserved, and there would be no reason for anyone to check on the trunk in Yankee's room, where it was stored.

Their timing couldn't have been worse. As Joe Bob and Opie entered the room and were lifting the heavy trunk onto the sturdy canvas sling, the schooner's whistle blew, and Yankee told Cook, who was in the kitchen at the time, "Go back to my room for the papers for the captain to sign. The men have waited so long this go-round that we'll all be needed to get the holds filled, and the sooner he signs that paper the better."

That's when Cook surprised them, and Opie was so angry that Joe Bob had to pull him off of Cook. He was hammering so hard on his head with the butt of his gun, that it was a wonder he didn't kill him. R.J. was so put out by the unexpected development that

137

he durn near spewed fire. "Well, did you have enough brains between the two of you to get any supplies? As long as they're on our tails, we might as well be running on a full stomach," he shouted as they headed south through the tangled underbrush, trying to manipulate the clumsy, canvas sling that held the heavy trunk.

****

Angrily, his stomach making him aware of the lack of provisions with its constant gnawing and aching, R.J. and Satan continued through the sweltering swamp. Suddenly Satan stopped. R.J. turned around to see what was wrong, and tried to pull him. He wouldn't budge. Then he felt someone or something watching him. He became cold - clammy - just like before a robbery - his pulse quickened, mouth became dry, and he experienced that same feeling. Even his eyes became dry and tight and he had difficulty blinking them, as he apprehensively scanned the area around him.

A loud, fluttering noise startled him and when he looked up he saw them. The trees were filled with turkey buzzards. Cold reality returned instantly. If there was one thing that R.J. Skinner hated it was a buzzard. He hated them, and he was also afraid of them, or what they stood for - Death.

Then he saw him, not twenty-five feet ahead of where he and Satan stood. His eyes were glazed and saliva was drooling out of each side of his gaping mouth. R.J. started to call to him, but at the same time Bunt raised his gun and pointed it directly at R.J. "My God, he's gone crazy!" he said as he called out to him. "Bunt, it's me, R.J.!"

But Bunt didn't stop his arm from straightening and taking dead aim. R.J. hit the water, trying to avoid the partially submerged cypress knees. He tried to get his gun out of its holster as he scrambled forward to get behind the tallest knees. Finally, he eased it out, and when he looked up to where Bunt had been, he realized that Bunt must have also taken cover, as he didn't see him. R.J. cautiously raised up to get a better bead on him and called to him once more. No answer and no movement. When he stood, he saw him face down in the red water. He slowly approached the still figure.

As R.J. got closer, he realized that Bunt must have passed

138

out...or was dead. He hesitated, then reached for his shoulder to turn him over, and when he did, he saw that Bunt's crazed eyes were rolled to the top of his head. It was then that R.J. saw his exposed leg. It was visible where the pants leg was torn above his old, worn, army boots. He had been snake bit. His leg was so swollen and discolored that, when R.J. saw it, he started to retch. Nothing but bitter bile came up from his constricted throat. He hadn't eaten in so long he was still heaving when he again heard the turkey buzzards in the trees above him, not willing to wait for poor Bunt to even get cold before attacking his miserably swollen body.

Bunt's horse was nowhere in sight. R.J. called for him but heard nothing, so he and Satan moved on, this time in a more northeasterly direction. He could hear the buzzards with their satisfied noises rid the swamp of poor child-like Bunt, and he made up his mind, right then and there, that he'd not be their next meal.

"If I get out of this swamp alive, I'm heading north and going back to Alabama. Gotta look up the Duke. Yep, I'm gonna first pay a visit to Miss Juanita, and then get the hell out of this God-forsaken state."

The hot sun was streaming through the sparse, tall cypresses as he and Satan neared the edge of the swamp. He scanned the area carefully as he approached the open glade of sawgrass in the event the posse had decided on the easterly route for their pursuit. There was nothing as far as the eye could see - just more grass and a few clumps of cabbage palms. R.J. turned Satan toward La Belle and Juanita

CHAPTER II JUANITA

"Nothing ever happens around here. Just nothing!" Said Juanita as she sat plaiting her long blond hair - not yellow blond, but white blond. Everyone commented on her hair. Everyone! Everyone! Frankly, she was tired of it. She never walked into Mr. Burns' Dry Goods that he didn't say, "I'll declare, Juanita, you have the prettiest hair in these Everglades." Sick of it, sick of it! Just once, and she meant just once, why didn't someone say, "Juanita, you've got the prettiest hands." And she intended to keep them that way, too. No rough callouses like her ma's. She would keep her hands nice like a lady and leave this place for good.

All the young men with their cow eyes made her sick. She'd just as soon kiss a big ole croaker as any of 'em. Mind you, they tried. Last social at the hotel that smelly Josh White did his best to get her outside. And her ma, well she had the nerve to suggest that that smelly old Josh drive her home. Made her want to throw up. "She does beat all! Just because Mattie White is her best friend, it doesn't give her the right," Juanita declared.

She was not uppity! No matter what they said. She knew what she wanted, and it was for sure not Josh White, nor anyone else in LaBelle for that matter.

She closed her eyes and leaned her long, heavy braids against the tree. Her place - her favorite place. The creek willows hung so low it was like being in a bright green cave, all clean and fresh, where no one could see her. She sometimes would come to her place and sit by the hour, just dreaming. Her ma got plumb put out with her, but she just had to get away from the house noise, and those chickens made her sick. They were so stupid that she hated tending them. She was not lazy, as her ma would have you believe. She was a good worker.

"I'd best be getting back," she thought. But Juanita continued to sit underneath the willows, reflecting on the unexpected excitement that rode into her humdrum life just a few short weeks ago. Her thoughts were on R.J. Skinner, the notorious robber. As she made circles in the cool water with her bare feet, she quickly resumed her remembering as she watched the circles grow out into the creek, getting bigger and bigger, then disappearing.

****

It had all happened so sudden like. She had been sitting underneath the willows, just lazing away the day. "My, but that cool water feels good. What if a big ole gator came slithering in and took a bite?" She laughed, and splashed loudly and made lots of noise to scare him just in case. Not that she was afraid. She just knew you couldn't trust a gator. She was suddenly startled by the sound of horses. First thing she thought of was the thundering herds, like in the many books that her friend, Lonnie, loaned her to read from his aunt up north. Must have been at least five of 'em. She'd never seen 'em before - strangers. "Now what on earth are they doing around here?"

Juanita ducked back into the sanctuary of her hiding place and parted the willow branches so she could get just a little peek. It appeared that the bearded one was the leader. He said something, and they paid heed to him. "Just like Preacher Catlett," she thought. She couldn't make out what he was saying. Someone's name must be Sheldon. He kept saying that name....then he would turn toward where she was hiding and she would duck back inside. He was saying something about Spanish gold and Punta Rassa and was calling one of 'em Opie. When she parted the branches again, he was facing her. All of a sudden she became scared. Not like when it was pitch black, but a kind of cold-all-over scared.

He had the blackest and meanest eyes she'd ever seen with coal black hair and beard. Just like what the Devil must look like. She couldn't seem to take her eyes off of him. He was squatting down and raising his voice, and he sure was mad at somebody. The one named Sheldon kept getting up, and the mean one would tell him to sit down. He'd do it, too. The one called Joe Bob said that he couldn't help it - it wasn't his fault, and that that fool Opie had to have the meanest streak of temper that he'd ever seen. The little one called him R.J. So that was who they were - the R.J. Skinner Gang!

They'd been talking about them at Mr. Burns's Dry Goods last week, he and Mr. McBain. Said as how he'd read about them killing the banker way over at Tater Hill Bluff. It was then that she realized they must be hiding out right in La Belle. Imagine that! R.J. was saying something about all that Spanish gold and Punta Rassa, where the cowmen drove their cattle and got paid gold doubloons. "So that's what they're planning - to rob the ranchers!"

141

Now she was scared.

She was leaning forward, straining to hear more, when the log she was sitting on slid out from under her, and she pitched forward. Before she could get back under the willow, one of them had her by the arm and was mumbling something about her being a spy and goodness knows what all.

R.J. bent down and turned her over. She was spitting and sputtering--dirt all over her face. He gently brushed the dirt from her cheeks and she bit down on that thumb as hard as she could. A searing flash of heat from his swift hand took care of that, and the tears started streaming down. He again brushed away the tears and dirt, and this time she opened her squinched-up eyes and met his curious black ones.

They just stared at each other. The one called Opie said she sure had pretty hair, and so help, she couldn't help but laugh out loud. Guess they thought she was hysterical. "Oh, God! I wanted some excitement, and it finally arrived, and then that fool Opie just had to comment on my hair. He's as dumb as Mr. Burns," she thought.

R.J. helped her up and in a military-like manner asked, "Do you live around here, young lady?"

Juanita started to respond, but before she answered he brusquely informed her that "My men have need of rations. We have been on a government expedition...a secret mission." His black eyes just stared at her as he let the importance of his message sink in. "You are not to inform anyone...and I mean not a living soul, not even your folks, about seeing us. We must have rations other than fish, salt meat and corn meal...."

"We raise chickens...lots of chickens...and I'd be happy to catch one of 'em for your supper."

R.J. saluted her and thanked her on behalf of the United States Government. He said it was her honor bound duty to commandeer those chickens and not to tell a living soul. She breathlessly informed him, "I'll be more than happy to assist the United States Government, Mister Officer, sir."

As Juanita crossed the pasture between the creek and her house she began planning how she could catch the chickens and get the supplies to the gang. She was so excited about the venture, she was sure her face was flushed with anticipation, and her ma would for certain sure suspect something was amiss. "Those chickens are so dagblasted stupid they deserve to die. What Pa wants with so many I'll never know," she said, bolstering her confidence.

Juanita got her apron off the nail by the back door and called to her ma. "Ma, I hear the chickens a-squawking - best I go see if there's a snake in the coop." Her ma looked at her kinda funny, then settled back in her chair and continued to snap the beans for dinner. "That girl might settle down yet. Never knew her to care if the whole barnyard got et up by snakes," she mumbled, as she smiled to herself. "The young are so antsy - especially Juanita. Not one bit like Bonnie. And Lordy, how she hates those chickens. She's right. They're squawking. Now where on earth is she off to? I'll declare, that girl will be my undoing!" she said as she watched Juanita, whose mouth was covered to hide her laughter, leave the coop and head for the creek.

"Would serve that gang right if I caught that dadburned rooster. Bet he'd be tough as whitleather. Or how about Pa's prize Plymouth Rock? I'll declare to the whole world, he thinks more of those ugly, squawking chickens than he does me. Always spouting off about 'em, and, to beat all, the first thing anyone ever asks him is - 'Well, Ben, how's yore prize Plymouth Rock doing?' Not once, 'Has Bonnie had that baby yet?,' or, 'Did Juanita win the elocution award on Display Day?' Never...'Well, Ben, how's Ovella and the girls doing?'"

"No - not a one of 'em. Always, 'Well, Ben, how's yore prize Plymouth Rock a-doing?'" And Juanita thought, "I'll just show 'em all!"

In order to get back to the creek and the gang, Juanita had to go through the pasture where her pa's Brahma bull was grazing. She sure didn't trust that bull, but she was so excited about her adventure that she just walked right past him, and him looking her right in the eye. She bravely tightened her apron around the squirming chickens and held her head high as she approached the men, who were squatting beside the creek where it widened and flowed into the river. She wasn't scared anymore.

The gang was still shouting angrily. They weren't a bit different than the men around the Glades, she observed. "Now wouldn't you think robbers and murderers would look and act different? But nope. They squat, too, just like every man I know. Why don't they sit, or at least stand? And always with a stick in

143

their hands. Men do beat all!" Juanita concluded as she studied the R.J. Skinner Gang while they plotted their robbery of the ranchers' doubloons at Punta Rassa.

The squawking chickens startled them. "They're sure strung up tight. Guess I'd be, too, if I'd just robbed a bank and shot a hole straight through a man," she said to herself. "And that R.J. --- boy, he sure can stare a hole plumb through you." But she didn't back down. She just stared right back at him. She wouldn't let him know her stomach felt like the creek edge slime on a still, hot day just oozing and circling out. But she was sure she had it in check. It was the only exciting thing to ever happen to her in her whole lifetime, and she'd be dadburned if she'd let an ole slimy stomach spoil it - not if she turned pea green.

R.J. got up and the others followed, all talking to her at one time. They wanted to know if anyone saw her stealing the chickens, and if she talked to anyone. Juanita informed them that "The chickens are mine to do with as I please, Mister." That little peewee of an Opie grabbed one of those Rhode Island Red chickens from her and proceeded to wring its neck, laughing all the while, and before it stopped kicking and jerking, he began plucking it. "That just shows the whole, entire world he's dumber than the dumb old chicken," she thought.

Juanita spoke up and told him, "Boil some creek water and I'll teach you the right way to fix a chicken, Mister." He didn't like that one little bit, but R.J. told him, "Mind the little lady and do what she says, Opie." He for sure didn't take to that either, and glared his dart-piercing stare clean through her. But Juanita smiled her satisfied, sweeter-than-honey smile right back at him.

Sheldon got some branches and banked some sand around the fire for the tub to rest on. It was going on dusk by the time the chickens were roasted. "They sure do need to rob a bank," Juanita thought. "Not a one of 'em seems to know the first thing about cooking. That R.J.'s the only smart one in the whole bunch." She continued her observation, "There they are - squatting around that camp fire, hot as it is. Skeeters aren't bad yet, but come dark they'd better have brought some net or they'll be eaten alive. And letting their horses eat the sawgrass! Bet they're gonna swell up and bust by mornin'." When Sheldon tied one of the horses beside the castor beans, Juanita yelled, "What on earth do ya think you're doing letting that horse eat those castor beans?" About that time that horse started spitting and sputtering and Juanita just shook her head. She told R.J., "The United States Government sure gave you some mighty stupid horses, Mister." He broke out laughing his head near clean off and just a-staring at her all the while.

Juanita didn't understand why R.J. kept looking at her that way - not mean like, or teasing, or like he wanted to kiss her, either. "That must be what Preacher Catlett means, when the Devil has you in his spell," she reasoned.

It's for certain sure that R.J. Skinner had her in his spell. She couldn't seem to stop lookin' at him.

"I'd best be getting back," she decided. "Ma'll ask me what on earth I've been doin' and I'll say, 'Just day dreaming.' And then Ma'll say that my chores're suffering, and that means my mind is lazy, and as how a woman with a lazy body and mind never in all the world would catch a husband. And I'll reply, 'I'd just as soon catch the plague as a husband any day,' and Ma'll get that sort of half smile on her face as she goes about her chores."

Juanita bet they went round and round on the same subject two or three times every blessed week, and it always was the same - nothing different. But this time she'd say, "I've been by the creek eatin' chicken with the R.J. Skinner Gang, and I'm not afraid of 'em neither." She bet her ma's mouth would drop clean down to her apron strings, and she smiled as she thought on it.

****

It was warm in her airless, small room. As she lay still, listening to the night noises, she thought she'd never get to sleep. She'd promised R.J. she'd get him some meal and coffee before daybreak. Her pa was such an early riser that she guessed she'd best tend to it as soon as they were abed. She heard her pa's breathing become steady and heavy, so she knew he was in a deep sleep. Tucking her muslin night shirt into her old work skirt, she pulled on her brown shoes, knowing she'd return before you could shake a stick.

Juanita had to be very careful about how much meal and coffee she took. Her ma measured every speck Mr. Burns sold her. If she said anything, Juanita had decided to tell her that she spilled some while fixing her breakfast - as how she had been so all-fired hot that she couldn't sleep, so she got up early to do the cooking. "That should satisfy her," she thought while she filled the cans from her ma's precious larder.

When she approached the campsite, she decided she'd best make some noise or that fool Opie would probably shoot a hole plumb through her. She was startled - "What's that? What's that noise? Maybe a hoot owl, "she reasoned as she peered through the night haze.

None of the gang stirred. They were just grey lumps surrounding the banked fire. The next thing she knew she couldn't breathe and her ma's coffee and meal cans went a-skittering all over the ground. "It's a good thing I put 'em in the tight-lid cans or that would have been the end of 'em," she thought, as her legs gave way under her, and she sank onto the damp night grass.

No one had to tell her it was R.J. She could feel the heat of him. This time Juanita didn't try to bite his hand as he removed it from her taut lips. She started to relax. She felt his hand begin to gently stroke her hair away from her face. Even though he was behind her, she could feel those piercing eyes stare that devil's look right into her brain, and her knees started to feel rubbery, and her legs began to tingle.

"He must have squeezed the breath out of me," she thought as she gasped for air. He held her as she eased around toward him on the soft grassy slope beside the water's edge. She heard no one else stir as she felt his heavily muscled arms wrap around her.

R.J. whispered softly that he was glad she'd come back. Before she could even tell him she'd got meal and coffee for their breakfast, he started stroking her long blond hair and saying, "Shhhhhhh," and her brain started swimming. Juanita remembered what that stupid Cleo Anderson told her - that she'd been kissed a dozen times or more, and she'd just as soon kiss a log, and that she didn't know what all the fuss was about anyway...

"Oh, God--I don't know why I can't think. I know my heart's goin' to bust right out of my body, and I'll never be able to walk again. My knees feel so strange - like there're a million needles poking in 'em. I know this is that devil's spell Preacher Catlett shouts about. He's having a hard time breathing, too. He keeps telling me, 'Shhhhh. Not a word'," and her mind blurred.

"Is this what Ma keeps saying I'll know one day when I marry? And Bonnie and Ma exchange those knowing glances and smile at each other secret-like?" One day she got so sick of hearing about how she'd know some day that she told miss smarty pants Bonnie Graves Martin, "Well, Miss, I already know. So there!" Bonnie went running off to tell her ma and when her ma questioned her, she told her, "I'm sick of everyone in this house whispering and keeping secrets from me," and she just got madder and madder and started crying and told her as she ran out to "Her Place" - "I'll never let any old man put his 'worm' in me!" Her ma did let her mouth drop to her apron strings that day, and Juanita didn't come home 'til after supper. By then smarty pants Bonnie Graves Martin was home and probably letting that old gold toothed Randolph Martin put his stinking, little ole worm in her, giving her ugly, dumb younguns like Blessed Jane Martin. She couldn't imagine anyone stupid enough to name their youngun Blessed Jane. But that's what those two named theirs.

He must have known her legs felt funny - that stroking sure soothed them. She didn't feel like yelling. She knew, at least she thought she knew, what he was going to do. "At least he doesn't smell like Josh White," Juanita thought.

"I never felt like this even when I came back from the dead. At least that's what Ma said. A lot of folks died with the typhoid that time, but I'd been spared. I remember feeling hot and rubbery - just like now. You don't suppose I'm going to die? The preacher said the evil shall perish. His hands are so hot, and he's kissing me all over."

"Is that moan coming from me? I can't seem to stop! I wish the world would just stop. I want to stay in My Place and never leave - and the night to hold still, and Preacher Catlett to get out of my mind, and R.J.'s devil eyes to stop staring at me."

Juanita's eyes were closed so tightly that they hurt, and she'd bitten her tongue 'til it was bleeding. The night air embraced her exposed, rounded body and everything felt warm and moist and without time. Floating...suspended. The uneven rhythm of his breathing whispered beside her as he lay spent.

She must have fallen asleep. The next thing she knew, the red sun was coming up over the awakening Glades, and through the early morning mist she could smell the lingering aroma of coffee.

But she was alone...the R.J. Skinner Gang was gone. Juanita sat silently underneath the creek willows. She smiled secretively to herself. "Mr. R.J. Skinner, I'll meet you again. I know it just as good as I know I'll not spend the rest of my life tending those dumb old chickens and married to a cow- eyed Glades boy - not Juanita Jane Graves, Mr. R.J. Skinner! Not Juanita Jane Graves!"

****

Juanita had never even considered telling her folks about the gang and the impending robbery at Punta Rassa. When word was received in La Belle about the daring exploit, and R.J.'s escape, she dropped what she was doing and as fast as she could ran for the solitude of the willows. This adventure was hers..all hers..and she wouldn't share this excitement with a living soul. Not a living soul!

She languidly stretched her rounded arms and smiled to herself with her new awareness - her new confidence. As she relived the exciting intrusion into her monotonous life, her mind lingered on the devil-black eyes of R.J. Skinner, who was making his way through the Big Cypress swamp toward La Belle... and her.

CHAPTER III   R.J. SKINNER

R.J. had no trade. He had never known his pa, and his ma had worked as a cook and cleaning lady in one of the big, fancy hotels in Montgomery, Alabama. R.J. and Joe Bob had been brought up in the streets of that city, and out of necessity and a need for excitement had learned the craft of survival by their cunning ways. When the conflict between the states came along, they anxiously joined up.

When R.J. reflected on the good times in his otherwise miserable life, the exciting War years were the only happy times he could remember. His mother had died of TB about two years before the War, not that it mattered to him one way or the other, since they had never been close. Actually, he couldn't remember her ever having held him. As far back as he could remember, he and Joe Bob had been looked after by Aunt Ruby, the big black woman who lived behind their shack and who watched over a number of neighborhood kids while their mas were at work. But by the time R.J. was eight or nine, he looked after himself and Joe Bob, who was two years younger.

R.J. had learned to steal at an early age. If he saw something he wanted, he took it. There was always a gang of rowdy boys hanging around him, following his lead. And when he said hop, they hopped. When the War broke out, they all joined the same company - Co. "B", of the 23rd Regiment of Montgomery, Alabama.

It didn't matter one way or the other who won the War to R.J. He just liked the excitement of it. He moved up in rank rapidly, as it was apparent to his superiors that he had leadership ability. He and Capt. Joiner took that rag-tag company and made it into one that the whole regiment was proud of. That's where he met baby-faced Bunt, Opie and Sheldon. Bunt was about eleven years old and was the 23rd's drummer boy, and Opie and Sheldon were hop-tos like Joe Bob.

When the War ended and they had surrendered in South Carolina, the five of them decided that there was nothing to return to in Alabama - so they headed for Florida, the last frontier. They went to the busy port of Jacksonville in the northeast corner of the state. Work on the wharves of the St. Johns River was plentiful, and R.J. and Joe Bob engaged in the first and last honest work of their lives.

R.J. liked being near the ocean and declared that he'd never live in a land-locked state. After working Jacksonville for about three years, they discussed moving to Louisiana and working the docks there, but before they could make up their minds where to relocate, fate took a hand in deciding their future.

Tough men worked the docks, and there was always some kind of altercation - day and night - with tempers high and fists, guns and knives fast to be drawn. One dark, cold February night after they got off work, they decided to spend part of their pay over at Laticia's Palace. It was Saturday night and their spirits were high and they wanted action. They returned to their boarding house and got all spiffed up for their night on the town - but especially for Laticia's best girls.

As they walked down Bay Street toward the Palace, they decided to first stop in Randy's to hoist a few ales. The smoke was thick, and it was noisy with the dock workers just off the 8 o'clock shift. R.J. never did find out who actually started the fight, but nine to zero it was that hot-tempered Sheldon, who never had any sense anyway. As R.J. and Joe Bob downed their first ale, they saw Sheldon squaring away at a big, burly docker. He and Joe Bob quickly left their spot to get to Sheldon before he got himself into a mess he couldn't get himself out of. But before they got there, the punches had been thrown, and all hell had broken loose.

R.J. didn't remember a thing 'til he awakened later that night in jail. Must have been twenty men in that miserable, stinking hole. He couldn't make sense out of what had happened, and Bunt was the only one who had any recollection of it.

"Randy sent for that constable the minute he saw Sheldon square away at that docker, R.J. Why, there wasn't hardly any punches thrown 'fore they was a swinging those billy clubs. We didn't have a Chinaman's chance! Honest we didn't," Bunt moaned.

Sheldon's hand was covering his left ear, the congealed blood concealing the torn, jagged part that had been bit off, and with a grimace agreed with Bunt. "That sonovabitch Randy jumped right in with those billies, R.J. Hell, we didn't need no constable...it was jus' a li'l ole fight. Hell, R.J." He was feeling miserable enough, so R.J. decided not to chastise him, but thought to himself - "This'll be the last time, you stupid bastard! I'm through with trouble..have had my fill," and proceeded to doze off again.

It was barely daybreak when all twenty of them were shoved

into heavy, wooden wagons. They had been chained together by leg braces and told by a big, black buck that "If'n I hear one peep..jes' one peep, out of a one of you, you'll be seein' out of but one eye." And he stroked his billy club as he glared his hatred at them. There was no doubt that he meant every word, and the men's expressions confirmed it as they sneaked a glance at each other.

They traveled through the streets of Jacksonville, passing blocks of burnt-out buildings that had been reduced to piles of rat-infested rubble when the city was burned during the War. They rode like that for two whole days, stopping only to let the convicts relieve themselves alongside the ox trail that headed west.

They were each given a ration of two flat corn pones and a cup of the vilest tasting soup R.J. could ever remember tasting. A lone water barrel was in the back of the wagon with a tin dipper hanging from its side, green from the sticky slime that was thick around the barrel's rim.

No one dared ask their destination. One of the men, still slightly inebriated from the night before, had made that costly mistake earlier. The big black took the end of his billy and, as threatened, did exactly what he said he would do. The man, shivering and shaking, was wrapped up in the back of the wagon, blood all over his face where his eye had once been.

It was almost dark on the second day out when the wagons pulled into a clearing, and as R.J. looked to the south of them, he realized why they had been brought there. It was a railroad camp. He had heard that a new rail line was planned for the central part of the state. Apparently, that bastard, Randy, had a deal with the foreman of the railroad to supply him with free labor so they could complete the line - and no doubt pocket the money themselves.

Joe Bob tapped him lightly on the shoulder, and when R.J. turned toward him, he coughed, put his hand over his mouth, and whispered - "That constable and Randy have really got something going, little brother. Every time there's a fight, they break it up, stick the men in jail, and hijack them out here to build their goddam railroad. A lot of gold exchanged hands, Joe Bob. A lot of gold."

The men were shoved into a long, narrow building. It was obvious that they were replacing a group that had recently vacated it. The slop jars were filled, some overflowing, and the disgusting stench in the airless room was almost unbearable. Huge green flies were making themselves at home on every cot. The few windows

151

were high toward the ceiling, and there was a door at each end of the building, with Black guards stationed at them, who were just as big, and looked just as tough, as the one on the wagon train.

R.J.'s men kept looking at him for guidance. He slowly shook his head as if to say - "not now." Thoughts of escape were not even entertained at that point.

The next day at daybreak, they were rousted out of their bunks and marched outside into the cool morning air to the cook's shed. The rations were some better, as cook had shot a turkey, and added it to the root vegetables he'd tossed into the large black kettle. But the coffee was loaded with chicory and so bitter that R.J. thought his mouth was going to turn wrong side out.

After they ate they were told to strip and line up so the guards could shave them - even their heads. "If'n there's one thing Mr. Tomlin won't tolerate, it's lice on his workers. Hop to, now, so's I can douse you with this lye water. Don't hurt none - just stings a little," he said as the naked, embarrassed men closed their eyes tightly and held their noses.

If R.J. hadn't been so miserable he would have found the situation amusing as well as clever - but R.J. Skinner was miserable. First, he liked his coal-black hair and the beard that he had become accustomed to even before the War. Second, he had liked the new blue suit he had donned to wear to Laticia's Palace to please the ladies there, especially Posey, his favorite. And third, and not least, he hated being bested by the larcenous Randy McDougall of Bay St., Jacksonville, Florida.

The very idea that he'd let that gin-swilling carpetbagger best him made his blood boil, and he salivated as he thought of all the ways he was going to encourage Mr. McDougall into an early demise. It might take a week - it might take a month - even a year - but the ultimate goal would be realized, and on that every man in that miserable fly-infested camp could lay a wager.

By nightfall they had pulled into another camp. The going had been rough, especially because "One Eye" - that's what the men had started calling him - had gone completely crazy, and the pot-bellied White guard had yanked him out of the wagon, and taken him off behind a stand of myrtle trees and, they surmised, slit his throat. When he came back toward the wagons, he was wiping his bowie knife on his already stained britches - his worm-eaten-teeth just a grinning at the wagon filled with subdued, beaten men.

This camp was no better than the last one, and in the same filthy condition. This convinced R.J. that he would not shake hands with the devil before he had a chance to rid this stinking, smelly world of a few of Mr. Satan's comrades. And from the looks of it, this Mr. Tomlin was his closest ally.

Daybreak arrived, and the pot-bellied guard came through with his club to hurry their awakening. He called out for all to hear that there would be clothing rationed for them to wear, that Mr. Tomlin liked to see his workers spit and spiffy, and that Mr. Tomlin, himself, was arriving at noon to inspect them. And arrive he did! He was dressed in white from his head to his toes. His carriage was coal black and spit-shiny, and his horses were the most beautiful pair of stallions R.J. had ever seen - matched and pure white. He was driven by a Black, who was dressed in a bright red uniform with the biggest brass buttons you can imagine. All the guards in the camp had put on identical red uniforms and shiny, black boots, and the workers wore dark blue shirts and pants and, at that point...no shoes.

The foreman, who was in charge of the camp, nervously opened the carriage door and was carefully explaining to Mr. Tomlin about the lack of shoes for the workers. The men had been lined up in a row, facing the road on which Mr. Tomlin arrived, and it was obvious on first sight that he was not pleased by their appearance. His pasty, bloated face became beet red as he glared at the long row of shoeless workers. He pursed his lips, and all he had to do to get total obedience was nod that pig-like face toward his driver, who then accompanied the shaking foreman to the back of the long, narrow building.

That was the last time they ever saw him. About five minutes later the driver returned to the carriage carrying the foreman's red uniform. He assisted Mr. Tomlin out of the carriage, and Tomlin waddled up and down the rows of workers, looking at each of them with his sadistic, beady eyes. He lumbered back to the carriage and was helped in. The driver flicked his whip once - the carriage turned around, and the prancing stallions returned by the same route they had come. The entire inspection took only fifteen minutes, but they were made to remain in line until the white hat of Mr. Tomlin was no longer visible.

From inside the foreman's cottage emerged the new man in

153

charge. It was the big, black buck who had accompanied the men to the first camp, and who had very quickly made an example of the mouthing man, "One Eye". His first order was to turn in their uniforms, "and they'd better be clean and folded!" he shouted in his deep, threatening voice.

By supper time, there wasn't a man in the entire camp who didn't have diarrhea. The stench in the filthy building was unbearable, and by morning, with the arrival of the pot-bellied guard, the men were so weak they could hardly stand. However, they were forced to march out into the cold, damp air with only half the workers managing to walk upright. The wagons had been hitched up, the bitter coffee and pone consumed by those who could tolerate them, and again they were loaded into the waiting wagons.

About a mile out from camp, they arrived at the work site. When R.J. saw the rail ties and huge mallets, he and the others sighed in relief. The back breaking job of laying rails was more welcome than being cooped up in the putrid air of the quarters.

R.J. couldn't believe what he was seeing! He shook his head, trying to get the mirage out of his mind, and looked up again. It was indeed his old army buddy, the Duke, and he was guarding the crew which had apparently preceded their arrival. Duke didn't recognize him and the others with their shorn heads and beardless faces, and when Sheldon nudged R.J. and Joe Bob started to speak, R.J. shook his head - "No! Lady Luck is smiling down on us at last, and no one is gonna rob us of this chance!" The Duke was their means of escape.

All day long his crew was removed from Duke's men, so R.J. couldn't let their presence be known. He was getting anxious but could not afford to get careless. There was only about an hour until dusk when he realized - "What if the Duke isn't here tomorrow?" He quickly hit on a plan. He was working alongside a big bruiser of a loud-mouthed Irishman, and didn't take to him anyway, so the plan he had in mind was getting more exciting by the minute.

R.J. purposely missed the spike he was pounding in. It barely glanced off the Irishman's foot, but R.J. was right - he did have a volatile temper, and the fight was on. All the guards, including Duke, backed off to watch the fracas, and the men were allowed to lay down their mallets and enjoy the respite from the back breaking work.

"God, I knew you were a tough son of a bitch, but gawd-a-mighty, you bastard, you gonna gouge out my eyes?" R.J. grunted.

So the time was now! He let out the 23rd's war whoop, and on signal, Sheldon, Opie, Joe Bob and even Bunt did the same, as they jumped in the fight. R.J. saw the Duke's mouth fly open and his eyes try to pierce through the crowd of workers who had joined in the fight. The guards drew their clubs and, after cracking a few heads, restored order...but R.J.'s mission was accomplished.

The Duke meandered over to R.J.'s work crew and pretended to be picking up some spikes that had scattered alongside him. "Skinner, is that you?" he said as he cleared his throat with a cough.

"You're goddammed right it is, you thieving bastard!" and the Duke left the group with a smile on his face.

Contact had been made, and R.J. hoped it was just a matter of time before he would make a move to help his fellow comrades from Company "B". They had joined up the same day and served the 23rd throughout the War, covering each other's butts more than once, and if R.J. Skinner had ever had a friend, it was the Duke. It was true that he looked after Joe Bob, and in his way loved him, but Duke was the only real friend he had ever had.

When the surrender came in South Carolina, Duke, whose real name was Leon Hempstead, headed back to Montgomery, or so R.J. thought. At least, that had been his plan. R.J. was very disappointed when Duke decided to return to Alabama, but he had kin there, and a girl, too. Somehow they both knew they'd serve together again, so there were no goodbyes on that quiet, foggy morning in South Carolina.

It'd been a long time since he had really thought of him. Duke hadn't changed much - a little heavier perhaps, but then so was he. Pickings had been real slim that last year of the War.

When "Pot Belly" Stokeley loaded up R.J.'s crew that night, Duke wandered over to him and loudly asked, "Stokeley, you and Speed going to work on this line tomorrow, or are you going to work one of Tomlin's turpentine camps?"

Stokeley shook his head, "Dunno, Duke. Mr. Tomlin done made Marvell the head man at Camp Number 9, and his words will pull these wagon ropes. You can bet on it!"

With that, Stokeley cracked the whip, and the boney, mistreated mules moved them back over the rough trail. While R.J. held tightly to the rough, pine siding, he had a smile on his face.

There was never a better team than Skinner and the Duke. Mr. Tomlin didn't stand a chance. "Yes, Mr. Pig-faced Tomlin, consider your days numbered," and with a satisfied smirk on his face, R.J. plotted his revenge.

He went to bed not noticing the green flies all over his bunk - not caring that his belly was growling for want of food - not noticing the heavy acrid stench of the lousy, foul air. He had a plan, and with that plan R.J. Skinner and the Duke were unbeatable. After all, they were the golden boys from Company "B" of the 23rd Montgomery Regiment. "Yesiree, Mr. Too-Fat Tomlin, the golden boys have arrived!" And he slept like he hadn't slept in months.

When Pot Belly called, "You miserable looking excuses for humanity! Get your arses out'n those beds!," the next day, he was witness to at least five of the wretches with smiles on their dirty faces.

It was, "Good morning, Mr. Stokeley," and "A beautiful morning, Mr. Stokeley," and "Oh, excuse me, Mr. Stokeley," and the plan was in effect.

The other workers picked up on the attitude of the Co. "B" boys with their pleasant exchanges and made the guards skittish, apprehensive, and nervous. Stokeley burst into Marvell's quarters and told him what was going on. Marvell automatically gave him his boot and told him he had to be coming down with the fever. But when he walked slowly to the screen door with his big, black belly protruding over his stained underdrawers, he could see that what that fool Stokeley was saying was true.

"Now what in hell is going on here? What in hell these White bastards gotta be smiling about?" And he, too, became suspicious. He called Speed over to the quarters door and asked him if he had seen any sign of a revolt, hidden guns, or knives or anything at all that would encourage those no-good skunks to be smiling, just like they were happy about being there.

Speed said that he was worried, too. He'd never seen anything like it in the six years he'd been strapping for Mr. Tomlin. Speed did Marvell's bidding and checked the bunk buildings thoroughly. He even dumped the foul smelling slop buckets to check 'em for any weapons. But nothing did he find. They were late going to the line that day, and even Marvell rode out to the line on his new black stallion to keep a check on things.

156

The plan was on target. Duke had also done a thorough job at camp Number 8. When he asked the other guards if they had noticed anything out of the ordinary, they replied that they hadn't. He then said that he suspected that there might be a plan of escape in effect. So he pretended to check the bunk house, and, of course, found nothing. But he had created the suspicious atmosphere he wanted.

The guards at Number 8 were so jumpy that they quickly got their workers to the line, and when they witnessed Camp Number 9's smiling workers happily swinging their mallets, they really got concerned. The workers from Number 8 soon picked up on their taunting and teasing 'til the guards couldn't stand it any longer and started working them over with their clubs to quiet them.

Duke took one of the guards aside and told him that someone should go tell Mr. Tomlin what was going on. No one volunteered, so he talked it over with Prior Cummins, his foreman, and Marvell, and it was decided that he would be the spokesman.

Now no one, but no one, ever called on Mr. Dagmar Tomlin with a complaint, suggestion, or for any reason at all. It was an unspoken law that Mr. Tomlin was unapproachable by the scum who worked for him, and Duke knew that he was taking a risk. But for the plan to work, the head man had to become confused, thereby undermining the effectiveness of his operation. The Confederate spies had used this strategy very successfully in the War when they infiltrated the Union camps and reported conflicting information regarding troop movement and locations to the Union officers. And when R.J. slipped Duke the folded up piece of paper with the combat plan on it, he could hardly contain himself. Perfect! He knew the plan would work. R.J. hadn't lost his touch, Duke humorously concluded.

The long drive leading up to Tomlin's pretentious, white-columned mansion was lined with manicured, sculpted boxwood and azaleas. On each side of the massive, black double doors, stood over-sized marble urns in a sentry-like position, filled with crimson geraniums and green ivy cascading to the red, brick porch. It was just as Duke had imagined it would be.

Before he got past the first cattle guard, a uniformed guard rounded the tall cylindrically shaped cedars on each side of the gate. Duke pulled up rein and extended his hand upward. He didn't recognize the guard, and when he stated his business, the white

157

faced guard almost went into shock. Duke had asked to see Mr. Tomlin's foreman, or whoever, to inform him of the trouble. He didn't want to disturb Mr. Tomlin personally, he said, and the guard thought that that was a very wise decision. He escorted him around back of the main house to the stable and told him to stay put while he went to the back door to give someone the message. While Duke was carrying out the guard's order, he took the opportunity to check out the surroundings of the slaver, Tomlin.

As he surveyed the layout, he realized the enormity of Tomlin's accomplishments. He had been able to put together quite a complicated system of commerce, and had obviously come out of the War a rich man, no doubt playing both sides against each other. His latest enterprise was apparently well thought out and lucrative. He had a string of twelve lumber-turpentine camps up and down the northern part of the state, and to expedite the delivery of the timber and by-products, he was building his own private railroad system between the camps and the main railroad depots.

What R.J. and his gang were unaware of was that the railroads they had been hijacked to build had absolutely nothing to do with the Savannah-East Coast line between Savannah and Jacksonville. And that Randy McDougall was but one of Tomlin's suppliers of workers. There was at least one getting-rich constable in each precinct of the three cities of Charleston, Savannah and Jacksonville.

Duke let out a low whistle as he shook his head in amazment. "What in Hell have I got myself into?

CHAPTER IV THE DUKE

Instead of returning to Alabama after the War as planned, Duke Hempstead had gone to Charleston to try to get some kind of employment. He was a proud man and didn't want to return home destitute.

Tired and thirsty after the long, dusty walk he gratefully entered the Isle Of Erin Saloon on the outskirts of town. He swung the much used door open and addressed the craggy face that was suspiciously staring up at him from behind the well rubbed bar.

"Where'd a worn out old soldier get a paying job around here, Mac?"

The man slowly responded, "Well, if you're not too worn out, Bo Jenson could use ya over to the #6 dock. Tell 'im that Joe Malarky sent you. 'ere, son. 'ave one for the Ould Sod and we'll down anaither for the fair city of Charleston," he said in his unmistakable Irish brogue as he handed Duke the tankard of warm ale.

"Don't mind if I do." Duke reached for the ale and raised it. "Here's to what should have been, Mr. Malarky, from the Duke."

"So it's Duke is it now? Joe's the name I'm known by," he stated as he raised his ale. They drank silently each deep in his own thoughts.

Bo Jenson hired Duke on, but the dock work proved to be unbelievably hard, so Joe began using him behind the bar. When he regained his strength, he began acting as Joe's bouncer, and remained in that position for almost two years.

One night when they were closing up, Joe turned toward him and asked, "Ya know Henry Watson? You know the one who 'as that big black mole on 'is chin? He comes in 'bout every month or so from down Savannah and Jacksonville way."

"Sure - I know who you mean. A fancy dude who always looks like he just walked out of Kahn''s Haberdashery."

"Yeh, that's the one. Well, 'e was asking me about ya the last time 'e was in here. Seems 'e's needing help guarding some convicts down Jacksonville way. Ah told him A'd speak to ya about it."

"Well, Joe - since your missus has fattened me up on that good mutton stew I'd probably be a match for any of Mr. Watson's ornery convicts. If the pay is right, I'd truly consider it. Yep - it's time I made my way out of here and headed on back to Alabama. Long past due, it is. Long past due."

When Watson returned to Charleston, Duke met with him. He was told that he'd be guarding convicts on a railroad crew down south. The pay he offered was more than he had ever imagined making. He jumped at the chance. They left the next day by train and arrived in Jacksonville that night.

The depot was crowded with the many travelers from the northern states. Watson and Duke had a long wait before an empty carriage arrived and drove them down the brick, lamp lit street that circled the river front and wound toward Laticia's Palace.

When Watson mentioned that he had a "very special treat" lined up for him on their arrival, Duke had no indication what the treat might be. The tinkling music from Bimbo's piano and the lilting laughter of the beautiful young girls reached them as they opened the carriage door. A smile played across Duke Hempstead's ready face as he followed the dapper Henry up to the heavy oak doors, set with oval glass etched with graceful swans cavorting amongst the lily pads.

Henry rang the bell and was quickly motioned in by a very effeminate young colored boy. Laticia, resplendent in royal blue silk taffeta that allowed the rosy glow of her oft used, flawless shoulders and full bosom to emerge from her corseted waist, greeted them warmly.

"Welcome back, Mr. Watson," she said formally, but Duke saw the special message in her darkly fringed, pale grey eyes. "I don't believe I've had the pleasure of meeting Mr......?"

"Miss Laticia, may I present Mr. Duke Hempstead of Charleston. It's his first visit to our fair city. He'll be joining Tomlin Enterprises come tomorrow, but of course I had to first introduce him to you, the fairest lady of all Jacksonville," he said as he bowed deeply, his hooded, dark eyes never leaving hers.

When Watson emphasized Tomlin Enterprises, Laticia's expression quickly changed from a delightfully practiced smile to a fleeting picture of fear. She recovered her composure momentarily as she extended her gloved hand to be received by Duke - but her reaction was not lost on him, and he wondered what it signified.

She immediately took his arm, holding it nervously as she turned toward Watson and said, "Beautiful Eloise should be a most royal welcome for our friend, Mr. Hempstead. Do you approve,

160

Henry, dear?"

"A most royal welcome, Miss Laticia. Indeed. A very royal welcome, my dear." She motioned toward a noisy group of patrons.

Emerging from the throng, and walking across the busy parlor toward them, was the most beautiful young girl Duke had ever seen. China blue eyes openly stared through coal black, thick lashes with a directness that amazed him. But when Laticia mentioned Tomlin Enterprises, the young girl's frightened manner was not as quickly masked as the madam's. The broad smile did little to quell his curious suspicions.

The sun had awakened the surrounding sky sooner than he had wished. He dressed quietly so as not to disturb the beautifully tutored Eloise. He studied her tousled black hair that almost covered the mountain of pale blue, satin pillows, and wondered what evil lay ahead of him that she and Laticia had so quickly acknowledged and just as bravely hidden.

He carefully pulled the door to and descended the richly carpeted circular stairway. Watson was patiently awaiting him beside the buckboard. There was no driver. They arrived at camp #8 early that afternoon and were greeted by Prior Cummins. Duke never saw Henry Watson again, nor had he been encouraged to venture from Tomlin's camps.

He had been quickly indoctrinated into the system and told as little as possible about the recruitment of the convicts. He didn't become overly suspicious until he saw a wagon filled with men arrive at camp their first day. He knew then that these men had not been in jail any length of time, since some still had on their Sunday best. All the pieces began to fall into place.

Tomlin had been able to successfully accomplish the building of his empire because of the types of men who were hijacked. The majority had served in the War and had lost touch with family and friends. They had migrated to Charleston, Savannah and Jacksonville because the shipment of timber and beef resumed almost immediately after the War, and there was work for the unskilled and unwanted - they just disappeared into the countryside never to be heard of again.

Duke had been planning his departure long before R.J. and his men arrived. Their appearance just reassured him of his need to return to Alabama to begin again. The timing could not have been better.

****

Duke was patiently waiting beside the stable when Tomlin's guard returned and escorted him into the rear entrance of the mansion. He kept shaking his head from side to side as he looked at Duke with disbelief - the nerve of this upstart. Duke tried to look straight ahead and not acknowledge the opulence that surrounded him - he'd never seen anything like it. The house was what he imagined a palace would look like, with massive furniture, heavy tapestries and lamps with figures as tall as a man holding the torch-like globes.

By the time he entered the library, he was scared. Just down right scared! The overpowering wealth surrounding him had undermined his otherwise extreme confidence, and he had to keep reminding himself that R.J.'s plan would indeed work. It had worked against the enemy and Tomlin was their enemy. Over and over again he said it as he followed the guard down that imposing, long, red hall.

Tomlin sat king-like behind the pretentiously ornate mahogany desk. He did not move or utter a word. The guard stood behind him and told Duke to state the problem at camps 8 and 9, and to be quick about it. The only movement in the otherwise still room was Tomlin's right hand, that extended out from the impeccable, white jacket. He wore a massive, ruby ring and sat tapping his fingers on the polished desk, not blinking, not making a sound, as Duke told him of the changed attitudes of the workers.

"Mr. Tomlin, sir, the workers are singing and laughing and acting real polite like. Marvell and me haven't ever been a witness to anything like it, sir. It's our opinion, and that of the other guards, that they're planning some kind of disturbance, and we thought someone should let you know, sir."

Not a word did he say as he sat there staring right through Duke. Duke was immediately escorted out by the guard, followed down the long roadway and carefully watched until the guard was positive that he was headed for the camps and out of sight.

How they got to camp before him, Duke couldn't imagine. But new guards were already assigned to 8 and 9 when he arrived. R.J. and the other workers put on a real show for them. They left that very night. That just reinforced Duke's belief that there had to

162

be a means of quick communication to make Tomlin's scheme workable. The telegraph had to be the answer and it was probably set up in Prior Cummins' cottage. Marvell and Cummins had no doubt telegraphed the main depot to warn them of Duke's visit. Tomlin had probably sent the new guards from the camps nearest to 8 and 9, even before Duke had departed from the plantation.

Duke had never been inside the cottage. Cummins was a quiet man and mostly kept to himself. He was an ex-cotton planter from up Savannah way and had worked for Tomlin for about six years. He seemed to be a cut above the other men and Duke had always wondered what Tomlin had on him. Duke knew he had to get inside to see if he was right. If he was, and they could destroy the system between the various camps and the main depot, which he was sure was right in Tomlin's mansion, they might stand a chance.

Duke had worked two other camps and had noticed that all the foremen's cottages were built high, with a steep, pitched roof, and always underneath tall trees. He had wondered why they were apart from the workers' and guards' buildings that were in cleared areas.

He could see no lines approaching Cummins's cottage and certainly couldn't afford to draw attention to himself by climbing any of the thickly branched trees that surrounded it. What complicated the situation even more was that Cummins seldom ventured outside and was not a talkative man. Moreover, Duke had been unable to get any word to R.J. concerning the telegraph.

He lay awake that night, trying to figure how he could find out whether a telegraph indeed existed. After a fitful sleep, he awakened with a plan - clear as a bell.

It was now or never! He had just finished his breakfast of pone, slab and coffee, when he let out a yelp and bent over, calling for help. In each camp there were four guards, one cook and one foreman. Dubie Crosley, the only other guard Duke liked at all, came over to see what was wrong.

"For Gawd's sake, Dubie! Get Cummins. I never had such pain!" Dubie ran to the cottage and soon he and Cummins came out. Cummins was putting his shirt tail inside his blue britches while he hurried toward the bunk house. Duke observed them from the small window. Cummins was never out of character - he took time to comb his straight brown hair and straighten his collar before they entered the narrow room. Duke was back on his chair, bent over

163

and moaning and groaning.

"Duke, I think you'd better lie down on the table so Crosley and I can examine you," he said as formally as though he were requesting Duke to please pass the butter.

"No sir, Mr. Cummins. I'm not going to let anyone but a real, bonafide doctor touch me. Can't you get word to Mr. Tomlin and ask him to send the Doc over?"

Cummins took his time returning to the cottage, no doubt trying to make up his mind what he should do. Crosley sat beside Duke just like a mother hen and finally Duke managed to feign sleep. When he noticed that Duke was resting some better, he went out to the line to tell Stokely and the others that they'd have to double up on duty, "'cause Duke's got himself a bad bellyache and the doc's coming out to check him."

He had timed his ride to Tomlin's, and it had taken about two hours. If the doctor arrived in about the same length of time, that would mean that he would have to have been telegraphed as it would have taken twice as long if Cummins had sent a rider for him. Sure enough, Doc rode up in less than two hours after Cummins left for the cottage. Duke was satisfied.

The doctor, a very amiable, soft-spoken man, examined Duke, and when he touched his belly, Duke let out a yelp. Doc shook his head up and down.

"As I thought! It would appear you have appendicitis. Have you had it before?"

Duke moaned, "No-o-o."

Doc prescribed that he rest, eat lightly and if the pain was no better by the next day he would return.

Duke needed help. He liked Crosley, but the man didn't seem to have much spine. He surely couldn't pull it off without someone's help. Duke knew there was no way that he would be allowed to ride out of camp. He and the other guards were prisoners - just like the workers. They had to have help from the outside, so Crosley's assistance was paramount.

They had to get word to the Union colonel in charge of the occupational army in Jacksonville, to inform him of Tomlin's slave camps. But what if he was in cahoots with Tomlin? Tomlin had obviously tapped into the terminals in Jacksonville, Savannah and Charleston in order to control his suppliers and constables. So, why not the Union colonel? It was a chance he'd just have to take.

That night, he decided to feel Crosley out. The guards had finished supper and Duke called him over.

"What ya need, Duke? You feelin' any better?"

"You know, Dubie, this morning I'd 've sworn I was going to shake hands with the Man upstairs," and Crosley said "Oh, hell, Duke, you too damned mean to die, and too ugly, too," and laughed while the others joined in as they surrounded Duke. But he got real sober acting and said, "No, Dubie, I'm serious. I'm not feeling a hell of a lot better, and if I die, not a one of my family would even know it. Hell, they don't even know where I am. Any of you got kin?" he said with questioning brow. He quickly went on before they could answer.

"Any of you let Mr. Tomlin know who to write or telegraph if something should happen to you? Hell no! You ain't done any such thing. Not a one of us." They all shook their heads in agreement.

"Crosley, you got any kin....?"

"Well, yeah, Duke. I got kin. I got a aunt who lives over near Darbyville, 'bout 30 miles from here. Got me a sister and two brothers up Savannah way."

"Crosley, do any of 'em know where you are?"

"Don't know that they do, Duke. I seen my Aunt Velda 'fore I joined up with Mr. Tomlin, but I ain't had no reason to talk to her since."

The others shook their heads as the realization began to sink in. "Well, maybe it's because I'm sick, but I just got to thinking 'bout all of us," and he looked pathetically at each one of them.

"It ain't right that we've all got kin who don't know where we are," and they all agreed.

"Crosley, seems that you're the only one who's got kin anywheres close around. Mine are way up Alabama way. Don't you think you ought to let your Aunt know where you are?"

"How am I gonna do that, Duke...?"

"Well, hell! You can write her can't ya? Or better yet, have Cummins let you telegraph her. I know there's a station in Darbyville."

Crosley looked at the others and shook his head. "I don't know if Mr. Tomlin's gonna like that, Duke."

Duke looked at him. "Good grief, Crosley, why not? What would he care if you wrote or telegraphed your aunt?"

"Well, I ain't ever seen anyone send no letters from any of the camps I've worked."

About that time Duke got up. He looked every single one of them dead in the eye. "Well, I might be dead tomorrow, so I'm gonna say it! We ain't a hell of a lot better off than the scum we guard. We get good pay, don't have anywheres to spend it and no one to send it to. If I die tomorrow, what's gonna happen to my money I've been savin'? It'll go right back to Tomlin. If I decide I want to go to Jacksonville for a night at the Palace, could I go?"

"When's the last time you felt a warm, rounded, sweet-smellin' woman between your legs? Answer me that! When's the last time?"

They looked at each other, and it dawned on them that Duke was right. Cummins was supposed to be saving their pay. Every month the pompous ass made a big to-do about putting it in the big leather trunk. Duke knew the seed had been planted. They, too, were prisoners - and finally, they realized it.

Duke let it sink in, and in a weakened voice said, "Crosley, if I don't make it, I want you to smuggle this letter out to my kin and get my back pay to them somehow. Do you promise, Dubie? Say you do! Please," he pleaded.

The next day Prior Cummins came into the guards' building - something he never did. He slowly went over to Duke and inquired about his health.

"I feel some better, Mr. Cummins. But I wonder if you'd do me a favor? I got a year's pay in the trunk, and I sure do want to know that if anything happens to me you'd see to it that my kin in Alabama gets it."

He raised his skinny eyebrows and proceeded to get a coughing fit the likes of which Duke had never seen. Duke shot a look at the guards, and their expressions told him that their suspicions were indeed correct.

He soon recovered his composure and replied, "Why, of course, Duke. I'd be happy to."

Duke thought he'd take it one step further. "And something else, Mr. Cummins. I've been with Mr. Tomlin for over a year now, and you know when I was real sick yesterday I got to thinking about the fact that I ain't had a woman in all that time. I'd be much obliged if'n Mr. Tomlin would let me take a little vacation, just for a few days mind you - just to visit Laticia's Palace once more before I die."

166

All the other guards agreed and excitedly chimed in, "Yeah, Mr. Cummins, we need a night on the town!"

With that declaration, Prior Cummins started to mumble and duck his head. He went from ramrod straight to an immediate slump, and retreated hurriedly to the safety of his cottage.

In two hours to the minute there were four of Tomlin's most reliable guards, brass buttons on red uniforms, riding into camp #8. They made for the guards' building even before going to the cottage, and had barely gotten off their worn out horses, when a breathless Cummins joined them. They didn't exactly burst in the doors, but abruptly passed by Crosley and went directly to Duke. The guard who had greeted Duke at Tomlin's plantation was their spokesman.

"Well, Duke, Mr. Tomlin sent us over to see how you're feeling. Doc Holden said he thought you might have appendicitis."

"I'm not sure exactly what I got, but I'm feeling right much better today."

"Well, Mr. Tomlin wanted us to make sure you're comfortable. Doc Holden will be back tomorrow to check on you." When he said that, his meaning was very obvious - Duke had better not be faking. Duke got the message, and so did the others.

He bit his tongue, but he knew he had to carry on. "You know, the men and me were talking, and we sure don't want to go to our maker without a farewell at Laticia's Palace. No sirree! We ain't had any time off in over a year, and since I've been feeling so sick I got to thinking about those warm, soft beauties at the Palace. Do you think you could burden Mr. Tomlin with just one little request for a couple days on the town?"

The guard's eyes dilated, his nostrils flared, his face got red as fire and he started coughing a dry cough as he bent over. The other guards went to his aid, but he pushed them aside and raised his head just enough to glare pure hatred at Cummins as he grabbed his arm and pulled him reluctantly toward the cottage.

"Gawd, Duke, you shouldn't 've said that," Crosley sputtered.

"Why not? We ain't the workers here. Ain't we free to go and come as we please?" he said as he looked at their disbelieving faces.

The guards soon returned, all smiles. The spokesman said, "Duke, how would you and the others like for Mr. Tomlin to have a few of Laticia's best girls visit the camp from time to time? He understands how lonely it must get for his men."

Duke looked him dead in the eye and said, "Oh, it just ain't the same," and he got all drifty-eyed. "Have you ever seen those sweet smelling girls glide down that circular staircase with the lamp light playing off their yeller hair and that big chandelier hanging down in the parlor with about a thousand lights all lit up? And Laticia herself has gotta have the littlest waist you've ever seen. Why both my hands could go around her and have finger space left over. Those blue shiny covers on those little gold chairs sitting all over the room and Bimbo playing that piano like his fingers had the St. Vitus Dance...just a hoppin' all over."

Everybody in that room was remembering their special nights at the Palace. "Oh, you tell Mr. Tomlin 'Thank you', but it ain't no way the same as being there alive and kicking and raring to go....is it boys?"

They left abruptly. Duke never thought he'd see the day Prior Cummins would get riled up, but riled up he got. He spit and sputtered and lit into all of them about how much trouble they were causing him with all their outrageous requests, and how his sister would never forgive him.

So that was it, Duke thought. Tomlin had something on Prior, and it had to be connected with his sister. But of course, he did not say what. A gentleman to the end, as Duke knew he would be.

Prior high-tailed it out of that bunkhouse and told Crosley that all three of them had better get themselves back out to the line, because that crazy bunch of "convicts" was still smiling and singing like a bunch of church-going women.

"Still on target," Duke thought. He had to get word to R.J. But how? He got Crosley aside and told him to tell Stokely and Speed that they all planned a trip to the Palace, compliments of Mr. Tomlin himself, and that they were welcome to join them, if they wanted to.

While Crosley was protesting, Duke said, "Hey, Crosley, what's the problem? If they don't, they don't. What's the harm? Give that old pot-bellied Stokely something to look forward to besides that swill they're feeding us."

As Crosley got into the wagon, he thought about what Duke had said, and he knew he was right. What's the harm? The food was awful and why shouldn't they have something to look forward to? But he sure didn't want them to know that he'd never even set foot inside the Palace. Just the thought of going to see all those things Duke talked about made him warm all over, and he sure did plan on going before he left this world. Yessiree! He sure did.

Stokely and Speed told Marvell about the impending visit to Laticias', and Marvell laughed so hard his big, black belly almost split in two. "There ain't ever been the day that Dagmar Tomlin would allow the scum of the earth to violate Miss Laticias'. Not ever been the day!" But Stokely and Speed told him that he was for once wrong, because the word had just come from Camp #8.

Marvell left them in a huff. When he got to the guards' house, he turned triumphantly around, and yelled at Stokely - "Mr. Stokely, I want you to know that Mr. Tomlin ain't given the O.K. on any visiting to Miss Laticia's. He only said that he might have some of the Palace girls visit you here at #9. But he sure as hell ain't given you no permission to high-tail it to Jacksonville!"

On that, even Pot Belly Stokely shook his head and said, "It just ain't the same, Marvell....it just ain't the same."

Marvell then knew he'd have trouble with the guards. So the #8 and #9 workers and guards were rebelling. As R.J. observed the goings on he saw the Duke's work all around him. He informed the others that they were on target - the rebellion was in progress, and the authorities were being undermined.

Duke told Prior Cummins the next day that he was much better, and that he, Crosley, Sam and Lamar planned on going to the Palace come Saturday. "You'd best telegraph Mr. Tomlin so's he kin get some help for you and Cook."

He said it in such a matter-of-fact way, that Cummins just shook his head, indicating that he understood. "And Mr. Cummins, we'd like some of our pay, so's we can have ourselves a good time." Prior Cummins didn't bat an eyelash when he said "telegraph." So Duke knew he was right. He also knew that there was no way they'd be allowed to leave the camps and travel any distance - probably be bush-whacked on the way.

The day was Wednesday. Duke told Pot Belly Stokely the plan. "We'll leave at dawn on Saturday, Stokely, and if any of the other guards want to tag along you'd better have Marvell telegraph Mr. Tomlin, so's he can send some more men to take your place. And you'd better get some spending money out of Marvell's trunk." Stokely and Speed got so excited when he said that, that they joined in on the workers' tunes. Duke sidled up to R.J. and slipped him a note with the proposed plan on it. After reading it, R.J. signaled Duke that he approved.

Saturday morning, about five o'clock, Duke arose - even before Cook was up - and sneaked outside. It was in his favor that Cummins was a quiet man who kept to himself, some days not venturing out at all. He silently rounded the bunkhouse and went toward the cottage. As he suspected, Cummins had the door bolted from the inside. Cat-like, he climbed up on the porch rail and deftly slashed the mosquito netting tacked onto the window. Knife between his teeth and barefooted, he peered in the window, but it was still too dark to see well. He slowly lowered himself into the room, taking a chance that the bed would be on the opposite side of the room.

Duke was in luck, but even if he had not been, with surprise on his side, he would have been able to take care of Mr. Prior Cummins. He got his bearings and could make out the layout of the room. Taking the rag and rope out of his belt, he gagged and tied the groggy man securely. He did not even struggle and Duke figured that he was just glad to be left alive. First, he lit the lamp then tackled the trunk. When the lid wouldn't budge, he asked Cummins where the key was. He nodded towards the dresser. Duke found it underneath a stack of letters, in the top drawer, that had definitely been written by a woman as they smelled heavily of perfume. "Probably from his sister," Duke thought. As he suspected, the trunk held very little money. The foremen probably showed them the same gold every month. What there was, Duke took. He took the gag out of Cummins's mouth, drew his knife and asked him for the code for #9, and for the main station, making it quite clear that he would gladly kill him if he gave him incorrect information. He had judged Cummins. right. The frightened bastard had a yellow streak a mile wide down his back.

He first telegraphed the main station to tell them that Duke had come down with an acute appendicitis attack, so the visit to the Palace was aborted, and the Doc should be sent for. The return message was loud and clear, "Good...let the bastard die!"

He then sent the second message, "I'll contact number 9." The answer came, "All right, Cummins." Duke telegraphed #9. Marvell answered and Duke signaled him that the guards from #8 would be leaving for there in about an hour, and that Tomlin said to let 'em pass. They'd be taken care of.

170

Duke gagged and tied Cummins, hurriedly climbed out the window, securing the net once again, and called to Crosley as he went in the front door of the guards' house. "Hey, ain't you men the ones going to the Palace with me?"

They got a move on, and Duke said, "Oh, Mr. Cummins gave me last month's pay for us to spend at Laticia's," and yelled over the commotion they were making, "We'll get our coffee at #9, men."

Before they left, Duke went into the little alcove off the worker's long room and gagged and tied Cook. Then he went to Beardsley, the first worker he came to, shook him, and put his hand hard over his mouth. He told him what was going on, and as he became more awake, he handed him the map he'd painstakingly drawn. He told Beardsley that he was to lead the men to the Darbyville station, but to give him a good head start. He hoped to have the Union Occupation Army at Darbyville by sometime the next day.

Duke knew that Beardsley had served under General Braxton Bragg in the War, and that he would be capable of controlling the workers. Beardsley gave Duke over an hour, then he unlocked the leg braces of the astonished men with the keys Duke had taken from Cummins, and they headed for the freedom road. Not a single man believed they'd make it.

CHAPTER V THE ESCAPE

Duke and the other guards arrived at camp #9 about an hour after daybreak. He immediately went over to the cook for coffee and put his head inside the workers' building to look for R.J. He was lying on his cot, arms underneath his head and grinning up at Duke.

"Hey, any of you see Stokely around here?" R.J. smiled and shook his head - no. His men glanced at him to get his reaction and R.J. nodded in the affirmative. The Duke was right on target.

Duke walked past the cook, turned and said, "He must be up getting his money from Marvell."

"I ain't seen him this morning, Duke," said the cook as he continued stirring something in the big, iron kettle.

Duke knew full well that that lazy Stokely was still in the guards' house, probably still asleep. He also knew that there was no way he'd be able to gag and tie that black bastard of a Marvell like he had Cummins. This was the most ticklish part of the entire plan and he was apprehensive, but it had to be done.

He looked to make sure no one was around as he climbed the steep steps, his knife drawn, and rapped on the heavy wooden door. No answer. In a disguised voice he said, "Marvell, it's Stokely. Lemme in. I wanna get our money."

He could hear him shuffling and then he slowly opened the door, half asleep. Duke could see past him. He'd already opened the trunk. He pushed in so rapidly Marvell didn't know what had hit that big, black belly as Duke sank the drawn knife all the way to its guard. Marvell's eyes bulged out in disbelief. At the same time Duke closed the door with his boot, got the keys, sack of gold, cut the telegraph wires and quickly closed the door behind him. The entire operation couldn't have taken more than two to three minutes. He was feeling confident as he approached the guard's building and called Stokely and the others.

"Hey, ain't this the day we're going to the Palace? Hey, Stokely, get yore fat, pot belly out here and get some coffee. Man, I'm getting anxious to see Miss Laticia and all those pretty yeller haired girls."

Grinning and shaking with laughter, they sleepily joined Duke and the guards from camp #8 at the cook's for their coffee, while Duke pushed in the door and tossed R.J. the leg iron keys.

172

R.J. and his men were quickly unchained. Duke pulled his horse around to the side by the cook's stand and removed the rope and knives he'd been able to stash there. He walked over to Stokely and his men.

"I'd be willing to bet, Stokely, that you ain't even got your money from Marvell. I'm beginning to think y'all ain't as anxious to get to the Palace as I am. 'Fraid you can't cut the muster? Been too long, huh Stokely? Bet you done forgot how, huh men? That big ole pot belly might just keep you from gettin' inside one of Miss Laticia's pretties."

As Duke teased the laughing men, they left cook's stand and started up the hill toward Marvell's. Duke opened the door and handed R.J. the rope and knives. Walking up behind Stokely he yelled, "Hey, you guys, wait up for me so's I can make sure you get enough money for Laticia's best ladies."

While Duke and the guards walked up the steps to the cottage, R.J. and his men gagged and tied the cook and Dubie and the other guards from #8. Duke reached Marvell's door first and said with an exaggerated sweep of his hands, "After you gentlemen."

When Stokely and the others saw Marvell's eyes rolled to the top of his kinky head and the blood all over his belly they turned toward Duke with their mouths hanging open. By then R.J. had joined Duke at the door and the two of them stood there, just like in the old days, grinning at the disbelieving men.

They gagged and tied them outside the cottage and Duke told them that when they managed to get loose that they'd best high tail it out of the territory, because Tomlin's men would never allow them to get to Jacksonville, or any other place, for that matter. They were as much prisoners as the workers. He then dragged Marvell's trunk out for all to see - turned it upside down and showed them that the money he held in the small pouch was all the money in it and that Tomlin never intended for any of them to leave those camps.

"We've all been duped, men, every last one of us, while that bloated toad sits in his ivory tower and laughs at us. Just like those bastard Yankees did. Just like 'em.".

Duke put the sack of money and the map showing them the road to Darbyville on Marvell's porch and told them that he was telegraphing the authorities from Darbyville about Tomlin's slave camps. He turned to the guards and wished them luck in his commanding army voice. "If you want to throw in with us, gentlemen, just follow the map to Darbyville."

R.J. straddled Marvell's black stallion, while Opie, Bunt, Sheldon and Joe Bob got the guards' horses and provisions from the cook and left #9 camp at a gallop. They would pass only two of Tomlin's camps on the way to Darbyville and Duke had worked both of them. The men would already be working the line, so they didn't expect to see anyone along the way - and they didn't.

A few hours later, they arrived in sleepy Darbyville. Duke didn't want to go to the local marshall, as there was a good chance that he was in cahoots with Tomlin. So he threw Opie over his horse, went into the telegraph office and told the young lady that he was Lt. Stevens of the Union Occupation Army and that he needed to let them know that he had captured the runaway.

"This message I'm sending, young lady, is in our secret code and I'd prefer that you not be a witness to it." The not very attractive, giggling girl joined R.J. on the front stoop and basked in the sweet talking he was laying on her. She tried to avert her eyes from the poor dead Opie. Duke made contact and received the message that a troop of soldiers would arrive within four hours.

Now, Opie was good at playing dead, but R.J. knew he had to have time away from the gathering crowd of curious townsfolk. So he said, "Now folks, this here is the property of the U.S. Army. Where's there a place I can put this low-down deserter till the Lieutenant gets here?"

Someone said, "Joe Stump'll let you house him in his barn over there by the stable."

So R.J. led Opie's horse into the barn, and not too soon either, as Opie's face was getting beet red. He dropped him into a pile of straw in the darkest corner he could find and found Joe Stump to tell him that the barn would be off limits to everyone but the Union soldiers.

"You'uns don't look like no soldiers to me, mister," said Mr. Stump, and R.J. replied, "Well, Mr. Stump, we are in disguise. If we were wearing our uniforms we'd never have caught this no good deserter, now would we?"

Joe Stump let that sink in a minute and nodded his head. "Well, yessirree, I guess you're right, young fellow."

So R.J. went to the corner to tell Opie he'd slip him some water and maybe something to eat from the boarding house kitchen

174

later. But for now, he had to play dead. Some curious kid just might take a notion to come in there and find out that he sure as hell wasn't dead, and then their arses would be hauled out of their in a sling.

Opie assured him that he'd play as dead as a doornail if he'd just get him some water and maybe, as a bonus for playing dead so good, that sweet little telegraph operator. He chuckled with his hand over his mouth to muffle the sound.

R.J. shook his head and said, "Opie, that little gal has probably given her favors to every available man in Darbyville. The only thing she could give you is a bad case of clap."

"Oh, go on with you, R.J. I was just foolin'". And R.J. said as he left the barn, "Like hell you were, Opie. Like hell!"

The boarding house dining room was not unlike the others R.J. and Duke had eaten in - bowls of good winter greens and butter beans, platters of corn bread and thinly sliced country ham, smoked just right, with redeye gravy to go on the saucer sized biscuits. R.J. told Duke that it was undoubtedly the best meal he'd ever eaten in his entire life. A month of swill not fit for a hog made him appreciate good home fare.

While they ate and slowly savored every mouthful, they relived some of their war time exploits, while keeping a watchful eye out the window. No activity as yet. The town was the same as on any other day. Suddenly, Joe Bob rode up and burst into the dining room. "They're here, R.J.! They're here, Duke!"

The empty plates were hurriedly pushed aside and their chairs scraped the rough hewn pine floor. They hurriedly left the boarding house. There were only six of them. Duke approached the young lieutenant and introduced himself and R.J. The lieutenant looked from one to the other in open suspicion. R.J. quickly and formally invited him to join them for coffee so they could give him their report.

Duke was very uneasy about dealing with one so young. He decided to take the lead and approach him in a strict, military manner. He was right in his appraisal of Lt. Godby. He was indeed a newly commissioned officer and a by-the-book man. R.J. followed Duke's lead, and after discussing the matter, the three decided on a plan. An agreement was satisfactorily reached, and the three men left the Darbyville Boarding House with a newly found respect for the military training from both sides of the Mason-Dixon Line.

175

As Duke and R.J. approached the barn, Duke turned to R.J., "R.J., he's green - a good man with book learning - but R.J., I'm worried - no field training. I'm not sure how he'll act under fire, and you can bet your scalded ass Tomlin will have his goons armed to the teeth. I can't believe the colonel sent only six men - but then he probably thought it was a wild goose chase."

R.J. agreed. They sat in the dark corner of Mr. Stump's barn and discussed the plan with Opie, Joe Bob, Sheldon and Bunt. Their concentration was interrupted by an unusual noise coming from the main street of town. Bunt ran to the barn door and started howling, "R.J., you gotta see this. R.J., you just gotta see this!"

The most rag-tag looking group a body could conjure up was strutting down the dust-swirled main street of Darbyville, Pot Belly and Speed in the lead. R.J. and Duke walked out of the barn, and on seeing them, tried their darndest to control their laughter, so the very dedicated "Workers and Guards Army" wouldn't think them unappreciative of their practiced efforts.

It was apparent that they had worked very hard on their marching all the way from camp #9. They had all served in the War, and proudly. As R.J. and Duke walked back to the barn, they were joined by Pot Belly and Speed. They made every effort to treat them equally and with respect. But it wasn't easy, and the derogatory facial expressions they got from Opie and Joe Bob were not appreciated. Even so, their arrival was a welcome break from the serious business of wiping out Tomlin's operation.

Lt. Godby, Duke, R.J. and their men, plus the mule-drawn wagons filled with the ragged soldiers from camps #8 and #9, moved out at daybreak the next day. Arms had been confiscated from some of the townspeople and the plan was in effect. By nightfall they had passed by four of Tomlin's deserted camps. When they came upon Camp #8, it had been completely razed, a burning hulk. They made camp alongside the tall pines and live oaks on the west shoulder of No Name Creek, and before daybreak Cook had started the coffee for the excited men.

It was decided that the guards and workers would be led down Dagmar Tomlin's long driveway by Lt. Godby, R.J. and Duke, with all the military bearing they could command.

As Duke, R.J. and Lt. Godby rehearsed the maneuvers again with Pot Belly, Speed and Beardsley, who were so filled with their new found importance that it was difficult for them to keep straight faces during the conferences, R.J. turned to Duke and said, as he shielded his face from them, "Gawd Almighty, Duke, I think we gave birth to three bloomin' generals." Duke roared, and it was all the more comical because of the intensity and seriousness of Pot Belly and the others.

Between camps #8 and #7, there was no contact with anyone. The entire area was deserted. As the men approached Camp #6, one of Lt. Godby's scouts reported activity in that camp. They were reported to be leaving the bunkhouses with mules pulling wagons loaded with supplies, and were headed north.

They were only about a mile outside Tomlin's compound, and R.J. and Duke were so keyed up you could feel the electricity. Their senses were aware of every sound and smell, of each subtle movement. As they looked at each other they were both remembering the anticipation of battle - not fear nor concern - just the thrill of the anticipated force.

Lt. Godby's scouts were given orders to scout the area directly around the mansion and report back immediately. It was obvious to the men that Tomlin was abandoning the camps and would no doubt make a stand at the hub of the wheel, his beautiful white columned home. They halted the march and awaited word from the two scouts.

It was toward mid-afternoon when the scouts rode in with their report. Tomlin had turned his home into a fortress, as predicted. There was so much activity on the grounds surrounding the house that it was difficult for the scouts to get a good idea of the number of men, or how many guns they had, or where the ammunition was stored.

Duke interjected his thoughts after the scouts told of their findings. He was positive that the two-storied house had a basement or cellar. When he had been there before on his mission, he had noticed on either side of the back door, two huge slanted ground doors. He had thought at the time that it wouldn't be necessary for Tomlin to have that large a root cellar, and he wondered what he could be storing there. He had seen the stable and the barn, and they appeared to be of average size. He was sure that there was a full sized basement that was probably used to store supplies: guns, ammunition, medical supplies and any other things needed during a siege. Tomlin was crafty and by his very nature would have prepared for any eventuality.

177

The plan the three men had formulated was sound, but a way had to be found to destroy the ammunition. Pot Belly Stokely wandered over to the three men, who were squatting underneath a big live oak. He interrupted and said, "I know I've got no business putting in my two cents, but I couldn't help but hear ya." He coughed, and his sneaky grin and his beady eyes would have betrayed him anyway, so he might as well have confessed.

"Well, if ya wanna know, I was trying hard to hear ya." R.J. exasperatedly said, "For Gawd's sake, Stokely, get on with it. We ain't got all day."

"Well, R.J., I always had a fondness for my red guard's suit Mr. Tomlin had us wear for inspections and the like. I just couldn't bear to leave it behind so I brung it, and so did Speed. Now if'n one or two of us would mingle in with all those guards all dressed up in red, maybe we could get into that cellar and maybe blow it up or something like that - if we had some gunpowder - that is - maybe, huh?"

Duke let out a small "Yeehaw," and said, "Stokely, you know R.J. and me was just talking about you havin' the makings of a Goddamned general. Weren't we, R.J. Yeehaw!" and they all joined in.

"With all the commotion around Dagmar Tomlin's compound, two more uniformed guards won't be noticed. And who were the dagburndest demolition experts in the 23rd? R.J. Skinner and Duke Hempstead. At your service, Sir," he added.

Pot Belly and Duke had about twelve inches difference in their waists, but R.J. and Speed were the same size. Duke threw the britches to Cook and told him to sew up the sides and he'd just tuck the too-big shirt in. He didn't want to draw attention to himself with a disheveled appearance. He had four days' growth of beard, and by the time he and R.J. got to the compound, it'd be almost dark. Their chances of seeing any of the guards who had come out to check on Duke's faked appendicitis attack were slim, since they were Tomlin's top men and would probably not associate with the camp guards.

They prepared for their mission further by rubbing soot from Cook's pot on their four days' stubble, and decided it best to wait till after dark to enter the heavily guarded compound. Good-byes and good luck were passed among the men, and R.J. and Duke started off on foot.

178

Duke knew that the stable was backed up to the south ridge of trees and felt that that was the obvious place for entry. Besides, he wanted to make darned sure that Tomlin's fancy rig and stallions were still there and that he hadn't made his getaway.

Spring was approaching, and new growth appeared on the maples and oaks, but a good thicket remained. As they crouched beside the stable, they could hear the activity of many men laughing and talking, but still could see no one. As they crawled in closer, they could hear them more distinctly. They were apparently bivouacked in the barn and stable.

R.J. tapped Duke on the shoulder when he saw the stallions outside the stable, and followed the sounds to the back of the house. Sure enough, the cellar doors were open, and men were going in and out, unloading boxes and kegs from the wagons and storing 'em in the cellar. It was now or never, their glances said. They sauntered over to one of the wagons and started unloading right alongside the others. When they walked down the steps into the cellar, their eyes almost bugged out. Never in all their army days had they seen anything like it - that whole place was an arsenal.

Hell, Tomlin could hold out for months, they realized. It'd take the entire US Army to budge him. They saw what they needed to see and worked their way over behind a tall stack of boxes next to the wall. It was easy to duck into the shadows that the lantern provided without drawing attention to themselves.

"One big problem remains," Duke whispered. "What if the doors are locked from the outside when they're through tonight? We'll have to wait 'til mornin', and we'll never be able to pull it off, Skinner."

"Besides, that bastard Tomlin will have taken off. I'm sure of it! It's now or never, ole buddy."

He abruptly left the security of their hiding place, and told R.J. to follow his lead. He rummaged around the boxes, appearing not to care who saw him, and finally asked one of the men, "Where the hell is the gun powder and fuses? He's gonna have our asses if we don't get a move on."

"Over there by the south wall back of the sand bags. They don't let up on you, do they?" the young guard complained.

Duke replied, "They sure as hell don't," and they walked hurriedly over to the gunpowder and boxes of fuses, and lifted as much as they could carry. They climbed up the cellar stairs,

179

mumbling about never getting a breather, not even for a swig or a smoke anymore, and the others chimed in in agreement.

It was a pitch black, starless night, and they rushed behind the barn to the safety of the thicket. Both sat down with a huge sigh of relief and rolled silently on the ground trying to muffle their laughter.

"Gawd, I can't believe you'd have the nerve to just up and ask that goon where they had stashed the gunpowder, Duke. I just can't believe it!" They spent the next hour reliving similar incidents in the War, and they both knew that they had missed the comradeship of those bygone years.

R.J. was the first to bring it up. "Hey, Duke, after we blow up old pig-face Tomlin's ass, you wanna team up again?"

The Duke took several minutes to think on it and replied, "R.J., we've had some good times and tonight's gonna be one more of 'em, if all goes well. But I now know that I've gotta get back to Montgomery one more time. Then, sure...well, Hell, there ain't never been a better team than we are," and he smacked him a hard one on the shoulder. As he did, R.J. thought to himself, "You know, I've never seen the Duke lose his temper. Not once. Not even a single time."

The sky lit up for miles around when the explosion interrupted the starless spring night, and the noise accompanying it was deafening. As planned, Lt. Godby, Bunt, Opie, Joe Bob, Sheldon, Pot Belly, Speed and Beardsley, with their guns drawn, led the workers and guards irregulars up the manicured lawn to the black, burning remains of Dagmar J. Tomlin and his mansion. The guards who had been asleep in the barn and stable did not even draw their weapons when they saw them approaching. Tomlin's empty black carriage stood beside the matched stallions, which were unconcernedly munching the fresh shoots of green grass.

R.J. and Duke came around the south thicket and joined them in the rear of the column, and as Duke passed the group of weary, red-coated, disbelieving guards, he turned to them and said with a straight face, "Oh, uh - thanks for the gun powder, men," and saluted them in his best military fashion. R.J. almost fell to the ground laughing hysterically, uncontrollably at his friend the Duke.

That was the last time they saw each other. Duke headed back to Alabama, and R.J. and his gang headed back to Jacksonville to take care of one Mr. Randy MacDougall. Unfortunately for them, Mr. MacDougall had disappeared from sight. So they robbed his replacement and then hit the Springfield Bank as a farewell to Jacksonville and Northeast Florida.

CHAPTER VI THE REUNION

It took R.J. and Satan almost two weeks of slow, torturous traveling to reach the creek willows and Juanita's place. He traveled by night and slept most of the day, and lived off of squirrel and fish, roasted with no salt or seasoning. It was long past nightfall when he walked Satan over to the spot where Juanita's cans had scattered all over creation, and as he felt the creek's grassy edge where it widened and flowed into the river, he could remember her soft, smooth, yielding body.

He lowered himself and moaned, "Oh God, this ground's gotta be the hardest ground in all of Florida," as he sat down on the firmly packed sand of the high bluff above the crooked Caloosahatchee River. Satan was skittish - had been ever since he got there. Now, R.J. knew if his horse was skittish, there sure as hell was a reason. He was rubbing his neck and quietly telling him to calm down, when out of the corner of his eye he saw something move in the tall maiden cane. He slowly, deliberately cocked his gun. He rubbed Satan's sweaty neck, trying to pierce the darkness for more movement. He was positive someone was hidden in the cane and willows that grew thickly at the mouth of the creek and on the sand ridge that edged the river.

Suddenly a rock whizzed past his head and he said out loud, "There ain't anyone in this entire world stupid enough to throw a rock at an enemy in the dead of night but Opie Miller. Hey, Opie, it's R.J." It never occurred to R.J. that it would be anyone else.

"R.J., oh Lordie! R.J., I was hoping! Oh, how I was praying it'd be you or Bunt or Joe Bob! Oh, R.J.!" and he fell at his feet. It was then that he realized that Opie was out of his head. While he stroked his hot, dry face, he told him reassuringly that everything would be all right.

Opie's horse wandered over toward them. He was probably starved half to death, too, R.J. thought, as almost every bone in Opie's body was tugging at his skin. He remembered that he still had fish in his rucksack, and slapped Opie, trying to revive him. When that failed, he went through the thick moon vines and down the steep bank to the river and got some cool water to bathe his face. When Opie finally came to, he gave him the fish to eat and he tackled it like a crazed animal of a man, only to throw it up almost instantly.

182

R.J. told him that he'd make their camp up underneath the willows and the cane that was tall enough to hide the horses, and that come morning he'd get them a meal fit for a king. As R.J. watched over him, Opie drifted off to sleep with a relieved sigh and a smile on his haggard face. He was a simple man and needed someone to tell him when to walk, talk and breathe. Poor dumb Opie. He had been a good soldier because he did exactly what he was told - never questioning a command or even thinking to.

Morning arrived when it shouldn't have. The soft drizzle on R.J.'s face made him turn over to shield it from the unwelcome light. He got up, kicked hard at a clump of maiden cane and bent it over the sleeping Opie. He took a look around and realized that they'd never had better cover, so he climbed back under the bent cane and moon vines into his damp bed roll and fell into an exhausted sleep.

Opie was swatting an insect and beginning to stir when R.J. awakened and realized he'd have to get some food for them and the horses. Opie hadn't been able to handle that wild land and was so weak that he'd be a real burden if R.J. didn't start foraging immediately.

His first thoughts turned to Juanita. He felt sure she'd jump at the chance to help him out again. The thought of that roasted chicken over the open pit under the star-filled night on the bank of the Caloosahatchee made him smile to himself in his remembering - especially after the hell he'd been through since. "But that remembering's not gonna help my poor empty belly and half dead Opie," he thought, as he climbed up higher on the ridge to scout his surroundings.

There wasn't much cover between the river and the Graves' small spread, once you got past the vine covered trees, just sawgrass, some custard apple trees, a few cypresses and rubber trees. But chance it he had to. R.J. took his rucksack off Satan and told Opie he was off to get some breakfast, but before he left he walked down to the river's edge and filled Opie's canteen with the cool water. He patted the still Opie and told him to stay put and he'd be back soon.

There was no activity at the Graves' place. But then he had slept late and their early morning chores would probably have already been done. He looked up at the sun filled blue sky. Must be near 10:00 o'clock, he decided. Mrs. Graves is probably preparing the dinner meal and Juanita was probably helping her. About then the kitchen door slammed and a fired-up Juanita Jane Graves came tearing out of there like a bucking bronco.

R.J. smiled as he looked at that yellow-white hair cascading down her back and that determined I'll-be-damned-if-I-do set to her spine. He'd never met one like her. Feisty, yes. Oh, yes, he'd broken a lot of feisty fillies in his time, but never the girl-woman Miss Juanita was. She was starving for excitement and adventure. As he peered through the parted cane he knew she'd be by his side come nightfall.

Mrs. Graves followed Juanita - her fists planted determinedly on each side of her flowered apron. He couldn't make out what she was saying, but he sure could tell by her actions that she was none too happy about Miss Juanita Jane Graves. He scrunched down in the cane and parted it just a little. Mrs. Graves seemed to be explaining something to Juanita.

There Juanita stood, teeth clinched and a scowl on her brow, with defiant hands on her rounded hips and tapping her foot. Oh, how he wanted to swat that bottom to see her get all riled up. Mrs. Graves turned abruptly and went back inside the small cabin. He quickly glanced around to see if there was anyone else about. He put his two fingers in his mouth and whistled loudly, standing up slightly as he did.

She didn't look his way. Guess she didn't hear me, he figured. He stood erectly and was about to whistle again when she turned. Her mouth flew open and she covered it quickly and began running toward him unashamedly, slowly at first, then at a faster pace. When she reached R.J., she stopped abruptly and said in a matter of fact voice, just like she had seen him yesterday, "Hey, R.J. How are you?"

Juanita lowered her deep, blue eyes for fear he'd see her embarrassment at her apparent anxiousness. He didn't let on that he had noticed, but her enthusiasm excited him and he wanted to take her right there in the bright morning light on that ridge of prickly maiden cane.

"I'm all right, Juanita. At least there's nothin' wrong with me that one of your Pa's Plymouth Rock chickens couldn't fix up."

At that, Juanita began to laugh, and he joined in as they gazed hungrily at each other. Juanita finally broke the mood. "I've been reading about you in *The Ft. Myers Times*. Said you and

184

your gang stole some gold. Is that true?" And the way she said it you'd have thought she was discussing the weather or what color dress she was going to wear to the social. R.J. just stared at her in total amazement. Most girls would be having some kind of fit about a robbery, but not Juanita.

He couldn't figure her out. She sure wasn't stupid. So he answered her cautiously, "Yes, Juanita, we did, but God knows we paid for it. Bunt died of snake bite in that miserable swamp and poor Opie is half-crazed over the ridge in the cane, and I don't know where my own brother is and no tellin' where that devil Sheldon is." He figured he'd play on her sympathy, but he needn't have concerned himself about her feelings.

"Don't have to worry yourself about Sheldon, R.J. *The Ft. Myers Times* said he'd been killed, and his doubloons recovered. But I don't know about your brother." Everything she said was matter of fact. If this is what happened, then so be it.

As he looked at her yellow-white tresses, he began stroking them away from her face. She knew she longed to put his arms around her - caress her, take her. But Juanita was a practical girl-woman with a logical and precise way of thinking, and not even the handsome bank robber, R.J. Skinner, could put a brake on her wheel of thought. Nor could he encourage her with those hungry eyes to stray from her determined pursuit.

"R.J.," she said simply and to the point, "You and Opie need food. I'll bring your dinner in about two hours. We'll need some kind of signal." They discussed their signal and then she was gone. Very cautiously, she took her time trying to avoid the hazards of the uneven pasture between the ridge and her house. R.J. watched her. He knew she could feel his eyes on her, but she didn't priss or sashay to tantalize him like most girls would.

Still bent over, he made his way through the itchy cane until he got back to the river's ridge. Opie had not stirred. At first R.J. thought he had fallen back asleep. But when he called to him there was no answer. It was then he saw the ants and flies swarming all over his mud-covered pants and R.J. knew his longtime soldier buddy was gone.

The two horses stood unconcernedly by, eating some wire grass they'd found underneath the custard apple trees. R.J., tears sliding down his cheeks, angrily kicked the clumps of cane, and in a frustrating effort, bent them over Opie's still body. He wasn't

185

a sentimental man, but he knew a part of his life had ended with Opie's death and he was saddened by it.

"I'll have Juanita bring a shovel before those God-damned buzzards find him!" he said, as he continued to angrily kick the maiden cane. Soon, Opie was covered by the huge mound. R.J., unashamed by his tearful reaction, shrugged his shoulders and went to the creek to bathe his streaked face.

He hadn't been there long when he thought he heard something. He dashed back up the bank to the cane ridge. It couldn't be Juanita because it was too soon, and she didn't give their signal. R. J. couldn't see a thing, but he could hear the approaching horse. He knew whoever it was would surely see the horses if they went over the ridge toward the muck land. If they did, he'd have to force himself to leave his sanctuary and take care of the situation. No matter who it was, he couldn't afford to lose the horses. Not now. He'd gone through too much.

The noise stopped. He couldn't hear a sound. Then he heard a horse whinny. He rose slowly from the midst of the thick cane, and as he did, Joe Bob appeared - standing not three feet from him with every tooth in his head gleaming. They rushed into each other's arms. R.J. stepped back and looked at his brother. Joe Bob looked great. He was clean shaven and none the worse for wear.

"God, Joe Bob, you even smell good!" R.J. exclaimed. He kept his fatherly arm around his brother's shoulder as they walked down to the river to water his horse.

"When you left, R.J., I wasn't sure I'd be able to make it alone. I couldn't go into that swamp. I just couldn't! So I circled around to the coast and headed north right back to Punta Rassa. I decided to follow the Caloosahatchee and ended up at Alva. Not much of a town - just a small settlement. Made out that I was a drifter lookin' for my long lost brother who had come to Florida to work on a ranch. Shoot - wasn't nothin' to it. Folks were real friendly like. Even got a job at the stable and, R.J., found me the cutest little ole gal you'd ever want to see. Rose is her name. Works for Miss Tatum taking in sewing, and helps out at the dry goods when they need her."

"Oh, R.J., she's some kind of sweet." He hit his thigh a smart slap as he gestured about Rose. R.J. smiled at him and said in a low voice, "I'm real glad for you, little brother. Real glad." He

186

glanced toward the mound of cane and Opie, and shook his head sadly.

"R.J., I sure hope you don't mind if I go back to Alva for her on the way back to Alabama. I'm already hankering for her, and it's only been a day."

R.J. looked at his brother - really looked at him. He, too, was tired of running. He, too, wanted to get back to Alabama and start a new life. His thoughts turned to Juanita then, and he and Joe Bob with their arms around each other turned back to the cane ridge. As they did, R.J. told him about Bunt dying that terrible death, and about Opie and what Juanita had told him she had read regarding Sheldon.

It was just the two of them now, just like they had started out. They sat on the ridge and talked animatedly. They wished that after they left the Tomlin compound they had headed right back to Montgomery with the Duke. They weren't any better off than they had been, except for the gold.

"But a price on your head don't take the place of freedom," R.J. said, and Joe Bob agreed. "It sure ain't a fair exchange, no sirree!"

R.J. quickly put his hand on Joe Bob's gun arm and told him not to move...it was Juanita bringing them their dinner. Then he started to laugh so hard at her pathetic croaker sound that she got plumb spitting mad and soon they were all three rolling in the maiden cane releasing their pent-up anxiety.

Juanita was the first to speak. "Where's Opie? I brought him something special."

The brothers looked at each other, and their saddened expressions answered her question.

"Oh well...it's good for well folks, too." she said philosophically. R.J. started to laugh so hard, he almost choked on Mrs. Graves' hot flaky biscuit.

"Juanita, so help me, you do have a way of putting words in their proper places," he finally said. Juanita just looked at him quizzically, not knowing what on earth he was talking about. "Yep, Juanita, your words are sparse, but right on target," and he continued to laugh as he greedily ate some of her pa's Plymouth Rock chicken.

She glared at him, not understanding his thinking. "Men do go on in the silliest fashion," she thought. "He must be suffering

187

from the sun and starvation."

R.J. and Joe Bob were so stuffed they could hardly move from their maiden cane bed. Juanita whispered to R.J. that she best get back before her ma missed her. He looked at her questioningly, and she nodded yes. Joe Bob pretended not to notice their silent exchange.

R.J. walked beside her up to the edge of the cane, then she hurriedly went over the ridge and out of sight. She had told him she'd return later with the shovel to bury Opie, but her words meant much more to him.

As they relaxed on the cane bed, R.J. stated that they had to make plans. Now! They had to have a plan and a backup plan for their return to Alabama. First, no one was looking for two men and two women. When he said that, Joe Bob smiled his gratitude, thinking of his Rose. Secondly, no one knew that they had been to La Belle except Juanita, and he knew she'd never tell a living soul. And no one at Alva suspected that Joe Bob was associated with the gang. So all that was in their favor.

They worked and re-worked their plan, sitting underneath the lively, green creek willows, while their horses ate contentedly nearby. R.J. was anxiously checking the sun's descent, wanting it to hurry its adieu over the Everglades, so his eager Juanita could warm his lair in the seclusion of the starless night.

Their plans completed, Joe Bob said he was going to take a little nap before Juanita brought their supper and shovel. He hurriedly walked past Opie's mound, not wanting to even glance in that direction. He kicked the root section of the tall cane, pushing it over with his boot, and when he was about to place his blanket over the prickly cane, saw someone appear below the ridge. It was not Juanita. He called to R.J., and said disgustedly that their plans would have to be changed - they had been spotted.

The medium sized man, about R.J.'s age, walked slowly up the ridge. He was whistling to himself and carrying what appeared to be rope and a bucket. R.J. hailed him, and the man looked around, following his voice, and saw them. He quickly walked over to them and introduced himself.

"Howdy. I'm Randolph Martin, Mr. Graves' son-in-law. Don't believe we've met. You a friend of the family?"

That was all the opening R.J. needed. Mr. Randolph Martin played right into his expert hands.

"No, we are not acquainted with Mr. uh - Graves did you say his name is? We were just passing by on our way up to Ft. Basinger." He gestured toward Joe Bob. "This is my brother Marcus, and I'm Luther, better known as Luke. We have kin up toward the Kissimmee Basin and thought we'd head that way come morning. We're just stopping momentarily to water our horses and ourselves. Marcus and I were wondering about the fishing in this glorious river. We've heard about the huge catfish that abound here...."

"Oh, yes!" he exclaimed. Well, Randolph Martin was a talker. He began a long, tedious and tiring account of the fishing in general, and his trotline business in particular. Apparently, he had his trotline up close to town, but his pa-in-law, who didn't take to fishing too much - he was really more into show caliber chickens, Plymouth Rock and Rhode Island Reds, more than fishing - thought he should try his lines off'n his property for a change. He got "cats" so big that one would feed his family for a week - and on and on he droned.

R.J. was holding rein on his patience, and Joe Bob was agreeing with everything he said and rolling his eyes at R.J. in disgust. Finally, R.J. spoke up, "Randolph, seems to me if you don't get that line out before nightfall, you might just come eye to eye with an alligator."

Randolph thought on that for it seemed like forever, and then agreed. He proceeded to wade out into the mouth of the shallow creek. He just kept going, turned around and yelled at the two of them, "See what I mean? You have to walk slam to the center of the river 'fore you get to good catfish depth," and as he said it, he stumbled and almost went under. He turned around again to report to the strangers, "See what I mean? Got lots of holes in this river."

He cast his corked trotline out, anchored both ends with big rocks and waded back to shore. In the meantime, R.J. and Joe Bob had a chance to talk about another plan. Joe Bob said, "Maybe if we cozy up to Randolph, we can get ourselves invited to the Graves' house for a real supper, and you can court your Juanita proper like."

A slow smirk spread over R.J.'s face. "That'd be just too easy, little brother. There are probably wanted posters on every wall in this whole state, with a description of us and our horses, for any

189

keen-eyed bounty hunter to latch onto. Joe Bob, I'm not thinking that's such a good idea."

Joe Bob insisted that it was just as good an idea as Juanita's leaving a note for her folks, telling them that she was running away to seek fame and fortune, and it wasn't no sense for them to come after her, 'cause she sure wasn't staying in "No two-bit Glades town." But then, Joe Bob didn't know Juanita, and R.J. figured that the Graves were well aware of their daughter's high-strung, stubborn-as-a-mule antics, and the "note" plan was Juanita through and through.

Randolph Martin talked all the while he was walking to the shore, but they paid no attention to his babbling until he said, "I'm sure my ma-in-law would be happy to have you for supper, since it appears you haven't provided for it."

But R.J. spoke up quickly and said, "On the contrary, Randolph, Marcus and I dined earlier. We had a delightful chicken dinner and have plenty left over for a nice cold supper."

"Now why's he putting on airs, I'd like to know," Joe Bob thought, as he glared at R.J. "He knows full well we ain't got no supper. Doggone you, R.J. Skinner!"

Randolph gulped and said with as much class as he could muster, "I'm indeed happy that you won't be doing without. I just thought that since I didn't see you startin' any fire or anything, you might be wanting."

R.J. walked up to him and extended his hand in a brisk, formal fashion to thank him for his hospitality before he said another word. Randolph's pale, vapid, blue eyes were impressed by the cut of the stranger, and his milky white hand tried to return R.J.'s gentlemanly handshake.

Joe Bob turned to R.J. as he watched him descend the cane ridge, and in a plumb disgusted voice asked him, "Why in tarnation did you turn down supper? The Lord only knows when we'll eat decent again! We could have got by with it for one time, R.J. Honest we could."

He smiled at him and replied, "My dear brother Joe Bob, fair Juanita will supply the R.J. Skinner Gang, better known as Marcus and Luther, with a sumptuous repast," and he prissed around and pretended to be a fancy gentleman, like in the plays they'd sneaked in to see in Montgomery, when they were both just lads roaming the streets. Joe Bob roared with laughter and slapped his knees

190

with amusement, as he sat down on the cane seat.

The sun seemed to take forever to set. The color washed sky made even R.J. and Joe Bob appreciate the spectacular beauty of the timeless Glades, and the miles and miles of shoreless grass, with only the majestic sabal palms interrupting its vastness.

Darkness was immediate once the sun set. They had taken their aired out blanket rolls off the willow branches, and had set up camp, before the light failed. Now that they were discovered, they could have a fire. There was no lack of broken limbs around the river bank, and plenty of dry grass with which to start it.

Joe Bob had placed large rocks he'd gathered from the river's edge to build a base for the hoped for chicken. But no Juanita. While he was tending the camp fire, R.J. busied himself making a cave-like tunnel in the midst of the maiden cane for his and Juanita's lair. He had carefully spread his and Opie's blanket rolls over the foot high cane, and was smiling to himself, when Joe Bob broke into his thoughts.

"She can't come 'til way past dark, R.J. You best not be expectin' her. You know her folks are probably suspicious of strangers, no matter what that dumb-ass son-in-law told them about us. You know full well they'll sleep anxious-like, and Juanita's a smart girl. She'll be awaiting their heavy slumber."

R.J. knew he was right. "It's just so long seemin' since good things have been mine, Joe Bob - so very long."

When he looked at R.J. in the dim firelight, he saw an unexpected tear slip out of the corner of his eye. His own heart tightened with concern at his brother's sadness.

Joe Bob had been the lucky one. He hadn't had to witness Bunt's and Opie's deaths, and he was relieved he had been spared. "R.J.'ll come out of this misery," he said to himself. "He'll be good as new in no time at all. I just hope he don't get the fever, like he did up Old Town way." They sure didn't need that right now, he thought, as he swatted the gnats that had begun to swarm. "Good thing they don't bite," he yelled at R.J. "Lordy, we'd be dead by mornin' if they did."

The fire had died down to bright, yellow-white coals in the rock rim Joe Bob had concocted. It was difficult for him to say goodnight, but he was so tired, he kept nodding and almost pitched right into the fire. R.J. was so quiet he was concerned. He wasn't used to him being like that. Finally, he just gave up.

191

"R.J., I'm just real tired. I'm almost sick to my stomach, I'm so tired. I'll just turn in," and he headed for the cane bed he'd made earlier. R.J. looked at him like he wasn't sure he knew just who he was. He blinked a few times, and his voice was far away and different sounding.

"Goodnight, Joe Bob," and no more.

Joe Bob went into the dark, away from the dim firelight, and smoothed out his bed roll, pulled the leftover flap of flannel over his lean, long body, and fell into an exhausted sleep. He heard the motion in the distance, but was too numb to move.

R.J. heard it, too. He was afraid to hope. He sat motionless, breathing shallowly. She appeared above the soft glow of the fire - ghost like - her golden tresses loosened and billowed into the shadow of the night. She wore a soft, angelic expression and called his name softly. R.J. thought he was dreaming, when suddenly she was in his arms, stroking his sad face, kissing his forehead, cheeks - lips. Lightly at first then hungrily, sensing his need of her with her keen animal instincts - his depression fueled her passion.

Morning arrived before Joe Bob could accustom himself to the glare emanating from the diamond ripplets that were shimmering on the deep, blue water's surface. He grinned and stretched, and rubbed the hard sleep out of his eyes on his way to wash up in the clear water. The tiny minnows swiftly darted to and fro away from his hands, as he teased them with the splashing.

When he turned to the ridge of cane and willows, the cotton fluffy clouds danced overhead, floating. "Today I'll be heading for my Rose," he addressed them. "My body knows it. We're Alabama bound!"

He was hesitant about approaching R.J.'s bed, so he busied himself gathering wood for a fire that might never see a coffee pot and meal - thinking if Juanita hadn't brought supplies, they'd have to do without.

On his way up the sloping embankment, he heard him call. Hesitant, he turned, and a soft smile warmed his entire body. R.J. was standing straight and tall, filled with his usual energy. Joe Bob wanted to let out the rebel yell, but restrained himself. The less ruckus they made, the better off they'd be. He walked toward him. Juanita was nowhere in sight, but Joe Bob knew she'd been there. He'd never seen such a change come over a man.

"Thought I'd check out Opie's horse for coffee and meal, R.J. My stomach is growling so hard it plumb woke me up."

"Don't have to, little brother. Juanita's corn dodgers will take the growl out of it," and he tossed him a couple he pulled out of his jacket pocket. "But you can get the water boiling for the coffee. I'm going to take care of Opie 'fore those red-eyed devils find him."

Toward morning, just before daybreak, he had walked Juanita back to the field next to her house, talking softly and planning their tomorrows. He found he could talk to her. He'd never been able to talk to a woman like he could to Juanita. Her directness just seemed to make it so easy.

It was daylight when she returned with the shovel. She quickly kissed him on his cheek, with both hands caressing his bearded face - then she was gone. "I think my Juanita's got some Florida bobcat in her. Lordy, she's quick to move - just like light." But she was also quick to think. As she rounded the corner of the kitchen, there was her ma, hands planted on her hips, getting ready to jump down Juanita's throat.

"Oh-ooo, Oh-ooo," Juanita moaned. "I didn't want to wake you and Pa, so I've been walking and walking out in the cool air. I think I'm coming down sick with something awful. My stomach is aching, Ma. Oh, how my stomach is aching!"

Mrs. Graves soon replaced her "Where in the world have you been, Juanita Jane Graves?" with "Oh, honey. Must have been that side meat in the greens we had last night. It didn't sit too good with me, either."

"Come in this warm kitchen this instant, honey. I'll fix you up with some chamomile tea and it'll soothe that ache away in no time. It's just that when I woke up, and you weren't anywheres about - well - I just didn't know where you had high-tailed off to this time. You know you've been so strange actin' of late. Your pa and me are real worried about you." And she put her motherly arm around her shoulder, and Juanita rested her blond head on her mother's breast, just like she had done since she was a babe, sixteen years ago.

R.J. told Joe Bob about his and Juanita's plan - he was in accord. They got the horses tended to, and were finishing up their coffee, when Juanita came tearing up that ridge with her hair flying out behind her.

"R.J., we've got to get out of here now! Right now!" and

193

as she was saying it, she was rolling up his bed roll. Just before she ran down the embankment, R.J. stopped her.

"Juanita! Hey, Juanita! Slow down! What's happened?" She looked at him, and the tears began to well up in her huge eyes. "That old Randolph Martin. That's what's happened! He came riding up to the house this mornin', just a bustin' to tell Ma and Pa about you. Your faces are plastered all over creation, he said. He was in Mr. Burns' Dry Goods, and lo and behold! When he looked up to pay for Bonnie's meal and coffee, darned if he wasn't staring right at the two gents he'd met at his pa-in-law's, and them making out like they were fancy dans, he said. Well, he proceeded to have Luellen telegraph the sheriff at Ft. Basinger to tell him he'd captured the R.J. Skinner Gang - at least two of 'em. Not captured exactly, but he could take them to their whereabouts. The reward is up to $300.00 now."

They looked at each other, and as Juanita told them the rest of the story, they quickly assisted her in getting all their gear on the horses.

"He rode real fast out here to tell Ma and Pa not to go to the river, since the two desperados were there, just a waitin' for a chance to rob them - maybe even kill them. Well, I spoke up and told him that he must be daft. That I'd been sick to my stomach before daybreak, and was out walking in the cool morning, and I'd walked up on the high bluff, where I could see a far piece, and sure wasn't no men or horses anywhere that the eye could see. As a matter of fact, I told him, I saw some fresh signs of some horses and that they were for sure headed for Ft. Thompson, and probably then on to Ft. Basinger, since there wasn't nothin' 'fore there."

Now Randolph didn't much like Juanita, but he knew she was smart about a lot of things, and that included fishing and trackin' - not one bit like his Bonnie. So it never occurred to him that she didn't know what she was talking about, or could be lying. "Oh, Lordie!" he said," I'd best be gettin' back to town to have Luellen telegraph Ft. Basinger to tell the sheriff that the killin' thieves are headed straight for them - I'd sure best be doin' that!"

When he left the kitchen door, her ma and pa walked out with him. Juanita proceeded to grab the only handy garment from her room - her night gown. She closed her bedroom door, and went outside after the three of them, and made it a point that they see her headed for the outhouse. But instead of going in, she pulled the door to and put a stick through the latch to hold it shut. Then she ran around behind it while keeping an eye on them.

When they went back into the house, she circled behind the chicken coop and the custard apple grove, through the north pasture, toward the ridge, and into the comforting arms of R.J.

R.J. looked at her with his black, heavy brow cocked, "Juanita, aren't they gonna miss you?"

She stood her ground. "R.J., Ma is busy cookin' dinner. When she looks at my door still shut she'll think that I'm in there. But - if the curious gets her, well, I put my pillows underneath the quilts so's to look like I'm there, and unless she bends down to check my forehead for fever, she'll not know I'm gone, now, will she?"

R.J. looked at Joe Bob - and Joe Bob looked at R.J. They both just shook their heads - amazed at Juanita's quicksilver mind.

In no time the three of them had straddled the loaded-down horses and were headed due west - away from La Belle.

Juanita didn't even look back.

CHAPTER VII CALOOSAHATCHEE

Juanita, R.J. and Joe Bob hurriedly left La Belle and headed west, following the ox-trail beside the Caloosahatchee River toward Alva. Joe Bob was getting anxious about his Rose. If posters were up in the La Belle store, they'd no doubt be up in the Alva General Store as well, he rationalized. He was concerned about Rose's reaction when she learned of his identity, and the closer they got to Alva, the more antsy he became. Juanita would glance at R.J., and R.J. would watch Joe Bob. They were all three tense as they trudged the overgrown road.

The towns along the Caloosahatchee were but small villages. They usually had a general store, blacksmith shop and stable - little more than wooden shacks. A few had a church and school, and the abandoned barracks, that were not much more than large stockades, were a reminder of the Seminole Indian Wars. The weary travelers who migrated to the southern part of the state to homestead a plot of land or to fish the many rivers, lakes and streams, had to camp in the wilderness until they could build a more permanent home.

The Seminoles had long ago abandoned their small settlements in the hammocks near the river, where the soil was high and dry, and where they had raised corn, melons, squash and pumpkin. In 1858 after the last excursion, most had moved into the sanctuary of the Everglades. But a small band of Creek-Muscogee speaking Seminoles had settled north of La Belle on Fisheating Creek, not far away. There were only a hundred or so, and they mostly raised cattle and farmed the beautiful, fertile land along the creek and harmed no one. Every spring the women and children would walk to La Belle to sell their buckets of blackberries and huckleberries. The sleepy village came alive with their colorful costumes and unusual hairstyles, and the young children of the settlement followed them through the town site, as they sold their berries from house to house. But not even an Indian had the trio encountered since they left La Belle. Not a living soul. Not a rancher. No one. Luck was their companion, Juanita decided as she looked up and down the trail.

Now, Juanita was a planner. It didn't seem to matter that her knowledge of the outside world was limited. She had never

196

traveled more than ten miles from home, when her ma took her to visit her aunt and cousins in Ft. Simmons, west on the river and just past Ft. Denaud, and her but ten years old at the time. Aside from that trip her wandering had been in reading the many adventure books her friend Lonnie had loaned her. But she seemed to know instinctively what path to take and had the derring-do to follow her instincts. She was undaunted.

They pulled up to a small hammock of cypresses and cabbage palms on the outskirts of the settlement. Dismounting in silence, they went about the business of gathering rocks and wood, and starting the fire for coffee. Juanita slid down the slippery, wet sand banks for water. Her active mind was working the entire time.

With her bucket filled with sweet, cool, river water, she joined the men and started the coffee. Joe Bob was fidgeting with his bed roll and almost anything else he could lay a hand to in his nervous state. She had planned to divulge her well-thought-out plan after she had soothed them with coffee and fried corn cakes. They had had no time to secure other provisions, but the smell of the boiling coffee and the sizzle of the frying corn cakes over the pine and oak fire soon reminded them of their lack of them, and they hovered around Juanita like a couple of hungry puppies.

Night had fallen sudden-like. It was overcast, warm and already damp with the evening's dew. The smoke from the glowing embers spiraled upward, warding off the swarms of insects. The men lit their pipes and snuggled in among the beds of fronds and Spanish moss. Joe Bob had piled their beds high to keep the damp Florida soil from seeping through their blanket rolls. Juanita knew the time was ripe. She slyly moved closer to R.J., and purposely leaned against his receptive shoulder.

"R.J.," she said sweetly, "I've been thinking. Since everybody in the whole state of Florida is going to be looking for us, maybe you and Joe Bob had better try to change your appearance."

R.J. answered, "Uh huh," drowsily.

"You know - maybe shave your beard, and Joe Bob could grow a moustache, and I could braid my hair real tight and hide it under a bonnet. Then we could get an ox and a cart and make believe we're a family. A real family, maybe, huh?"

Joe Bob spoke up, "Hey, Juanita, I've always wanted to grow a moustache, but I haven't seen R.J. without a beard since Darbyville," and he chuckled at remembering R.J.'s shorn face at

197

Tomlin's camp - he'd looked just like a plucked chicken.

But Juanita persisted, "What do you think, R.J.? I could go into Alva and tell them our ox had died and the wagon broke down on the outskirts, and how we needed to be outfitted again." She turned to Joe Bob, "And, Joe Bob, I could go see Rose, to tell her where we're camped, and at the same time, I could look around for the wanted posters and buy provisions. What do ya think, R.J.? I've really been thinking on this."

R.J. thought a while, then he circled his heavily muscled arm around her small waist, jumped up, pulling her up with him, and swung her around and around. Her tiny feet flew through the black, Florida night, as he and Joe Bob laughed like a couple of school boys.

"You know, Joe Bob,' he said breathlessly, "If Juanita Jane Graves had been a general in our Army, the South would most certainly have won the War." And he pulled the laughing Juanita down with him onto their secluded bed. Their laughter soon ceased, and Joe Bob tried to remember the softness of Rose as he lay in his bedroll. He finally dozed off to the night calls of the chuck-will's-widows and hoot owls, to dream of his love - his Rose.

He awakened during the night, put another pine knot on the dying fire, and listened to the wind rushing through the trees overhead. He was too restless to sleep. Dawn would soon arrive, and Juanita's plan would go into effect. He was concerned and apprehensive as he lay there. Finally, sleep invaded his fragmented thoughts.

The sky was getting pale over the cabbage palms when Joe Bob awakened. He hummed to himself as he gathered the firewood, and excitedly called to Juanita and R.J. as he went down the river bank for coffee water.

After eating their meager breakfast, Juanita gathered up R.J.'s hairbrush and the strips of cloth she had cut from her under drawers, and slipped away to the river's edge. She dampened her long hair in the night-cooled water. Sitting on a fallen oak log, she untangled it, and began the arduous task of braiding the long tresses. The sleepy, dark, river water along the shallow edge cooled her toes as she painstakingly mastered every braid.

She sensed rather than heard R.J.'s approach. He was quietly still, but she could feel his piercing black eyes follow her every move. Instead of making her nervous, it heightened the excitement

198

of the moment. She slowly turned, and their eyes met. There were no words, only the quiet stillness of an empty forest at the dawn of day. R.J. knew that as long as he lived he'd never forget that picture of Juanita, straddling the fallen live oak tree beside the Caloosahatchee, braiding her waist long yellow-white hair, with her powder blue muslin skirt hiked above her soft white knees and her tiny feet curled in the shallows of the river.

The quiet was shattered by the sound of an approaching wagon. Juanita was the first to react. She deftly tucked the last braid up under the large roll of braids circling her head and ran up the uneven river bank. Turning toward R.J., she said, with her finger on her moist lips, "Shhhh, R.J. I'll handle it." Her rounded hips moved rhythmically as she approached the wagon.

R.J. said to himself, "I'm sure you will, Miss Juanita - I'm sure you will," and a warm smile transformed his stern face. "You know, she's right. The beard goes," and he stroked it as he ducked behind the thick brush on the river's sandy bank.

There were four people in the wagon, a man and woman and two children, a boy about twelve and a girl just around eight years, she thought. As Juanita approached them, they called the mule to a halt.

She smiled up at them and bid them good morning. Then she explained, "My husband and brother-in-law are taking a cool bath in the river. We've come a long way, all the way from up Tater Hill Bluff, lookin' for a place to homestead. Went down the Kissimmee to the Big Lake, and then someone told my husband about the settlements along the Caloosahatchee. We thought we'd look over this way before deciding where to settle," she said, casually.

The man and woman were taking all this in and nodding. The man spoke first, "We come from over Olga way. Got a small spread south. Have about twenty beeves and do a small farm. My sister over by Ft.Thompson took sick, and we're headed over there to help her out. She's got three small children and no husband."

Juanita asked them about the towns of Alva and Olga, and the woman finally spoke, "Got a nice church at Alva and a school, too. Plenty of good hearted people to help you if you've a need...so I've been told."

She spoke so softly it was difficult for Juanita to understand her. She was probably only about thirty years old, but looked more like forty, with bad teeth and a pasty, coarse complexion. Life in the frontier could be plenty hard on a woman, with the never ending work and the insufferable heat taking its toll. As she looked at the woman, Juanita decided then and there that she would have a better life than that....Yessiree! She'd do a whole heap better than that poor, old woman. She bid them good-bye, and they slowly headed east toward Ft. Thompson.

Juanita joined the men in the thicket, and told them about the passing-of-the-day conversation with the family. R.J. patted her on her backside and referred to her as his little actress. Just as proud as a peacock he was of his Juanita. She was coming along real good.

The bonnet she had fashioned from the leg of her bloomer had turned out amazingly well. As she packed Opie's roan, R.J. softly confided in her. "Juanita, Joe Bob sure thinks a lot of that girl, Rose. You'll probably find her at the dry goods store, but if for some reason she doesn't want to come back with you, please, for his sake, try to make her understand his need of her. I've never seen him act this way about a woman. He sure is in love, Juanita." And when he said it, she knew that he, in his way, was telling her how he felt about her.

She never doubted R.J.'s love. What she doubted was his ability to get to Alabama without causing a commotion so bad that they'd all end up on the end of a rope. He was smart and clever, but he was a bulldog for excitement, and it would seem to her he attracted it the same way a tall pine did lightning. They had promised that they'd make themselves scarce while she was gone, and R.J. also promised he'd be clean shaven when she returned. But she was still worried as she rode toward Alva.

She tied the roan to the post outside the dry-goods store. Just inside the front door there was a horseshoe-shaped heart-pine counter. There were shelves filled with boxes of every description behind it, all the way up to the ceiling. Buckets and whips and lanterns and goodness knows what all hung from the cross pieces. The store was half way on the river bank, and the other half hung out over the river, and was supported by tall pilings. Staggered platforms descended to the river, and after a lot of rain, the lower platforms were submerged. As much business was done by customers arriving by boat as by wagons, she observed.

The gray-haired, elderly woman behind the counter ap-

200

proached her. "Howdy, what can I be heppin' you with, young lady?"

Juanita smiled ever so sweetly up at the tall, thin woman, her observant eyes not missing her flour sack dress, with its blue cornflowers in patches all over. Over that, she had a stained, white, work fabric apron that went all the way to the floor, and smelled strongly of fish. A big pocket across her little bulging belly held tools. She guessed they were for scaling fish, as small opaque fish scales were stuck to her unkempt hair.

"My husband and brother-in-law are camped 'bout two mile east, and one ox died on us and the wagon axle broke. Had that bad luck all in one day. Can you imagine? Anyways, Ralph sent me to fetch some supplies and to inquire 'bout buyin' a ox, and maybe even a new wagon, if'n him and Jack can't get the old one to workin'," and Juanita's innocent blue eyes would have melted the hardest heart around.

The old woman said, "Now, now - little lady - you shore done had more'n your share of trouble, haven't you? Well, Miss Tatum will be heppin' you get fixed right up - soon's I get this fish off'n my hands."

She went out the back door with Juanita following her, threw out a bucket that was attached to the piling by a rope, drew up some clean river water and rinsed off her hands. There were several boats moored to the pilings, and several more out in the river. Fishermen were bringing in their morning catch to sell to her.

Miss Tatum waved and called to them, wiped her still smelly hands on the soiled apron, and followed Juanita back into the cool shade of the store. Juanita rattled off the list of supplies they needed. Miss Tatum talked motherly-like to her the entire time she was fetching them. Rose was nowhere in sight, and she decided she couldn't just ask about her. She was going to have to come up with some tall thinking about the new development. It never occurred to her that Rose wouldn't be at the dry-goods store.

Well, she thought, she'd just have to give it a go and see what happened. "This sure seems like a nice town, Miss Tatum. I've been tryin' to get Ralph and Jack to settle down in one place, but the two of 'em have got the wanderin' feet. I'd like to find me a nice settlement with a school and church and young people - you know, about my age."

The stage was set for Miss Tatum, and she fell for it like

Juanita was hoping she would. "Well, Missy, you've found your spot. We got quite a few young people right here in Alva. Now, you take Rose for instance. She helps me out from time to time right here in the store. She's just about your age. Ain't married though. Then there's Jeanie Farmer. She married last spring to a nice, young man over close to Olga - 'Bout mile and a half up stream. Then there's Lucy Hawks - lives with her folks just west of here. Got lots of young people here about," and she continued to measure out the coffee, meal and grits.

Juanita continued, "It's been over a year since I even talked to a girl my age. I just get plumb lonesome for woman talk, I'll declare I do."

Well, that's all Miss Tatum needed. "Well now, don't you fret. Rose'll be comin' back from the house any little ole minute. She just went to fetch our dinner, and I'd be obliged to you if you'd share it with us. She's been mopin' around here for goin' on four days - ever since that Joe Roberts up and left in search of his brother. It'd do her a mite o' good to have someone to talk to, I'm thinkin'. Yep, a mite o' good."

Juanita eased her fretting. She walked around the store, acting like she was trying to think of what else they needed, but she was actually looking for the wanted poster. She was taken aback when she saw it. There was only one of them, but the likeness was unmistakable. She knew Rose would now know who Joe Roberts was. The reward was $300.00, just like Randolph Martin had said it was.

Miss Tatum saw her studying it, and spoke up in a hushed tone, "That R.J. Skinner Gang stole the doubloons right out from under Yankee's nose - right over to Punta Rassa. Um-m-m. Now that is some mean bunch of men. Imagine that! And in broad daylight, too."

It then occurred to Juanita that Miss Tatum didn't recognize Joe Roberts as Joe Bob Skinner. It was hard for her to understand how she could escape seeing the resemblance, but then, maybe her eyes were poor - and then again, him being alone, and not the least bit suspicious acting while living amongst them like he did - well - she just shook her head, amazed at the stupidity of folks.

The bell rang out back, and Miss Tatum walked to the door and yelled out to the fishermen that she'd just be a minute, and for them to go ahead and weigh up their catch and she'd be there

202

directly - just as soon as she finished with her customer. As she was talking to the men, Rose came in the front door, carrying a covered basket containing their hot dinner. She was a pretty girl, with light brown ringlets framing her round, rosy cheeked face. Her soft, calf-brown eyes were deeply fringed with dark lashes, and she had a beautiful, dimpled smile, which she used to greet Juanita, who could readily see why Joe Bob had fallen in love with her.

Rose's drab, gray, homespun dress was covered by a bright, red-checked apron. She lifted the heavy basket up on the counter, and Miss Tatum introduced her to Juanita, who said her name was Sally Burns, and she again explained about the ox dying and her other problems. Miss Tatum turned to Rose and said, "Rosie, why don't you fetch another plate out from the back for Sally, and we'll just have us a nice dinner, and you girls can get in some girl talk. I got to check out Cooter and Snooks' catch and get 'em in the shade 'fore I salt 'em down."

Rose and Juanita pulled the small pine table away from the counter and removed the boxes, so they could put the fried mullet, grits, hushpuppies and mustard greens out - still plenty hot.

Rose explained, "I just live down the road by the stable, so I usually fix our dinner and bring it over." Miss Tatum put her head inside the back door and said, "You girls don't wait for me. Cooter and Snook must have fished the whole river. Never saw such a mess o' mullet."

So Rose and Juanita sat down on the up-ended boxes and ate their dinner. Juanita was having a hard time being polite. She wanted to pick up that fish and devour it. She was already sick of corn cakes. She had to feel out Rose quickly, before Miss Tatum returned. She brought up the R.J. Skinner Gang in between bites. "Miss Tatum was tellin' me 'bout the excitin' robbery over to Punta Rassa. Whew! I bet those folks were scared near 'bout to death - and in broad daylight, too. Imagine?"

Rose looked off then, and when she turned back to face Juanita, she said, "I'm sure I would have been scared, too, but when you look at their faces real keen like, they don't look so awfully mean - at least to me they don't. Maybe there was only one mean one, and the others were scared of him, or something like that."

"So, she knows, or at least suspects, that Joe Roberts is part of the gang. I'll have to tell her. There just aren't two ways about it. I'll have to tell her," Juanita thought. She lowered her voice

203

and looked her right in the eye, "Rose, I'm not Sally Burns. I'm Juanita Jane Graves and I'm not married to Ralph Burns. I'm travelin' with R.J. Skinner and his brother, Joe Bob, or, as you know him, Joe Roberts."

Rose's round face went sad as she lowered her velvet brown eyes and allowed a tear to slide down her pretty face right onto her dinner. She bit her lower lip and lifted her chin and said to Juanita, "I knew it, I just knew it. Nobody else around here even suspects who Joe is. I knew something was wrong, the way he just slipped away without a word," and she wiped her runny nose and tear-streaked face on her checkered apron, trying to compose herself before Miss Tatum returned.

Juanita went on to explain to her their plan, and that Joe Bob wanted her to join them. She just sat, and shook her head from side to side. "Rose, Joe Bob truly loves you. He's not a killer, or mean, or anything like that. The only thing he and R.J. have done wrong is they robbed a bank and stole money. They neither one ever killed a single soul. It was that dumb, stupid Sheldon who killed the banker in Tater Hill, and he's already paid dearly for that."

But Rose just sat, numb-like, and shook her head. About then, Miss Tatum came in, and the conversation had to change. She looked at Rose and said, "I'll declare, Rose Shorter, are you comin' down with the grippe again? You're lookin' plumb peaked."

Rose forced a smile and said, "No ma'am, I'm feeling right good. Just got some smoke in my eyes, and they're still smartin'." And when she looked at Juanita, she shook her head slightly from side to side for the final time.

"Sally here is goin' to be needin' an ox, and probably a wagon, too, Rose. After you're finished with dinner, why don't you take her over to Tom's to see what he can do to fix her and her menfolk up? I can mind the store, while you two get acquainted. She's just plumb lonesome for girl talk, ain't you, Sally?" and she chuckled as she remembered how hungry for girl talk she'd been, when she and her folks landed in Alva, and there were just three families living there and no one for her to talk to.

They ate the remainder of their meal in silence. Miss Tatum shoved the girls out, explaining that she'd tend to the cleaning up. As they walked along the ox trail and crossed over past the thicket of scrub oak and palmettos to the stable, Rose told Juanita that she'd help them all she could, but that she just couldn't bring herself to run off with Joe Bob. She didn't hold with stealing, but she did indeed love him. There had never been another, but she just couldn't go with him, and she wept quietly as she said it.

Juanita understood that some girls just couldn't stand excitement. Bonnie was like that. Just wallowed in the day to day humdrum life, not needing nor wanting anything else. "Oh, Lordy! I'd dry up and die if that's all there was. I'd just dry up and die," she thought, as she listened to Rose.

Rose walked over to Tom, who was busy repairing a saddle, and explained the needs of the stranded family. Tom told her he knew that Leon Hawks had an ox he'd be willing to sell, and probably a wagon, too. Since all his younguns but Lucy had moved over to Ft. Myers, he wouldn't be needing that extra rig. Tom said he'd be glad to drive over to have a look at it, and talk to Leon, if she'd like.

He turned toward Juanita and said, "You fetch yore husband over to check the soundness of the ox on the morrow, Miss."

Juanita told him that she was much obliged and that she'd do that very thing.

She and Rose returned to Miss Tatum's, and she had Billy, the hired boy, strap the supplies onto the roan. She took the pouch of doubloons out from under her frock top, where she had tied them securely around her waist, and paid Miss Tatum. Before she left Alva, she gave Rose's arm a reassuring squeeze, and smiled as she told her she understood her decision.

To herself, she said, "I just hope and pray that Joe Bob will. Oh my, how I dread telling him." And all the way back to camp, her manipulative mind churned out probable solutions.

The brush was thick all along the river. In some areas, the sharp bends of the river made it practically impassable for any sizeable boat, except the oft-used wet-ass boats. The majestic oaks, with their thick Spanish moss, hung low around the bends, and made it impossible to see if there was a boat approaching from the opposite direction. So all the river boats were equipped with bells. All the way back to camp Juanita could hear the different bells toll musically across the quiet of the land.

She slowly trotted the roan, thinking and figuring . But a solution escaped her. Joe Bob was new to her, and she didn't know just how to figure him. She knew he was quick to laughter, but usually that meant quick to anger as well. She didn't sense any devil bursting to come out of him, however. By the time she and the worn-out horse arrived back to camp, her decision was made. She grunted her croaker sound, trying hard to not laugh, and as she did, the two of them appeared. She had to stifle an exclamation quickly in her throat as she looked at R.J.'s beardless face, plucked just like her pa's prize winning Plymouth Rock chickens before they hit the boiling pot. His eyes were questioning, and she forced herself to smile sweetly, all the while wondering just how long she could hold a lid on the belly laugh that was clawing at her throat to be unleashed.

Joe Bob's eyes were also questioning. He was so het up that she wondered if she'd be able to control him. R.J. took the roan, and as she slid off of it, she told them it looked like they would be able to get the ox and wagon. But Joe Bob wasn't interested in whether they could get them. All he wanted to know was if she had seen Rose and what she might have said.

She assisted them in removing the provisions from the roan, chitchatting all the while about her adventure.

Finally Joe Bob could stand it no longer. He burst out, "Juanita, did you see Rose, and what did she say? Ain't she comin' with us?" He was strung up so high that Juanita got the key to his lock. She lowered her big blue eyes down to her feet, and she shuffled her work shoes under her blue work skirt, and finally, when she slowly and deliberately raised her eyes to his worried inquisitive ones, she let her lower lip begin to slightly tremble, and whispered, "Joe Bob, your Rose is plumb afraid." She quivered. She rolled her eyes toward heaven, and continued when she saw she had him captivated. "Oh, how she does love you, but, Joe Bob, she's just downright scared of a future with you. She just doesn't have a speck of adventure in her, Joe Bob. She's a stay-at-home lady doing her dailies and going to church, and that's all she wants. If you didn't have a price on your head, she'd be Mrs. Joe Bob Skinner in a wink, but, Joe Bob, there's a heap big price on your and R.J.'s heads. Every quick trigger-finger and bounty hunter in the whole state of Florida is after you. Now, you know your Rose don't want to be married to that kind of life. Now, Joe Bob, you rightly know that."

He was kneeling before her, with his head at her knees, and she stroked his contorted face as he sobbed uncontrollably. R.J. was in the shadow of the spreading live oak, taking in the show Juanita was orchestrating. He was shaking his head with an I'm-not-believing-this-woman-of-mine smirk on his pink, bare face, as she continued easing Joe Bob's misery.

Finally, she pushed him out in front of her, and firmly said, "Joe Bob, or Joe Roberts, or whatever you're known by, it's time you came to terms about which road your life is going to traverse."

He brushed the sliding tears from his red eyes, blinked at her once, gulped a big gulp, and shook his handsome face up and down. He stood tall in front of her, all six feet of him, and looked down at the diminutive Juanita. His face reflected the determination necessary to overcome his deep disappointment. He quickly turned in the direction of R.J., and said, "R.J., let's get packed and head for Alabama. Soon is not fast enough."

R.J. came out from the shadows. A loving concern softened his strong features. He spoke to Joe Bob and Juanita in his determined voice, "We'll follow the plan Juanita has laid out for us. It's a good, solid plan. First light of day we'll check the ox and wagon, and if they're sound, we'll be on our way."

The following dawn the trio purchased the ox and wagon from Leon Hawks and headed for Alabama. With luck and good weather they should arrive in Montgomery in eight or so weeks. Joe Bob and R.J. had mapped out their route, skirting the main towns along the way. They took turns accompanying Juanita into the various settlements to purchase supplies. The wanted posters were everywhere. They were in every trading post and stable along their route, but with R.J.'s shaven face and Joe Bob's new moustache and Juanita's hidden tresses, no suspicions had been aroused.

Their plan was to get to Montgomery, contact the Duke, and head West. A very relaxed and unconcerned trio pulled up to the camp on the banks of the Suwannee River on the outskirts of Old Town at Two Mile Bend. It was the same site where Sheldon had made sport of shooting poor Tag in the fall, and where R.J. had come down with the terrible bout of fever. He looked around and sighed wearily. He realized that the only good thing to happen to him since then was discovering the enchanting Juanita Jane Graves.

BOOK FOUR:

THE RETURN
TO
OLD TOWN

CHAPTER I THE MEDICINE SHOW

Jonah had tried, in every way he could contrive, to make Layke appear inferior to his dead pa while Layke was away on the drive those six long weeks. But Berta was well aware of Jonah's scheme, and she understood his need to place Reuben on a high pedestal. After weeks of listening to him downgrade Layke, she had heard enough, and came to his defence.

"Jonah, I'll always love your pa. He was a wonderful man, and," she continued, "I wish he were here right now, but, Jonah, he isn't! He's dead, Jonah! Do you hear me? He - is - dead!"

"Turn your face toward me when I speak to you, Jonah. Please," she pleaded. "It has taken me over four long, hard years to accept that. Why won't you even make the effort?" But he would not look at her, and refused to listen. He stood woodenly.

She decided to pursue the subject. "Now, I know you don't like Layke. You've made that loud and clear for all of Old Town to hear. You think he can't come up to your pa in any way. I'll accept that, Jonah. But for me, Layke Williams is a fine, honest, hard-working man, and I love him."

"Do you hear me, Jonah? I love Layke! And when he gets back from the drive, if he asks me to wed, your remembering of your pa is not going to stop us. Because, you see, Jonah, I'll never stop remembering your pa either."

Jonah glared at her, trying to make her feel guilty with his unrelenting stare. Berta looked pathetically at her middle son, and shook her head from side to side as she said, "I wish you were more like your pa, Jonah. He would have wanted me to be taken care of and loved and protected and happy and not have to work so hard. It's too bad you don't have more of his fine qualities ... "

"I am like my pa!" he screamed, as he ran from the kitchen. He turned, "Everyone says so, and I can protect you a helluva lot better than that gimpy Layke Williams can. Everyone but you says I'm just like Pa!"

He opened the door, and in a low voice, barely above a whisper, threatened, "...And I'll see to it that you won't ever have the chance to replace Pa...I swear it!"

Berta ran toward the door shouting, "What did you say, young man? What did - you - say?" He slammed the door hard and ran to the quiet and solace of the barn, not to return to the house until the next morning. He came into the kitchen, carrying a pail of Rosie's rich milk, and acted just like nothing had happened. But he had not said Layke's name, nor had he acknowledged that he existed, from that day - except once.

His jealousy was unleashed in a torrential outburst when Layke brought the pony, Fiddlesticks, home to Wes. Berta had never seen such fury. His unhealthy, protective attitude toward Wes had been a worry ever since Reuben died, but this new, uncontrolled anger was something that she just didn't know how to handle. She tried to put it out of her mind, telling herself that time and patience and prayer would heal the problem - but in her heart, she knew better.

****

Summer had come early the year of '78. Only one week into June, and the oppressive heat had already taken its toll on Berta's strength. Layke had been back from the drive for weeks. "When he was gone for so long I seemed to have difficulty remembering his voice. But now that he's back, it seems he was never away," she thought, while she went about her daily chores.

She sang softly, as she finished with the dinner preparation. SuSu was in the dark of the parlor, in her make-believe world, when Berta called her. She had finally come to the conclusion that SuSu's behavior was normal for a shy child, and that when she was able to take her into town more often, and she became acquainted with the other girls her age, she'd come out of her shyness, and her personality would develop, just as her Aunt Bertrice's had. She seemed to have better color this year, Berta observed, and had finally begun to fill out. Berta patted her rich, red-brown hair as she passed by her.

Since Layke's return, Berta used her finer dishes and her pretty linens. Wes picked wild flowers for the table, and SuSu arranged them. Berta felt that she had a special talent that way. She was quick to learn her stitches, too, and was already crocheting edging for Berta's many embroidered pieces. SuSu took down the dinner plates, and began to set the table. As Berta watched her go about her chore, she was amazed at her grace and self assurance. She never had to be concerned about SuSu breaking her good pieces.

212

Berta began dishing up the bowls of yams and early peas. When SuSu saw her, she went out the kitchen door to the barn, and called Jonah, who was building a cart for Fiddlesticks. When she no longer heard the hammering, she knew Jonah had heard her. Layke and Wes came around the side of the chicken coop, with Tag trying to keep up with their steady trot. They all gathered at the pump to wash up, and though there was no open animosity between Layke and Jonah, Berta could sense Jonah's consummate hatred. It frightened her - this obsession he still would not free.

And how much longer could she and Layke deny their love for each other? Berta knew his patience was wearing thin, and though their denial heightened the excitement of their relationship, he was a man of deep passion, and his needs were strong. Jonah would have to be dealt with. But how? She felt that they needed his acceptance, if not his approval, to be truly happy.

****

The McCoy Dry-goods Store was always busy with the townspeople of Old Town. Davis and Palmer, along with their wives, stocked a good store, for the size of the town. The drummers who came to call peddled everything from headache remedies to lemon drops for the children of the area, and the furniture bought by most of the townsfolk was ordered out of the many catalogs the McCoys' kept at the store. But even with the well-stocked shelves, they couldn't compete with the elixir-of-life products the medicine shows hawked when they performed in town, usually in the summer or fall of the year. The summer of '78 was no exception.

There was not much excitement in the small rural settlement - a birthing, a death, an accident on the range or river. But when the plumed, horse drawn, colorful wagons arrived in town, the entire population descended on the vacant lot between Stucky's Boarding House and McCoys', and the excitement was high. In less than an hour the performers and hawkers would have the wooden benches set out, the platform skirted with red, yellow and bright blue flowers with peacock designs. "It's bright enough to make a blind man see," someone observed. It didn't matter that the reds were beginning to fade and the edges fray.

The children were warming every bench long before dusk arrived. The lanterns had been lit and hung from tall posts sunk

213

around the rectangular stage, while the performers were behind the wagons, perfecting their tricks and acts of magic.

The deMoyas had played Old Town in years past. There were Pierre, the younger son of the family, and his black and white spotted dog, Delilah, practicing the hoop jumps. Beside him were Dom, the patriarch, and Mama Orlean, who were working on their hawking techniques to the delight of the gathered audience. The older son, handsomely dark Etienne, was the family balladeer and musician, and Aimee, the youngest family member, who was the tumbler and tightrope performer, who also accompanied Etienne in their soulful duets.

Word had come from Fannin Springs that the medicine show should be in Old Town that Saturday, and Layke had promised the family that he would make arrangements for them to attend. Minna Haglund's oldest daughter and son had promised to tend the stock for the weekend, so the trip would be possible.

Miss Trudy had got their rooms ready and was as excited as any youngster in the audience about the colorful and entertaining troupe's show. Every room was rented, and she had given up her own quarters to the Charlie Beattys and their daughter, Agnes - the boys would use their blanket rolls underneath some of the huge live oaks alongside the river. After sampling the elixir-of-life on Saturday night, they'd probably sleep like the dead - probably straight through their dad's sermon on Sunday morning.

She knew Charlie would be long winded in the pulpit, if he partook of any of the deMoyas' Sweet Elixir, that was purported to have magical powers, handed down in their family from the old country and brought to the bayous of Louisiana by their great, great grandfather. It didn't seem to matter to anyone there that the magical concoction was over 50% alcohol. Mama Orlean supervised the mixing and bottling of this precious, golden liquid in the back of their painted wagon, with Aimee assisting in the filling of the bottles and Pierre slapping on the labels as fast as she handed them to him. It didn't take much to excite the simple folks of Old Town.

This was the carnival atmosphere that greeted Juanita, R.J. and Joe Bob as they rode into town Saturday afternoon. They had become a typical traveling family those past weeks, and the humdrum existence was telling on them. The excitement of passing the time of day in a settlement as small and sleepy as Old Town

214

was better than watching the lazy rivers lap their banks, or bacon fry or coffee boil, Juanita decided.

Juanita had heard R.J.'s and Joe Bob's tale of the Duke and the blowing up of Tomlin's empire too often. She'd heard R.J. cry out in the night, and finally, after several nights of having been awakened by his cries, he had told her of Bunt's death. She needed a respite. "I have to have a change, or I'll go stark raving mad!" she declared. "I might just as well have stayed in dull, old La Belle."

But when they rode into town and she saw the crowd gathered around the show wagons, her heart gained an extra beat. She started salivating and her hands began to tingle. She quickly turned from R.J. as she slipped out of the wagon. Like a child she was amongst the crowd with her mouth open, hands clapping, and laughing as loudly as the girl beside her. She didn't realize that R.J. had joined her. She was transported to an exciting world - the world she had thought she would invade when she left home.

He studied her flushed, child-like face, with its easy laughter, and as he did, he knew that with all her seeming maturity and methodical organization, her most endearing quality was her desperate need for excitement. "She is the same as I was - oh, so long ago," he thought.

He sadly turned from her, and proceeded to McCoy's to purchase their supplies. He was tired. "I must be getting old." He laughed to himself when he realized that his behavior was exactly the same as every other customer in the store. He passed the time of day, paid for the purchases, stored them in the wagon, and searched the amazingly large crowd for Juanita and Joe Bob. They had not left their spot. He decided to join them.

****

Layke looked down at Berta. Both her hands were in his big strong ones. At last they were alone. It was a rare occasion when they were given that privilege. He had brought the last of the valises upstairs to Trudy's front room and told SuSu and Wes to go join the other children for the show, and they had luckily found seats on the reserved front benches. Jonah had jumped off the back of the buckboard at the edge of town and gone goodness knows where.

Layke pushed the bedroom door closed, and Berta came

215

hungrily into his waiting arms. He let her go, trying to catch his breath, and in a husky voice said, "Berta, we'll not wait any longer. I'll speak to Charlie tonight. I know you'd like for Jonah to accept me, but honey, I've done all I can. He'll not stand in the way of our happiness any longer. You'd best go to McCoy's to select your wedding dress fabric as soon as the performance is over.

She looked at his handsome face and sweetly said, "I know it hasn't been easy for you, and I'm just as impatient as you." She reached up on her tiptoes and kissed his eyes, cheeks and mouth, and burst out giggling, as she added, "Layke, I selected the pattern and fabric my very first visit to town after you left on the spring drive."

"Mighty sure of yourself, weren't you, young lady? Why, I just might have found someone more to my liking on the drive. Maybe that beautiful, gorgeous, ravishing lady, Ruby Thomas - Queen of Punta Rassa."

They fell laughing onto Miss Trudy's feather bed, and when they heard her approach the door, Berta spoke up, "Come on in, Trudy. Mr. Williams has decided to give up the throne for a commoner bride, and we're setting the big day."

Trudy burst in the room. "What on earth are you talking about, Berta McRae? What throne?" Her robust arms extended to envelop them, and she wished them every happiness.

Layke turned to both of them and exclaimed, "I just hope she's a fast seamstress, Trudy. My patience has run out."

"I put the last stitch in it last night, Layke. I'm real fast!" Berta and Trudy roared with laughter at the astonished look on Layke's surprised face.

He pulled her lithe body up from the bed, and held her close to him, and Trudy brushed a joyful tear from her full cheeks, saying, "It's settled. It'll be next Sunday. The Townsends will be returning, and the entire town will be turned out."

But Berta said, "No. We want a quiet ceremony in your front parlor, with just our closest friends attending. Don't we, dear? Trudy...Jonah still refuses to accept Layke, and the less fuss the better. Frankly, I'm not sure how he'll react to the news. He's so unpredictable. It frightens me - this uncontrollable temper of his.

But at the moment Layke wasn't concerned with Jonah McRae's feelings. He was only concerned with Berta's happiness,

216

and he didn't want to share her with the entire town - she was too precious to him.

****

Frankie Brewster turned to Jonah and said, "All right, Jonah, have it your way!" and he stalked off to join the Haglund boys. "Gosh," he complained, "That Jonah McRae is sure peculiar. He never wants to do anything but sit around and mope."

Jonah stood self-consciously at the edge of the laughing crowd. As he looked around for SuSu and Wes, his eye caught sight of Juanita. Her long braids had slipped out from under her bonnet in all the excitement, and went unnoticed. He was thinking that he'd never seen such beautiful yellow-white hair, when he glanced at the men sitting beside her. They were the only strangers in the crowd.

He knew. Somehow he knew. He studied R.J. and Joe Bob very carefully, and the lump just got bigger and bigger in his throat. He didn't know what to do. He didn't dare say anything to that slow-talking Frankie or the Haglund boys. As he stared at the trio, his quick mind began formulating a plan. He had planned to camp out with Frankie and the others anyway, so his ma wouldn't miss him. His decision was made that minute. He'd show them! He'd show all of them!

He and Old Red would follow them to their camp. This was his long-awaited opportunity. This was his big chance to prove to his ma that she didn't need Gimp Layke Williams around. If he was man enough to capture dangerous killers and collect the reward, he was sure man enough to head up the spring drive and South Spring. There'd be no need for that gimp to hang around. It'd be just like before - before his pa died. In his naive meanderings, Jonah never believed that his ma could love anyone but his pa. He figured the only reason she wanted Layke around was to run South Spring, so her life could be easier.

****

Juanita couldn't remember when she'd had such a good time. Pierre was having Delilah, his trick dog, jump through three colorful, fringed hoops. He had her dressed up like a clown, with

217

a big double ruff around her furry neck. The crowd loved it. While the applause was dying down, Dom and Orlean deMoya came out on the platform and began telling the captive audience about the miraculous cures of the Orlean Salve. They inferred that the lame would walk - it would cure lumbago, consumption, and just about any kind of misery a person could have. One of the liquored up young bucks asked, "Will it cure my sick cow?" and the audience howled with good natured merriment.

But Old Dom and Orlean were so serious in their response, that a hush soon fell over the crowd as they explained how the miracle salve was discovered. Many hundreds of years ago, or so they would have them believe, in a cave in southern France an old crippled hermit discovered a soil that held minerals so rich, that when he fell into an exhausted sleep on the damp soil in the cave one night, his crippling disease was cured. The next morning, when he awoke, he could straighten out his bent legs, and he experienced no more pain.

He wasn't an educated man, but he was smart in the ways of people. He had lived by his wits for many years, since he'd been left destitute. It would seem an evil uncle had stolen his inheritance, and he had spent his entire life wandering from town to town, living off what he could scavenge.

The next morning as he was coming out of the cave, with his strong, straight legs, a caravan of gypsies was passing by. He wanted to share his miracle with someone, so he joined them. As he sat around their camp fire that night, eating the first hot meal he'd had in some time, he saw the good in these simple, traveling people, and decided to share his discovery with them, on the condition that they would never divulge the whereabouts of the cave, and would use the soil only for the good of mankind.

Those gypsies were the Orleans' and deMoyas' ancestors, "And to dees day," Old Dom explained, "De heart of dees miracle salve come from dat faraway secret cave in my old country" The audience let out an "Ahhhhh", in unison.

Jonah had the only sober face in the entire audience. His eyes never left the three strangers on the fifth row, not even for a second. They were his future...they were his miracle...not the Orleans' Miracle Salve.

While Pierre and young Aimee deMoya wended their way through the audience, selling the salve and collecting the money in their money pouches, the swarthy, dark Etienne played his guitar and sang a ballad in French. There wasn't a girl-woman in the audience who didn't immediately fall in love with the mysterious foreigner, with his warm, soothing, baritone voice, singing about they knew not what in the beautiful, lilting language.

R.J. glanced at Juanita and knew she was not conscious of anyone or anything but Etienne and his promise of an intriguing life. He wasn't jealous. Actually, he was relieved. He was tired. He was tired of running. He was tired of camping out, never knowing his tomorrows. He was anxious to get to Montgomery to look up Duke and get settled in the West, but realized that Juanita was too adventurous to want a settled, day-to-day life.

As he watched her, a soft smile come over his face. He reached for her hand and startled her. "Oh, R.J., he sure sings nice, doesn't he?" She squeezed his hand, and immediately returned her gaze toward the handsome Etienne.

Aimee joined Etienne in a duet, and there wasn't a dry eye amongst the ladies, and some of the old timers shed a few, too. Layke, Berta and Trudy were standing in the back of the crowd. They didn't see Jonah, who was in the shadows away from the lantern light.

Aimee was the grand finale act with her daredevil feat of walking the tightrope that had been strung between McCoy's store and the Stucky Hotel about twenty feet in the air. She was a slight, pretty girl of about fifteen, and had changed into a shiny, gold, satin costume with a silver and blue fringe across the bodice. Juanita thought it was the prettiest thing she'd ever seen. Her long dark brown curls glowed in the lantern light, and as she ascended the ladder Etienne and Pierre held for her, Dom and Orlean deMoya went into their "moaning act", calling to her in French to be careful.

She would hesitate every few steps, and the audience had mixed reactions as to whether or not they wanted her to attempt the frightening and dangerous feat of walking the rope. When she got to the top of the ladder, there was a small platform that held a beautifully draped parasol. She stood erectly proud, holding the parasol high over her head. The audience broke out in a thunderous applause, but only for an instant.

Everyone there, except Jonah, held his head high to gaze at the beautiful Aimee...breath held...not a sound, not a whisper escaped their lips. She deftly placed her tiny feet on the rope and balanced her slight body, teetering from side to side with the aid of the parasol, thrilling the crowd with every tentative step. When she took her final step, the audience stood to applaud her, relieved.

Etienne and Pierre ran the long ladder to McCoy's for the smiling Aimee to descend, while Dom and Orlean rushed to her side with obvious relief to reassure her. Not wanting the audience to lose their appreciation, they hurriedly walked through them, passing their hats to collect the coins, before the crowd dispersed. When Etienne stood next to Joe Bob and Juanita and put his almost-full hat in front of them, Juanita's heart beat so loudly she was sure R.J. would hear it. But she brazenly dared to raise her beautiful big inviting eyes up to Etienne to gaze at him longingly.

Her coy half smile was not lost on Etienne, nor on R.J., who knew his Juanita pretty well. He was enjoying her liveliness and her awakened excitement. "I'll take advantage of Mr. Etienne's magic," he thought, with a sneering smile. Juanita was an apt student, and a hunger grew within her the likes of which R.J. had never witnessed. Yes, his Juanita was an eager and adventurous pupil, and he knew that if he was not alert, Mr. Etienne deMoya would be the recipient of R.J.'s masterful tutelage in the future.

He squeezed her arm hard, and she looked at him quizzically. " He knows," she thought. "R.J. Skinner doesn't miss a thing, and he knows of my desires. But in his devilish way he's enjoying my excitement." She returned his squeeze on his taut muscled arm, and her eyes spoke of a later promise.

Joe Bob was talking up a storm. He was so excited about the show, that he'd bought every remedy the deMoyas were hawking. R.J. laughed at his eager, boyish manner.

"If I'm not careful, you two'll try to talk me into buying a fancy wagon so you can put on your own show. I saw you drooling over that fancy little costume that Miss Aimee was wearing. I bet you'd be beating off every man from here to Alabama if I let you show yourself off in one of those, Miss Juanita."

And she smiled up at him and teasingly replied, "Why R.J., would you be jealous if I did?"

"Not in the least, Juanita. Not in the least. I'd gladly help you beat them off, and I'd take a special pleasure in beating off Monsieur deMoya...a very special pleasure."

A tiny chill ran over her, but she continued to smile, not letting on that she was conscious of his meaning.

220

****

Jonah was having difficulty keeping them in sight, the crowd was so thick. He saw Layke's tall figure above the crowd and quickly ducked back of an exiting group of people. He panicked when he resumed his position in search of the Skinner Gang, for they were nowhere in sight. He pushed and shoved his way to the outside of the crowd, and there they were, heading for their wagon across from McCoy's.

Jonah took that precious time to fetch Blackie and Old Red from behind Miss Trudy's, not looking right nor left. He immediately came around the porch and waited in the shadows for them to start the return to their camp. The lantern hanging from the wagon made them an easy target to follow on the two rut road, that also led to South Spring. He kept his distance and realized that if he was discovered, he'd just explain that he was on his way home. The road they traveled was the only one leading directly to South Spring from town.

He figured that they would make camp at Two Mile Bend, where the road that lead to the Haglund's property curved north of the river and branched off from the main road. It was not usually used by strangers, but mostly by the two families. He remembered that the Gang had camped there earlier on their way south because that's where one of the thieving bastards had shot poor Tag.

Every time he thought of Tag, he wanted to take out his gun and mow the two men down but he had to be very careful as he didn't wish the Graves girl any harm. Word had come over the telegraph about a month ago that she had been kidnapped by them, but there was some suspicion that she had willingly accompanied the brothers. There was no price on her pretty, blond head, so the reward remained at $300.00.

As Jonah had suspected, they turned north on the Two Mile Bend road. He slowed Blackie down, and Old Red was at his side. Seemed to Jonah that Red was showing his age lately. He was slow to retrieve his kill, and Jonah found himself saying, "Come on, Red. Come on old boy." But he was a good dog. He had inherited him from Young Reuben when Reuben moved up to Rose Head. Red hadn't really belonged to anyone in particular. His pa had trained him, and they all had used him for hunting. He was just the family

221

dog, and Jonah was mighty glad for his company, even if he wasn't the dog he once was.

The gang pulled up about a quarter of a mile off the road. Jonah could hear their easy laughter and thought to himself that they wouldn't be laughing so much after tomorrow. There was a stand of black gum trees west of the road and a clearing to the east that was protected from any northeaster by a thicket of pine, oak, hickory, sweet gum and cedar. A little, lazy creek, known as North Prong, ran beside it on its way to the Suwannee. The area had been a favorite picnicking spot for the McRaes when Reuben was alive.

Jonah felt confident as he pulled up and got off Blackie. He petted Old Red and told him to stay. His plan was to wait until they were asleep and sneak up on them right at daybreak....at first light, so he could see a little better and catch them before they were fully awake. He felt no fear as he went about preparing his bed.

He kept his distance, got his bed roll off Blackie and made out a grassy clearing beside the trail. It was a clear night, with the half moon darting in and out of the hovering clouds. Even as excited as he was, he easily dropped off into a deep sleep. "Hunting men ain't no different than hunting game," he thought smugly, with a satisfied smile on his naive, young, beardless face, not suspecting the danger that surrounded him.

****

Berta and Trudy covered up the two exhausted children, and as they tiptoed out and gently pulled the bedroom door to, they squeezed each other's hands. Berta had made many acquaintances since coming to Old Town eighteen years ago, but Trudy Stucky was her truest and dearest friend. And as she thought of that, it occurred to her that Layke could say the same.

They went into the warm kitchen. Trudy pulled the coffee pot from the back of the stove and stoked the fire.

"Berta, why don't you go to the porch to see if Layke would like a hot cup of coffee to go with this pecan pie?"

"Hmmmm, Trudy, that sounds good. When on earth did you have time to make a pie?" she said, amazed at her friend.

Trudy bent almost double with laughter. "Berta, I didn't bake it. Earline Haglund made it. As soon as she found out that Layke

222

was staying the night, she got those hands busy. Why, I didn't have the heart to tell her that he was sure 'nuff spoken for and that even one of her pies wouldn't help her to Layke's heart. Besides, she does indeed bake the best pecan pie I ever sank a tooth into." And she shook all over as she and Berta laughed. Trudy used her apron edge to protect her plump hand from the hot coffee pot handle, and proceeded to fill the tin cup, as Berta joined the men on Stucky's front porch.

Layke was deep in conversation with the gypsy troubadour at the end of the porch, and a group of fascinated townsmen were gathered around them. He was telling them about life on the Louisiana bayou. There were no other women about, so Berta decided to slip back inside and leave the men to their conversation.

"Trudy, he sounds so interesting that I didn't want to disturb Layke," she whispered, as she pulled her toward the windows that separated the parlor from the front porch. "Let's sit right here and eavesdrop," she said, holding the plates of pie and coffee, while Trudy pulled the brocade parlor chairs next to the windows.

Etienne was telling his captive audience about his youth in the swamps outside of New Orleans. It wasn't until he was almost ten years old that he saw a road or a horse or most anyone other than family members. His Uncle Pierre was instrumental in moving the family out of the bayou. It seems that he got on the wrong side of the law and was hiding out with the deMoyas. He lived with them for over a year and talked them into following the tradition of their ancestors, and they had been a traveling family ever since. He gave Etienne his first guitar and taught him how to play, and Aimee how to balance the rope.

"It was very difficult when we first started out, because the War was in progress. But we felt that we brought the poor people a respite from the misery of war, so we continued to play the small towns as we traveled west. Since the War's end we've traveled in Alabama, Georgia, and, of course, all over beautiful Florida. Uncle Pierre saw to it that we children were schooled by providing a tutor, Leonidas, who traveled with us until his demise a few years ago. And Uncle Pierre...well, unfortunately, he took a fancy to another man's beautiful wife and ended up on the receiving end of a knife." He laughed as he added, "He died with the same fervor for life as he had lived, and went to the world beyond with a satisfied smile on his face, we have been told."

223

The men convinced Etienne that they'd sure like to hear some of those foreign songs. Trudy and Berta sat back, closed their eyes and when Layke came into the parlor, seeking Berta, he was surprised to find the two sleeping soundly with empty plates and coffee cups balanced on their knees.

Berta opened her eyes to his loving, humorous expression. They didn't disturb Trudy, but sneaked into the kitchen to be alone. The soft ballad Etienne sang, the pale light of the moon and the loving warmth of Trudy Stucky's kitchen was a perfect setting for their amorous doings.

As day broke a soft gentle breeze fluttered the lace curtains in Trudy's front bedroom. Berta lay there, not wanting to disturb Trudy, who was snoring softly beside her. Wes and Susu had hardly moved from their exhausted sleep all night long. Berta was remembering Layke's restrained passion of the night before and wondering in her woman's way what their lovemaking would be like once they were married. She wasn't embarrassed or ashamed about her thoughts. Berta had had a wonderful, warm relationship with Reuben, but now she was a woman in the prime of her life, whereas with Reuben she had been a girl-woman, fearful and ashamed of her own desires and yearnings. Her love-making with Layke would be full, unleashed. He was an experienced man, having known many women - or so the stories went.

Trudy had told her about the cow towns and how the girls would fight over sharing his bed. It didn't surprise Berta. She wanted him the minute she laid eyes on him, but the remembering of that moment was shattered by Wes jumping on the foot of her bed. He always awakened with a smile. Such a happy child, so unlike Jonah and SuSu. Young Reuben had been the same, she remembered.

Berta tried to quiet Wes, but Trudy sat straight up in the brass bed and said, "Berta McRae! What do ya mean allowing me to sleep this late? Dear Lord in the mornin', it's past daybreak and I've a house full of mouths that'll be screamin' for their breakfast!" and they jumped up hurriedly and pulled on their dressing gowns.

Trudy poured a bowl of water and quickly splashed her face, smoothed her gray hair with her damp hands, grabbed her apron off the oak chair and rushed out the door - all the while Berta was laughing uncontrollably at her antics.

Trudy stopped, turned around and exclaimed, "You're mighty

frisky actin' this mornin', Berta. Just what went on in my kitchen last night, young lady? You have that cat-that-swallowed-the-canary look on your face," and she pushed the door to as Berta heard her chuckling all the way downstairs.

"I love you, Trudy Stucky. I love you almost more than I loved my own ma," and she hugged SuSu, who had just awakened, and pulled Wes close to her. She had never been happier.

CHAPTER II THE CAPTURE

Jonah awakened before first light as he knew he would. He took Blackie down to North Prong and watered him and gave Red a couple of corn dodgers out of his saddlebag and told him to stay. He was no more nervous than he'd have been if he were going quail hunting.

He decided to approach the camp by the ox trail, as the brush was dry this time of year, and the noise it would make might awaken the sleeping gang. He figured Joe Bob would be out for sure if he partook of any of the Elixir of Life that he purchased the night before, and the girl didn't appear to be an early riser - she looked like the lazy kind to him. The only one who concerned him was R.J. He couldn't figure him out. Light was appearing over the stand of tall pines to the east of their camp as Jonah hung close to the high brush and approached the campsite. He heard nothing and smelled no smoke. He was not more than twenty feet from the wagon that partially blocked his view of the sleeping figures. Squinting through the early morning haze, he tried to make out their exact position. His gun was ready, and he had brought plenty of rope from the family wagon.

He was surprised that he wasn't the least bit scared, but this was like stalking a dead animal. To make it exciting there had to be fear, he realized, and was obviously disappointed because it was so easy. As he cautiously rounded the wagon, he lifted his gun and pointed it at the sleeping mounds.

When he said, "I've got you covered, you----," his gun was effortlessly wrenched from his arms and a strong, steel-like arm encircled his neck, holding his head in a vise grip. The breath went out of him, and he was pushed down hard on the ground with such ferocity that his face was partially buried in the sand. He felt the heavy boot crush him hard in the center of his back, and felt no more, just floating blackness.

When he came to, he was vomiting and aching all over. "Oh Lordie..Oh Lordie," he murmured, looking around as he raised his throbbing head, and saw Joe Bob leading the ox and wagon into the heavy brush and Juanita sweeping the ground around the old camp fire. She scowled at him in disgust. Not a word was said while they methodically went about the business of clearing camp.

226

R.J. lead the horses to the trail while Juanita swept the tracks away, then held the reins as he approached Jonah. If he had missed fear before, it sure visited him now. R.J. bent over and picked him up by the shirt collar like he was a sack of corn. Now, Jonah was not a small boy. He was built square and solid like his pa.

"Oh, Lordy!" he thought. "What've I got myself into? I've never seen such devil eyes before. They didn't look like that last night at the show. He looked just like everybody else and was so gentle with the girl."

He was slung up onto the front of Joe Bob's horse, his head shoved down and wrenched to one side. That's when he saw Old Red tied tightly to a tree. He wouldn't have noticed him but for his whimpering. He struggled against the rough ropes, but they seemed to get tighter and tighter with every effort. He could still hear Red's pathetic howl as they rode off with Blackie tied to the back of R.J.'s horse.

Jonah's muddled mind was trying to figure out when his ma would miss him. They wouldn't even be getting back to South Spring until nightfall because Layke had arranged for the Haglunds to tend the stock while they were in town, and if his ma didn't see him, she'd just figure he'd gone back to South Spring. They wouldn't start looking for him 'til the next day at the earliest, and goodness knows where he'd be by then.

Red's howling was getting fainter as they trotted through the over-grown trail. Jonah knew that if someone didn't fine Red soon he'd die for sure. Joe Bob yanked his head straight back, pulling his hair so hard that he cried out. He shoved a wad of cloth into his open mouth. He could feel the rag gag him as he tied it tight behind his head. He was going to be sick... Oh God...He moaned and squirmed and almost choked before Joe Bob loosened the rag and he vomited the bitter bile - then blacked out. The strange sound he heard was his own whimpering. He pitched forward.

****

Layke accompanied Berta and the children to church, not that he was a church-going man, but because he knew it would please her. The little church was filled with the many townspeople who had stayed overnight, leaving someone at home to tend their stock, as Berta and Layke had done. As Miss Trudy had predicted,

Charlie Beatty was especially long-winded, and those pews were rock hard.

After services were finally over Trudy asked Berta and Layke to have dinner with her before going back to South Spring, so they could discuss the up-coming wedding and make plans. And since there was no rush to return, Berta helped Trudy with the chicken and dumplings and the serving of the guests. They leisurely washed the mountain of dishes while Layke and the children visited with the guests on the porch. No one was concerned that Jonah hadn't shown up. When Berta didn't see him, she assumed that he had ridden Blackie back to South Spring, as he had often done in the past without saying good-bye.

Trudy interrupted her thoughts, "Berta, do you suppose Jonah went back home? I haven't seen that young man since ya'll arrived yesterday."

"Oh, he's probably gone on home, Trudy. You know he doesn't take to folks easily. So unlike Reuben, or the rest of us for that matter," and she thought no more about it.

After the dinner dishes were done, they joined Layke on the porch. There was an air of expectancy as they animatedly discussed the wedding plans. It was decided that they'd wed two weeks from that date, after the Townsends had gone on to Cedar Key and the town was back to normal.

Berta hated to tell Trudy good-bye. They hugged each other tightly, then Layke assisted her into the buckboard. When they passed by the medicine show wagons she asked Layke why the deMoyas were still there. Layke had grown fond of Etienne and had spent quite a bit of time with the family.

"They needed to make some wagon repairs, hon, and the Old Towners have treated them so warmly that they decided to stay here 'til they're completed," he said as he waved to Etienne, who was in front, assisting Dom with the repairs.

"Oh, Layke!" she said excitedly, "Wouldn't it be fun to have them stay at South Spring? Put some life into our dull lives. Please, Layke. Why don't you ask them?" And Berta stroked his arm affectionately, eagerly awaiting his response.

"Put some life into our lives, young lady? My, my. I was under the impression that the soon-to-be Mrs. Williams was having a great deal of fun. Why just last night as I held her in my arms, I could have sworn that she was having...."

"Layke Williams, you shush..the children." Layke turned the buckboard around and winked at Berta.

He was amazed at her perception. Etienne was one of the few men he'd found a true companionship with since leaving the army. "You're quite a woman, Berta McRae..quite a woman," he whispered as he kissed her finger tips tenderly and gazed into her smiling eyes.

He jumped down from the buckboard and Etienne met him. He wore a perplexed expression as Layke approached him, but when they emerged from the wagon he and Orlean and Dom were all smiling. They hesitated, then shyly came over and thanked Berta for the invitation, which they gratefully accepted.

"Then it's all settled," Berta stated, while trying to calm Wes and SuSu, who were beside themselves with excitement.

"Oh, yes, missy. We'll happily spend a short time wit you. Orlean and Aimee will not be witout heppin' you wit de chores. Nosirree.. Dey are not lazy women. Dey will be much hep," Dom assured her.

When they arrived back at South Spring, Berta was a little surprised that Jonah had not returned. But she rationalized and told Layke, "Well, you know Jonah. He'll be home directly. He's always concerned about who's handling Rosie. He'll be home shortly, I'm sure... probably went fishing with Frankie or some of the other boys."

****

Pierre and Dom were driving the lead wagon slowly. They were in no particular hurry, so they leisurely took their time enroute to South Spring. Orlean was riding in the back of the second wagon, and she and Aimee were attempting a new fortune telling scheme in hopes of supplementing their meager income, while Etienne drove and encouraged their efforts. When they came to the fork at Two Mile Bend, Etienne said the South Spring Ranch was north of the river, so they turned north. They had gone only a short distance when they realized that the road was much too overgrown to be the correct one, so they continued 'til they came to a clearing that was wide enough for them to turn around.

When Aimee heard Old Red whimpering, she went to investigate.

229

"Pierre...Etienne...come quickly! It's a dog and something is very wrong with him. Poor thing," she consoled him, stroking his back as they helped her untie him.

While Aimee ran to the creek for water, Etienne and Pierre discussed in low tones, so as not to distress the women, what could have happened. It was obvious that the dog was mistreated. No one hobbled a dog and tied him around the neck as well. No water..no food. They were perplexed and concerned and decided to take him on to South Spring with them to discuss it with Layke. Perhaps he could identify him. They had no way of knowing that Red belonged to the McRaes.

An hour later they rode up to the South Spring gate with Red riding on the front seat of the wagon. He had eaten very little and Aimee was soothing him with her soft French when Layke and Wes approached the gate. Layke knew the minute he saw Red that something was wrong with Jonah, and Etienne read the fear and concern in his eyes.

Layke was the first to speak. "I see you found Old Red. Why, we were just talking about his and Jonah's whereabouts." He winked at Etienne and shook his head, gesturing toward Wes to let him know that he didn't want to talk in front of the boy.

"Here, Orlean, let me help you down. Berta has a nice cup of tea waiting for you and Aimee. The men and I have a number of things to discuss. Wes, show the ladies in, son."

"Oh, Layke! It's just into the kitchen. Golly, I never get to do anything. I'm not a baby anymore, you know." But he did as Layke had asked and grumbled all the way up the path while Orlean tried to smooth things over by telling him about Delilah's new trick. Wes kept looking around at the men, who were in deep conversation. He knew something wasn't right, and as soon as he had shown the women in, he rapidly ran back to the men.

He overheard Pierre say, "He meant to...there is no doubt, Layke - abandoned wagon and ox and the poor dog. Something is amiss."

Dom spoke up, "Dere was no sign of anybody. We looked all 'round. Nobody dere, Mr. Layke."

"What's wrong, Layke? Where's Jonah?" Wes worriedly asked. "Now, son, there's nothing to be worried about - yet. We were just discussing where Jonah could have run off to without Old Red. That's all."

230

And Wes, with the wisdom of the very young, stated matter of factly, "Jonah wouldn't have gone off without Old Red, Layke. Something's happened to Jonah. He must be hurt or something. We better hurry and tell Ma." And with that he spun around and was yelling for Berta as he ran toward the house, with Layke right behind him also yelling. "Wes... Wes...Slow down, son. We don't know anything yet. Don't get your mother upset. Hey..wait a minute!"

"Gracious me, what is all this commotion, you two? Why our guests will think we're a bunch of barbarians." But her smile disappeared when she saw Layke's expression, and before he could say a word, she shouted, "What's wrong with Jonah? Layke, tell me! Is something wrong with Jonah?" Her hand went to her mouth to restrain the scream she was sure would come.

"Berta, now don't get upset before we know the facts. Here," he said as he sat her down at the kitchen table. "We'll discuss this in a calm manner. There is probably nothing wrong with Jonah. It's just that the deMoyas have found Red...."

She listened as he told of their discovery. Very calmly she asked, "Has anyone heard of the whereabouts of the Skinner Gang lately?" She said it coldly and with a quiet deliberation.

"Now, Berta, you're overreacting. We don't even know if Jonah's missing. Just because he didn't come home...and Red was tied..doesn't mean that..." He held her close and declared, "We'll find him, darling. We'll find him. Please, don't, my precious one..." She could no longer control her tears.

Orlean and Aimee accompanied Berta to her room as the men continued to discuss the facts. Finally, Etienne asked Layke about the Skinner Gang. He had heard of their exploits, as had everyone in Florida, but he really didn't know much about them. When Layke mentioned Juanita, Pierre piped up and asked excitedly, "Did you say her hair was white? They were there. I know it! They were right there before our eyes. Up front - in about the fourth or fifth row. The young one had brown hair and a moustache and plenty of money. Why, he bought at least a dozen bottles and jars and I wondered at the time if perhaps someone in his family was very ill. I was going to inquire afterwards, but they disappeared. They weren't at McCoy's and they didn't go to the Stucky porch like most everyone else did. The girl had very long braids and they kept coming out of her bonnet. I'm sure, Layke.

231

I'm positive!"

When Pierre said that, Layke remembered the fright he felt
when Tag was shot, and he felt the same empty, helpless feeling
at that moment. He looked up and Berta was staring at him soberly.

"What are we going to do, Layke? What?" and she was in
his arms, sobbing, as he consoled her with his strength. "We'll take
care of the situation, hon. Don't you fret. They'll be taken care
of this time if it's the last thing I ever do!" His fists were throbbing,
bloodless, as he shouted his threat.

It was decided that Layke, Etienne and Pierre would ride into
town to sound the alarm, and that Dom would remain at South
Spring with the women and Wes.

While the men saddled up their horses and got their gear
ready, Orlean and Aimee sat with Berta and exchanged small talk.
SuSu and Wes, bored with the inactivity, finally coaxed Aimee into
accompanying them to the side yard to teach them some tumbling
tricks.

When Layke returned to the kitchen, he quickly went to
Berta. "Berta, Jonah is a smart young man and an expert hunter.
I'm positive he'll be able to handle himself. Etienne and I think
we know what happened." She was about to interrupt when Layke
put his finger on her lips and said, "Shush, young lady, 'til I've
explained."

"Jonah must have recognized the gang on his way back home,
and decided to attempt the capture by himself instead of riding back
to town for help. I'll speak to Frankie when we get to town to find
out more about Jonah's activities last night. Then I'll send someone
to Ft. Fannin to telegraph the Crosstown and Rose Head sheriffs.
We feel sure that the gang will head north and out of state as fast
as they can. Berta, I know they're a dangerous bunch, but I've never
heard of the brothers' hurting anyone. If you remember, Ruthie
Townsend said that it was the others who were the real scoundrels.
Remember, hon?"

As he held her, they gazed out the kitchen window. Wes
and SuSu were playing with Aimee, Delilah and Tag as though
nothing was wrong. Layke whispered that he was positive that
Jonah would be home soon, a wiser and humbler young man. His
strong, comforting arms eased her around to face him. Berta felt
numb all over. Even though she and Jonah didn't see eye to eye,
she still loved him and understood his fright and deep need of

232

approval.

"We must leave now, hon." Berta did not respond. She just shook her head as she bit her lower lip apprehensively. They walked together, hand in hand, toward Etienne and Pierre. Then all three silently mounted their horses and galloped through the south gate. They turned and waved to the six statue-like figures, lined up in a row, motionless, as they swiftly rode toward Old Town.

****

Frankie Brewster rubbed the sleep out of his eyes and told his ma that he didn't feel any too good. Luta laughed at her trying-to-be-a-man fifteen year old son and said, "I can't imagine why, Frankie Joseph Brewster. You drank enough Elixir of Life to cure any ailment you might catch for the next umpteen years," and she reached for his ear while he yelped good-naturedly and rolled out of bed. They were having a later-than-usual breakfast and discussing the medicine show and how brave Aimee deMoya was, and also how pretty. Bud Brewster was teasing Frankie about what a fancy figure she cut up on that tight-rope, and the entire family was in high spirits that Sunday morning.

Luta turned to Frankie and said, "I thought Jonah was going to spend the night with you and Earl. What happened, son?"

"That Jonah is a real strange sort, Ma. He said he was, and then, when the tightrope act was over, well, he just acted like he didn't even know I was there, and kept staring at that bunch of strangers like he was in a trance or something." He reached for another hot biscuit, and Luta passed the butter and cane syrup to him, not that he needed it. "Frankie is sure busting out of his britches," she thought, "But Lordy, I love to see him eat."

Bud spoke up, "What bunch of strangers, Son?" And with a mouth half filled with biscuit, dripping with butter and syrup, he said, "You know, that pretty blue-eyed girl with the long yellow-white braids and those two men; they were sittin' 'bout in the middle."

"No, I didn't notice 'em, but seems to me you sure noticed the girl." He laughed at his son and winked at Luta, then continued. "They were probably from Cedar Key area, or maybe Newberry."

Luta told her family that they'd better get hopping 'cause Charlie Beatty was never late for services, and she proceeded to finish up her morning chores before dressing her hair. She'd been dressed for church long before her family had awakened that June morning.

****

When Berta and Layke had left for South Spring after dinner Sunday, Trudy had Leander pull some greens. "These are probably the last of the spring crop," she thought, and sat on her front porch preparing them for the next day's meal. She was reflecting on the visit with Berta when Bud came loping up from the stable with, no doubt, a problem. Trudy saw trouble spread all over his face half way down the road.

"Now what?" she wondered out loud. "I sure hope Luta ain't been expectin' and is losing it. You would've thought she'd have said somethin' about it. It's gotta be bad. He sure is troubled." She got up from her rocker and met him at the first step.

"What in God's creation is the matter, Bud Brewster?" He caught his breath and began stuttering. That was indication enough for Trudy to realize just how frightened he really was, because Bud stuttered only when trouble came calling.

"Trudy, i-it's the Skinner Gang. T-they were r-right in our m-midst, r-right here last n-night."

Trudy took him by the shoulder and set him down on the steps. "Calm down, Bud, for heaven's sake! You've gotta be kiddin' a person. Right here in Old Town, indeed! Maybe you've been partakin' of too much sweet elixir, Bud." But Trudy could tell as he got his breath and began to explain that that was not the case.

"We were havin' breakfast, just talking about one thing and another, when Frankie mentioned that Jonah was a starin' at a group of strangers at the medicine show, and one of 'em was a pretty blue-eyed girl with long yellow-white braids. Well, Luta and me didn't think a thing about it 'til just now. He hadn't finished his chores yesterday, so I told him to clean up the rest of it 'fore night fall. He came a runnin' into the house, all blusterin' like, and we finally made out what the matter was. He said that those folks Jonah was starin' at was the R.J. Skinner Gang!"

Bud was getting the proper reaction from Trudy. Her mouth was wide open in disbelief, so he continued. "Well, we laughed at first so he ran into the stable, pulled the "Wanted" poster off the wall, and when I saw it, Trudy, I just wasn't sure. You know? I

234

really didn't pay that much attention to the crowd. There was just too many folks for me and Luta to have remembered them."

"Get on with it, Bud! Then what happened?"

"Well, I just couldn't remember. So I took the poster over to Palmer and Davis and showed it to them. I can't believe it, Trudy! Frankie was right...Palmer took that poster to the back to show Davis and sure 'nuff, he said it looked just like the two of them...the brothers, you know. He said it definitely was the gang. And the girl was with them. You know, the one from down La Belle way...the one that ran away with them."

She jumped up as quickly as she could, and left the pan of greens sitting on the porch to wilt while she accompanied Bud to McCoy's. Palmer and Davis were fidgeting nervously as they showed Trudy the poster and described the men and the girl. She was inclined to believe them.

"We'd best send someone over to Fannin Springs to telegraph the sheriffs in Rowland's Bluff and Rose Head, so's the folks there will be on the lookout. That gang is probably high-tailin' it out of the state as fast as they can go."

Wasn't long after that when Layke, Etienne and Pierre arrived in a cloud of dust to tell them about Jonah's being missing and finding Old Red hobbled at Two Mile Bend and the abandoned wagon and ox. In no time the entire town had been alerted and within half an hour the posse had been formed.

They decided to ride north toward Crosstown. There was well over an hour of daylight left but word was that the sheriff was already investigating a killing at a turpentine camp west of town and wouldn't be able to assist them.

Layke was worried. He figured that the gang had a full day's head start on them. Frankie reminded him that they probably figured that Jonah wouldn't be missed 'til tonight, and that no one recognized them. "Shucks, Layke, we got a real good chance. After all, the sheriff from Rose Head has already been told and we got a good couple hours to get on their no good tails."

"Think you're right, Frankie. They're probably so sure of themselves that they're taking their own sweet time." He tousled Frankie's straw-colored hair and thanked him. "Bet they're only a half day ahead of us," and he put the spurs to Bucko.

****

235

R.J. had never seen Juanita act like this. She was so put out by that young whippersnapper spoiling her plans that Joe Bob told him he truly thought that if they didn't keep a keen eye on her she'd do that boy in. R.J. laughingly agreed with him. She was so upset with the turn of events that she had broken out in red splotches all over her face and arms. And that made her even madder.

They had continued with their original plan to go north, but now would have to skirt the towns along the way and live off the land. Juanita was thinking that that meant more old corn cakes and coffee, and that really got her going. Most of the provisions had been left in the wagon to lighten the load, enabling them to make better time. They stopped only occasionally to remove the gag from Jonah so he wouldn't choke on his own vomit. It was decided that the following day they'd allow him to ride his own horse if he continued to behave himself, but thought they'd best keep him blindfolded and have R.J. lead him.

They made camp beside a small creek about forty miles north of Old Town. R.J. figured that they were about four hours southwest of Rose Head where he knew there was a telegraph but wasn't concerned, as he was sure no one would miss Jonah 'til the next morning, when he failed to show up at his farm. Even if someone had recognized them, it would take time to organize a search party.

He was feeling very confident. "We'll be up and out by first light, and north of Rose Head before anyone is the wiser, Juanita. You can get that scowl off your pretty face, young lady, and come on over here so R.J. can soothe those old welts." She turned from him abruptly and said through gritted teeth, "When are we gonna let this brat go, R.J.? Far as I'm concerned you can tie him up right now and let the bobcats and wolves have a go at him. He's just holding us back - slowin' us down. What're you gonna do with him, anyway?"

"Thought we'd take him on to Georgia, Juanita," he said in a low voice. "Keep him blindfolded the whole time, and by the time he gets help, well, we'll be half way to Montgomery and the Duke." R.J. had been counting the time 'til he could ride with Duke again. He'd been so weary lately.

She shook her pretty head and continued to scowl at Jonah and said loud enough for him to hear her, "Well, if I had any say-

236

so in the matter, Mr. Skinner, I'd feed him to the wild animals," and very dramatically added, "That's the fate he deserves, sir." Jonah was surprised that the girl was talking like that. He was beginning to think that she was more to be feared than the two men.

He couldn't be sure which route they were taking. He thought it would be north, but in his weakened condition, and with his head feeling like a whole herd of beeves were doing a dance in it, he wasn't positive. He knew they'd gone through the hammocks, probably in Lafayette county near the salt marshes. He couldn't make out how long they'd been on the trail since he'd been out a lot of the time. But, when they made camp that night, he could tell that they were way north, probably close to Rose Head.

He kept saying to himself - "Now what would a wounded animal do in a case like this? He'd play dead, that's what he'd do. Now, they know I'm not dead, but I'm gonna play as near dead as I can to throw them off guard. Then tonight when we make camp I'll take advantage of the thieving bastards' stupidity."

In his muddled thinking, in and out of blackness, Jonah blamed Layke Williams for all his problems. "If it weren't for that wife-stealin' gimp none of this would have happened," he thought. Over and over the hatred he felt for Layke seemed to bolster his will to stay alive. He was determined to capture the gang and prove to his ma that he was indeed just like his pa - a take-charge person, a courageous man.

****

Sheriff Walker, from Rose Head, had been alerted about Jonah at six o'clock Sunday night. When he got the news he had his missus telegraph the sheriff over in Rowland's Bluff, only to find out that he was in Live Oak on a case. So he'd have to rely on his own men and the posse from Old Town, if they could get there in time to assist them. Along with his oldest sons, James and Hiram, he rode out to the Arrants' and Bishops' farms south of town, and chose to spend the night at Uncle Bob Bishop's spread about ten miles south of Rose Head.

The Arrants boys and John and Russell Bishop gave him a total of ten men, and they left the farm long before daybreak Monday morning. They had arranged their signals and split two men to a team. Figuring that the gang would be smart enough to

237

use the old turpentine camp roads, they spread out to the west and to the east. There wasn't a boy or man among them who wouldn't be glad to shoot to kill the despised gang members. The only problem they faced was the safety of Jonah and Juanita. They would have to be very careful with their aim.

Riding up from the south, late into Sunday night, Layke, Etienne, Pierre and the other four townsmen were up and headed north after only a few hours of sleep. They were about four hours outside of Rose Head when the sun rose over Cook's Hammock, and the pine, cypress and oaks were edged with the clear red of a Florida sunrise.

It never ceased to amaze Layke. The clarity of the colors at daybreak and day's end were like he'd never seen before. In Tennessee the haze of the mountains defused the depth of color, and it wasn't 'til he left the hills that he saw what the balladeers had been singing about for centuries.

They had ridden for another hour when they heard shooting in the distance. That's all it took. They put their spurs to their mounts. There was no mistaking the gunshots in the distance...but whose? The sheriff's or the gang's? Sheriff Walker and his men were expected to be close by about nine or ten o'clock.

Layke turned toward Etienne and shouted over the noise of the horses, "I hope and pray, for Berta's sake, that Jonah hasn't been harmed. But I fear for him. Those men have to be desperate. If Walker has spotted them, then it's kill or be killed or the hanging rope. They don't have a chance, and from the sound of it, those aren't signal shots - someone's being shot at."

The seldom used, deep rutted road was overgrown with weeds almost to the men's shoulders, so they were slowed down. Bud Brewster pulled up rein beside Layke and Etienne when he heard Layke.

"Now, Layke, I know you're worried, but remember, Jonah has been hunting since he was knee high, and knows the way of animals. And those Skinners ain't nothin' but animals, I'll allow."

Layke appreciated Bud's concern and agreed with him, making the necessary replies to show it. "Yes," he thought, "The people of Old Town are indeed caring people."

Again shots rang out. This time clearer and obviously closer. Layke called the men to a halt so they could put their plan into effect. One of the men had to alert the sheriff of their position.

Young Frankie Brewster volunteered. After securing a strip of white cloth onto the barrel of his gun, he made his way toward the posse and periodically shot it toward the sky. Layke and the others moved slowly in the direction of the shots.

It had gotten hilly about a quarter of a mile back, and since Layke had been on many a cow hunt in that area when he worked for the Mansards before moving on to the Wilpole's in Rowland's Bluff, he knew the terrain. He thought that Sheriff Walker probably had the gang backed up to one of the many tiny lakes or creeks, and if he had been able to raise a large posse, they would have surrounded them.

They heard Frankie sing out his contact yell, so they knew he'd gotten through. Layke sighed with relief. He'd not been overly concerned about Frankie because he knew he'd travel the roadbed, and the gang was most likely holed up downhill among the dense woods beside a lake. It was the posse's good fortune that they had been spotted where they were. If they'd gotten even a mile farther north there would have been sparse piney woods for them to make time over, and as tired as the Old Town posse's horses were, they would not have caught up with them 'til late in the day... if ever.

****

Juanita had taken Jonah's gun from his saddle, and was squatting down beside the lake's edge among the cattails and flags that grew thick all around the small lake. "It'd be just my fate to be shot dead beside some old no-name lake," she said over and over. "I can't believe R.J. was dumb enough to think we had all the time in the world. He should have tied up that nosey kid along with his dog so's they both could have starved to death. That's what he should've done!" she thought as she kicked the sand furiously.

Her stomach was growling so loudly she could hardly feel the heavy beat of her heart. "God, ain't there a squat-down place in the whole state of Florida that there ain't ants?" she moaned as she brushed the stinging black ants from her scratched-up legs. She pushed down her stockings to crush one that had found its way down around her foot. "I can't believe that we'd allow a dumb, bratty, crybaby mess us up so bad."

Joe Bob had Jonah tied up, feet and hands, beside him, face down in the damp, sandy ridge next to the lake. He moved up about

239

six feet to the heavier brush, but there was just nothing between him and the dense woods for protection, he realized. "Gawd," he thought, "They came upon us so sudden we were lucky to've found cover at all."

R.J. had been in the lead with Juanita back of him. They were going at a good trot when two men appeared coming toward them down that back road. R.J. turned around and told Juanita to stay calm and pass the word that he'd handle everything. Joe Bob pushed Jonah's head down, pulled the old black felt hat over his head and pulled the blanket over him. When they got close to the men, they reined in. R.J. was the first to speak.

"It's sure good to see someone way out here," he said with great concern. "We've got a snake-bit lad with us, and we're wondering where there's a town nearby with a doctor. We cut and bled him, but he needs help bad."

The younger of the two spoke up and said, "You're about three hours outside of Rose Head. Doc Loomis is the doc there and he'll take care of your friend. He's a good man. Good-day to you. Just keep on this road 'til you come to that big, flat topped cypress 'bout half hour's ride up. Take the fork to the east, and you'll be there 'fore you know it," and they passed the gang by, acknowledging Juanita with a tip of their hats and a "ma'am."

The three of them looked at each other quizzically. They weren't sure if the men were hunters or part of a posse. They proceeded north at a good clip, nervously excited, gun fingers on ready at the least motion from the passing men.

James and Hiram wanted to open fire, even if it meant shooting them in the back, but the girl was in between the two of them and obstructed their view. It was clear that Jonah was in the line of fire as well. They quickly turned off the road into a thicket of myrtle and briars, and sent off their signal shot. The noise resounded over the sleeping marsh land to the east. They heard a responding shot... it came from due north of the site.

Hiram watched the departing gang's reaction when the first shot rang out. They hurriedly pulled up rein, and on the responding shot they instantly disappeared into the heavy brush to the west. James and Hiram hit the overgrown road again, and could see two of the posse coming toward them - it was the Bishop boys. Hiram greeted Russell and told him to stay put 'til the other posse members caught up with them while he, James and John pursued the gang,

240

and he was to tell the posse to be very careful because they still had the McRae boy, and the La Belle girl was riding with them as well. "And she sure is a looker, too," added James.

Hiram rolled his eyes upward and shook his head at his brother's inappropriate remark, and James hung his head, but he had a smile on his young, beardless face as he did. "She sure is a looker," he thought. "You can't blame a person for lookin', Hiram..."

They could hear the gang's horses thrashing in the distance. As they listened, James' mind was on Juanita. He sure hoped her soft white skin wasn't being scratched. That would be a crying shame, he thought as he chopped his way through the devil-thorn vines that were hidden among the moon vines. They could cut a person so he'd bleed to death if he didn't clear his way first. James and Hiram were aware of that, and never went on a cow hunt without their machete-like knives. There'd be times a maverick would be hung up so bad that if they didn't cut it free, it'd just about starve to death, or panic, and the heavy, sharp thorns would rip its hide, sometimes two or three inches deep.

****

When the Walker boys showed up and Joe Bob shoved Jonah's head down on his mount and covered him with the blanket, Jonah's mind began to clear, but he was afraid to yell or fidget. He wanted to appear resigned and scared. And if the truth were known, he was scared. He heard the exchange of words, but they were muffled by the hat and blanket, so he couldn't make out what was said. But when the shots rang out he heard them loud and clear and was almost tossed off the horse when Joe Bob turned around abruptly and hit the brush.

He could feel the devil-thorns cut clean through his heavy britches' legs and the sticky blood began to run down his shins. Joe Bob was cursing every other breath about how they should have left him back there to die, that he'd been holding them back from Alabama ever since the snot-nosed little wimp had tried to play the "big man."

His tone of voice gave Jonah a cold fright he'd not felt up 'til then. As scared as he was he had actually thought that he'd be able to play the hero's part, but the posse's arrival squelched that. Now he had no purpose. He was at the gang's mercy, and

241

if they weren't shot dead they'd be hanging on the end of a rope by nightfall. That he was sure of.

They had not removed the blindfold, but he knew he was near water because he could feel the murky sand when Joe Bob yanked him off the horse and kicked him hard, rolling him down the sandy embankment. Only the heavy stand of cattails kept him from going into the sun-drenched, green slime on the lakes edge.

The sudden barrage of rifle shots startled him. It was all around him - bullets singing past him. He heard the horses whinnying with fright and R.J. cursing and yelling at Joe Bob, telling him to go farther south into the stand of cypresses for better cover. He didn't know whether to listen or to shut everything out. He couldn't help anyone, especially himself, and the little boy that had been locked away for four long, miserable years cried out for help. But there was no help. He drifted off...

When Layke got to Jonah he thought he was dead. He hesitated, then tenderly rolled him over, holding his own breath all the while. Carefully, he removed the blindfold and gag. Young Frankie Brewster was beside him - he slowly called his name...no response. Layke cut the tight rope from his trussed hands and tried to rub the warm life back into them. Jonah's closed eyes began to flutter, then opened to the tear-filled eyes of the despised Layke Williams.

He spoke barely above a whisper some unintelligible words, cleared his throat and started to sob as he raised his weakened arms toward Layke. They held each other, sobbing, rocking back and forth, and Layke called him, "Son." There wasn't a dry eye among the rescuers who witnessed the unlikely reunion, especially among those who knew of the hatred that Jonah held for Layke.

Layke picked him up and carried him up the lake's ridge. He asked Frankie to get him some water from his canteen, and then he sat on the white, lake sand and bathed Jonah's tear streaked face as he cradled him in his arms, talking softly to him while telling him about his mother's concern, and about how all the townspeople were holding a prayer vigil at the church, praying for his safe return. Jonah smiled sleepily, relaxed in Layke's protective arms and drifted off to sleep to the sounds of "bravery," and "courageous" and "hero".

CHAPTER III THE HANGING

Old Dom deMoya drove Berta into Old Town while Orlean and Aimee remained with Wes and SuSu at South Spring. He nervously spoke in his broken English all the way to town. Berta answered a word or two, but mostly sat - numb. She had been just too upset to stay, feeling absolutely helpless and needing to be doing something - anything - to keep her mind off of Jonah.

It was Orlean who suggested that Dom drive her to town so she could be there to welcome her son on his return, and Berta was grateful for her perception and her understanding mother's ways. While they quickly embraced, Aimee helped her pack a few items, in case there was a wait of a few days, and Orlean assured her that she was not to worry.

"Me and Aimee know de ways of de leettle ones, Missy. We can tend de milk cow and cheeckens to please you and Meester Layke, so you run along and await your boy." Berta held her weathered hands in gratitude as Dom helped her into the buckboard, and as she thought of Orlean's strange beginnings and the things her wizened, old eyes had seen in her wanderings, she reflected on their conversation of the previous day while she and Dom made their way to Old Town.

When Berta first saw her at the medicine show, she had thought she and Dom must have been the grandparents of the others, but Orlean explained, as they relaxed in the warmth of Berta's kitchen, that she and Dom believed that they'd never be able to have children, and had resigned themselves to their fate. She was in her early thirties when, to their amazement, she conceived Etienne and five years later they were surprised by Pierre's appearance. She had always wanted a girl, and her prayers were answered when Aimee was born five years after Pierre.

That's when her brother's son, Pierre, came to live with them, and was responsible for their leaving the bayou country to begin the nomadic life that had been enjoyed by their forebears. They soon began to love the life of the wanderer, for it gave them a chance to see the world beyond the confines of the bayou, and to make friends along the way, and the children were able to be schooled. But she and Dom were getting along in years, and it wasn't as easy on them as it had once been. Dom kept talking of finding a place to settle, but the children loved the excitement of

243

the gypsy life and wouldn't hear of it.

****

Trudy met Berta on the porch with her comforting arms extended, and while holding her close, told her of the vigil being held at the church. She had wanted to attend, but since half of Old Town was there she'd be needed more in the kitchen than the church, she explained.

She released her and said, "Now, Berta, it's too soon to have heard anything at all. I know that Layke will get word to Fannin Springs just as soon as he knows anything. Now don't you fret. You've got to keep your mind occupied and your hands busy, and put yourself and Jonah in the Lord's hands."

While she was encouraging Berta to occupy herself, Trudy eased her into the kitchen, pulled up her padded rocker and handed her a bowl of polebeans that were overflowing their container, and forcefully suggested that she sit right down and get to work, knowing that the busier she was the better.

Before they had a chance to get settled, Luta Brewster came dashing into the kitchen, out of breath, and said in a halting voice, "Bo Lutes just rode in from Fannin Springs - and, Berta - they found Jonah...he's all right and so is everyone else." She rushed to continue. "The gang was captured just south of Rose Head and they're bringing 'em in. Should be here by noon tomorrow," and she sat down hard on Trudy's kitchen chair, exhausted by the long harangue.

Berta, Trudy and Luta sat, all three sobbing with relief, while Old Dom stood in the doorway brushing the tears from his wrinkled, leathery face, and over and over again, with his head raised toward the heavens, he jabbered away in his broken English, making the sign of the cross repeatedly.

When they all calmed down, he approached Berta and asked if it would be all right if he drove the buckboard back to South Spring to tell the good news to Orlean and the rest.

"You're a dear, thoughtful man, Dom deMoya. A dear one," she said as she gratefully embraced him, and walked with her arm around his gnome-like figure opening the creaking, screened door between the parlor and the porch that was already filled with the loudly enthusiastic townspeople.

****

Juanita was hot, filthy, and exhausted from the trials of the past two days. She had but one comfort, and she held to it with all the passion a desperate person could cling to. The night before - it seemed so very long ago - as she and R.J. lay side by side in their blanket rolls, apart from Joe Bob and the boy, he had held her close - not passionately as she would have preferred, but almost fatherly. He told her about growing up in the slums of Montgomery, and how he had cared for Joe Bob and often stole, that they might have food and clothing. He went on and on.

Juanita was so exhausted she just wanted him to go to sleep. Then he said - she thought he said - "I'd like for you to have a better life." He let that declaration sink in, then continued. "And I'd appreciate it, Juanita, if you'd take some of the doubloons, just in case something happens to me and Joe Bob. It really would ease my mind a lot if you would do that for me."

Juanita's eyes widened in the night, and she whispered in response, "But, R.J., I wouldn't even know what to do with all that money. I'll declare I wouldn't," and she snuggled up closer to him so she could feel his warm breath on her cheek.

"Juanita, I'm sure you'll be able to think of something. That is, if anything happens and we get separated from each other or something like that. I've put half of my share in a canvas bag. You can strap it underneath your saddle with a blanket around it so's not to injure Opie's horse. Juanita, that'll be your insurance in case some one recognizes us." He waited for her to respond, then hurriedly added, "They'll not harm you 'cause you've done no wrong. What d'ya think, honey?"

She was taken aback. Never in her busily scheming mind had she ever dreamed of this...Never! "I don't know, R.J. I just don't know," she whispered. "Somehow it just doesn't seem quite right."

Oh, how he loved this girl's mind. He could hear the wheels running round and round inside her beautiful blond head. He held her close, her head on his muscled, cushioned chest, and whispered softly, smiling his knowing smile, "My little Juanita....this is R.J. Would I want you to do anything that was going to harm you? Now, would I?"

He had just iced the cake. He could feel the relief ease out

245

of her, as she appeared to reluctantly accept his generous offer. Holding the doubloons close to her, Juanita Jane Graves soundly slept the night away with not a care in the world. A triumphant smile played across her full lips as she slumbered softly beside R.J., who gazed into the dark night, listening to her rhythmic breathing, content at last.

****

During the battle for their lives it never occurred to Juanita that she might be harmed. She was going through the motions of survival - loading, shooting and reloading automatically - in a trance. She couldn't see who she was shooting at, just where the shots came from. Finally she just got tired of it - sick and tired. So she put the gun down and sat there in the sun-drenched lake sand and watched those blasted black ants crawl up and down her scratched up legs. Her face was down in her hands when finally she gave into the strain and began to sob. That's how Etienne found her.

At first he thought she was hysterical, but she soon began to shudder and just as quickly stopped altogether. He walked around her, and in his heavily accented voice stated, "I'm Etienne, and I'm here to take you home, Miss."

Juanita recognized his voice immediately and shuffled her old, brown shoes in the sand, busily brushing the ants off her stockings and slowly - deliberately - she raised her beautiful, dark fringed, blue eyes up to the handsome young man's face that was hovering a very short distance above hers.

Etienne gulped, cleared his throat and repeated, "I'm Etienne, and I'm here to take you home.." but before he got the "Miss" out, she had extended her small white hands up toward him, and he simultaneously bent to receive them.

He'd never in his entire life seen anyone so beautiful - all pink, white and gold. The girls he had known before had been dark in color. She looked so fragile and lost sitting there, but when he took her hands he was surprised at the strength in them.

"I'm Juanita," she said in her soft, lilting, Southern voice, and Etienne deMoya could not take his eyes off hers. It was Pierre who broke the spell.

"Etienne, Layke wants us to go to the farm north of here to get a wagon. Jonah is too weak to sit a horse. Hey, Etienne,

246

are you coming or not?"

"Oh, yes, Pierre. I'll accompany you in a moment. I'll first assist Miss Juanita to her horse and ask Frankie to care for her needs. If that is satisfactory, Miss Juanita?"

Oh, how she loved to hear him talk. She'd never heard anyone with an accent before. "He talks just like he sings," she thought. She lowered her eyes and sweetly replied, "I'm much obliged, Etienne. I am very weary after such a frightening experience. Thank you for your kindness."

As she lowered her head, she saw R.J. out of the corner of her eye grinning at her. And she thought, "If that isn't just like Mr. Smarty Pants, R.J. Skinner, laughing his devil's laugh at me and him on his way to the hanging rope, too. It's just like him to laugh at a girl who's trying to be polite. But I'll not give him the satisfacton of knowing I even saw that devil grin of his. Nosirree...not one ounce of satisfaction." She quickly looked the other way and ignored his mocking grin.

When she could no longer stand the suspense, she turned around and saw the sheriff leading him and Joe Bob with their hands tied tightly behind their backs. She got a catch in her throat, but immediately recovered her composure and decided that they deserved their fate. After all, they had robbed banks and goodness knows what all. They were led south on the trail they had just traveled. But this time it was not to the freedom of Alabama and the west, but to Old Town and the noose.

Juanita Jane Graves kept her eye on them 'til they were out of sight. She sighed - shrugged her shoulders and said with finality, "Well, that's that....."

"Miss," one of the men asked, "Do you wanta wait for the wagon? You look plumb done in. And it's no wonder, after what you must've been through."

She politely said, "No, I would prefer to return to Old Town now. But I do thank you for your concern. That's mighty nice of you." There was no way anyone was going to separate her from Opie's horse and the doubloons.

Sheriff Walker had removed the saddlebags filled with doubloons from R.J. and Joe Bobs' horses and had placed them on Blackie, Jonah's horse, for safe keeping. There was speculation among the men as to how much was in them. He told them that some of the money belonged to the bank in Tater Hill and some to the man in Cuba, who had put up part of the reward, and that he'd sent Dubs Bishop back to Rose Head to telegraph both of them to let them know the desperadoes had been captured and that they were being hanged in Old Town.

When Etienne and Pierre returned with the wagon, Etienne was disappointed that Juanita had decided to return with the posse and immediately told Pierre and Layke that if they didn't mind he'd ride on ahead to catch up with them. His anxiety was not lost on Pierre, but Layke, who was so concerned about Jonah, had not noticed the intimate exchange between Etienne and Juanita.

Layke had not been able to awaken Jonah long enough to drink but a small amount of water. While he was waiting for the wagon to return, he had boiled some strong coffee and had been able to force some of the hot, black liquid between his relaxed lips. Jonah coughed and sputtered, but Layke forced some more down him.

"Jonah, you've got to drink some, Son. You want to be strong for your hero's welcome, now don't you?"

Jonah managed to sigh a little before falling back to sleep. Layke had seen this reaction in the War. The doc called it "shock," and he knew he was going to have to force feed him all the way back to Old Town. He was sure he'd kept nothing down for two days, as the stench of vomit was all over his clothing before Layke changed it and replaced it with his own shirt. It swallowed him but at least it was clean. It was washed by Berta's loving hands, and he warmed at the remembering of her gentleness and how relieved she'd be that Jonah was not harmed.

Etienne caught up with the posse about an hour after they'd made camp. He didn't see Juanita anywhere. He was getting anxious, but didn't want to appear so. He walked around the camp talking to one man and then another. R.J. and Joe Bob were securely tied up and sitting beside the sheriff and his boys, and Etienne thought that that was the logical place for her to be. Finally he could stand it no longer so he asked Frankie Brewster, "Frankie, did the yellow haired lady disappear into the night?" and laughed as he gestured into the darkness.

"Heck no, Etienne. She's sleeping with that old horse of hers. You'd think that nag was made of gold the way she treats it. But she said that it was her only reminder of home and the good life before she was kidnapped. Don't she have pretty eyes, Etienne?"

"Well, yes, Frankie, her eyes are very pretty - very pretty indeed," and he quickly moved over to where the horses were corralled. He didn't see her at first, as the glow from the fire did not extend as far as the corral. Then he saw her. She was curled up alongside some creek willows with her saddle underneath her head, resting on her smoothed out blanket roll. He hesitated, not wanting to appear forward, and as he abandoned the idea of approaching her, he turned and started to retreat to the fire and the men surrounding it, when she called to him.

"Is that you, Etienne?"

"Yes, Miss Juanita. Frankie Brewster said I'd find you here. I just wanted you to know of my sorrow regarding your ordeal."

"Oh, Lordie. I could listen to him talk all night long. He sure has a way with words, not like the dumb old Glades' boys, or R.J. for that matter. His voice kinda sparkles with little ripples like the Caloosahatchee after a soft spring shower with the sun shinin' on it." But aloud she replied simply, "Well, Etienne, you're a true gentleman to be carin' about little ole me. Yes, a true gentleman," and she invited him to sit beside her for a spell, as she was so very weary and would soon retire for the night. She patted her blanket, gesturing for him to sit down to join her..

Etienne sat on the very edge. At first he was uneasy, but as they conversed about one thing and another he found he was feeling the warmth of Miss Juanita, who was all of a sudden right next to him. He licked his hot, dry lips, and before he could bid her goodnight she was in his arms. Her lips hungrily found his, and as they broke apart Etienne stood up suddenly apologizing for being carried away by her sweet beauty, exclaiming that he had not meant to take advantage of her loneliness at such a time.

Juanita was breathing short, gasping breaths and decided she'd allow him to languish in his passion for a few more days. But she silently declared, "That's all I'll allow you to have, Etienne deMoya... a few more days and then you'll know what a woman really is."

She soon fell asleep under the black night, dreaming of a gold, silver and blue-fringed costume with her yellow-white hair blowing gently in the breeze, high above the applauding crowd, as she thrilled to the resounding applause, Etienne below her singing a beautiful ballad with his arms extended toward her....And she could feel the excitement and the thrill of the unknown.

249

Etienne lay beside Frankie staring into the camp fire, and every lick of flame bore the beautiful Juanita's likeness. His arms were resting underneath his black, curly hair, and his dark eyes formed intriguing images of Juanita - she was seated beside a blue waterfall like the one painted on the canvas backdrop behind their stage. "When I return to South Spring," he thought, "I must approach Dom and Mama Orlean about having a painting done of Juanita. She could be placed on the large rock in front of the deep blue waterfall with her glorious hair cascading down her back. Maybe in a mermaid costume..." and on and on his imagination created romantic settings for the beauteous Juanita... Never lustful - always in loving, protective images as he idolized her from afar. Finally, he drifted off into a heavy slumber, still dreaming of pink and white, soft skin above the silver mermaids costume.

"Boy howdy! Etienne, you sure sleep like the dead," Frankie commented as he shook him. "You'd better get a move on. They've already broke camp."

Etienne's first conscious thought was of Juanita. "Has anyone ridden out, Frankie?"

"Oh, no. It's just that you'll miss coffee if ya don't hurry up. Number one camp fire has already been snuffed out."

Etienne continued rolling up his gear and quickly filled his tin cup with the smoking liquid. Blowing into the cup, trying to cool it, he scanned the active crowd searching for Juanita.

He walked through the throng and skirted along the outside. The men were high with excitement and already rowdy about the anticipated hanging. But, no Juanita. He ran down the sand bank to the still stream. The cool water felt good as he splashed it on his dark face and ran his wet hands through the thick, dark mass of curly hair, wiping his tanned hands on his britches legs as he ran up the other side toward the gathered posse to get his horse. Still no sign of Juanita. He was getting anxious. Frankie had said no one had left camp, but he realized that the sheriff and his sons and the prisoners were gone.

As Etienne frantically looked from one area to the other he caught a glimpse of her. He sighed with relief as he quickened his pace, and was soon beside her, insisting that she allow him to assist her with the saddling of Opie's horse. Juanita didn't want to appear rude, and certainly didn't want to get his suspicions aroused...but no one...absolutely no one touched that blanket - not even sweet,

250

gentle, handsome Etienne deMoya. She loved to say his name, ...Etienne deMoya... My, what a beautiful name! ...Juanita Jane deMoya... Yes! Juanita Jane deMoya.

Juanita said sweetly, but emphatically to his waiting response, "A lady must learn to look after herself in this God-forsaken wilderness, Etienne."

After placing the heavily laden blanket on the horse, she turned her soulful eyes up toward the dejected troubadour, and softly said in her most engaging Southern voice, "I'll allow ya to hep me with this oh so heavy saddle, though. But I do feel, Etienne, that I must carry ma share of the burden. In the future...that is, if you and I have a future together...I'll do the lighter work, more ladylike - like blanket the horse - and you may hep with the heavier, more manly chores, such as saddling the horse. Would that be too much to ask of you, Etienne?"

Etienne was overjoyed at the prospect of helping Juanita in any way...even the smallest task would be a pleasure. And when she looked up into his warm brown eyes, she knew she had him on her hook, and she wasn't about to let him go.

"Oh, no, Miss Juanita. I would deem it a pleasure, as well as a privilege, to be allowed to assist you in any way at all. Do not hesitate to call on me..even for the most menial tasks," and he raised her tiny hand up to his eager lips.

She was beside herself with excitement. "Oh, how gallant he is. He's just like the men in the books about the knights and their ladies." But, she said simply, and with great confidence, "Oh, I won't, Etienne. I'll call upon you whenever I have a ... special..need," and as she said that her eyes spoke of unfulfilled promises, and Etienne's dark face allowed a blush to show when he realized he was staring at her with his mouth open with desire.

He quickly coughed, placing his hand over his mouth, and excused himself to resume saddling Opie's horse.

Gently he assisted the petite Juanita onto her mount and made haste to saddle his own horse to accompany her to Old Town and the hanging.

****

Trudy, Berta and Luta had just finished washing the dirty dishes. There had been nearly seventy people dining at the boarding

251

house, and the three of them were completely exhausted from cooking, serving and cleaning up after the throng.

"Berta, I'll finish wiping off the tables. Why don't you just get yourself up those stairs and put on that pretty blue dress Orlean brought for you? Now, you want to be pretty for your heroes' return, don't you?" Trudy asked. "And, Berta, take a little rest before you get all gussied up. You look plumb done in, dear."

Berta walked slowly around the table and put her arms around Trudy and said, "You are undoubtedly the most wonderful friend a body could have, Trudy Stucky." And she kissed her cheek and tiredly ascended the straight, narrow stairway to the front bedroom.

As she looked around the room, she thought, "I've spent more time in this hotel lately than I have in the eighteen years I've lived in Old Town." She smiled happily to herself as she slowly dressed for the hero's welcome Old Town had prepared for Jonah. She washed her face placing the cool cloth on her tired eyes and dressed her golden hair before going downstairs to join the gathered townspeople from Crosstown and Fort Fannin Springs.

She heard someone say, as she entered the room, "I heard tell that the banker's family from Tater Hill plan to be here for the hangin' if'n they'll postpone it 'til tomorry." And another voice replied, "Yep, and I heard that the Cuban has done and upped the reward money to $400. How about that? That young McRae boy is gonna be the richest fifteen year old around these parts, I'll vow. They said that the Cuban was giving him the reward 'cause of him being so brave. He didn't even care that he didn't exactly capture them." And on and on they tried to outdo each other in their "I heard tells." The town was bustling. You could feel the excitement in the air. Little Old Town had never had anything as exciting as a hanging. The last true happening had been when the Haglund girl ran off with the medicine show performer and her folks thought she'd been kidnapped - but she hadn't.

Yes...the R.J. Skinner Gang had sure turned sleepy Old Town into a veritable town of excitement. What with Tag being shot, and the Townsends being kidnapped, and now - the ultimate - the hanging of the most notorious gang ever. Why, they had raped...robbed banks...murdered folks in cold blood...and the talk went on and on.

There was someone occupying every available sit-down spot,

252

and they were filling the air with their exclamations and innuendos. The milk cows were left on the farms unattended. The chickens had to scavenge for their own food. Entire towns were emptied as their folks attended the "Big Event."

And as a special bonus, they would get to see the beautiful, white-haired girl the gang had kidnapped from La Belle. It was not known whether she had accompanied them voluntarily or was indeed kidnapped. The town was divided in their opinions regarding Juanita. Some said her hair was to her knees, and was the color of spun gold. And then there were those who said she at one time had had coal black hair and that because of the shock of the kidnapping, they'd heard that it had turned white...and on and on the jugs were passed and McCoy's Dry Goods had plumb run out of tobacco.

****

Luta ran over to the Boarding house. All flustered, she declared, "If Bud and Frankie don't get back soon, Trudy, I declare I'll not be responsible for what I'm plannin' to do to the next half-drunk man who gives me trouble at the stable. They're swarmin' all over just like flies at a cane squeezin'. I jus' can't handle 'em!"

Trudy told her, "Don't you fret, Luta. As soon as I'm finished up I'll be over to set 'em straight."

As Luta started back to the stable, wiping her hands on her apron and pushing her hair wisps back from her face, hot and exhausted and thoroughly angry, she heard the horses approaching from the north. There must have been fifty children leading the arrival with their hijinks, jumping, shouting and yelling.

"I'll declare!" Luta said to herself. "The whole state of Florida has got to be here in Old Town, and look at all those raggedy kids. Not a one of 'em with any more manners than a billy goat at a clothesline. I'll declare!" and she rushed into the stable to make sure the rafters hadn't started tumbling down from all that rambunctious riffraff from up Crosstown way.

She didn't know if her ears had ever taken such a beating as from the abusive language from those turpentiners. "If my Buddy had been here... well, I dasn't think what would have happened. That's one thing about my Buddy - he don't hold with cussin' around women folk. He sure would have had his hands full today," she

253

declared as she joined the gathered crowd. They were all craning their necks, trying to get a good look at the R.J. Skinner Gang.

Someone yelled, "I see 'em! I see 'em!" "Oh, my," she heard a woman say, "I've never seen the devil in person before. Look at those beady, black, devil eyes, would ya?" And another said, "Where's the girl? I wanna see the girl. I come all the way from down Otter Creek, and I wanna see that yeller-haired girl they kidnapped." There was no let up.

The town was so fired up that when Sheriff Walker pulled up and raised his arms toward the heavens to silence them, he could not be heard. Hiram took out his gun and shot it up in the air. That did it - the whole town inhaled, then, relieved, they exhaled in unison.

"Now," said Sheriff Walker, "I know you're anxious to get on with the hanging, but we've got to wait for our hero, Jonah McRae, to arrive. Layke Williams is bringing him by wagon 'cause he's pretty much exhausted. Now, you know if Jonah hadn't recognized these two varmints they'd probably have got out of Florida unbeknownst to any of us. But he took it upon himself to go after them single handed. And, well, ladies and gentlemen, here is the result of his bravery," and he pointed to the Skinner brothers with a great flourish. The crowd didn't know whether to cheer, boo, hiss or clap, so there was a very mixed response to Sheriff Walker's speech.

No one questioned whether Jonah should have sought help in Old Town when he recognized the Skinner gang. They just assumed that he didn't realize who they were until they turned off the road and made camp at Two Mile Bend, where the deMoya's found Old Red hobbled, and that he was brave enough to attempt the capture himself.

James and Hiram dismounted and took the tied-up prisoners with their heads hung down over to Palmer and Davis McCoy's to ask them if they would be so kind as to supply the rope for the lynching. Well, the McCoys were beside themselves at being singled out for such a great honor. It was probably the most wonderful thing that had ever been asked of them. It never occurred to them that since they ran the dry-goods store that it was the logical place to get rope. All they knew was that the sheriff had asked them - the McCoy brothers.

He next asked where the most secure place would be for the

prisoners while they waited for Jonah and Layke to arrive. Bud Brewster rode forward and told him, "Sheriff, I'd be honored, indeed, to have them held in my blacksmith shop..."

"Oh, Buddy!" Luta shouted, putting her hand over her gaping mouth as she anxiously worked her way through the crowd to get to Bud. When he saw her, he dismounted and they embraced right there in the middle of the street. She was so proud to think that they'd be a part of the happenings that she was afraid she was going to have a fit right in the middle of all those folks. The other posse members joined their awaiting families and the crowd began to chant, "Where's the girl? Where's the girl?"

R.J. and Joe Bob were shoved into Brewster's Blacksmith Shop. They could hear the chanting crowd. R.J. looked at Joe Bob and said sarcastically, "My Juanita is finally getting the attention she so rightly deserves," and he laughed his devil laugh as Joe Bob joined him.

Hiram turned to them and told them, "Shut up your thieving mouths! This is a town of God fearing and law abiding folks, and they don't need to hear any of your murderous talk."

R.J. winked at Joe Bob, and he returned the wink. "It's over," R.J. thought. He was, in a way, glad it was over. He really had not looked forward to going West. He was disappointed in only one thing, he sure had wanted to see the Duke again. On that, he was sorry. But he couldn't think of another single reason to go on. He'd done everything he'd ever really wanted to do. After the War, everything just sort of let down. Blowing up Tomlin's compound was the only exciting thing that had happened to him in a very long time. That truly satisfied R.J., that and meeting a girl as complex and as enticing as Juanita.

She was undoubtedly the most scheming, manipulative, self-centered...warm, passionate, adventurous woman he'd ever known - and he'd miss her. Oh, how he'd miss her. He just hoped that when he got to the other side, he could peek through a keyhole at Juanita and observe her goings on. He didn't know anything that would give him more pleasure than to continue observing that beautiful girl-woman play her game. Yes, he'd truly miss Juanita Jane Graves.

****

Etienne was riding beside Juanita as they rode into Old

Town about twenty minutes after the others. The gathering let out a thunderous applause and yelled their enthusiastic greeting. At first Juanita was frightened, but Etienne held Opie's horse firmly, and they both calmed down. She held her head high, as high as a princess in a story book, and as she had planned while back at camp, she loosened her beautiful long hair with a dramatic twist of her hand. As it tumbled gloriously down her back, the awaiting crowd gasped and then yelled their approval.

Etienne's expression was unmasked as he worshipped Juanita with his warm brown eyes for all to see. It was not lost on Pierre and Mama Orlean, who looked questioningly at Pierre then back to Etienne. She sensed trouble.

R.J. whispered to Joe Bob, "She came and she conquered," and he laughed at his Juanita's entrance to Old Town.

Joe Bob's head was bowed. "R.J.?" he paused before going on. "R.J., are you scared of the rope?" and he raised his head to study his older brother's face while awaiting his answer.

"No, little brother...I'm not. I guess I've always known that the rope would crack this ornery neck of mine. There's just one thing that I'm concerned about." He pondered before going on, "And it's what I've seen happen every time I've witnessed a necktie party...."

"What's that, R.J.?" "Well, little brother, I'm afraid I'm gonna piss in my drawers," and he didn't smile when he said it.

Joe Bob started to laugh, but when he saw how sober R.J. was he changed his mind. "Well, I'm scared, R.J., and I know damned well that I'm gonna piss in mine. The only decent thing I've done in my entire life is to love Rose, and I couldn't even have her. I just wish I could've found her a long time ago."

"Little brother, you just keep thinking about your sweet Rose, and I'll think about my bitter sweet Juanita, and maybe they'll get us through this thing without us pissing in our drawers," and then they both roared with laughter.

James Walker, who was guarding the door of the blacksmith shop, turned abruptly and stalked over to them, "What's so funny, you thieving bastards? You won't be laughing so hard when Pa puts that big ole scratchy rope around your no-good necks, I bet," and he glared at their now sober faces.

The minute his back was turned and he resumed his guard's position at the entrance, they broke out in laughter again. James

256

turned abruptly, but made no comment as he shook his head in disgust at their behavior.

Juanita and Etienne rode slowly through the crowd. He dismounted, took her reins and held the jittery horse while she lowered herself. She was shaking. The realization of the impending hanging finally caught up with her. He started to take the horse around to the back of Stucky's Boarding House when Juanita stopped him.

"Etienne, no!" she said sharply. "This is all I have in the world. What if something happened to him?"

"Juanita, would I allow anything to happen to your only possession? Look at me, Juanita. I'm Etienne deMoya, and I care for you, and whatever happens to you and yours." And as he looked down at her, he held her quivering chin with his large masculine hand - but oh, so gently. Her tears started then, and she clung to him with all her strength.

This time Juanita was allowing an honest emotion to emerge unashamedly. Etienne stroked her beautiful hair and kissed the top of her head while speaking soothing phrases in French to calm the trembling Juanita. Their only witness was Pierre who had followed them behind Stucky's to tie his horse as well. He wasn't exactly spying on them, but he was concerned by Etienne's obvious infatuation with the girl. Etienne had known many women intimately, he knew. They fell in love with him at every town where they performed. He was a handsome, dark man and his beautiful voice attracted every girl-woman in the audiences. But it was always they who pursued Etienne - not he they.

Etienne's happiness was very important to Pierre, not because he was the older brother, but because it was he who acted as a father to him and Aimee. It was Etienne who Pierre would turn to for any advice. It was Etienne who patiently taught him how to ride a horse, shoot a gun, to survive. It was Etienne who explained to him how to love a woman. And Pierre was concerned. He knew down deep that Juanita spelled trouble for the deMoya family, and he was going to protect Etienne from her scheming, knowing ways as he would expect Etienne to do if the situation were reversed.

Etienne turned to Pierre and smiled gently. Pierre took all three horses and tied them to the post. He turned back toward him and Juanita and said, "Sheriff Walker set the time of the hanging for sundown," and he reluctantly walked away from the embracing couple.

Finally Juanita was able to control her emotions and she and Etienne parted. "Thank you for understanding. I'm not usually such a big crybaby. Honest I'm not! But I've been under such a strain and now that it's almost over, well, I guess I just let loose..that's all."

"Oh, ma cherie, I understand the ways of a woman. And you have my permission to come to me with any problem, no matter how small." And as he patted her hand, Juanita's big blue eyes teared once more as she thought, "Etienne, you just solved all of my problems, if you only knew. Yes, all of my problems," and she went up on her tiptoes and kissed him sweetly on his willing cheek.

They were interrupted by the tumultuous roar from the hundreds of people lining the road into Old Town. Juanita was hesitant to leave her doubloons, but he pulled her with him as they hurriedly joined the packed throng on Stucky's porch.

Layke and Jonah were being mobbed as their wagon inched along the rutted road. Layke was trying to protect Jonah from the well-wishers, but Sheriff Walker finally had to stop the onslaught. He climbed the ladder beside Brewster's and fired his gun into the air. Then James and Hiram had to follow suit once more in order to silence the unruly crowd.

Layke stood up in the wagon, put his hands up in the air to quiet them and said, "I know how proud you all are of Jonah's bravery, but you must understand that he is very weak from his ordeal. I beg you to please let us continue to the hotel so his mother and family can tend him. He needs a lot of rest. When he's well again then you can give him a proper hero's welcome. Thank you, and now if you will please just step back from the road so we can proceed, we'd be much obliged."

Berta, SuSu and Wes were all on Trudy's porch awaiting them. Tears of pride dampened Berta's beautiful face. She could contain her joy no longer. She pushed the bystanders aside, stating, "Let me through, please. I'm his mother. Please let me through..."

She finally got to Layke. He dropped the reins, jumped down from the creaking wagon and embraced her, kissing her forehead and cheeks until someone in the crowd hollered, "Why don't you kiss her proper-like, Layke Williams?" so he did, and for such a long time that the crowd loudly shouted their approval. When

258

Berta finally broke away, there was no doubt in the minds of anyone there who the next bride would be in Old Town.

Layke lifted Jonah's listless body out of the wagon. He was barely conscious, but recognized Berta and the children and seemingly went back to sleep. Trudy went to him, examined his closed eyes and told Layke, "Take him up to my room immediately, Layke. This young man needs attention - fast."

As they went up the stairs, Trudy went to her kitchen and began brewing some chamomile and rose hip tea. Her heavy body juned around like a young girl's. She had seen Jonah's symptoms before, and when Layke told her that he reeked of vomit when he got to him, and that he'd been gagged, she knew the poor lad had not had any liquids - probably nothing at all for two whole days, and with his constant vomiting was probably dehydrated.

Trudy went to the foot of the stairs and called up to Berta, "Berta, I'm coolin' the rose hip tea. What I want you and Layke to do is try to make him walk. Get him up and try to keep him awake. Talk to him!" and she rushed back into her spicy smelling kitchen and added the honey to the tea, pouring it from one cup to the other in order to cool it more rapidly.

When she reached Jonah, Berta looked at her and shook her head, "He's not responding, Trudy. What should we do?"

"Here, let me have him. Sit him upright in this straight backed chair."

Jonah's head fell forward onto his chest. Trudy had Berta lift his head and tilt it backwards. They took rags and tied him securely in the chair. Then she forced his mouth open, and spooned the warm tea into it while holding his nose, forcing him to swallow. It took almost an hour, but Jonah consumed one and a half cups of Trudy's tea.

It was mid-afternoon when Jonah opened his eyes to gaze at a very worried group of people. Trudy had been able to force down more of the sweetened liquid, and they were all exhausted from the effort. The very first thing he said was, "Hey, Layke...I gotta go:.I gotta go real bad," and the relief in their laughter brought a smile to his parched lips and childish giggles from SuSu and Wes who had joined them upstairs.

****

259

Layke went to the window when he heard all the commotion coming from the dirt road in front of the hotel. He called to Trudy and said, "Trudy, who are those men?"

She went to the window, pushed back the lace curtains and in an almost inaudible voice said, "For the Lord's sake! That's the turpentine crew from all the way to Gainesville - old man Pritchard's gang, and they usually mean trouble, Layke."

"Not today, Ladies. Not today! I've had all the trouble I can tolerate!"

He left the room swiftly and went out the kitchen door to his horse, got his bullwhip and walked around to the front of the boarding house. Over half the crowd had dispersed by then. Most of the men had retired to the river's edge to sleep off their abundant dinner and spirits so they could be lively and fresh for the sundown hanging.

The seven men were hooting and hollering, their horses prancing and just as excited as their riders. They had raised so much dust that Layke could not see where the sheriff and his sons were, but he figured they were at Brewster's. So he proceeded to walk slowly down the main road with his bullwhip in hand, tall, ramrod straight, eyes dead ahead toward Brewster's. The women quickly took refuge in the various buildings while the few men who remained were so curious about the expected conflict that they hung around on the porches, for this would be a bonus to the hanging. They knew that Layke Williams didn't pack a gun, and all had heard of his accuracy with the whip. The air was electric as they watched him approach the drunken gang.

The men angrily pulled their horses to the side of the road, cursing in loud voices. It was obvious that they were liquored up. The one they referred to as Mesquite was showing off more than the others. When Layke uncoiled his bullwhip and started cracking the dust spittles in the road, he reared his horse up on its hind legs and galloped around Layke - around and around, taunting him with his antics.

Layke was getting more furious by the minute. He turned toward Mesquite and started cracking the whip, missing him by only inches every time he popped it. Mesquite pulled his horse up and looked toward his men for assistance. The anger on his contorted face was frightening. But Layke was not deterred. As he had told Berta and Trudy, he had had his fill of trouble for one day, and

260

it would take more than this trash to destroy the peace he felt he deserved after such a harrowing experience.

Determined, he walked toward the gang. "Mesquite!" he yelled. "This is a God-fearing town and there're women and children all around us. Now, you decide right here and now whether or not you're gonna cause me and them any grief, 'Cause I've had my fill of trouble for one day, Mister." He drew closer to them, his whip coiled in his hand, anxious to be unleashed.

No answer did he get from the grumbling men. Layke saw Mesquite's hand move slowly and inched toward his sidearm. He instantly uncoiled his whip and struck. Mesquite, amazed by the lightning swiftness of Layke, grabbed his arm where the barb had cut through his shirt. The blood oozed out, staining the sleeve. He yelped as he saw it and turned toward the others for assistance, but the noise from behind them caught their attention...

The town had reawakened and the music of the calliope filled the tense air. The lead wagon with Juanita sitting on the seat beside Etienne, Pierre and Aimee startled the rowdy men. Dom and Orlean's wagon followed close behind and the town's children were jumping and shouting while hanging onto the colorful wagon, easing the tension.

Mesquite and the other men reluctantly moved their prancing horses to the side of the road to allow Layke and the medicine show wagons to pass. Layke and Etienne exchanged grateful looks and, on Layke's part, relief. The gang's boisterous behavior had been outshone by the parade, and when they realized they weren't going to cause a commotion they soon headed for the woods.

When Layke saw them depart, he turned to Etienne and said, "They've probably got their jugs stashed away and will return more liquored up than they are now. We'd better keep an eye on them - I don't want anything else to upset Berta, Etienne. She's had as much as any woman could stand."

"We'll be close by, if you need us Layke. They're a wild bunch all right." What he didn't say was, "That Mesquite's likely to try to get even, and I must be on the alert for my friend. I don't trust that one! Not for a minute."

Layke coiled his whip and they headed back for the boarding house. Etienne and Pierre began setting out the benches for the evening's show, and Orlean and Dom ran over to Layke to inquire about Jonah.

261

"How ees our young Jonah doin', Meester Layke?" Dom inquired. Orlean chimed in quickly, "Oh, Meester Layke, we were so worried..Mees Berta ees a very luckee woman to have her son home again." Layke thanked them for their concern and thought, "How quickly they've become a part of South Spring. I must invite them to stay for the wedding. I know I'd be expressing Berta's wishes as well."

He held their hands in his and expressed his gratitude for their help during his absence. "Berta and I would be honored if you could stay for the wedding. It would mean a great deal to us..."

"That would be perfect, Layke," Etienne interjected. "I want to begin Juanita's training for the high rope act immediately." They all stared at him in complete surprise, all except Pierre. He knew she'd been working on him. "So now she's going to be a performer," he thought. "My - my - my - she'll break her pretty neck," and he couldn't conceal his amusement.

"I believe Juanita will be an asset, Mama. She's very beautiful and indeed willing, and she has no place to go. She's ashamed to return to her home. She said she had heard that her parents believed that she had intentionally run away with the gang, and she just doesn't feel she can return to them under those circumstances."

He hurried to add, "She can share the wagon with you and Aimee. I know she will work very hard, and I'll be fully responsible for teaching her, Mama," he pleaded, begging Orlean with his eyes.

Orlean looked up at her tall, handsome son with her wise eyes, and she knew that Etienne had made up his mind and there would be no dissuading him. "Eef dat ees what you wish, my son, den dat ees what weel be. We weel welcome de girl eento our family, and she weel be treated as one of us."

Etienne's warm, giving nature was very precious to Orlean. She meant what she had said to her son, but what was left unsaid was, "But I weel keep a very close watch over de girl, my son - a very close watch. Otherwise, she weel bring harm to all the deMoyas. I feel eet in my heart." He put his strong arms around Orlean and kissed her on both cheeks affectionately.

Aimee was thrilled at the prospect of having a "sister" and having her share the wagon. She thought she was the most beautiful girl she had ever seen - all golden. She rushed after Etienne and happily explained, "Oh, Etienne, I'm so excited about having Juanita join us. She is so beautiful. Please, oh please, let me help make her costume. It should be blue and silver, and I'll sew millions of tiny brilliants all over. Oh, Etienne! I feel like it is Christmas, and you've given me the most beautiful gift I've ever seen. Thank you...thank you!" "Wait a minute, young lady," he laughingly said. "First I must teach her the high rope. And I'll need your assistance, ma cherie." He pulled her dark curls and playfully squeezed her lithe arms. "There is no one in the world more beautiful than my own Aimee...not even Juanita," he whispered to her.

"Etienne, she is a golden girl. Etienne..oh, Etienne, can we call her 'the golden girl'?"

"She shall be called 'Cherie', little one, but between the two of us, we shall call her 'Golden Girl'," and they walked arm-in-arm to the wagon to inform the awaiting Juanita of the news.

****

The afternoon sun ducked behind the tall sand pines that edged the field behind the few buildings that were Old Town as the quiet, whispering on- lookers gathered around the site of the big event - the big oak behind McCoy's store. The dark clouds rolling in from the east would bring the afternoon rains, and from the looks of them, high wind as well. When the sheriff soberly led R.J. and Joe Bob out of the blacksmith's shop to the awaiting tree, the crowd was hushed - even Mesquite and the rowdy gang were subdued in anticipation of the hanging.

R.J. turned to Joe Bob and said, "Head up, little brother, it'll be over in a snap," and he laughed quietly as he stared at the gathered throng. He was looking for Juanita, but she was nowhere to be seen.

Their horses stood beside the dangling nooses, and Hiram and James, who were going to be given the honor of swatting their rumps, stood stiffly beside them. Jonah had been assisted by Layke and Berta to the deMoyas' wagon so he could sit up high on the front seat to have a uninterrupted view of the proceedings. As they walked through their midst, the crowd burst out with a thunderous applause of approval for the brave young man. Jonah turned weakly toward Berta, and smiled as she put her arm around his waist and hugged him to her. Layke was busily scanning the crowd for Mesquite and his gang, his arm never relaxing from the coiled whip at his side.

R.J. was not that concerned about being hanged. But he was real curious as to where Miss Juanita Jane Graves was. "Now, where could she be? Surely she wouldn't miss the event of the decade," he thought. Then he figured that wherever the French troubadour was, then there would be his Juanita. And sure enough as he looked toward their wagon, she emerged from within with Etienne by her side. His arm was around her waist. R.J. smiled.

Juanita saw him at that moment. She was put out with his smiling right at her. "Now why is he doing that?" she questioned. "Grinning at me like a chessy cat. You'd think that he'd think enough of me to try to show some..some eh, dignity. Good grief! R.J. they're hanging you!" and she scowled at him. He was delighted by her reaction and continued staring at her, much to her consternation..

Charlie Beatty was all decked out in his funeral frock coat, Bible in hand. The sheriff called for the crowd to be quiet, and asked Charlie to read from the good book. And did Charlie read! He must have read ten long passages. The crowd was getting impatient, and finally someone yelled, "Charlie, the sun's been down near half an hour. Ain't ya ever gonna let these two shake the devil's hand?" Mesquite started to yell, but when he glanced at Layke, he changed his mind. Layke relaxed his arm and held Berta's hand tightly.

Charlie finally wound down and after a forever seeming length of time, he "Amened." Sheriff Walker then proceeded to tell the assembled crowd about the heinous deeds for which the R.J. Skinner Gang had been responsible, and laboriously continued to expound on the subject of law and order and the duty of a sheriff.

Again, from the midst of the anxious crowd, someone yelled, "Good grief in the morning, Sheriff! we gonna have us a hangin' or ain't we? Look at them thunder clouds - we all gonna be drenched if'n ya'll don't get a move on." So the sheriff proceeded with the business at hand. He turned to R.J. and Joe Bob and asked them if there was anything that they'd like to say before departing this world.

Juanita was positive-sure that R.J. would say something embarrassing, 'cause he kept those devil eyes staring plumb through her. Finally, he turned toward the sober crowd and with that devil's smirk on his face said, "Not right this minute." He paused and

264

added, "Maybe afterwards," and laughed his practiced evil laugh to the absolute astonishment of the good people of Old Town.

Hiram and James were given the nod, and as the crowd held its breath, they swatted the horses. A gasp..and an "ahhh" escaped the multitude.

"Oh, my Gawd, R.J.!" Juanita exclaimed in unison with a commanding clap of thunder and hung her head in disgust and shame when she saw the dark stain coming through their britches. "What'd he have to go and do that for?" she lamented as she quickly retreated to the sanctuary of the wagon. Etienne was directly behind her to comfort his "Golden Girl."

Satan and Mister, R.J's and Joe Bob's horses, stood underneath the spreading hanging tree, unconcerned, their swishing tails stirring up the visiting flies, while their masters' still bodies dangled beside them. Rain and wind rushed in, washing the dusty, flat palms. The sporadic gusts meshed their gray-green fronds against each other as R.J.'s and Joe Bob's suspended bodies whirled around and around. The stinging rain fought its way underneath the canopy of the oak tree.

The crowd quickly dispersed and sought shelter. Most sought comfort from the jug, others in the retelling of the tales about the R.J. Skinner Gang's exploits.

****

Trudy stirred the bubbling grits, her mind going a mile a minute. The sun was not yet up when she quietly sneaked out of bed. Berta, sleeping soundly, did not stir. Trudy Stucky needed time to think - to be alone. She reflected on the past year since Layke's arrival and was amazed at the changes in all their lives. "Old Town was a dead little town 'til he came riding in. It'll never be the same again... nor will he. He's still got the gnawing though - I can see it! He'll be someone in this state someday, mark my word, with Berta right there helping him, and they'll be needin' me more than ever."

She rocked, peering out the screened door and watching the sun announce the beginning of the day. The rooster stopped his crowing and his hens began their clucking when Trudy went to the coop, scattering corn in front of her. She pushed her hair back and looked toward the heavens.

"They'll be needing Your help, too!"

Preview

The continued romance of old Florida
in the compelling series

The Floridians

By: Ann O'Connell Rust

Palatka

The second novel of

The Floridians

(to be published in fall of 1989)

The author cleverly intertwines the lives of these
daring pioneers, who courageously attempt to
tame the last frontier — Florida

Palatka

BERTA ... Berta awakened very early. She lay quietly, barely moving in her thin muslin gown. Her mind restlessly flitted from one inconsequential happening to another, never fixing itself for even a moment.

"Dear Lord in the morning! Why am I so restless? This should be the most perfect day in my life ... my wedding day."

She immediately thought of Layke. "I wonder if he's awake, and if he's as restless as I? I wonder what your thoughts are on this special day, my husband?"

Lazily, she curled up under the light sheet and turned on her side facing the drab, faded wallpaper. She remembered when the cabbage roses had been so bright and cheerful that they helped lighten the otherwise dull life at South Spring. Berta allowed her thoughts to ease back to her wedding night with Reuben. It was vivid now, where as just a short time before it had been blurred, hazy, beyond recall.

Oh, she had been so very young and innocent, and goodness knows, she was totally inexperienced. "Reuben, bless his heart, knew it. And he was so understanding." She could still remember their drawing room with the low ceiling and walls covered with deep red brocade. The plush seats, when pulled out, made a very comfortable bed. She closed her eyes and slightly smiled, allowing the bygone impressions to again form.

She did not become Reuben's wife until after leaving Uncle Jock's and Aunt Lawanda's home in Jacksonville. They had nervously talked, non-stop all the way from Macon to Savannah, holding each other lovingly, tenderly, and had continued their journey on the Florida, Atlantic & Gult Central Railroad from Jacksonville, to Lake City. By then, they were so comfortable with each other that their love-making was beautifully natural.

Berta sighed, then began smiling devilishly to herself, and said profoundly as she leaped from her bed, "Today's my wedding day, and there will be no delaying my becoming Layke's wife — of that I'm positive!"

She blushed as she covered her smile. "I'm grateful that you don't know what I'm thinking, Layke Williams. I'm sure you'd think me very unladylike, but I'm enjoying every minute of it," she thought as she removed her floral wrapper from the foot of the bed. She draped it over her bare shoulders and went barefoot into the kitchen.

Layke abruptly rose from the ladderback chair, knocking it over with his anxiousness. Berta flew into his waiting arms. He kissed her eyes, her cheeks, then hungrily on her eager, moist lips. After a forever-seeming time, Berta breathlessly pushed him away.

"Is this a preview of what I may expect tonight, Sir?" He threw his dark brown mane back and laughed heartily.

"No, Madam, not even a smattering of what you can except. I have ordered something for Madam Williams that is very special."

269

Berta looked very serious when she gazed into his laughing eyes and exclaimed, "This is undoubtedly going to be the longest day of my entire life, Layke Williams. I wish we could be alone right now — this very minute."

"Not more than I, darling. Not more than I ..."

CALLIE ... Excitement was in every pore of Callie's long, muscled body. Thom would be at the state fair! He had been very faithful about writing, and she had replied. The letters were mostly concerned with the crops, weather and ranch life in general and inquiring of her health. But in every letter he added his own brand of humor.

There wasn't much doing at the Tall Ten in early August. The crops had long ago been harvested, and they'd not be seeding the close-in pasture until fall after the heavy summer rains. So her pa decided it was time for the entire family to take a trip, and at the same time give Jay a chance to strut, to show off his animal exhibit. "Slick and Jam can handle whatever comes up, and Mattie'll see to it that no one goes hungry. And, shoot, Kate's been working on that sunflower guilt for going on four years, so it'll get her going on finishing it so she can enter it in the fair," he reasoned.

It would also give him a chance to see what the other ranchers were doing to improve their stock. He knew Jordan Northrup and Pierce would be there because they'd talked about it during the spring drive. Jordan's Big Lake spread, south of Ft. Basinger, was the talk of the camps. It wasn't as large as Tall Ten, but his experiments with grasses and breeding were becoming known all over the state.

When Parker asked Callie if she was going to enter the calf roping event, she changed the subject real fast. Later in the quiet of the evening when he and Kate first went to bed he mentioned it to her. She chuckled and said, "Why James Parker Meade, you're getting old and forgetful. Don't you know that Thom Garvin will be competing in that event? Now how would it look if Callie up and beat his time? You know that she's sweet on him, don't you?

"For pete's sake, you women have always gotta have your daughters sweet on some no-good lout! Why, the next thing I know you'll be saying she's sweet on Clay Willett!"

"And why not, Mr. know-it-all? I for one think that Clay Willett will be quite a catch one of these days. He's intelligent, handsome, talented, and mark my word, he'll be someone big for all to see. Why just the other day, Callie said that he's planning on a writing career."

"Well, I for one hope so. If he's thinking of marrying my daughter he sure couldn't feed her beans on what that skinflint Jeeters pays him."

"Well, J. Parker Meade, now did I say or even hint that Callie had marrying on her mind? Why, she's just now getting into the swing of courting and here you go and get her married off before she even learns the first thing about it!" and she turned over in a huff.

270

JUANITA ... Juanita, lying sleepily on the narrow straw-filled pallet, watched Aimee dress her long, rich brown hair. It was so thick that she wondered how on earth she would be able to weave it into the figure eight French rolls in the back. Juanita felt so tired — she'd had a fitful night's sleep. She knew that she'd been completely immersed in her training for the tight rope act, so maybe that was the cause. And watching R. J. and Joe Bob hang did prey on her mind, much more than she thought it would. But she felt so tired this morning that she was glad there was no practice.

Aimee turned to her and said, "Juanita, I'll dress your hair if you'd like. I've always wanted to, ever since I first saw you."

Juanita lazily sat up and yawned, stretching her shapely arms in the air, and lackadaisically replied, "Oh, all right, Aimee. If you really want to."

Aimee had noticed how withdrawn she had become lately. The only time she showed any enthusiasm was when she practiced on the rope. "But then," she thought, "she had had a very frightening experience with those terrible kidnappers. It's no wonder," and she reached for Juanita's brush to begin untangling her golden-white hair that was badly matted from her restless night.

Orlean parted the canvas curtain that was nailed to the back of the wagon affording them some privacy. Peering inside the darkened interior, she too noticed how quiet and still Juanita was. "Are you not feeling well, Juanita?" she questioned as her knowing eyes studied Juanita's sullen face.

Juanita turned toward her, the cramped wagon leaving little room to maneuver and smiled sweetly at Orlean, declaring to herself, "She'll never like me — not in this world or in the next. She's jealous of Etienne's feelings for me, the old crone," but she said, "Oh, thank you for asking, Mrs. deMoya. I think I just need a good tonic, that's all."

Aimee's quick humor broke the strained atmosphere. "How about the 'Elixir of Life', Juanita? It cures all ills," she said with elaborate theatrics.

But Orlean de Moya did not join in in their sarcastic merriment. She seriously looked at Juanita and asked, "Do you teenk you should chance de journey eento Old Town een your condeetion, Juanita?"

"Oh, I'm just feeling a little poorly, that's all. I'll be fine as soon as I have some breakfast," and she squinted at Orlean, trying to mask her true feelings, as the brightness of the glaring July sun intruded into the soft light of the wagon.

Orlean dropped the canvas curtain and stumbled as she began to run toward the house. She had to get away from the girl — the ungrateful girl — the girl who would bring shame to her family. "I was afraid of dees. I was afraid!"

She reached the porch and out of breath gasped, "Now Etienne weel nevair let her go — nevair!"

271

About the author:

Ann O'Connell Rust is a native Floridian, a "cracker". Her parents were pioneers in the Everglades in the early part of the century. Her father, Frank O'Connell, moved to Canal Point on Lake Okeechobee to work on Conner's Highway — the first hard road into the Glades. Conner was a friend of the West Palm Beach O'Connells, and young Frank wanted to be a part of Conner's thrust into the mysterious Glades. There he met Onida Knight, one of the beautiful Knight girls, whose father had homesteaded their land the previous year, and opened his own Knight's Grocery and Dry Goods Store in Canal Point. Luther Knight ultimately became a farmer/rancher and her father, a farmer, deputy sheriff and chief of police in Pahokee.

After schooling in Palm Beach County schools, Ann embarked on a very successful career in modeling — in Miami and New York City, where she met and married Allen, an FBI agent, and followed him to Puerto Rico, New Mexico, Washington, D.C., Mexico City and finally back to her love — Florida.

She has had an on-going love affair with romantic old Florida all of her adult life and three of their five children live in the state.

She is the owner of two modeling schools and talent agencies in Orange Park and Jacksonville and since her retirement has devoted all her energies to writing and sharing her love of this magnificent state. She and Allen spend their time between their home on the St. John's River and their ranch in Wyoming.

Are you unable to find *"The Floridians"*
in your book stores?

Mail to: AMARO BOOKS
5673 Pine Avenue
Orange Park, Florida 32073

Please send check or money order (No cash or C.O.D.s)

I enclose $_____for books indicated.

Book Title:_____

_____

Number of books: _____

Name:_____

Address: _____

City: _____

State:_____

Zip:_____

Please enclose $12.95 per book plus $1.00 each for postage and handling. Florida residents add 6% sales tax. Please allow 6-8 weeks for delivery.